# LINKS

Mary O'Conor

TOWN
HOUSE
DUBLIN

First published in 2004 by

TownHouse, Dublin
THCH Ltd
Trinity House
Charleston Road
Ranelagh
Dublin 6
Ireland

www.townhouse.ie

1 2 3 4 5 6 7 8 9 10

ISBN: 1-86059-222-8

Printed by Creative Print & Design (Wales) Ltd, Ebbw Vale

Mary O'Conor is a psychosexual therapist and relationship counsellor who lives and works in Dublin. She is a frequent guest on radio and television and her bestselling book *Sexual Healing* – a self-help guide to sexual problems – was published by TownHouse in 2002. She also writes a weekly newspaper column. She is married to concert pianist John O'Conor and has two sons. *Links* is her first novel.

Also by Mary O'Conor

*Sexual Healing*

*For John, who supports me
in everything I do*

# Acknowledgements

The idea for *Links* came on a snow-bound and therefore golf-less weekend in Woodstock, Co. Clare in the company of Emer Keeling and Marian Benton, so thanks to them for entering into the spirit of the fantasy. It was fitting then that they were also with me on a more successful golf outing to Lahinch when Treasa Coady called to tell me that once more she was going to have faith in me and would publish *Links*. Thank you to Treasa, and to everybody at TownHouse, particularly my patient and ever-cheerful editor Penny Harris. She did a great job and is a true romantic at heart. Thanks to my son Keith for the IT support and my son Hugh for the encouragement of a fellow writer. To both Ted McDermott in Dublin and Brian McCaffrey in California go my thanks for sharing their urological expertise. Thanks to my brother Mahon – a wonderful golfer who has always been encouraging even during my worst days on the golf course. Thanks to my teacher Gillian Burrell for her eternal optimism. Thanks for the friendship to everybody in Delgany Golf Club and particularly to my buddies Ann Boyle, Eileen Broderick, Joan O'Connor and Susan Lennon. Long may the fun continue! And a very special thank you to Reynaldo Catapang who does such a wonderful job in running our house thus enabling us all to get on with our sometimes alarmingly hectic lives.

# PROLOGUE

'LOOK, I DON'T CARE HOW MANY TIMES YOU ASK ME, I AM not going to another goddamn reception!' Kevin's voice was growing louder with every word until he was almost shouting at Madeleine, who stood before him with gritted teeth. 'I have enough of these networking functions to go to in my own job without having to chitchat at someone else's,' he added sourly, turning to check out his reflection in the mirror as he knotted his tie. 'You say you told me about it last week,' he continued with his back turned to her, 'but I don't have it in my Palm Pilot, so I really doubt that you did. I'm not going and that's that, end of discussion.'

'I can't get over how selfish you're being!' Madeleine threw back, fighting to keep the tears that were welling up behind her eyes from falling. 'How many boring dinners have I sat through for you? This is important to me Kevin – it's the first European deal I've won for the company, and you know how hard I worked to get it. A little support wouldn't hurt.'

She had wanted to explain to him that they never got to spend any time with each other any more and how this would be an opportunity to do something together. She wasn't sure, though, if she could control the tears threatening to spill down her cheeks if she continued talking, so she said nothing.

'Which part of NO do you not understand? I'm not going Madeleine, OK? I hate these things.' With that, he grabbed his black leather briefcase off the table and glanced impatiently at his watch.

'Shit, look, I'm late for work now. I'll talk to you later.'

Madeleine glared after Kevin as she followed him from the bedroom to the dimly lit hallway. He tried to put on his coat hurriedly, struggling with the sleeve. Almost as an afterthought he turned back from the door and tried to plant a peck on Madeleine's cheek, which she avoided. Pretending not to notice, he grabbed his keys from the hall table and with a slam of the door he was gone.

Madeleine was shaking with upset and anger, and could no longer hold back the tears that had been waiting to fall all morning. She hated leaving arguments unresolved, especially with Kevin, and now she was going to have to wait until she saw him that night to settle things between them. In an effort to snap herself out of her miserable mood, she looked around for something to take her mind off him.

'Well damn him, anyway,' she said out loud, hoping that she might feel as unconcerned as she sounded. She had wanted so much for him to be there with her tonight, and while it was true she wanted him for the support, another part of her couldn't help wanting to show him off. Nobody at work had met Kevin, and she knew that they'd be impressed by his tall, statuesque figure and dark features. Hadn't she fallen for it all herself? He could certainly be arrogant and stubborn at times, but he could also be absolutely charming – although she had to remind herself after arguments like this that she really did love him. She would just have to make up some lame excuse that he had to go out of town on business.

Deciding to put it out of her head for the time being, Madeleine concentrated instead on what to wear. She knew that she wouldn't have time to come back to the apartment between work and the reception, so she went into the bedroom and started pulling things out of her wardrobe that would be suitable for both. After discounting everything twice, she surveyed the pile of expensive clothes strewn across the bed, and finally decided on a very flattering black Donna Karan trouser suit with a crisp white blouse. She would change the blouse later for the lovely cerise Richard Lewis camisole she had bought the last time she was home visiting her mother. The camisole was beautifully cut and emphasised just enough of her full breasts to hint at sensuality, without revealing too much – perfect for the reception. The colour would lend a touch of vibrancy to the black suit too, and would look amazing against her golden tan and sleek blonde hair. Finally she selected the patent leather, high-heeled Charles Jourdan ankle boots to add a touch of subtle sexiness to her outfit.

'Even if Kevin isn't going to be there tonight,' she thought to herself, looking at the stylish ensemble on the bed, 'I'm not going to let myself down.'

As she was going to be working late that evening, Madeleine decided she didn't need to get to the office early this morning. Instead, she would take a leisurely shower and read the morning paper before going in. She would even have breakfast, which she usually didn't have time for.

After what seemed like a blissful eternity, she emerged from the bathroom feeling like a new woman. The steaming hot water and the silky body lotion had helped to smooth away all thoughts of the argument, and her anger and tears had evaporated. With Kevin's soft dressing gown snugly wrapped around her and a fresh white towel in a turban around her head, she poured herself a fresh cup of coffee and popped a croissant into the oven to heat.

Settling back into a comfy armchair, Madeleine flicked on the television and was momentarily baffled at the pictures unfolding before her. One by one, the images on screen began to register in her brain, though few seemed to make sense. There, in a blaze of fire and engulfed in thick, black voluminous smoke was Kevin's beloved World Trade Centre. Footage of frenzied confusion, people screaming, running through the streets to avoid the growing danger of collapse, flashed across the screen. With a numb sensation seeping through her body, Madeleine clutched the armrest and lifted herself out of the chair. As coffee spilled from the cup onto the floor, she stood as if transfixed, not wanting to see more, but unable to turn away from the screen. As tears began to well up once more behind her eyes, she reached for the phone and tried dialling Kevin's mobile. She listened with increasing panic as an automated voice told her that his number was unavailable, and then she crumpled to the floor, all thoughts of the reception, the clients and their argument forgotten.

*September 11, 2001*

# CHAPTER ONE

*March 2002*

'MRS CASTELLANO, YOUR CAR IS HERE.'

'Thank you, I'll be right down.'

Replacing the receiver on the hook, Madeleine glanced around the opulently decorated room one last time to make sure she had left nothing behind. She picked up her bags, closed the door, and padded across the plush beige carpet to the nearest lift. The lift attendant greeted her with a smile and the elevator music was gently soothing as they descended to the foyer of Fitzpatrick's hotel.

She had decided to spend her last few nights in the hotel, as the couple to whom she had leased her apartment wanted to move in immediately. It suited her perfectly, really. Having made the decision to move back to Ireland, Madeleine had found herself growing increasingly impatient to leave New York, and moving out of the apartment had felt like the first step.

She relaxed back now in the luxurious leather seat of the chauffeur-driven Mercedes she had ordered, which seemed to her to be the height of idyllic decadence – she wished she could afford to travel first class all the time – and stared dreamily out the window as they drove across the Triborough Bridge on their way to the airport. She found herself once again startled at how strange everything looked without the dominant Twin Towers. Although she had spent the last six months trying to get used to the gap in the once-so-familiar skyline, Madeleine could never forget the damage the attacks had done both to her adopted city and to her life. She had cried so much over the last six months, sometimes at the most unexpected moments, that she had begun to wonder if she would ever stop. When Kevin died, her mother had wanted to come over to be with her, but knowing how much she hated flying, especially on her own, Madeleine assured her that she would be well taken care of by her friends in New York and that she would be home soon. In fact, it had taken much longer to get everything finalised than she had originally expected, but eventually the day had come when Madeleine was heading home to Ireland. Home to a new beginning. She knew she would miss a lot about the place, though – good friends, the constant buzz of the city, and most recently her new career in the PR firm. Everyone had advised her not to do anything permanent for the first year, so leasing her apartment had seemed a good compromise. Secretly, though, Madeleine felt that leaving the city was exactly the release she needed from her guilt. She had never forgiven herself for the dreadful way things had ended between her and Kevin. For her, remaining in New York would have been a constant reminder of their argument, and the feeling, irrational or not, that his death had somehow been her fault.

Madeleine's thoughts snapped back into focus as the driver smoothly pulled up outside Terminal 4, opened the door for her and lifted her matching luggage out of the trunk. She remembered how Kevin used to tease her when she called it a boot, telling her boots were what she put on her feet. Making her way into the departures area, she wondered how long it would take before every little thing would stop reminding her of Kevin. She decided that this was not the time to think back on the past, but to look to what lay ahead, and so she strode purposefully forward and through the large revolving doors.

Everything seemed so different from when she had been an Aer Lingus hostess. It was all so modern and impersonal now. When two girls in green and blue uniforms walked past her, though, Madeleine felt a sudden rush of familiarity, and already began to feel as if she was at home. As she took her place at the check-in desk, she met a familiar face. Amelia had started hostessing just as Madeleine was leaving to work for the PR firm.

'Go right ahead to the premier lounge, Mrs Castellano, and enjoy your flight,' the younger woman said, smiling amiably at Madeleine over the desk.

'Mrs Castellano' had never really suited her, but it felt even stranger now that Kevin was gone. She would use her maiden name, O'Connell, when she got back to Ireland, Madeleine decided, as she went through to the departure lounge, picking up a copy of *Vogue* on the way.

Just as she placed a glass of Ballygowan on the table beside her and began reading an article on weekend makeovers, a voice from behind startled her.

'Madeleine?'

The man's voice sounded familiar. Slightly disconcerted, Madeleine turned around to find herself looking into a pair of instantly recognisable cornflower-blue eyes.

'Donal!'

'I thought it was you, but I wasn't sure. I saw you going into the newsagent's and could've sworn I was seeing things. It's been quite a while.'

'Yes, yes it has,' she stuttered. 'It must be about ten years?'

It was exactly ten years, and she knew it, but after all that had happened between them, she wasn't going to give him the satisfaction of knowing she had been counting. She had imagined this moment so often, but despite all the scenarios she had run through in her head, she now felt totally caught off-guard.

Looking at him a little more closely, she could see that age had been kind to him. He still had the same wonderful olive skin and that seductive smile that made Madeleine melt every time she saw it. Although he was only thirty-five, a few flecks of silver-grey were already noticeable in his dark hair, and little crinkles at the edges of his eyes had materialised. Madeleine couldn't help wondering how they had appeared – through stress or laughter? Stress most likely, being married to Judith.

'Are you going back to Dublin?' he asked tentatively, and Madeleine realised with a start that her mind had begun to drift.

'Mm, ah, yes...'

Oh, why couldn't she appear poised and collected? She coughed to clear her throat, and then almost whispered, 'And you?'

'Yes, yes, I am. I was at a conference in Boston, then some meetings in New York and I'm on my way back home now.'

For a second Madeleine thought he even looked bashful – she wasn't the only one caught off-guard.

'This *is* a surprise,' he went on, not taking his eyes off her. 'It's really great to see you, Madeleine – you look terrific, as always.'

Madeleine could feel the colour rising in her cheeks. She couldn't bring herself to say anything, and prayed silently for their flight number to be called, a phone to go off, or anything else that might take the focus away from the two of them staring at each other. At last Donal broke the silence. He ran his long, tanned fingers through his hair and gave a small cough.

'I don't want to sound presumptuous at all,' he said, 'but would you mind if I checked with the receptionist at the desk and see if we can sit together? You know, catch up a bit... what row are you in?'

'2C,' Madeleine blurted out, before really considering that she was committing herself to six hours of painful reminiscing – she'd be a nervous wreck by the time they flew into Dublin.

Donal went to talk to the receptionist and Madeleine took a large gulp of Ballygowan. Her throat was suddenly so dry. She couldn't believe that after all this time he could still evoke such a reaction in her. She had really thought when she married Kevin that she was well over him. Clearly not.

'Oh, and Madeleine… what name should I say your ticket is under?'

Madeleine looked up and saw that he had turned to face her again.

'It's just that I heard you got married to an American a while back, and I wasn't sure…' he trailed off sheepishly.

Their eyes met in an ardent gaze. Madeleine was struck by the irony of the situation. After all they had been through together, and now he literally didn't know her name. There was so much he didn't know…

## October 1988

'Well, Kay, if you'd asked me a few hours ago, I would have bet you any amount that I'd hate the opera, but I was wrong. Very wrong, in fact – it was great! Who ever would've thought that those warbling women were actually telling a story!'

Kay tried to suppress a giggle, and turned away from Madeleine in mock offence.

'No, seriously, Kay, thanks for inviting me – only for the fact that you forced me to, I would never have come.'

'You're welcome,' said Kay, 'but don't think I don't know that you really came for the fashion, and not the music at all. Sure, how often do we get to dress up in evening gear without the risk of getting beer spilt all over our outfits?' Madeleine's friend was clearly remembering the disastrous Freshers' Ball of the previous year. 'I knew that once you tried it you wouldn't find it too bad. There really is more to life than sex, drugs and rock'n'roll you know!' she continued, raising her pretty chin slightly, and adopting the superior tone of the nuns in St Theresa's.

'Well, so far I've only had the rock'n'roll and some "heavy petting" as Sister Agnes used to call it, but I live in hope!' Madeleine replied, laughing.

The two girls had been best friends since school, and scarcely needed the champagne they were given at the interval to send them into fits of gossiping and laughter. The night was turning out to be great fun, better than even Kay had imagined it would be.

It was really by chance that they came to be at the Wexford Opera Festival. Kay's parents, who were avid opera-goers, had been delayed on a flight from Spain and at the last minute phoned Kay to see if she'd like to go instead. Madeleine was staying with her for the weekend, and the friends had planned nothing more elaborate than a video and a takeaway for the evening. The opera sounded like a far more enticing alternative.

Kay still had her debs dress, and she found one of her sister's for Madeleine, and the two had left the house in a frenzy of excitement, not really knowing what the night would hold in store for them.

The festival atmosphere was electric. The otherwise unremarkable little town was transformed, with fashionable couples sipping drinks outside bars, and a murmur of speculation over who would win the critics' favour filled every bar and auditorium.

Once the final curtain had descended over the stage for the last time, the girls gathered up their coats and, with little hesitation, they agreed that the night was too young to end. Following the crowd out of the theatre and into the bustling street, Madeleine and Kay soon found themselves standing outside White's Hotel. The noise coming from inside suggested that the nightlife was worth coming to the festival for, more than the opera itself. As the girls opened the heavy door to the lounge, laughter and the sound of tinkling glasses tumbled out to greet them. After a few polite 'excuse me's and ineffective tapping on shoulders, Madeleine and Kay could see that the only way to get to the bar would be to push their way towards it. Squeezing past a group of people heatedly discussing the merits of that evening's soprano, and ducking under trays of drinks being passed over people's heads, they finally reached the busy counter.

Laughing and smiling together, the two girls were unaware of the attention they were receiving in the room. Madeleine, whose tall, slim figure was crowned by sleek long blonde hair held up in golden pins, was radiant in azure silk. Kay, more petite than her friend, looked equally glamorous in her scarlet Chinese dress, with a seductive slit to the thigh. Madeleine looked cool and sophisticated and Kay, with her dark-haired bob, was the picture of mischief. They were like chalk and cheese.

'I don't think we're ever going to get a drink,' Madeleine muttered in exasperation, as the overworked barman passed them by yet again.

'I know, a body could die of the thirst around here.'

The girls turned around to look up into the wonderfully blue eyes of a tall, dark-haired man. For a moment, Madeleine was speechless. She had never seen anyone so handsome in all her life.

'Sorry, how rude of me, Donal O'Sullivan's my name. I've just put an order in myself, can I get you anything? You could be waiting all night otherwise.'

'That'd be great, thanks. We are both drinking white wine.' She thought it would be pushing her luck to ask for the Dom Perignon she had been enjoying so much earlier. 'Oh, and Madeleine is my name... very pleased to meet you.'

Donal had just reached out to shake Madeleine's perfectly manicured, slender hand when Kay coughed tactfully.

'And yes, eh, I'm Kay,' she said, shooting a look a Madeleine for not introducing her. 'Also a pleasure,' she added with a playful smile.

She knew though that as far as this race was concerned, she wouldn't even make it off the starting blocks. It was clear that

Madeleine had already won: Donal's eyes were glued to her, watching every smile and tilt of her head.

A few minutes later, the three of them were carrying their drinks back to Donal's table. When they reached it, Donal introduced them to a couple already sitting down.

'Madeleine, Kay, these are my good friends, Ray and Betty Barnes, otherwise known as those who will have to make it up to me for dragging me out to the opera!'

Betty reached over and gave Donal a friendly slap on the wrist.

'And this, as I'm sure you've gathered, is Donal O'Sullivan, otherwise known as the most ungrateful soul on the face of the planet.'

Settling back into her seat, Betty squashed up beside Ray on the deep red velvet seats to make room for the two girls.

'So, when you're not busy being an ungrateful soul, what do you do?' Madeleine asked, taking her first sip of white wine.

'Well, I've been studying in the US for a while, but now,' he took a modest bow, 'I'm a qualified urologist.'

Trying to look suitably impressed, Madeleine smiled her congratulations at him, though when Kay nudged her in the ribs and quietly asked what a urologist was, Madeleine had to admit in a whisper that she really didn't know.

'He sorts out men's, you know, problems,' Ray answered out loud.

'You mean if there's something wrong with their…'

'Yes, Kay, thanks, I think that's probably what he means.'

Realising that all eyes were on her, Madeleine humbly thanked Ray for his explanation, mortified, and went back to sipping her wine.

Noticing the vague unease that had settled over the group, Betty smiled and asked in a friendly tone, 'So what do you two do?'

Thankful for the change of direction in their conversation, Kay answered enthusiastically that they were both studying arts in UCD.

'Oh, I was in UCD before I went to the States. Is that old lady who sleeps on the steps of the science building still there?'

'No, but she was probably before our time, I'd say,' Madeleine answered, to the delight of Ray and Betty.

'You've met your match in her, I'm afraid, Donal,' Betty said.

As the conversation continued, Madeleine found herself looking at Donal more and more. He really was extremely attractive and he was one of the most easygoing people she had ever met. He had them in fits of laughter as he recounted tales from medical school and from the rugby pitch, each more outrageous than the last.

They discovered they had a mutual interest in golf, too. Madeleine's father had started her playing when she was very young. Donal refused to tell Madeleine what handicap he played off, though, making the excuse that he hadn't had much time while he was studying in the States to get much practice in. Without thinking, Madeleine put her hand on his leg and laughingly remarked what a weak excuse that was. The smile faded from her face, however, as they both became acutely aware of her touch, and for a moment they just stared intently at each other. In the quiet that surrounded them in the busy bar, Madeleine drank him in. From the dark tousles of his glossy hair, and his broad, muscular shoulders, Madeleine's gaze travelled down his torso to his long, athletic legs and back to his captivating stare. He was well over six feet, and despite his earlier protestations that he didn't like dressing up, she thought he looked unspeakably sexy in his tuxedo.

Soon afterwards, a shout came from the bar that last orders were being taken. Madeleine realised that they had been chatting for hours and, when she looked over at Kay, her friend winked suggestively. Surprisingly, though, when the lights came up fully, the Barneses and then Donal stood up to find their coats.

'Time to head for bed, I think,' Betty said, stifling a yawn.

'Yes, I'd suppose we'd better...' Donal looked down apologetically at Madeleine. Barely able to hide her disappointment, Madeleine stumbled through the goodbyes and promises of meeting up again in a haze of confusion.

Outside, when the girls were alone again, Kay couldn't help blurting out, 'What happened there, Mad? I thought that would be a dead cert.'

'Don't ask me! Men are weird. Who knows what goes on in their heads.' Madeleine spoke jokingly, but she couldn't disguise the letdown she felt at his abrupt departure.

Trying to ease her friend's disappointment, Kay joked: 'I was sure you were going to have your first "older man" relationship, you know, give those nuns something to worry about!'

Madeleine couldn't help but smile. 'And did you see that he didn't even have a wedding ring on? I must be losing my touch!'

'Well you know what they say, plenty more fish in the sea and all that, and you did have the attention of almost every male in the bar tonight, so I wouldn't worry about it.'

'Speaking of fish…' Madeleine said then, nodding towards a convenient fish-and-chip shop.

Kay smiled and put her arm around Madeleine's shoulder, 'Well, we never did get our takeaway this evening did we?'

## March 2002

Having successfully changed his seat allocation so that they were sitting together, Donal arrived back to Madeleine, smiling.

'All set,' he said, his voice sugary with the anticipation of spending the whole journey next to Madeleine, 'and apparently we're boarding now. Are you ready to go?'

'Just give me a minute to run to the ladies,' she replied. If she was going to be sitting beside him for the next six hours, she reckoned a moment alone to gather her thoughts wouldn't go astray. Anyway, she needed to check quickly in the mirror to make sure she was looking OK.

They boarded the aeroplane and as soon as they had settled into their seats, an immaculately groomed air hostess came round to offer them champagne. Madeleine took the fluted glass with a grateful smile. This whole experience was unnerving, and she thought a little alcohol might be just what she needed to calm herself down.

Madeleine soon found that conversation with Donal was much easier than she had expected it to be. For the first hour of their journey they chatted around neutral subjects, such as Madeleine's mother, Donal's job, but inevitably, the question Madeleine had been dreading arose.

'So did your husband remain in the States or is he already in Ireland?' he asked, looking a little anxious himself at what the answer might be.

Trying to control the shake in her voice, Madeleine told him how Kevin had been killed, and how her life had been so drastically turned upside down afterwards that she had decided to come home to Ireland. She omitted, however, to mention anything about their argument, or how they had left each other angry that morning – it was enough that she had to remember it herself. She didn't want anyone else knowing about it.

'Oh, Madeleine,' he said compassionately, 'I am *so* sorry, I had no idea. You know that had I known I would have contacted you, or written, or... I don't know... something.'

His sincerity was obvious and Madeleine was touched that even after all this time he still cared so much for her.

'Thanks, Donal, it was really, truly awful. I honestly don't know how someone is meant to get over this kind of thing, but I suppose I feel that going home is a step in the right direction.'

Madeleine stared at her hands. She couldn't look at him, she found, when she spoke about Kevin. She was startled when Donal reached his hand up to her face and softly stroked her cheek.

'I *am* sorry Madeleine.'

For a moment they just looked into each other's eyes and Madeleine felt every old feeling she ever had for him come rushing back.

15

'Anyway,' she said as he dropped his hand, 'how have *you* been? Obviously doing well for yourself, jet-setting first class all around the world! And, eh, Judith, how's she?'

The question that had been in the back of both their minds since they met was now hanging in the air between them. Madeleine almost wished she could take it back, turn time back to the minute before, when he had so tenderly touched her face. Now, a marked change had come over him. Gone was the Donal she knew so well, and in his place sat a tense, uptight man she didn't recognise.

'She's well, thank you, working hard as usual.'

'And, eh, your children...?' Madeleine asked, already knowing what the answer was. Kay had told Madeleine what had happened after Donal married Judith, but she desperately wanted to know if he would tell her the truth.

A long silence ensued.

'None,' he said in a sober voice, not daring to look at Madeleine's reaction.

She sat motionless, overcome with the emotion of hearing it from Donal's lips, and paralysed with its significance all over again.

'Don't ask,' he pleaded, and something about the desperation in his request made her silence the questions forming in her head.

Thankfully, the static tension between them was relieved by the rattling of the food trolley coming towards their seats. With something else to focus on other than Donal's momentous revelation, Madeleine was grateful for the distraction of fixing the tray in front of her. With dinner to focus on, they both relaxed, and before long were back talking about more general topics. He told her that he was now captain of Redcliff Golf Club, and asked if she still played.

'Well, speaking of Redcliff, my dad never could accept that I was gone to America for good, so he kept up my membership. I

16

kept it up myself after he died last year, I suppose just because I knew that's what he would have wanted me to do.'

Donal knew just how much Madeleine's father had meant to her, and smiled encouragingly, noticing how her voice quietened as she mentioned him.

'As for getting to play in New York, though,' she continued, 'I did play a bit in a friend's club, but not as much as I'd like. And, of course, there was the occasional trip in winter to Florida to get a bit of practice down there. You know how competitive I can be?' she asked with a teasing grin, thinking back to how they used to play together.

'Well, then, we'll just have to wait and see whether standards have slipped or not when we get back! We should have a game up in Redcliff whenever you're free.'

'That sounds great,' Madeleine said, hardly able to keep the smile from her face. She'd have to be careful, though, she thought. He had broken her heart once before, and the stakes were higher now: he was married.

After a surprisingly delicious meal of juicy dill-seasoned salmon, with pecan tortes drizzled with butterscotch syrup to finish, Madeleine drank the last of her champagne and drifted off into a troubled sleep. She dreamt of arguing with Kevin again, only in this dream they weren't alone. Here, Donal and her father looked on disapprovingly, and Madeleine was vaguely aware of feeling that she had somehow let them both down. The rattle of the breakfast trolley roused her, though. Sleepily, she brushed her flaxen hair from her face, and became conscious of the comforting smell of Donal's aftershave – still Polo Sport.

He was still asleep. It took all of her willpower not to lean over and kiss his face, or run her fingers through his thick, dark hair. He looked so peaceful. Surprising herself, she suddenly found herself angry with him. How *dare* he look so peaceful and sleep so well after all that had happened between them, after leaving her heartbroken and forcing her to create a new life for herself in

New York without him. Seeing him begin to wake, though, Madeleine busied herself with smoothing the creases in her trousers. She soon became aware of his eyes following her every movement though, and she looked back at him again.

Grinning, he sat up straight.

'Hiya, Mad,' he said affectionately, allowing his leg to relax beside hers.

'Hiya, Don,' she replied as they had done so very many times, the warmth of his leg beneath his pinstriped trousers dissolving all traces of the anger she had felt just minutes before.

Their respective cars were waiting when they came through customs. Putting down his bags in the arrivals hall, Donal gave her his business card and mobile number.

'So, who knows, I may see you on the course,' he joked, but Madeleine could see the sincerity in his face as he said it.

Leaning down, he kissed her on the cheek, lingering just longer than he had to. Then, picking up his bags, he said goodbye.

'Not if I see you first,' she thought to herself, as she watched him walk through the glass doors. She was still amazed at how he could affect her so powerfully, even now.

'Who knows what moving back to Ireland might mean for me?' she mused, as she picked up her own bags and went out to the taxi.

Dawn was breaking over Dublin as the car glided noiselessly along the motorway. It was a nice crisp morning, and Madeleine decided that this was a good omen for her return. She opened the window and took a deep breath of the cool air that blew in on her face. She had got so used to the smog and noise of New York that this drive in from the airport made her appreciate just how much she had been yearning to get back to Ireland. Thankfully the driver hadn't tried to strike up a conversation. He'd left her to her own thoughts and hummed away quietly to the radio.

Her mum, already up and waiting for her, opened the door before Madeleine even had a chance to ring the bell.

'Oh, Madeleine, it's so good to see you, love!' she said, wrapping her arms warmly around her daughter. 'Sure, look at you!' she exclaimed, feeling Madeleine's waist. 'You're hardly in it, have you been eating at all, child?'

'I'm grand, Mum, honestly, they *do* have food in New York, you know.'

Madeleine's mum gave her a squeeze and her voice softened. 'I know, love, sure I'm just worried about you. You've had a rough old time lately of it haven't you?'

They were interrupted by Snowy the cavalier King Charles spaniel, yelping with excitement at their feet, and the two of them laughed.

'He looks like I feel,' Madeleine's mum said with a smile. 'Now, you come on into the kitchen.'

Now that she was home, Madeleine felt the loss of her dad more acutely. She desperately missed him and even now somehow expected him to come in from another room to greet her. It was almost two years since his death and Madeleine couldn't help noticing that her mum looked a bit older, thinner and a even bit more stooped since she had seen her last. Her parents had been a very devoted couple and seemed to have become even closer after her dad had taken early retirement.

Undoing the large white buttons of her crimson coat, Madeleine took it off and hung it on the end of the stairs. It struck her suddenly that both she and her mum were widows. As she watched her mum filling the kettle at the sink, Madeleine saw how frail she had become. Was it age that did that, she wondered, or loneliness? Putting the thought out of her head, Madeleine followed her mother into the kitchen and settled herself on her favourite armchair beside the Aga.

'You'll have a cup of tea I'm sure,' her mum said. 'You must be parched after the long flight.'

'I'd love one, thanks,' Madeleine said and smiled to herself. She saw that the kettle was already on and there was a plate of scones sitting on the table ready to be eaten. She had forgotten that her mother's offer of tea was never a question she expected an answer to.

Madeleine sank back into the soft cushions of the armchair, and Snowy jumped up immediately into her lap.

'Well, Mum, how've you been?'

'Fine, thanks, missing your dad, of course, but sure I don't think that's ever going to change. And what about you, love, how are you doing?' She looked at her daughter, concerned at the huge ordeal she had been through. Since it had happened, they had spoken often on the phone, but the sense of distance between them had sometimes made Madeleine feel even lonelier.

'Oh, Mum, it's been awful!' she said, surprising herself at the vehemence with which she said it. As soon as it was out, Madeleine realised that she had been bottling up almost all her feelings since Kevin's death, and now she felt like she needed to get it all off her chest.

As if sensing her distress, Snowy began to lick the tears that had begun streaming down Madeleine's face. Her mother came over to her, gently lifting Snowy back down on to the floor and sat beside her on the edge of the armchair. As her mother put her arms around her, Madeleine crumpled, feeling like a little child again, as she pressed her face into the crook of her mother's neck. The tears flowed and her mother comforted her, rubbing her hair and making little soothing sounds, giving Madeleine as much time as she needed to cry.

Eventually the tears stopped and Madeleine started to talk, tentatively at first, as she re-lived that fateful morning. Then, taking a deep breath, she told her mother what she had told nobody else until now.

'Mum, I can't explain how terrible I feel. When Kevin left that morning we'd just had a big row because he wouldn't come to a reception I was organising for my new clients. I was so mad at him for not supporting me, and for being so pig-headed, even though he could see I was seconds away from crying. And then I wouldn't kiss him goodbye, Mum, and he left in a temper, banging the door on the way out. I never saw him after that.' Fresh tears stung her eyes.

Her mother took Madeleine's face in both her hands. 'Now, listen to me, your father and I had countless arguments, but it doesn't mean we loved each other any less. If anything, it made us love each other more, because we got through them. No one's going to deny that the way things ended between you wasn't hard, but you have to realise that a last encounter does not reflect your whole relationship.'

Seeing her daughter so upset made it easier for Madeleine's mother to comfort her with any words she could. In truth, though, the few times she had met Kevin she had found him arrogant, and not as sensitive to Madeleine as he should have been. Still, it wasn't her place to say it then, and she certainly wasn't going to say it now.

'You've got to remember the good times together, how you made each other happy,' she said, stroking Madeleine's hair as they talked.

'But did I, Mum? Did I make him happy?' Madeleine looked into her mother's eyes, anxiously looking for reassurance. 'I wonder if I was a good wife at all,' she continued, 'and that makes me feel even worse.'

Madeleine didn't know if she should mention Donal and how she had travelled home from the States with him. Her mother had never fully approved of their relationship and when he broke her heart, there was no doubt where her sympathies lay. Still, Madeleine felt that if she didn't get everything off her chest now, she might not say it again.

'I sometimes think,' she started quietly, 'well, that maybe because Donal was the first real love of my life, that I never

21

really got over him. That maybe I feel I should still be with him. You know that if I could have married him I would have,' she said, looking up beseechingly at her mother, 'and then I wonder how could I have been a good wife to Kevin at all if I still had feelings for someone else.' The end of Madeleine's sentence tapered off almost into a whisper as she felt her mother stiffen at the mention of Donal.

'Well, now, I think that you have enough on your plate to deal with at the minute without bringing Donal O'Sullivan into the equation. Anyway, I think that you are being very hard on yourself, love. I know how much you loved Donal, and I know how much he hurt you when you broke up. You just have to remember that you rebuilt your life after it happened, and now you have to focus on that again. One of the great things about the future, Madeleine, is that no one knows what it holds, you'll just have to take things as they come.'

Madeleine realised that while her mum wasn't exactly supporting her feelings for Donal, she wasn't condemning them either. As she said, no one knew what was around the next corner. She would just have to plan her own life as best she could, and if Donal was meant to fit into that, she'd soon find out.

Getting up from the side of the chair, Madeleine's mum went over to the teapot on the cooker and poured them both another cup.

'Now, drink this like a good girl and you'll feel better. You're home now.' She kissed the top of Madeleine's head.

Madeleine smiled at her gratefully through watery eyes. 'Oh, Mum, you don't know what a relief it is to get that all out in the open,' she said.

'I do know,' said her mother. 'Sometimes it's a great help to talk. And you know that I'm always here for you.'

They continued chatting for a while until Madeleine began to yawn. She had lost a night's sleep through the time difference and, all of a sudden, she felt totally jet-lagged. She had got some sleep on the plane, but it had been brief and troubled, and Madeleine now felt that the only place she should be was in her bed.

Her old room was just as it had always been, with its pink wallpaper and floral carpet. Her mum had turned on the electric blanket for her, as she used to do when Madeleine was younger and had been out late. As she climbed into her warm bed, she remembered one night, when she was a teenager, when she had stayed out so late with Kay that her bed was too hot to get into when she got home. Hearing her mum coming down the hall, though, was enough to make her jump into the roasting bed fully clothed, her heart pounding for fear of being caught up so late.

Madeleine smiled. It all seemed so long ago. She turned over and snuggled into her pillow with thoughts of happier times, and it wasn't long before she fell asleep.

* * *

When she woke, the sun was pouring in the window, bathing her whole room in glorious yellow sunlight. She lay for a few moments just wallowing in the warmth and comfort of being home again, and for the first few waking minutes, she almost forgot her worries. Lifting herself out from under the snug bedclothes, Madeleine could hear the radio in the kitchen and, opening the door to the landing, she was greeted by the delicious smell of brown bread and fresh coffee. After a relaxing breakfast, over which Madeleine's mum filled her in on all the local gossip since she had last been home, she had a shower and phoned Kay.

'Madeleine! It's so great to hear from you, how long have you been home?' Kay shrieked down the phone, delighted to have her friend back.

'I just got in this morning,' Madeleine replied. 'I was just ringing to see if you'd have time to meet an old friend for coffee?'

23

'If I'd have time? Are you mad? Of course I have time. I've already organised for the au pair to look after the kids for the afternoon, so after I pick them up from school, I'm all yours.'

'OK, then, why don't we meet in Bewley's for a coffee and a good old chat? Would three o'clock suit you?'

'Three. Right. Perfect. Oh, I can't wait to see you!' Kay was talking so fast Madeleine could hardly keep up with her. 'We really have so much to catch up on,' Kay continued excitedly. 'Let's just hang up now and save all our news for three. Right so, three, see ya!'

Madeleine heard a click and the buzz of the dial tone.

She found it difficult to believe that Kay now had three children, all under the age of seven. They had remained close ever since college and had both followed a similar route in going to work for Aer Lingus as hostesses after they graduated. Since giving up work after Holly was born, Kay had stayed at home to be a full-time mum. Madeleine knew, though, that life had grown steadily more difficult over the years, as Ed's drinking gradually worsened. In many ways, Madeleine felt that her coming home could help them both. She needed Kay to support her, to provide friendship and a sense of normality for her after all she had been through over the past few months. And Kay, Madeleine knew, would also appreciate a good friend to talk to. Despite the fact that she was usually bright and cheerful when they spoke, Madeleine knew that it was only a façade. Coping with Ed, as far as Madeleine could see, had gone far beyond marital duty. He treated her badly, he neglected the children, and Kay was miserable.

As Madeleine stood outside the busy café waiting for Kay, she couldn't believe how much Grafton Street had changed. The city had become fashionable and touristy, and the young people walking around had all the confidence of well-paid jobs and promising careers. For a second, Madeleine wondered what would've happened if she had stayed. Would a well-paid job have made up for the heartache of having to see Donal constantly with his glamorous wife, Judith? No, she thought to herself, moving to New York had been the right thing to do.

'Madeleine!' Kay called, spotting her as she came round the corner from Clarendon Court.

'Madeleine, oh, you look wonderful,' Kay exclaimed, as she got closer, and the two of them hugged each other with such affection that it brought tears to Madeleine's eyes. They had constantly been on the phone to each other since 9/11, and emailed regularly, but seeing each other face to face was more emotional than either of them had imagined.

When they finally broke apart, Kay took Madeleine's hands in her own. 'I'm just so sorry,' she said. 'I'd give anything to have you back under different circumstances.'

'I know,' replied Madeleine, 'me too, and thanks for all the calls, Kay. I would never have survived without them. Come on, let's go inside. I've been dying to come to Bewley's since I got home, and I think I might even have a sticky bun for old times' sake!'

With steaming cups of coffee and sticky buns in front of them, the two were soon engrossed in catching up.

'So, where to from here, or should I save that question until you're home more than a day?'

'Well, I have given it some thought, and my plan, I suppose, is not to have a plan. I think I need a little time to sort out what I want to do about staying here long-term, or going to back New York, and that just seems like too momentous a decision to be tackling at the moment. What is top of my list of priorities now, though, is to find an apartment.'

'But what's wrong with staying at home with your mum for while? If I was given the option of having my meals served up to me and my washing magically cleaned without me so much as having to hang out a single load, I know where I'd be staying!'

25

Madeleine looked at her friend, and tried to see how sincere a plea was hidden behind Kay's joviality, but couldn't figure it out.

'I know what you mean, and I'm not disagreeing with you. I think that we're both used to having our own space, though, and that by the time I actually find an apartment, we'll both be ready for me to move out.'

When Kay didn't say anything, Madeleine grew worried that things at home had taken a serious turn for the worse since they last spoke.

'Kay, I'm sorry, we've been sitting here discussing my woes for the last two hours, and we haven't once talked about what's been going on with you.'

'Oh, you know me, Madeleine,' Kay said with a smile, 'always something going on in that mad house I live in, but nothing you'd need to be troubling yourself with, you've enough to be thinking about without me prattling on about family life.'

Although Madeleine could see that there was something on Kay's mind, she decided that it would be better to leave it for another day, there was no point in pressing her for information she wasn't ready to give.

'I know what we'll do!' Kay said suddenly, lightening the mood. 'You still have your membership in Redcliff, don't you?'

'Yes, but I haven't played the course there in about four years, so I'd hate to think how rusty I'd be.'

'Well, Tuesday is still ladies' day, so why don't you come up with me next Tuesday? We can have a round – I promise I won't tell anyone if you're way over par at every hole! – and I'll be able to introduce you to a few people as well.'

'Oh, I don't know, Kay. I don't know that I'm ready for all that yet, maybe I should wait a while until I'm a bit more settled in?'

Kay was having none of it. 'Now, now, Ms O'Connell, we'll have none of that reticence,' she said, jokingly. 'You'll be fine, really you will, and the sooner you start playing the better.'

Madeleine could see the sense in what her friend was saying, but was still reluctant to agree. 'Eh, I don't know, Kay...'

'Good, that's settled then,' Kay said with a finality that allowed no room for further discussion. She looked at her watch. 'Oh my God, is that really the time?' she said taking a last gulp of her coffee. 'I really will have to go or they'll be wondering if I'm ever coming home.'

Just then, a waitress walked past their table and Madeleine signalled for the bill, but Kay insisted on paying.

'My treat,' she said putting a hand on Madeleine's arm, 'and welcome home.'

Outside, after they had hugged each other goodbye, Kay reminded Madeleine again about the following Tuesday. 'No excuses, now!' she said with raised eyebrows, turning around again to catch Madeleine before she went.

'OK, OK, no excuses!'

The mention of Redcliff had got Madeleine wondering whether she might see Donal up there, and an unexpected tingle shot up her spine. She knew that Kay would be up in arms at the mention of his name, just as her mother had been, so she had decided to keep quiet about meeting him. She didn't know how she felt herself about seeing him again, so she couldn't even contemplate having to explain it to someone else.

The more she thought about it, the more Madeleine was glad Kay had pushed her into playing on Tuesday. The practice would do her good, and besides, she always loved going up to Redcliff. She was daunted, however, at the thought of having to get to know so many new people. Well, one person in particular, actually. Donal had mentioned that Judith spent all her free time up in the club these days, and there was only so long Madeleine would be able to avoid her.

# CHAPTER TWO

*Tuesday – Judith*

'OK, I'M RELYING ON YOU THEN TO TAKE CARE OF IT,' JUDITH snapped icily down the phone to her assistant, Carol. 'As usual, leave a message on my mobile if there are any problems, but as I've basically taken care of everything anyway, I'm assuming I won't have to hear from you until tomorrow.'

Barely allowing her beleaguered assistant to draw a breath to agree with her, Judith cut her off again.

'And I'll be on the golf course all morning, so if something does arise, I won't be contactable until lunchtime at the earliest. Have you got all that now?'

'Yes, that's no problem, Jud...'

'Good. Bye then.' Judith hung up abruptly.

When she needed to be, she could be absolutely charming, but Judith saw no reason to charm her assistant. Employing her in the first place was consideration enough, she thought, and paying her well bought Judith the right to dismiss any notions Carol might have had about small talk or niceties.

For eight years now, Judith had run an extremely successful and exclusive interior-design business. Looking around her living room, she congratulated herself once again on her exceptional taste and her talent for capturing all that embodied style and elegance in a room. Georgian coving perfectly framed the rococo designs covering the ceiling. She had painted the walls pale blue to create a delicate backdrop for the large eighteenth-century armchairs facing the impressive fireplace. And the ornate mirror between two vases of lilies above the mantelpiece was the perfect focal point for Judith's guests to congratulate her on.

It had been said of Judith that she took more pleasure in things than in people. She found it easier to manipulate colours, textures, fabrics and furniture to suit her taste than those around her, whom she couldn't rely on to conform to her plans. She also knew that others questioned her relationship with Donal. He, who was so easygoing and friendly, was the opposite of everything that defined Judith. Indeed, his old friends Ray and Betty Barnes made no secret of the fact that they couldn't see why he had married her at all. Judith, however, had learned long ago to categorise anyone who didn't agree with her as beneath her, and so lost no time in worrying about them.

Judith had found it easy to be successful. She was undeniably beautiful, and exploited it to her advantage in every way she could. Her hair fell in brunette cascades down her back and glinted with copper when it caught the light, reflecting the chestnut brown of her almond-shaped eyes. She also took immeasurable pride in her perfect size ten figure, thanks partly to sessions with a personal trainer at six thirty, three mornings a week. She also had regular appointments at the beautician's and in the hair salon, and was rarely seen looking less than absolutely immaculate. Men were in awe of her, and women wanted to look like her. Coupling this power over people with a bearable dose of superficial thoughtfulness, Judith had quickly learned how to control the tastes and, by extension, the purse-strings, of her growing clientele.

Just as she replaced the receiver on the hook, Donal put his head around the door. 'Judith, just letting you know I'll be off in about five minutes. I should be home fairly early for a change. Will I see you this evening?'

She looked up at him critically. 'God almighty,' she said, resting one hand jauntily on her hip, 'wouldn't you think that, as captain of the golf club, you would remember that Tuesday is ladies' day? You know I always go back to the club for dinner on ladies' day, and so you should be able to work it out: I won't be home until about eleven, Donal.'

'Oh, sorry, I forgot what day it is. I'll just take something out of the freezer for myself, so, to have later.'

Donal was about to close the door, when he had second thoughts.

'Actually, Judith, I might meet Jim for a pint and something to eat if he's free. I haven't seen him in ages.' With that he closed the door behind him and left Judith alone again.

'Whatever you like,' she thought to herself. As long as his little soirée with Jim didn't interfere with her plans, she really didn't care what he did for the evening.

'Don't forget, we're having a dinner party on Saturday night,' she called out. She must remember to decline her own invitation to that charity auction in Dublin Castle. 'I know how busy your schedule is, so I thought I might remind you,' she said, following him into the kitchen. 'The Turners have already said they're free that night, I have provisional yeses from the Bakers and the O'Mearas, and Tom and Lucy Cahill will be in the south of France until Friday morning, but they have said they'd be delighted to come.'

'I know, I haven't forgotten,' Donal replied, and turned back to buttering his toast.

He had no trouble remembering the date of Judith's dinner parties, but what he did have a problem with was remembering where he had met the guests before. Saturday's line-up, for example, could go either way. Tom and Lucy and the Turners were old friends – well, acquaintances really – but he had only met the Bakers once before at a medical function, and trying to place the O'Mearas was proving to be a bit of a problem.

'So what's the reason for this one, then?' he asked, aware that he'd probably regret the question. Judith never held a dinner party just for the sake of seeing friends, there always had to be some ulterior motive – a new contact one week, a prospective wealthy client the next.

Somehow, though, Judith had become known for her dinners, legendary in fact. To be fair, Donal thought, she did put a lot of planning and effort into them. The planning however, never moved past the dining room. As far as Judith was concerned, the kitchen was a space to be decorated, not to cook in.

'That's what caterers are for, darling,' she had said once, when Donal asked why she never cooked for her own dinner parties, regardless of how many, or how few, were attending. It was a throwback, no doubt, to her own privileged upbringing, which had moulded her sense of superiority from a young age.

'No reason at all,' she lied now, and Donal decided not to pursue it.

Taking his piece of toast with him, he rummaged in his pocket to find his keys.

'See you later, then,' he said and, giving Judith a peck on the cheek, he was gone.

After casting an eye over the 'to-do' list she had made for the day to make sure that everything was in order, Judith went up to her bedroom to finish getting ready for golf. As she entered the room, she paused momentarily to congratulate herself on the wonderful job she had just done in redecorating it. The walls were papered in subtle lilac, which complemented beautifully the deep purple satin bedspread; the ceiling was pristine white, and the minimalist furniture she had chosen for the room was also white. Little crystal cups of snowdrops adorned each of the side tables beside the bed, and, irritated because they weren't completely symmetrical, Judith nudged one glass just a millimetre or two into place. No one could deny that it was an opulent makeover, and the brocade chaise longue by the large bay window added the perfect touch of languor to give the room a slight aura of decadence.

Judith treaded noiselessly across the deep, alabaster-white carpet to the adjoining bathroom, to add the final touches to her flawless makeup. As she swept the mascara wand of ebony black through her long thick lashes, she decided that she would be extra nice to Aisling Turner in the coming months. She had gathered from something Donal had said that Aisling was going to be nominated as next year's lady vice-captain, and Judith shrewdly reckoned that Aisling, in turn, would be able to nominate the one after that. Smoothing amber gloss over her full lips, Judith looked at her reflection in the mirror. She had strategically befriended all the right people in Redcliff who could further her position within the club, and now she felt she was closer than ever to getting the title she had been coveting for years. She wanted more than anything to become lady captain of Redcliff. And what Judith wanted, Judith got.

## Tuesday – Linda

'Jean, darling...'

There was no reply.

'Jean, you asked me to give you a call before I left this morning and it's half eight now.'

Silence.

Shaking her gently by the shoulder, Linda looked lovingly at her daughter as she reluctantly opened her eyes.

'Thanks, Mum,' said Jean, sleepily stretching one arm at a time out from underneath the cosy duvet. 'I'll be up now in just a sec.'

'So, how did last night go?' Linda asked. It had been Jean's first time working on a live programme the night before and Linda was keen to find out that it had all gone smoothly for her.

'Oh, yeah,' Jean replied, as if she had forgotten herself how it had gone. 'It was great, actually, I loved the buzz of the live studio, but I was absolutely whacked afterwards.'

She threw back the covers and hopped out of bed.

'I've to go back in tonight, to work again, so they must have been happy with me... Oh, it's freezing out here!' she added with a shiver, looking longingly back at her bed.

'Don't you even think about it!' Linda said, smiling at the look on her daughter's face.

'OK, I'll just take a quick shower, and I'll be down then.'

Back in the kitchen, Linda sat down to finish her muesli. Her husband Ian was already at the table filling in the *Irish Times* crossword.

'She'll be down soon, she's just having a shower. Apparently she had a great time last night,' Linda said, taking the last spoonful of her cereal and putting the bowl in the sink.

'That's great,' said Ian looking up happily from his paper. 'I knew she was a bit worried about it.'

They had both been concerned that the night should go well. Ever since she had started to work as a production assistant in RTÉ, Jean had really blossomed, and the worry of the past few years had slowly begun to fade into the background. For four years prior to seeking help, anorexia had dominated Jean's life and it had been an unbearably anxious time for them all. Linda had taken early retirement from the school where she had been headmistress, and was glad then, when it was needed, that she could devote all her time to helping her daughter get better.

Once Jean was firmly set back on the road to recovery, Linda had accepted the position of lady captain at Redcliff. Much as she loved it, she couldn't help feeling sometimes that it wasn't dissimilar to being a headmistress. She found that she had more trouble dealing with members on the golf course than she ever had with children arguing in the playground, but she loved the fact that it was such a mixed crowd. Trying to encourage the shy and quieten the brazen among the members was something Linda felt more than qualified to deal with. She knew how difficult it was to join a club where everybody else knew each other, and she had decided when she took the position that this was something she would try to make easier for the new members.

What had surprised Linda was how fast it was all going. A year was a very short time in which to achieve everything she hoped, and the first three months seemed to have already flown by. Speaking of flying, she thought, looking at the clock on the wall, she had better hurry up so she would make the ten o'clock draw.

'Have a good day,' she said to Ian, leaning over him to give him a quick kiss.

'Yeah, you too, love, enjoy your game,' he replied, looking up at her from his paper, only to catch the back of her stylish slim figure and blonde bob as she rushed out the kitchen door.

Shouting a goodbye up the stairs to Jean, Linda closed the door behind her and went to pick up the battery for her golf trolley, which she had left charging in the garage. She hopped into her Volkswagon Golf – a present from Ian last Christmas in honour of her captaincy – and, pulling out of the long driveway, headed off to Redcliff.

## Tuesday – Kay

Kay looked angrily at the figure lying in the bed.

'No I'm not calling in sick for you again. I said on Friday that it was the last time I was going to do that for you and I meant it.'

Whatever sympathy she used to have for her husband on these occasions had vanished. Somewhere between his sharp-tongued abuse as she woke him, and the distasteful smell of beer that wafted around the darkness of the spare bedroom, Kay had decided that she wasn't going to humour his requests, or his excuses, any more.

'I'm sick of all of this, Ed. I'm your wife, not your mother, so if you want to ring in sick, then do it yourself,' she said with what she hoped sounded like vengeful authority. 'It's time you got your act together for God's sake.'

Walking away from the bed towards the door, Ed groaned from the depths of the duvet.

'Ah, Kay,' he mumbled, 'I feel like shit. No, I feel worse than shit. You *have* to call in for me. I'm meant to chair a meeting this morning too, and I'm in no state to do it. Especially as the old man's going to be there and he's a right pain in the arse about being on time and prepared and all that bullshit.'

As Ed trailed off the end of his sentence, he turned in the bed to face the wall, which Kay knew meant that he considered the conversation to be over.

'You can say what you like, Ed, it's not going to make a difference this time,' Kay muttered, walking away.

Ed lifted his head slowly off the pillow and looked around at his wife through bloodshot eyes.

'What the hell are you making such a song and dance about it for? It's a phone call, Kay. I'm not asking you to give me a kidney.'

'I'm not making a song and dance about it. I'm not doing anything about it. Literally. No phone calls, no excuses, no Solpadeine. Just look at the state of you, Ed, you're a disgrace.

'Look, I told you already what happened last night,' Ed started. 'I can't go to Martin's stag party in Galway with the others because that's the weekend of Holly's First Communion, and you know I'd never dream of missing that. So, I met Martin last night instead, just to have a meal and a couple of drinks – it wasn't my idea to go to Lillie's for a last pint, you know, that was all Martin's plan.'

But Kay wasn't listening, her mind had wandered off, thinking about Madeleine. If she could survive such drastic changes to her life, then maybe Kay could do it too. Further hardening her resolve to ignore Ed's slurring pleas for help, she opened the door to escape the stale air of the bedroom and went out into the landing.

'OK, OK,' Ed said, sitting up a little straighter in the bed and raising his voice, 'so I had a bit too much to drink last night, but I wasn't driving and I came home, didn't I? Jesus, my head hurts,' he finished, rubbing his hand over his forehead.

Seeing that Kay was continuing to walk down the stairs, Ed decided that she had just seen sense and was probably going to call the office for him that very minute.

'Food poisoning would be a good excuse...' he called out to an empty hall, but no response came back to agree with him.

Ed always seemed to be able to justify his drinking, Kay thought to herself as she went into the kitchen. What worried her more was the fact that he needed to justify it so often. She had tried numerous times to bring it up with him, but he always avoided the conversation. 'Lighten up, Kay,' was a phrase she had got used to hearing, and she was mildly surprised that she hadn't heard it from him that morning.

Actually, in that regard, Ed was right. She did need to lighten up – in fact it was exactly what she needed. Life seemed to have got very difficult all of a sudden, and Kay was sick of it. She was aware, however, that her burden wasn't going to get any lighter as long as Ed was drinking. Although she didn't quite know what she was going to do about it yet, she knew quite definitely what she *wasn't* going to do. She would not make any more phone calls for him. He could tell the children himself why he hadn't turned up to yet another school play. And she would move all his stuff, permanently, into the spare room.

Her youngest son, Dominic, was crawling around the kitchen floor with a cracker clenched in one of his chubby little hands. Kay picked him up and told the others to go and get their school bags. Claudette, the new French au pair, was at the counter, getting together packed lunches for Holly and Mark. She smiled at Kay.

'Yez, Dominic, 'ee very much like eez crackers, *non?*'

'Yes, but you manage to get it all over your face, don't you, y'little monkey?' Kay said, wiping Dominic's face with his bib and smiling warmly back at Claudette. She knew that Claudette must have heard Ed come in drunk during the night, and also probably heard him shouting from the bedroom earlier, so Kay appreciated that she didn't make an issue of it, now that the two of them were alone.

Kay looked at her watch. It was already eight thirty. She handed Dominic over to Claudette and helped Holly and Mark with their coats.

'Have you both got your lunch boxes now?' she asked, eager to get them ready and leave the house. She did not want to be around when Ed got the phone call from work asking where he was.

'And you have fun with Claudette until I get back,' she told Dominic, giving him a kiss and mouthing 'thank you' to the French girl as she backed out the door.

The other children were already in the Jeep, waiting for her.

'Peace at last,' she thought to herself, as she settled back into the car after dropping the kids off at school. She could hardly wait to see Madeleine again. She had been so excited at their last meeting she could hardly talk, but a couple of hours out on the golf course would give them plenty of time to chat.

It hadn't been until Madeleine came home that Kay realised just how much she had missed her. Phone calls and emails had sustained their friendship between Madeleine's visits home, but nothing compared to being able to call around to see each other whenever they wanted to. Kay felt her problems were never as daunting when she had Madeleine to discuss them with, and she knew that her friend would give her more confidence to deal with them than she could ever muster on her own. Ever since their college days, they had been used to daily contact, and, when they both joined Aer Lingus after college, they always looked forward to working the same flights.

Kay knew that there was nothing she couldn't tell Madeleine, who had been there to support her through one of the hardest times in her life. When Kay's parents had told her that Declan, the one true love of her life, was socially beneath her, and that she couldn't see him any more, it was Madeleine who encouraged her to ignore them. Kay's parents had considered Declan to be from 'the wrong side of Killreeny' and constantly spoke about his uncultured accent and undesirable address in front of their daughter in the hope that it might dissuade her from seeing him. Despite Madeleine's ardent protestations that her parents were wrong, however, their nagging eventually took its toll on Kay. She became tired of lying about where she had been every time she saw him, and keeping his name out of every conversation she had with her parents weakened her determination to defy them. Eventually Kay's parents forced a chasm between her and Declan, and she spent many desolate months teary-eyed, asking Madeleine how it had all gone so wrong.

When Ed appeared then, shortly afterwards, with his good looks, flamboyant personality, wealthy background and the blessing of her parents, Kay was swept off her feet. She hadn't known at the time that alcohol was what kept his flamboyancy afloat, or that wealth, ultimately, could not secure Kay happiness. This realisation dawned on her too late, after the first couple of years of marriage, when excuses for being late or not coming home at all became more and more frequent.

It was to Madeleine that Kay turned when things got really bad, and they would sit up talking into the early hours of the morning. Madeleine was the only person that Kay really opened up to, and they often discussed what her life might have been like if she had ignored her parents and married Declan in the first place. Kay knew from mutual friends that he had never married, although judging by the photographs in the society pages, he was never without a beautiful girl on his arm. After a short certificate course, Declan had started up his own business in IT support, and later branched into web design when he saw how big the market was for it. Since then, his business had gone from strength to strength, and it wasn't long before the media's social diarists started photographing Declan around town. His striking good looks and his shrewd head for business put him in the spotlight as one of Dublin's most eligible bachelors, and it was difficult for Kay, and her parents, to avoid hearing about his success.

Thinking back on old boyfriends, Kay remembered Donal, and wondered whether Madeleine ever thought of him any more. As she drove along the winding coast road, it came to her that he was now the captain of Redcliff. Thank goodness today was ladies' day, she thought to herself. It would buy her a little extra time to prepare Madeleine for the possibility that, sooner or later, she would have to bump into him. Although Kay hadn't heard Madeleine talk about Donal in quite some time, she knew that her friend had never got over him. Donal had broken her heart, and he had had to pay for that by being forced to marry a woman he didn't love. Redcliff was a small club, though, and Kay reckoned that it was only a matter of time before the past got dragged up, and Madeleine, Donal and Judith would all have to face each other.

## Tuesday – Nessa

'I think I'll try the new Atkins diet,' Nessa said, looking over her magazine at James who was coming in the door fastening his dressing gown.

'Hmm...'

'The Atkins diet, I just read an article all about how Melanie Griffiths lost loads of weight on it, and it said she could eat anything she wanted to.'

'What are you going on a diet for?' he said coming over to Nessa and kissing her neck. 'You're lovely the way you are.'

'I know *you* think I'm lovely, darling, and I do appreciate that, but all the people at the fundraiser next month aren't going to think I'm quite so lovely in my Sonia Rykiel dress when the zip won't close.'

'Why don't you just buy a bigger dress, then?'

Judging by the look Nessa fired across the table at him, James realised that his question mightn't have been the wisest one to ask.

'What I mean is, those designer dresses are always smaller than normal dresses, so maybe you just need to get a bigger size... but that'd be the dress's fault and not yours, honey, you know?' he said, hoping to have dug himself out of a hole.

'The dress's fault? Well, at least you tried!' Nessa smiled at her husband's well-intentioned efforts to make her feel better. 'No, but seriously, I have to get into that dress somehow, and I'm fed up of Weight Watchers. Counting points all week and avoiding all of the things I adore, only to go back to the poxy Weight Watchers' scales and find out that I've put on two pounds.' Nessa drew a breath. 'No thanks.'

James watched Nessa as she piled her home-made marmalade onto thickly buttered white toast.

'Besides, the last time I was going to a meeting, that toffee-nosed cow, Heather McCarthy, just happened to be walking past and stopped to talk to me in that sneering, skinny little way of hers.'

'How exactly does someone stop to talk in a "skinny little way"?' James asked curiously, knowing that he wasn't going to get a logical answer.

'That's not the point, James, the point is that she just couldn't help looking down her bony nose at me in my new velour tracksuit, and smirking as she asked me where I was going.' Nessa was irate at the memory of the encounter, and as she continued talking her voice picked up vehemence with every sentence. 'Her! Standing outside Weight Watchers, asking *me* where I was going, when clearly, *clearly*, she heard me saying to Linda in Redcliff the other week that I was going to try it. Silly cow.'

'So, eh…' James wasn't quite sure what he should say. 'Were you talking to her for long?' he ventured, still not one hundred per cent certain he shouldn't be trying to change the subject.

'Well, didn't she only tell me that the greatest aid to weight loss was strength of character and will power?' Nessa said aghast, sitting back in her chair and taking another bite of toast. As a drop of butter fell and trickled down her sweatshirt, she began again in a calmer, more rational tone: 'I wanted to tell her that I had strength of character in abundance, because that was all that was stopping me from smacking her over the head with my points–counter booklet.'

James gave a small laugh.

'Anyway,' Nessa continued, licking her lips for a smudge of marmalade that had gone astray, 'I've just decided that Weight Watchers isn't for me. And besides, the Atkins diet doesn't require you to stand on a scales in public or make you contend with the likes of Heather McCarthy either, so I may as well give it a go.'

James looked at his wife as she picked up a crumb from her plate with one finger whilst simultaneously pouring a cup of tea with her other hand. He knew that no matter how often he said it, he could never get Nessa to believe that he really did love her the way she was. He had first met her when she was working as a secretary in his father's firm, and had been instantly attracted to her bubbly personality and small, curvaceous figure. She would wear tight skirts that clung to her shapely hips, which James's eyes used to follow around the office until she caught him at it, which made her blush.

Happy as James was with her figure, though, Nessa was equally unhappy with it, and was constantly trying out new diets in the hope that she could still eat what she wanted and lose weight. In the fifteen years they had been married, she had never fallen below eleven stone, but despite her best efforts, Nessa knew deep down that even the most beautiful Sonia Rykiel dress couldn't motivate her to slim.

Nessa liked to blame her mum. 'My ma's idea of a diet was less chips,' she told James once. To other people, though, Nessa simply said it was in her genes, on her mother's side, but she rarely went into much detail. In general, she avoided talking about her family and her upbringing, preferring to keep the life she had now separate from the life she had had when she was growing up. Nessa's mother had raised eight children on her father's small income and it was often the case with clothes, and particularly with food, that quantity was more important than quality.

Although Nessa had huge respect for her parents, she always knew that she wanted more for herself than to bring up a houseful of children and struggle to make ends meet. So, at sixteen, she left school and took a secretarial course at night, paid for by temporary work in Dunnes Stores as a check-out girl. Soon after that, she got a job in James's father's business, and she wasn't long working there before she asked James out on a date. Nessa had been attracted to him since the day she had started at the firm, and toyed for days with the idea of asking him out. She had figured from the way he followed her around with his eyes all day that he wouldn't say no, and she was right. James was delighted, if a little taken aback at the invitation, and spent the rest of the afternoon with a grin on his face. James never had a problem with her less than privileged background, no more than with her weight, and it was Nessa herself who placed the taboo on talking about it. She always kept in touch with her family, but she rarely spoke of them to the friends she and James had made. No matter how unfounded her fears, Nessa was always vaguely worried that they might turn their noses up at the class difference.

One thing that Nessa was forever grateful to her upbringing for, however, was her lack of pretension. Knowing that wealth was a luxury not everyone could afford, Nessa had an acute sense of how lucky she was. So, when she heard that a friend of hers was volunteering for charity work, she saw it as an opportunity to give help to others who hadn't been as fortunate as she had been in improving her lot. She volunteered as well, and now it was a charity event, a fundraiser for the children of Chernobyl, that was pressing so heavily on her mind. She had worked extremely hard helping to organise it and she wanted more than anything to look fantastic on the night. She imagined how the stunning – if currently too small – jade green dress would look against her sparkling blue eyes, and she had got golden-blonde highlights through her short brown hair especially for the occasion too.

'Oh, well,' she sighed, 'there's always the reliable little black dress from last year's annual golf dinner if the green one refuses to stretch for the occasion.'

'What are you thinking about? You look a million miles away,' James asked, watching Nessa as she held her toast precariously in mid-air.

'Thinking about? Oh, nothing. Actually, before I forget, though, I wanted to check with you about Florida.'

They had bought an apartment in Belleair Beach a few years previously, and for some time now, Nessa had been trying to think of more ways to use it.

'Are you still on for going there when the boys get back from school at Easter?'

'Sorry, honey,' James said, his forehead crumpling into a slightly worried expression. 'I forgot to mention it to you yesterday. I have some clients coming over from Germany to look at the new stock, and Dad won't be there, so it looks like I'll have to stay. Would you go over with the boys on your own?'

James asked the question with more than a hint of uncertainty in his voice. Their two sons, Gavin, who was fifteen, and Alan, thirteen, had made it clear after the previous trip that they didn't like spending all of their holidays in Florida. Although Nessa would have loved to have them, she did appreciate that her sons wanted to spend time at home as well. Going to boarding school was something they only tolerated at best, Gavin especially. Nessa knew that cutting short their time with their own friends over the Easter holidays was hardly fair.

'We're not using that place half enough, you know,' Nessa said, mentally counting up the number of times they had been there in the past year. 'It sits there for months on end with nobody in it, and I just feel like it's such an awful waste of money.'

Nessa glared at James, as if willing him to come up with an answer there and then as to how they could get more use out of the apartment.

'*I* know!' she exclaimed, much to James's relief. 'Maybe I'll get some of the girls together from the club and see if they'd like to come with me for a golfing holiday.'

Delighted with herself, Nessa sat back with a satisfied smile.

'Sounds like a good idea to me,' James replied, quietly thrilled that there hadn't been an argument over his not being able to go.

'Right, on that note then, I'm off to Redcliff,' she said, standing up. 'I might even mention it to a couple of the girls while I'm up there today. See you later.'

Taking half a piece of bread from James's plate, which he looked like he wasn't eating, Nessa left in a flurry of excitement, leaving her husband to his paper, and peace.

## *Tuesday – Catriona*

'Now, you remember everything I told you about etiquette on the golf course don't you?' Mike asked, not waiting for an answer. 'The person with the lowest handicap goes first, make sure you don't get into anyone else's line of vision, especially on the green, put your trolley pin-high, mark your card at the next hole, call people through if you lose your ball and don't ask for advice – it's not allowed.'

Catriona looked around her as if hoping that someone might pop out from behind the couch and explain to her what exactly 'pin-high' meant.

Mike was gathering together some work files he had brought home to prepare for his meeting that day, and in between shuffling and reorganising, he looked up at her again.

'Did you get all that? Seriously, Cat, in golf it's not just about your swing and your putt you know, it's all about the little things as well.'

'Yeah,' Catriona agreed vaguely. She was still wondering how a trolley could ever be higher than the pin, and images of golfers holding huge bags of clubs up over their heads elevated above the flagpole made her begin to laugh.

Mike put down the folder he was holding.

'It's not funny, Catriona. If you understand the rules of the game, you'll be able to play it better,' he said, and went over to put a supportive arm around her shoulders.

'It's OK, Mike, I've been repeating everything you said in my head, and it'll be grand.'

Catriona had been trying hard to share Mike's enthusiasm for golf for months now, but hadn't once succeeded in getting excited about a game. 'And anyway, I really think I'm getting better, so maybe today I won't need to ask other people for help like I did the last time.'

Catriona found her mind wandering off golf to how best they could redecorate the kitchen. Since she had moved in with Mike two years ago, she had begun to make changes around the apartment to make it feel less like his bachelor-pad and more like their home. At first, she only added things she knew Mike couldn't possibly disagree with – a vase of flowers in the hall, some matching cushions for the couch – but gradually, as he showed signs of liking the improvements, Catriona became more adventurous. She bought colourful prints and pictures for each room, and last month she had ruthlessly stripped down the tired pastel wallpaper in their bedroom and instead painted the room a luscious ruby red and put tall black wrought-iron candlesticks in the corners. To her surprise, Mike was delighted with the changes and encouraged Catriona to keep going. With free rein then to do as she wished, Catriona had decided that the kitchen would be next. If golf was Mike's passion, then cooking was hers, and she had seen the perfect chrome blender in town at the weekend, which she was sure would look incredible in the new kitchen.

'... and so all you'd have to do in that situation is aim for the top of the pin over the edge of the bunker and firmly strike the ball with a sand wedge.'

Realising that Mike was still talking about her game, Catriona refocused her glazed expression. 'Yes. Of course, my um, sand wedge, that would do it, wouldn't it?' she replied, biting her bottom lip and hoping that he hadn't noticed that she didn't have a clue what he was talking about.

She hated this bloody game. Not only could she never get the hang of all the rules and the etiquette, she was just no good at it. She hated everything about the game, from the irritatingly uncomfortable sun-visor she had to wear, right down to the stupid-looking 'hats' everyone loved to cover their woods with. Mike was totally addicted to it, though, and for that reason, and that reason only, she persevered.

Two Christmases ago, an elated Mike had handed over an envelope to Catriona, who received it with equal excitement. She was hoping that it would be a voucher to take the Ballymaloe cookery course she had been dropping so many hints about. One of the new chefs who worked in the restaurant with her had spent the previous six months training there, and from what Catriona heard from him, it was a priceless experience. What she found instead, though, on opening the envelope, was a series of golf lessons with Gillian Burrell, and a voucher to be redeemed for a set of golf clubs. Her heart sank. But knowing how much it meant to Mike, Catriona put on a brave face and tried as best she could to enjoy his present. Despite all the lessons she had taken, however, she knew after the very first one that there wasn't even the hint of a natural golfer in her.

To Catriona's distress, some months after her lessons ended, Mike came home one evening and eagerly told her that he and a few of his friends in Redcliff had put her name forward for a five-day membership. He was so keen and obviously delighted with himself, she just couldn't let him down. His piercing blue eyes were looking into her own in anticipation of finding the same enthusiasm there, and Mike, who usually maintained an extremely smart appearance, now looked slightly dishevelled in his excitement. As he told Catriona about her nomination, a strand of his dark red hair flopped over his lightly freckled forehead, and his well-toned body was almost tangibly tingling with the thought of having Catriona in Redcliff with him.

Catriona knew that it would have to be a waiting game. She couldn't tell Mike that she didn't want membership to Redcliff, so all she could do was hope that the application would be unsuccessful. Much to her disappointment, however, she found out the following January that she had been accepted, and ever since then had prayed for torrential rain each Tuesday. She felt that she reached new levels of incapability with every visit to Redcliff, to the point where she was sure she was getting worse instead of better. She couldn't bear the constant humiliation of mishitting her balls into the dense growth either side of the fairway, or watching with equal gloom as yet another ball plopped and slowly sank into one of the many lakes around the course.

Catriona knew, though, that she couldn't put all of her golfing failure down to a simple dislike of the game. It also had to do with her innate lack of self-confidence. She never felt comfortable in the clothes she had to wear for Redcliff, and pulling the trolley full of clubs always felt awkward and unnatural to her. If she was totally honest with herself, Catriona also knew that she only kept playing because she was afraid that if she didn't, Mike might find someone else who would. She realised that this wasn't really very likely to happen, but still she couldn't seem to shake the doubts that lingered permanently in her mind.

Apart from cooking, Catriona never gave herself any credit for being talented, or interesting, or even attractive. What everyone else saw, though, behind her low self-esteem and insecurity, was a heart of gold, and a subtle sense of humour that attracted friends wherever she went. Catriona believed that there really wasn't very much she was good at, which made it very difficult for her to muster up any enthusiasm for things she was unused to – especially golf. She didn't realise, either, that behind her glasses were two dazzling emerald green eyes, under her baggy jumpers was a beautiful hour-glass figure, and tied up permanently in a pony-tail was a mane of thick, almost black glossy hair.

Accepting that there was no possible method of delaying any longer, Catriona went to find the keys to her car. With Mike gone into the kitchen to get himself a cup of coffee, she had a little time to think back on the snippets of his advice she could remember. She hoped to God it wasn't an open draw today. Last time there was one of those, she had been drawn to play with an insensitive bitch who criticised her every swing and hand position on the golf club. She'd even had the nerve to ask her if she'd ever thought of having a lesson.

'Oh, please let it be a class draw,' Catriona thought to herself, knowing that if it was she would only have to play with people who had a similar handicap to her.

'It still mightn't be any fun,' she mumbled to the empty room, 'but at least there'd be a lesser degree of humiliation to endure.'

'Right, well, good luck this morning, Cat,' Mike said cheerily as he came back, bearing a delicious-smelling cup of coffee, 'and make sure you give me a call on the mobile to let me know how you scored.'

'Of course I will.' She smiled at him, looking much brighter than she felt. 'And you have fun working, too.'

As she reached up to hug him, Catriona looked out the window at the bright blue sky and streaming sunshine, and felt that even the elements were against her. Today's weather was yet another sign, she felt sure, that fate was having a laugh at her expense. With a small sigh, Catriona turned to leave for Redcliff.

## Tuesday – Marie

Marie stepped out of the shower and wrapped a large cream cotton towel around her. The steam was floating in swirling clouds through the bathroom, and she stood for a moment luxuriating in its warmth. Today was going to be a great day, she decided, opening the door and going through to her bedroom. Ladies' day, as far as she was concerned, was the best day of the week. With any luck, her usual rendezvous with Ciaran would be on the cards too, and they could have a quick shag after she came in from the eighteenth. Even thinking about it turned her on.

'That's what doing without it for so long will do to you,' Marie considered, 'but what fun making up for lost time!' she thought to herself with a wicked grin.

When she and Billy had broken up two years ago, Marie soon found that the single life was a lot more enjoyable, and a lot less lonely than she feared it would be. For a start, sex was proving to be much more plentiful than it had ever been when she was married. In fact, for the last few years of their marriage, sex, Marie reckoned, had been virtually non-existent, as it became increasingly apparent that Billy wasn't interested in her. It turned out shockingly, and secretly a little to Marie's relief, that Billy wasn't interested in having sex with any woman, but was most definitely interested in having it with men.

It had been a difficult time for them all. Their middle son, Eugene, who was himself gay, had seen his father in a gay bar and outed him in a row with Marie. What followed was something of a cacophony of melodramatic arguments. Marie shouted, Billy wildly denied, then confessed, then wept loudly, and Eugene stealthily sulked in the corner, fuelling the situation with spurious comments whenever he thought the passion for arguing was dampening. Eventually the fracas was silenced, when Marie hurled a decanter of Chivas Regal across the room and struck the marble mantelpiece. As shards of crystal rained down around their feet, everyone stood, frozen, until finally Marie, very quietly, asked everyone to leave. Within two weeks, Billy had taken his belongings and moved into a rented apartment nearby, and Eugene announced that he was going to live in town with his partner – a magnificently wealthy man twenty years his senior.

At fifty years of age, Marie considered it was about time that she sorted out her own life, or at the very least, started having some real fun again. She had known for years that their marriage wasn't making either her or Billy happy, and so letting him go had felt like a release for both of them. She also found, to her surprise, that she didn't even miss him. With her daughter Sinéad working in the States for the summer and her eldest son John living in a room on the UCD campus, she felt she could do whatever she wanted. She could walk around the house naked if she liked, without reprimanding looks from her husband or castigation from her sons. With no one to answer to, she could spend outrageous amounts of money on clothes and shoes and bags and beauty treatments if she wanted to, and best of all, for the first time in a very long time, she could have thrilling, breathtaking sex with younger men.

It didn't take long for Marie to get used to her new, blissfully self-indulgent lifestyle. Even after the separation, she still held a fifty per cent share in Billy's construction business, which ensured her an excessively generous deposit in her bank account every month. All that was required was a perfunctory thirty-minute appearance in the office three days a week to remind everyone that she was still the boss, leaving the rest of her time free for golf – and for Ciaran. Watching his fantastically toned body move around as he worked behind the bar in Redcliff gave her a huge rush of excitement, and the fact that he was fifteen years younger than she was added to her sense of secret, forbidden pleasure. She knew that, as soon as he took his break, they would be having incredible sex in the dark storeroom, trying to muffle the sounds of their ecstasy from the four-balls sipping Perrier in the bar lounge – that was if Ciaran didn't have time to slip up to her place for a quickie.

Marie had always been particular about her appearance, but now, especially before she went up to Redcliff, she took extra care to look radiant and ravishingly sexy. Her tall, womanly figure exuded confidence and style, and the energy of her viva-cious personality always guaranteed her an abundance of attention from both men and women.

Just as she finished smoothing the Paloma Picasso body lotion over her lithe figure, Marie looked at her reflection in the full-length mirror. She smiled to herself as she admired the Brazilian wax she had got yesterday at the beautician's and thought once again how lucky she was. Naturally slim, it only took the daily rounds on the golf course, two yoga classes a week, and exhilarating sex with Ciaran to keep her figure toned and supple. As she opened the large Victorian wardrobe, Marie imagined Ciaran discovering the Brazilian wax that he had encouraged her to try. She couldn't wait to surprise him with it today. Slipping into her new deep scarlet La•Perla underwear, she smiled to herself. Having money had a lot of advantages, and so did being separated. God, she loved Tuesdays!

# CHAPTER THREE

DRIVING HER MUM'S OLD NAVY VOLVO THROUGH THE LARGE entrance at Redcliff, Madeleine felt as if nothing had changed. It was almost eight years since she had last played there, and everything was exactly as she remembered it, from the wisteria that crept up around the pillars of the gate, down to the worn patches of gravel on the road crunching beneath her tyres. Although her dad had often suggested on her visits home that they go up for a game, Madeleine was somehow never free to go. Either the weather was too bad to play, or Kevin's grief-stricken face at the thought of spending the day with Madeleine's mother dissuaded her from going. But now there would never be another opportunity to have a round with her dad, or the chance to rescue Kevin from endless cups of her mother's tea.

Rolling her eyes up to the sky, Madeleine quietly thanked her father for keeping her membership up while she was in New York. She had never realised how much she would need it. After her conversation with Kay, Madeleine decided that she was going to get back into playing regularly. She reckoned that not only would it give her a bit of much-needed practice and take her mind off everything, it would give her the chance to get out of the house a bit more. Much as she relished the idea of sitting in her pyjamas on the couch for hours on end, Madeleine knew that it wouldn't be any help if she was to move on with her life.

Passing through the avenue of blooming rhododendrons, Madeleine drove on to the clubhouse and parked beside Kay's black Jeep. As she stepped out of the car, Madeleine realised that she was actually a little bit nervous. She knew that there would be changes on the course, but for the most part, she looked forward to the challenge. Meeting a different group of members, however, was something she did find daunting. What if she played terribly and the other women thought she was holding the game up? At least Kay would be there to introduce her, she thought, as she walked towards the ladies' locker room.

Kay had arranged for them both to play in the rumble that morning with another woman called Marie, who, Kay had assured her, would be more interested in talking to Madeleine than in assessing her golfing skills. As Madeleine stood reading the notice board while Kay entered their names in the competition, she desperately tried to remember the format for a rumble.

'I can't remember, Kay,' she whispered in a slight panic into her friend's ear.

'Can't remember what?'

'What happens in a rumble.'

Kay laughed and, taking her friend's arm, she led Madeleine over to a seat.

'Right,' she said reassuringly, sitting down. 'We each play our own ball throughout the game. The best score is taken for the first six holes, the two best scores are taken for the next six, and then all three scores count for the last six. Got it?'

'Ah!' Madeleine said as her face lit up, 'they play it in the States as well, but just call it a different name. I can't believe I didn't remember that – must be the nerves.'

'You'll be fine, I keep telling you. Anyway let me introduce you to a few people.'

Standing up, Kay and Madeleine walked over to a glamorous-looking woman with stylish ash-blonde hair who was sitting on the wooden bench putting on her golf shoes.

'Madeleine, this is Marie O'Neill, our partner for the rumble today.'

Madeleine reached out to shake her hand and found herself instantly smiling back at Marie's friendly expression and energetic greeting.

'Madeleine! It's wonderful that you've come up today. I've heard all about you. I'm sure Kay's just given me the tip of the iceberg, though. You can fill me in on all the juicier bits when we start playing.'

'Well,' Madeleine said, 'I'm not sure how fascinating you'll find my life, but if it's a laugh you're looking for, then you'll only have to watch me play. It's been a while.'

Marie's throaty laugh was infectious and Kay grinned at Madeleine.

'Well, that'd definitely make us stand out from a certain other group I could mention,' Marie said, half under her breath, looking towards a rather chic-looking group of women heading out the door. Madeleine followed her gaze to the three women leaving the room and her heart skipped a beat. Turning around to thank another lady for holding the door open was Judith. Although she had only seen her once before, more than ten years ago, Madeleine still recognised her instantly. A flicker of recognition flashed through Judith's eyes also, but she left the room still wondering how she knew the new woman.

Kay introduced Madeleine to a few more members congregated in the locker room, and then the three of them walked out into the glorious morning sunshine.

'So, Madeleine, what handicap do you play off?' Marie asked as they waited by the front of the clubhouse for another group to drive off the first tee. 'I know Kay here has six on me and plays off a twenty-two, but alas I don't think I've budged from twenty-eight in the last two years.'

'Well, seventeen when I left New York,' Madeleine replied cagily, 'but I won't be playing off that today. I haven't been on a golf course in about eight months.'

54

'Ah, sure, it's like riding a bike isn't it, or a man for that matter – once you get the hang of it you never forget!'

Madeleine had to consciously close her mouth as Kay turned around to laugh.

'Right, girls, we're off!' Marie called out swinging her driver in the air, and walked up to the first tee. Following suit, Kay and Madeleine walked over to the tee box after her and prepared for the game to begin.

Because of the format of the rumble, Madeleine was able to loosen up and ease herself into playing again. Given that only one of them had to have a decent score on any of the first six holes, she wasn't under any real pressure to play well, and even relaxed enough to laugh with the others when her second drive flew wildly into the thicket beyond the small lake on the left of the fairway. Marie, on the other hand seemed to master every drive and had an unerring judgement when she got to the greens, sending each of her balls like a magnet straight towards the pin on the putting green.

After a few holes, with each of them netting respectable scores, their conversation turned to the other players on the course. Marie gave Madeleine and Kay the latest gossip on everyone playing around them, pausing only to take a breath or hastily hit her ball. Were it not for the fact that she was proving to be an excellent golfer, Madeleine would have thought that Marie only came up to Redcliff for the socialising. She seemed to be passionate about everything she talked about, and the round was passing in a blur of laughter and shock, with Marie swearing at her golf ball time after time for flying into bunkers.

As the three of them waited for the group in front of them to tee off the fifth, Kay asked tentatively how things were at home for Marie.

'Well, it's funny you should ask that, because I was only thinking to myself yesterday that this feels scarily like the calm before the storm.'

'Why, what's on the horizon that has you so anxious?' Kay asked, pulling out her driver.

'Well, my niece, that's my sister's daughter, she's getting married next month,' Marie started, 'and my precious middle child has announced that he's bringing his partner to the wedding. Still, nothing to be anxious about once I have two stiff gin and tonics before the ceremony.'

Madeleine looked at Kay questioningly, wondering if she was the only one who didn't see what there was to be so worried about.

'You see,' she continued, glancing over to see if the other group had moved on, 'Eugene, my son, is gay, and took great delight in telling me that his "plus one" for the wedding was going to be Ken – his forty-two-year-old boyfriend. Did I mention that Eugene is only twenty-two?'

Madeleine and Kay looked at each other uneasily, not quite sure what they should say to Marie.

'Still, it could liven up the party a bit, and the shock might frighten that poker out of my sister's arse, if only briefly.' Marie laughed to herself at the image of her older sister's rigid composure collapsing, as she watched her truant nephew dance raucously to 'Dancing Queen' with his boyfriend.

'My sister's husband is a member of the Knights of Columbanus, and I just know that he'll be uncomfortable with the whole thing. When it comes to that pair, I tell you, straight-laced isn't the word!'

With that, she walked up to the tee box, and set her ball down.

'God, you'd hardly get a word in edgeways!' Kay said, giggling, as Marie drove powerfully off the tee.

'Yeah, but she's terrific, though, isn't she?'

'Great shot!' they said in unison as Marie walked back down to them.

'Thanks. I find it's wonderful to work off all my aggravation on the golf ball,' she said with a satisfied sigh, adjusting the Velcro on her glove.

As they walked towards the fifteenth hole, Madeleine had an idea. 'I was just thinking about our score – we're not doing well enough to win the rumble now, so why don't we put a little wager on the last few holes for ourselves? Whoever has the most putts on the last four holes buys the drinks?'

'Wonderful idea!' Marie exclaimed. 'Although my playing seems to have been deteriorating since the tenth, so it might be my round. Still, a gin and tonic sounds like the perfect way to finish up the game, so I'm on.'

'Yep, I'm definitely on for that as well,' Kay said, taking out a tee, 'but I'd have to disagree with you, Marie. Judging by the way I've been playing today, I think it'll be me buying the drinks.'

'They say that gin makes you depressed,' Marie said as Kay walked off to take her shot, 'but I only find it makes me horny.'

She was so matter-of-fact about saying this that Madeleine wondered if she had heard correctly, but didn't want to ask her to repeat it. Thankfully, she was saved the embarrassment of commenting, as Marie asked her what she drank.

'Well, white wine's usually my tipple, but after today's round, I think it'll be a vodka.'

Madeleine thought that she deserved the vodka as a sort of celebration – she had played better then she had hoped for her first time back in Redcliff, she had had a brilliant round with Kay and Marie, and she felt she had survived seeing Judith at the clubhouse surprisingly well. All in all, a good start to what Madeleine hoped would be a good decision in coming home.

To Kay's delight, she played superbly on the last four holes, and gleefully gave her drinks order to Marie.

'OK, girls,' said Marie, after a disastrous final hole, 'the drinks are definitely on me – and I can hear the ice and smell the lemon already!'

With that, they shook hands, and in high spirits, headed towards the clubhouse.

# CHAPTER FOUR

ONE PERFECTLY CHILLED GIN AND TONIC AND A TOASTED sandwich later, Marie hummed to herself as she drove the short distance home from the club. The wheels of her Mercedes whirred soothingly beneath her as she indicated into the driveway. Pulling up towards the wine-coloured Virginia creeper covering the front of the house, Marie stepped out of the car and unlocked the front door. As she imagined Ciaran's big, masculine hands roughly, but tantalisingly slowly undressing her, she hoped it wouldn't be too long before he appeared.

Making her way up to the bedroom, Marie wondered what the other ladies in the golf club would think if they found out about her and Ciaran. She had no doubt that they would be outwardly shocked, but she knew also that they would be secretly jealous if they found out what they were missing. Ciaran's tall, strong physique had attracted the attention of almost every female member in Redcliff, and Marie couldn't help feeling sorry for everyone else who still had to put up with the mundane sex she herself had been used to. Still, she considered, slipping on a pair of black stockings, they can find their own après-golf amusement. Ciaran was not someone she was planning to share.

For the second time that day, Marie thought about how lucky she was. She had a fabulous figure, wonderful friends and a younger man to satisfy her voracious sexual appetite. As she sprayed a touch of Chanel No. 5 on to her slender neck and stood admiring herself in the mirror, Marie heard her mobile phone ring downstairs. She ran down to get it, and before she had a chance to say a word, she heard Ciaran's voice whispering down the line that he was waiting outside. Placing the phone on the hall table, and straightening her skirt, Marie opened the large yellow wooden door to see him leaning casually against the pillar.

'Hello again,' he smiled, as he brushed past her, just close enough to rub his shoulder lightly against her breasts.

'Hello yourself,' she replied, closing the door behind him as he placed one hand seductively on her waist.

Within seconds, Ciaran had slipped his fingers beneath her red cashmere sweater and was caressing the small of her back. Expertly, without saying a word, he undid the zip of her black silk skirt, while Marie ran her fingers teasingly through his thick blond hair, her mouth finding his. As her skirt dropped to the floor, Ciaran's tongue slid between her lips and they kissed hungrily. He grabbed both her buttocks in his hands, and no words were exchanged as he lifted her up and she wrapped her legs around his muscular waist. Marie's excitement grew as she kissed him, allowing herself to be carried over towards the stairs. As if too impatient to go all the way up to the bedroom, Ciaran climbed only a couple of steps before putting her down and eagerly pulled off her sweater. He paused momentarily as he eyed her lacy red and black underwear, then unhooked her bra and started to kiss her breasts. Yearning for the feel of his skin against hers, she quickly pulled his black T-shirt over his head and grabbed his warm, firm body close to hers.

'God, this feels so good,' she panted, as she arched her back to meet him.

'So does this,' he teased, running his finger along the inside of her silky thigh.

Lifting herself up so that he could slide off her thong, Marie waited expectantly for his reaction to her newly acquired Brazilian wax.

'You got it done!' Ciaran exclaimed. 'Bloody great!'

Moving her legs apart as he ran his tongue down from her navel, Marie let her head fall back and groaned as he probed deeper and deeper.

'Don't stop,' she whispered. 'I could stay like this all day.'

But Ciaran was determined to prolong her excitement, moving back up her body just as she felt she was going to scream with pleasure, lightly kissing every inch of exposed skin. Unable to wait any longer, Marie reached up to unzip his trousers. She caressed his firm erection, and relishing his helpless enjoyment and teasing him with her mouth, played with him just long enough to bring him to the brink of ecstasy. They were now completely naked and Marie could wait no longer – she wanted to have all of him. Motioning him to lie back, she climbed on top of him and, locking him into her gaze, she straddled him and then finally, wonderfully, he was in her. She started to move, slowly at first, and then thrusting harder as his hands reached up and cupped her breasts. Moving together, quickly and rhythmically, within minutes, they breathlessly reached a rapturous climax.

'Wow,' Ciaran said, his voice wheezing with exertion, 'that was incredible.'

'And we never even made it to the bedroom,' Marie replied, lying back on the plush red stairs.

'Sure, it doesn't matter where we do it,' Ciaran said, looking at the discarded trail of clothes they had left behind.

'No, I don't suppose it does!' she laughed, as she collected her skirt from the hall floor and put it on. Getting dressed, she fleetingly thought about how different things had become – Billy would have been too worried about the discomfort of the stairs to have ever contemplated having sex there. Picking up Ciaran's T-shirt, Marie playfully threw it at him as he lay on the stairs with his eyes closed, recovering.

'Come on,' she said. 'Get dressed and I'll make some coffee before you head back to work.'

Filling the percolator with water, Marie could hear the rustling sounds of Ciaran getting back into his clothes. She smiled as she thought yet again about how fantastically lucky she was. She loved the fact that their relationship was so delightfully uncom-plicated. Neither wanted a serious commitment, or any sort of commitment for that matter. This was sex, pure and simple, and both were agreed that the more they had of it, the better. When they first started sleeping with each other, Marie had noticed the visible look of relief that had swept across Ciaran's face when she mentioned she had already had a hysterectomy. Ciaran made no secret of the fact that babies were not on his agenda, at least not for the time being, and Marie was as averse now to babies and commitment as Ciaran was. She'd had enough difficulties trying to untangle the mess that had become of her own marriage – only insanity would make her trade her current arrangement for that chaos again.

Thirty minutes later, having had their coffee and more sex, this time on the kitchen table, a thoroughly sated Marie stood at the door watching Ciaran speed off in his old coupé. Walking back into the house, she went into the kitchen to set upright the chair they had knocked over. A leisurely breakfast, a relaxing round of golf, and Ciaran to liven up lunchtime – this was definitely a habit she could get used to.

\* \* \*

Kay had really enjoyed herself at the rumble that morning. Stopped at the traffic lights, she looked at her reflection in the mirror and noticed, for the first time in ages, that there was a rosy glow to her cheeks. She actually looked really happy for a change. The weather had been perfect, Madeleine had played well and relaxed enough to have a good time, and a round with Marie was always great fun.

Rushing to make it to the school in time to pick up Holly and Mark, Kay cursed at the lights, as if hoping that they might hear her and turn green. As she flicked through the radio stations, Kay's mobile rang. Seeing Ed's name flashing up on screen, she contemplated not picking it up. She knew, though, that if she didn't answer this time, he would just keep trying, and so she lifted her phone reluctantly out of the bag on the passenger seat.

'Hi, Ed,' she said, hoping her voice didn't relay the anxiety she felt.

'Why the *bloody hell* didn't you ring in for me this morning, you inconsiderate cow?'

Kay didn't say anything. She knew there was more to come.

'I mean, I spoke to you about it, you said you'd do it...'

'Well, actually, I didn't...'

'*You said* you'd do it, and then what happens? *I'll* tell you. What happens is that my boss rings me up sounding like a bear with a sore arse, wanting to know why the hell I didn't turn up for the presentation this morning. Well, why didn't I turn up, Kay?'

Ed's voice was shaking with anger, and Kay could tell by his mood that he'd probably had a drink or two already.

'I'll tell you *fucking* why – because you're lazy, and you're useless.'

Hearing a silent pause at the other end of the phone, Kay reckoned that most of his anger was vented, and decided it was probably safe to talk.

'I never said I'd call them, Ed, you just assumed. I told you I wasn't going to make any more excuses for you.'

'Yeah... right. Anyway, I'm not going to be home for dinner tonight either. There are some clients coming over, so I've been asked to take them out. And seeing as you ruined everything this morning, Kay, don't even try to moan about this.'

Knowing there was no answer that would placate Ed, Kay stayed silent.

'We're going to some meal thing, so I'll be home afterwards – shouldn't be late.'

With that, he hung up the phone, leaving Kay drained of the good humour she had felt earlier on.

Hearing a car beep behind her, Kay realised that the lights had turned green. Moving forward, she replayed the conversation she had just had. She knew now what would happen later on. Ed wouldn't come home at a reasonable hour as promised. He would come home after everyone was in bed and then wake them all up again by drunkenly knocking things over in the dark. She had already decided to move all his stuff into the spare room. She must do it, and remember to find the key to her own, once she got home.

Kay had become used to the perpetual feeling of disappointment in her husband and their marriage, but what never ceased to surprise her was how she was able to deal with it all with such detachment. She couldn't quite remember when she had begun to stop worrying about his welfare, but somehow she now found herself in a position where she simply didn't care what Ed got up to. Driving up to the school gates, she saw very clearly, for the first time, that she didn't love her husband any more.

\* \* \*

She felt like such a fool. And what was Mike going to say when he found out that she had turned up at the golf club but didn't get to play? As Catriona sped through the gates of Redcliff, she thought back over the morning. Apart from feeling like an idiot herself, she could only imagine what the other ladies in the club would think of her turning up and leaving again.

Catriona had arrived in plenty of time for the nine-thirty draw. Or so she thought. She put her name in the entry book, filled out her card and left it in the usual spot for one of the committee to do the draw, just like she had done on her previous visit. Whatever sliver of confidence she had felt when she arrived, though, completely vanished as she noticed that not one single other member was doing the same. As it approached nine forty-five, it became clear to Catriona that there was no draw. Trying to occupy herself for even a couple of moments, so as not to look so totally uninformed, Catriona bent down to re-tie her golf shoes. Slowly, as other women came into and swiftly left the locker room, it dawned on her that perhaps they had already arranged who they would play with. Fearfully walking over to the notice board, she saw to her distress, in bold black type, that this morning's golf would be something called a three-person rumble.

'What the hell is that?' Catriona thought to herself, desperately looking around her to try and catch the eye of a friendly looking member. Wishing the ground would open up and swallow her, she changed back out of her golf shoes into her ankle boots. She kept her head down and played with the zip until she was sure that the crimson red that had flooded her cheeks had subsided back to a paler, less conspicuous colour. She really did hate everything about this stupid game.

Catriona walked quickly outside, only barely controlling the urge to run, collected her trolley and opened the boot of her car. She realised that she was attracting some strange looks from golfers walking up to the first tee, so she tried to make her actions look purposeful in the hope that maybe she wouldn't look as stupid as she felt. In an attempt to make it look like she had gone out on her own at dawn, Catriona put her trolley in the boot, and got into the car with all the poise she could muster. Speeding back down the driveway, she wished to God that she never had to go back there. She didn't know what was worse, though – leaving the club without having played, or having to tell

Mike about it. The same questions would be waiting for her when she got home: How had she played, what was her final score, and, worst of all, had she enjoyed herself. Tears stung the back of her eyes as she anxiously ran through excuses in her head that she felt she could give Mike with a straight face. Maybe she would go to the driving range to get some practice in instead, so the morning wouldn't have been a complete waste?

'Oh, who are you kidding, Cat?' she asked herself, her stomach tightening at the thought of spending the rest of the morning repeatedly swinging her golf club at a ball that refused to do what she wanted. Catriona's handicap was forty-five – the highest anyone could play off – and Mike had optimistic hopes of her cutting it down to thirty by the end of the season. At the rate she was going, though, Catriona reckoned she would be lucky if she managed to make it to forty-four. After all, if she couldn't even figure out how to take part in a rumble, she didn't think she'd have much chance of improving her game enough to actually play in one.

She would much rather go into town. A new cookery book had just come out and Catriona was dying to get her hands on it. She could imagine nothing nicer than to buy the book and then sit in some quiet café to look through its scrumptious recipes. She could even decide what she would make from it for dinner that evening and pick up the ingredients on the way home. She imagined the smell in the kitchen of the previous night's pasta with sun-dried tomatoes, and roasted pine nuts in her goat's cheese sauce, and her mouth began to water. 'That's it,' she decided. She would cook up something delicious to mollify Mike's reaction to her not playing golf, and she would sacrifice the driving range for a glorious morning in town. Cooking, she thought to herself – that was her passion, not miserable golf.

\* \* \*

Wandering around the room with a cup of coffee in her hand, Linda moved between tables of members eating soup and sandwiches. She had decided to make a particular effort today to get to talk to everyone. As she was coming up the driveway that morning, Linda had seen Mike McCarthy's girlfriend race past her in the opposite direction. Having spoken briefly to her in the past, she knew that Catriona had yet to play a round and enjoy it, so Linda resolved to try and make things easier for her the next time she came up. For a start, an introduction to some of the less ruthlessly ambitious golfers in the club might persuade Catriona that Redcliff wasn't so bad. Redcliff could be an unwelcoming place at times, she knew. Only this minute, she had caught Judith stealing a glance at herself in the mirror behind the bar.

'Yes,' she reflected, 'a little less time indulging the aspiring lady captains around here, and a little more time spent encouraging the novice golfers is what this place needs.'

Walking over to Nessa, who was heartily tucking into a juicy burger and fries, Linda allowed herself a seat at the table. She had been chatting for nearly an hour, and was dying to sit down.

'No, but seriously,' Nessa was saying, 'I've read all about it, the Atkins diet really does let you eat food like this. Now, I wouldn't have a dessert of course, but this is all grand.'

Linda smiled at the others around the table as Nessa took a large bite of her hamburger.

'Oh, I know, ladies,' she said with a grin, 'but it does help if I at least tell myself I'm on a diet. It's those genes you know, the fat ones, there's just nothing I can do about it!' Nessa winked as she popped another chip into her mouth.

At this, everyone burst out laughing. Nessa had toyed with several excuses over the years, but she seemed now to be fairly settled on the gene theory.

'Lady Captain, I was just saying to the others here about arranging a trip to Florida at Easter. James and I have a place there, and seeing as it has the most amazing golf courses around it, I thought maybe we could get a group together to go. Would you be interested?'

Linda's face creased into an anxious frown. 'Oh, Nessa, that sounds marvellous, but I just don't think I'd be able to get away from here at all. Between meetings, visiting captains and supporting team events, it's almost impossible to leave Redcliff for any decent amount of time.'

'I think you worry too much, Linda. Sure the lady vice-captain could look after all that, you're not chained to the place, you know. Anyway, I don't think anyone in the club is likely to condemn you for having a little extra-curricular fun outside of Redcliff.'

'Hmm, I don't know. Ian was saying only the other day that he hardly gets to see me any more. His retirement doesn't seem to have made much difference, really. I thought that we'd be driving each other mad by now with seeing so much of each other,' Linda laughed, 'but since I became lady captain, I see even less of him than I did before he retired. Don't get me wrong, I love the job – it's just very time-consuming, and I don't think it would be fair to Ian to swan off to Florida for a week and leave him at home.'

'Oh, that reminds me,' Nessa said, momentarily thrown off the Florida topic. 'I saw Ian last Friday in that new restaurant on Baggot Street. I've been meaning to go there for ages. What did he say it was like?'

'He, ah, well, he said it was very nice. Yes, em, said the food was lovely,' Linda said awkwardly.

As the others chatted easily between themselves about the restaurant, Linda felt a vague feeling of unease. Where had she been on Friday night, she wondered? She had no recollection of him mentioning going out to this restaurant, and she was sure that she would have remembered it if he had.

Making her excuses, and promising to think about the Florida proposal, Linda got up from the table and went over to talk to another group of women. It wasn't like Ian to keep something from her, especially not something like this, she thought to herself as she approached the next group of smiling faces, but she wasn't going to think about it now. It was probably nothing anyway, Linda decided, she would just ask him herself when she got home.

* * *

Madeleine threw her jacket on the chair by the door as she came into the warm kitchen. Her mother had already started to make lunch, and the smell of quiche wafting through the air reminded Madeleine of how hungry she was. She had opted out of eating in Redcliff because Kay had had to leave early to pick up Holly and Mark. Without much else planned for the day, she saw no sense in rushing a toasted sandwich at the club when she could have the delights of her mother's kitchen at home.

'So, how did you get on?' her mum asked as she sat down at the table.

'I'd a great time, actually. Seems silly now to have been so nervous beforehand, and it was brilliant to be back playing in Redcliff.' Madeleine wanted to add that it wasn't quite so brilliant seeing Judith again, but she knew she couldn't bring it up with her mother.

'I'm exhausted from all the walking, though. Guess I'll just have to go up more often to get fit again.'

'And what about the other members, did you recognise many of the faces?' her mum asked, setting place mats down on the table.

'One or two...' Madeleine replied, not wanting to discuss it further, 'but no one I'd know well enough to talk to. I'm so lucky to have Kay, really. Otherwise I'd be a bit lost up there.'

As she watched her mum potter around the kitchen getting things ready for lunch, Madeleine worked up the courage to bring up a subject she had been dreading for days.

'Between getting back into golf,' she started, 'and catching up with old friends, all I need now is an apartment and I'll be set,' she said, anxiously awaiting her mother's reaction.

'Sure, what do you need an apartment for? Aren't you grand here?'

Whatever hopes Madeleine had entertained that this might be easy were forgotten as soon as she saw the hurt look cross her mother's face.

'You know I just love having someone else to cook for, love,' her mum continued. 'And Snowy adores having you around as well.'

'I know, Mum, I know, but I'll have to find a place some time and now just seems to me to be as good a time as any. Sure, I'll be home all the time to see you, and you'll be able to cook for me then.'

The silence in the kitchen told Madeleine that this was not something her mother had been prepared for, and she felt awful.

'Mum, you know I love it here,' she said beseechingly, 'but I just think we're both probably used to living on our own, and I'd hate to start stepping on your toes.'

Madeleine knew she was throwing out weak excuses, but it was all she could offer. Given that she really wanted to move out because she was beginning to feel suffocated by the constant mothering, she knew she couldn't tell her mum the truth. It had been wonderful to be home, but Madeleine knew the time was right now to move out on her own.

That afternoon, she explained the whole situation to Kay on the phone.

'I kind of feel like I'm seventeen again and I've done something to annoy my parents.'

'Oh, you can be sure she knows as well as you do that it's right for you to move out,' said Kay. 'She just can't admit it because she's your mother. And besides, it's common knowledge that she'd happily look after you for the rest of your life if you'd only let her!'

'I know, I think I'd just forgotten how powerful "the silences" could be, and I wanted to tell someone else so I could reassure myself that I'm doing the right thing.'

'Of course you are. Don't let this dissuade you, Madeleine. You never planned on staying at home for long anyway.'

'Thanks, Kay. I won't be going anywhere, though, unless I can find an apartment that's bigger than a shoebox and doesn't smell of damp carpets.'

'They've all been that bad, eh?'

'Bad isn't the word. One landlord told me that showers were still something he was looking into, but "honestly, the place is a real gem",' Madeleine finished, impersonating the short bald estate agent who had shown her around an apartment in Blackrock the previous afternoon.

'Why don't you try one of those specialist agencies that advertise in *The Irish Times*?' Kay asked, mildly surprised that her friend hadn't tried this option before now. 'All you have to do is tell them how much you're willing to pay and where you'd like to live and they do the rest. Simple.'

'Kay, you're a genius,' Madeleine exclaimed. 'I forgot all about that, I'll get on to it in the morning.'

Two days later, Madeleine found herself being shown around number seven, The Beaches – a bright, airy apartment in a five-storey block on the seafront in Dún Laoghaire. It was perfect. As soon as Madeleine walked into the place, she knew she was standing in her new home. Although it wasn't very big, it had everything she needed, and each room was tastefully decorated. The living room was painted in an off-white, with three beautiful little oil paintings on the largest wall, and it had a wonderfully soft, deep-pile dark blue carpet. The rest of the apartment had polished wooden floors throughout, and the pale, cherry-pink bedroom with bunches of lavender on the pillows was like something from an old country cottage. Standing in the living room, looking out at the amazing view overlooking the harbour, Madeleine knew that she had to take it.

\* \* \*

'That's a pretty good computer you've got there.'

Madeleine turned her head to see that the man beside her waiting for the lift had directed the comment to her.

'What? Oh yes, this – well, I hope so! You see, I've just moved into number seven, and I swore to myself that before I bought anything else, I was going to get myself a laptop. It makes me at least feel that I'm organised.'

'A good choice,' the man said. 'You mightn't be able to cook with it, or even sleep on it, but at least you'll be online!'

Madeleine laughed, but missed her chance to take a good look at him as the doors to the lift opened in front of them.

'I'm grand once it's up and running,' Madeleine said as the lift hummed its ascent, 'but I have to admit, I'm fairly useless at getting everything connected in the first place – I'll have to talk nicely to my friends.'

Shifting his weight onto his other foot, her companion surreptitiously offered his services. 'Well, if you need a bit of a hand setting it up, I'm in that line of business and would be more than happy to help you out. We could call it a moving-in present?'

'Oh, no, I couldn't ask you to...'

'I don't mind, really, I'd be more than happy to do it.'

The bell pinged quietly, announcing that they had arrived at Madeleine's floor, and for a brief moment, neither quite knew what to do.

'Eh, this is me.' Madeleine spoke up eventually, as they both looked out of the open lift.

'Oh, right, well listen, here's my card,' he said, frantically digging a small rectangle of cream card out of his pocket, 'call me if you need any help getting your computer started.'

Madeleine's 'thank you' was cut short as the lift doors closed over, and she found herself standing in the hallway smiling ridiculously at the small card she held in her hand.

'Thomas Killeen, *IT Technical Consultant*. Well, Thomas,' she thought to herself, 'I might just have to take you up on that offer.'

Letting herself in the door, Madeleine was struck once again with how lovely her apartment was. She couldn't believe how much things had changed for her. If anyone had told her a year ago that she would be back living in Ireland with a place of her own – without Kevin – she would never have believed them.

'Kevin,' she said aloud to the empty room. For the first time in ages, Madeleine realised that she hadn't thought of him all day. She felt guilty – how could she forget him like that? But she wasn't forgetting him, she told herself as she took the computer out of its box, she was just getting on with her life.

An hour later, Madeleine threw down the incomprehensible computer manual in despair and looked at the phone.

'Could I ring him?' she asked herself, still not convinced it was entirely appropriate to call another man so soon after Kevin.

'Get a grip, Mad,' she said sternly to herself. 'Stop thinking and just do it. Sure, didn't he offer to help?'

When the phone rang in Thomas' s apartment, he said a silent prayer that it would be that fantastic blonde from the lift. He picked up the receiver and cautiously said hello.

'Hi. Thomas? It's Madeleine from downstairs. I met you in the lift earlier today.'

'Of course, glad you rang. So how are you getting on with that new computer?' Thomas said with as much machismo as he could manage. He didn't want to betray too much of how he felt.

After all, it was very possible that she hadn't been quite as smitten as he had been by their encounter.

'Well, I'm not having much luck with it, actually,' Madeleine replied, a little worried from the tone of his voice that maybe she shouldn't have called at all. 'Would it be too much to ask you to come and have a look at it?'

'I'll be right down,' he said, dancing round his kitchen with the cordless phone, trying to control the excitement in his voice, 'just give me five minutes.'

Once she had hung up, Madeleine searched out some candles from the bottom of her cupboard and placed them around the room. She told herself that it was just because she hadn't found a lampshade to cover the bulb yet, and that candlelight would be less harsh. She couldn't think up an equally credible excuse for putting a bottle of Chardonnay in the fridge, though, and, deciding not to dwell on it, rushed into the bedroom to put on a fresh T-shirt.

'Thanks a million for coming down,' she said as she let Thomas into the apartment. 'I hope I didn't take you away from anything important?'

'No, no, not at all, I'd nothing planned for the evening anyway.' Thomas lied, ignoring the fact that he had just cancelled going down to the local for a pint with his friend, Jim. 'Now, where's this computer of yours?'

Shortly afterwards, with her laptop set up and ready to go, Thomas joined Madeleine on the couch. She was finding it incredibly easy to talk to him and she couldn't help but be attracted to his strong handsome looks, with his dark brown hair and sparkling blue eyes. Surprising herself, Madeleine suddenly found herself saying that she had enough food for two if he'd like to stay for dinner.

'I should warn you that it's nothing fancy, spaghetti carbonara, but I do have a nice bottle of wine in the fridge, which would make up for any shortcomings of the meal.'

Madeleine couldn't believe she was being so forthright.

Thomas, on the other hand, couldn't believe his luck. He didn't think it likely that this gorgeous creature cooked supper for just anybody. At least he hoped not.

'That sounds lovely, thanks, and believe me, you could make toast and it'd still be better that anything I could cook up!'

Madeleine smiled at him as she went into the kitchen, leaving Thomas on the couch to stare after her in admiration.

After she had popped the spaghetti in boiling water, and took the eggs, cream and bacon out of the fridge to get ready for the sauce, Madeleine went back into the living room and filled up Thomas's wine glass.

'Here's to my first guest,' she said, raising her own glass, 'and to what I'm sure will be a lovely evening.'

'The pleasure is all mine,' Thomas replied, engaging Madeleine in an intimate stare.

Slightly unnerved by the feelings that were flooding through her, Madeleine rose from the chair, and stuttered that she had to make the salad.

'It's just lettuce and tomatoes,' she explained, as she carried her wine into the kitchen. 'I hope that's OK with you?'

'Perfect,' Thomas answered, not sure if he had read the situation correctly – had he misread her attraction, he wondered?

Over dinner, Madeleine explained her reasons for coming home from New York, and that she was still dealing with getting over Kevin. Pouring them both another glass of wine, Thomas also revealed that he had just broken up with his girlfriend of two years, but he seemed disinclined to give the reasons for the spilt. Madeleine didn't relish the thought of being quizzed too intently on her past either, though, and so didn't push it.

After what seemed like only minutes of conversation, Madeleine looked at her watch and realised that it was already nearing midnight. She couldn't believe how the time had flown.

Noticing her stifled yawn, Thomas got up and said that he had to be getting back to his own apartment.

'Thanks for such a great evening, Madeleine. We'll have to do it again some time, only seeing as it'll be my turn to cook, we might have to go to a restaurant. Culinary skills were not something I was blessed with.'

'That sounds lovely,' Madeleine said, also getting up from the couch, 'and if requests are allowed,' she suggested boldly, 'Indian is my favourite.'

'It's a deal, then.' Thomas smiled with relief. He hadn't been entirely sure she'd agree. 'Why don't you give me your number and I'll give you a call in the next few days so we can arrange a date?'

At the mention of the word 'date' they both felt slightly uncomfortable. The whole evening had been so informal that it didn't seem right to give it an official name.

Trying to rescue the situation, Madeleine went to find a piece of paper to write her number on, and when she returned, the atmosphere between them had eased.

'Right, well, I'll talk to you in a couple of days then,' Thomas said, opening the door to the hallway.

'I'm looking forward to it,' Madeleine replied with a smile, impulsively reaching up to give him a kiss on the cheek.

After he had gone, Madeleine leaned against the door, running through the events of the whole evening in her head. She couldn't have wished for a such a lovely evening, and with another date on the horizon before the end of the week, Madeleine saw the prospects unfolding before her looking better and better.

# CHAPTER FIVE

'SO HOW WAS TODAY'S GAME?' THOMAS ASKED, AS THE waiter left the table with their order. Madeleine and he were once again happily ensconced in the small Indian restaurant. Eight weeks after their first date there, it had become a firm favourite.

'Not too bad, thanks, and the weather was beautiful too.'

'Well, I'm glad to see you're getting back into the swing of things.' Thomas said, chuckling to himself at his own joke.

'Oh, very funny,' Madeleine replied, playfully throwing a napkin at him across the table.

Since that first evening in her apartment, Madeleine and Thomas's relationship had developed quicker than either of them had expected. The more they got to know each other, the more they found they had in common. Despite how well things were going, however, constant anxieties niggled at the back of Madeleine's mind. Was she developing a relationship too soon after Kevin's death, she wondered, and almost more troubling, could she be using Thomas to stop herself from thinking about Donal? Deciding that she was probably worrying too much about things, Madeleine kept these fears quiet, and hoped that if she didn't address them, they would eventually go away. Besides, she thought, she really did enjoy being with Thomas and their easy conversation certainly made a change from the arguments that had become so frequent with Kevin.

Madeleine did have one slight problem, though. Two months had quickly passed, but at best, all she could call their relationship was a perfect companionship. They hadn't had sex yet, and she was beginning to wonder if there was something wrong. There had been plenty of opportunities, but every evening, just when Madeleine was ready to take their cuddling on the couch into the bedroom, Thomas would invariably say that he had to leave. Was she imagining the chemistry between them? Had she been misinterpreting all of the smitten glances he had thrown her way when he thought she wasn't looking? Whatever it was, his lack of amorous behaviour was beginning to make Madeleine paranoid, and she didn't know how long she could go on without saying anything to him.

The arrival of two steaming hot curries reeled her thoughts back to the present.

Thomas looked at her expectantly. 'So, what do you think?' he said, leaning slightly forward so that the blue of his eyes twinkled in the candlelight.

'Sorry,' Madeleine stuttered, a little confused, 'say that again?'

'A weekend away – what do you think? You see, I have to go down to Limerick for a sales conference on Friday week, and I thought that maybe you could come down on the train that evening to meet me?'

'That sounds like a brilliant idea!' Madeleine answered, unable to stop herself from thinking that maybe this was what he had been waiting for. Perhaps he wanted the first time they slept together to be special, and so had put it off until they went away.

'And I was thinking,' Thomas continued, 'that since you said before that you've never been to Clare, and neither have I, we could hire a car while we're down there and do a bit of exploring.

We could even spend a night there if you wanted to, and travel back to Dublin on Sunday?'

'Oh, that sounds perfect!' Madeleine said smiling, and taking Thomas by surprise, leant across the table and kissed him.

* * *

The next day, Thomas was sitting opposite his GP looking decidedly uncomfortable.

'I know you don't need me to remind you that the prescription I gave you at Christmas was the last one I was giving you, Thomas. Really, I'm not trying to be unfair here, but I'm putting my foot down this time.'

'But like you said, it could just be the diabetes?' Thomas pleaded.

'Yes, I said it *could* be the diabetes, but I also said that it could be happening for a variety of other reasons too. I gave you that letter of referral to see the consultant so he could rule those other things out. And, not only that,' she said, pointing her pen at him, 'I can see that packet of cigarettes in your shirt pocket, so you needn't bother trying to tell me that quitting is going well.'

Thomas sat in his chair like a scolded schoolchild.

'I'm aware that this is going to sound like I'm preaching here – but please believe me when I tell you that there's really nothing I can do for you if you're not going to help yourself.'

'OK, I'll give you the smoking thing, but I'm sure that those other problems are nothing another prescription of Viagra wouldn't fix,' Thomas said, raising his eyebrows with uncertainty. He knew he was treading on thin ice.

'I'll tell you what I'll do then,' Dr O'Reilly sighed, 'I'll give you a prescription – four pills only, mind – on the condition that you let my secretary book an appointment at the urologist's while we have you here.'

Thomas had been arguing, without success, for the last half an hour trying to get the doctor to fill the script for him, and so decided it would be wise to just take what she was offering him now. At least, he thought, it would get him through the weekend with Madeleine.

Dr O'Reilly's tone softened.

'Look, I really don't want to alarm you unnecessarily, but I do think this is something that needs checking out. This is the second time you've come to me with the complaint of having blood in your urine, and now, with this back pain you're telling me about, it's best to have Donal take a look at it.'

'Donal?'

'Sorry, Donal O'Sullivan, the consultant I'm referring you to. He's an excellent urologist, and an extremely easy person to approach, I'm sure you'll get on fine with him.'

Fifteen minutes later, with his cigarettes thrown in the rubbish bin and an appointment made with Donal O'Sullivan for Wednesday week, Thomas walked into the chemist's. He felt like he was going to pick up gold dust. He had better make the most of the four tablets, he thought, as he imagined having Madeleine to himself for the whole weekend. Thomas had been getting more and more anxious lately – it was hard to mistake the look of confusion on Madeleine's face in the evenings when he left her to go back to his own apartment, and he didn't want her to think that she was the problem. It wasn't owing to a lack of desire on his part either – Thomas couldn't remember the last time he was so attracted to a woman – but past experiences had sown the seeds of apprehension to the point where almost all of his confidence was gone. He had never told Madeleine, but sex, and Thomas's increasing inabilities in that department, had been a major factor in the breakdown of his last relationship.

Taking his prescription from the pharmacist, he considered his conversation with the doctor. Thomas realised he had been stupid to put it off for so long, but he honestly thought that as the bleeding had stopped for a while, maybe the problem would go away on its own. But it hadn't gone away, and Thomas knew he would have to get over his fear of doctors to sort it out once and for all. The fact that he was absolutely dreading his visit to this Donal O'Sullivan didn't make it any easier. It was one thing to discuss his sexual ability with the doctor he had been going to his whole life, but the thought of telling it all to a stranger wasn't appealing. At least Dr O'Reilly's receptionist hadn't been able to make an appointment until next week – it would give him a bit more time to get used to the idea. Besides, there were more important things to be thinking about in the meantime, this weekend for a start. Patting the Viagra supply in his coat pocket for reassurance, Thomas smiled to himself in anticipation. He had been looking forward to the weekend for ages, and not even an appointment with the consultant was going to dampen his enthusiasm. A whole weekend of pleasure and having Madeleine all to himself – he couldn't wait!

* * *

The following Tuesday being the first Tuesday of the month, Madeleine and Kay played together in the monthly medal. This was the most important competition of the month, so for a change, concentration took precedence over conversation out on the course. Both were rewarded with creditable scores, and satisfied that they had played well, decided to treat themselves to a glass of wine. After they had showered and changed, the two women sat up at the bar with their self-congratulatory drinks before going in to have dinner. It was a ritual that Madeleine had almost forgotten about, but was delighted to slip back into. Every Tuesday, those who had played during the day all got together that evening for dinner, and Madeleine was quite looking forward to meeting the other members again. Kay was totally relaxed and enjoying herself too – Claudette had agreed to look after the children for as long as she wanted, so for once, there was no pressure on her to hurry home.

Deep in each other's conversation, neither of them noticed Donal as he approached the bar.

'Madeleine, Kay, what a nice surprise!' he exclaimed, a genuine smile stretching across his face. 'I've been keeping an eye out for you, Mad, since the flight back, but haven't seen you around. Can I get either of you a drink?'

'Oh, no, thank you, we're fine, really. And, well, I've just been coming up on Tuesdays since I've been home, so eh...' Madeleine's voice trailed off as she became increasingly aware of Kay staring at her. 'Yes, em, Kay, I forgot to mention to you,' she said looking a little flushed, turning to her friend, 'that I bumped into Donal on the flight home from New York.'

'Oh, really... did you?' Kay's voice was ever so slightly higher than its usual pitch.

'Yes, it was quite an unexpected coincidence,' Donal admitted to a startled Kay. 'I haven't been in the Big Apple in ages, and yet the one time I do go, I meet Mad on the way home.'

'So what brings you up here on ladies' day, anyway?' Madeleine continued, aware of Kay's palpable confusion and yet not wanting to finish the conversation with Donal.

'Oh, you know, the usual, meetings to arrange more meetings which might lead to a meeting where we actually get something decided.'

Kay couldn't help but notice the flirtatious laugh that played on Madeleine's lips as Donal spoke.

'Honestly, I never realised when I took this job just how many meetings there'd be. And the dinners!' he laughed as he patted his stomach ruefully. 'The position should carry a government health warning!'

'Ah, yes,' Kay interjected, 'all those delicious free meals must be a real hardship to endure.'

Despite the laughter, Madeleine couldn't decipher whether or not there was a jeer behind Kay's remark, but knowing that her friend was only doing it to protect her, she let it go.

'We should try to get a game in together, Mad, if you're free some time?' he suggested.

'I'd love to,' Madeleine replied. 'We can arrange it next time I'm up if you like.'

'Perfect,' he said, his eyes lingering just a moment longer than they needed to. He checked his watch. 'Shit, it's already half four, I'd better go, looks bad if even the club captain can't turn up on time!' he said, throwing a glance over towards the committee room. 'Oh, yes, before I go, though,' he added, turning back to Madeleine and Kay, 'Judith is arranging some sort of birthday barbecue for me here in the club next Saturday, if you're free. I'd love it if you could both make it – eight o'clock.'

'Sounds lovely, thanks,' Madeleine said, covering Kay's non-committal silence.

And with that, Donal smiled, said his goodbyes, and ran across the bar to let himself in the already closed door of the committee room.

'Well, you are a dark horse,' Kay said as soon as Donal had closed the door behind him. 'You never mentioned that you met him on the way home from the States.'

'Well, it was nothing really, we just bumped into each other at the airport,' Madeleine replied.

'And here I've been these last few weeks trying to protect you from bumping into him up here, and you knew all along!' Kay said aghast.

'Look, I'm sorry. I just didn't bother mentioning it because I didn't think it was important.'

'So,' Kay said in a more conspiratorial tone, 'how do you feel about him now?'

'You needn't start worrying! It's all water under the bridge. You seem to forget that I moved on and married Kevin. I'm long over Donal O'Sullivan.'

'Hmm…' Kay said, not wholly convinced.

'Anyway, did I tell you that I'm going to Limerick with Thomas the weekend after next?' Madeleine asked, trying to change the subject. She knew she wasn't a good liar at the best of times, but when it came to Donal, she was dreadful. Madeleine was sure that the others must have seen her chest thumping with her racing heartbeat as she was talking to him, and she felt she was barely able to keep her voice from shaking. Switching the conversation away from Donal was the only way to hide her anxiety from Kay. Besides, if Kay did find out how she really felt, she would only disapprove. It was easier to say nothing.

'No, you never told me that,' Kay said excitedly. She had been about to take a sip of her drink, but instead, put it back down on the table again as she digested the news. 'Tell me more – is this going to be the big seduction then?'

'Well, I don't know about that, but I'm keeping my fingers crossed!'

'Limerick's hardly the most romantic place in the world, though, is it?' Kay considered.

'Kay, I wouldn't care if he took me to a tent on the top of a mountain... we've been with each other for *eight weeks* now!'

As the two women laughed, Madeleine realised that the wait had suited her.

'Maybe it hasn't been a bad thing, though,' she said pensively. 'It does seem quite strange to be with someone else.'

They had spent many hours on the phone in the evenings discussing how Madeleine felt about sleeping with Thomas – a part of her just couldn't let go of the guilt she felt about betraying Kevin.

'I know, it's always strange at the beginning when you're with someone new,' Kay said, putting her hand on Madeleine's shoulder, 'but, especially when it's with someone you like as much as Thomas, it's something to look forward to as well.'

'Yeah, you're right. Anyway, don't listen to me! We've been having a wonderful day, let's not bring the mood down now.'

'You're welcome to bring the mood down any time you like,' Kay said with an encouraging smile. 'Do you know, I can't even remember the last time Ed and I had sex?' she continued. 'He's always out with clients, or just too drunk to even try.'

Madeleine didn't say anything. She knew her friend wasn't expecting her to defend Ed, but neither did Madeleine want to condemn him. After all, Kay was still married to the man.

'Mind you, it was never any good with him,' Kay went on, 'or not in comparison with Declan anyway. God, we were incredible together,' she said with a smile, remembering the days when they hadn't even bothered to get out of bed. 'We were so in love, I thought that life couldn't possibly get any better.'

Madeleine frowned. The reality that had become of Kay's ideal had been a lot harsher than either of them could have imagined.

'You know, sometimes I wonder if I did the right thing by listening to my mother. From the moment she met Declan she never stopped talking about how unsuitable he was for me, and yet, she never got to know him. But parents know best, don't they?' she finished bitterly, with a sardonic smile.

'Do you ever see Declan these days?' Madeleine asked. In all the time she had been in New York, Kay had never once mentioned bumping into him.

'No, I haven't seen Declan since that horrible night when I broke up with him.' She shuddered at the memory of the pain she had gone through for months after the split. 'I do see his picture in the papers the odd time, but never in the flesh. All this talk about sex, though, makes me realise just how much I miss that flesh!'

Madeleine laughed and glanced furtively around the bar.

'If the ladies of Redcliff ever listened to our conversations, Kay, they'd be scandalised.'

'I know! Sex and flesh and orgasms – you're right, they'd be horrified.'

Putting her empty glass on the table, Kay stood up. 'Come on into the dining room, all this talk of sex is making me hungry.'

As they walked towards their table, it seemed to Madeleine that Kay was friendly with almost every member they met, and as she was introduced, she wondered whether she would be able to remember all the names. There were, however, a few people she recognised from her last visit. Nessa, for a start, with her larger-than-life personality and apparent appetite to match, wasn't easily forgotten. She greeted Madeleine with a warm, enthusiastic smile as soon as they approached the table. Sitting next to Nessa was a very pretty, shy young girl wearing glasses, called Catriona. As Madeleine was introduced to her, she sensed that Catriona was probably the quietest of the group. Her timid 'hello' was barely audible, but there was a welcome in her eyes. Yes, she thought to herself, she would really enjoy getting to know these people.

Sitting down, Madeleine took off her blue linen jacket and hung it on the back of the chair. As she finished straightening the sleeves behind her, though, she felt the burning intensity of somebody's stare watching her every movement. Looking up, she just caught Judith turning back to her own conversation, but despite the polished elegance of her appearance, Madeleine noticed a definite air of unease about her.

## November 1991

'Oh God, I'm so sorry! Hold on one second and I'll get a cloth,' Madeleine exclaimed, and rushed back towards the galley. In the two years that she had been with Aer Lingus, she had never spilt a single drop on a passenger. Never, that was, until now. She had just upended an entire cup of coffee all over the very expensive trousers of a man in first class.

'I really can't apologise enough,' she said, as she returned with a cloth. 'I don't know what happened, and I can't even blame the turbulence,' Madeleine added with a weak smile. She was all too aware that the senior hostess was hovering nearby, and could only imagine what was going to be written about her in the flight report. 'Damn it anyway,' she thought to herself, sponging up the liquid that was now spilling onto his seat. Flustered and apologetic, Madeleine finally looked up and noticed that the man didn't look the slightest bit annoyed or distressed.

'Didn't we meet somewhere before? I think it was the Wexford Opera Festival, wasn't it?'

Madeleine was totally taken aback. As recognition seeped through her memory, though, she realised he was right.

'Em, yes, I think we did,' she answered, relaxing a little now after the coffee debacle. Oh, what was his name though? she wondered to herself, hastily trying to scan back over the conversation they had had. At least he had it easy – she was wearing her hostess name badge.

'It was medicine!' she thought suddenly to herself. And she was sure he had said that he played golf too.

'So how's the golf going?' she asked with relief. She mightn't be any good with names but at least she hadn't drawn a complete blank.

It was his turn to be impressed.

'Wow, not a bad memory!' he said, oblivious to the growing interest of the other passengers around them. Neither did he notice the inquisitiveness of the senior hostess, who was unobtrusively edging towards them to see what was happening.

'Look, I really am so sorry about this, it's honestly never happened before,' Madeleine said, indicating the sodden patch on his trousers.

'Must be my lucky day, so,' he answered, with a mischievous grin. 'Listen, tell you what, why don't you make it up to me by coming out to dinner tonight? You are staying in the city aren't you?'

Madeleine considered the offer for a moment. Under normal circumstances, she would never accept a date from one of the passengers, but she decided that this was a little different. It wasn't like she'd never met him before, and she had just destroyed his trousers... not to mention the fact that she thought he was gorgeous. And... *Donal*... that was it!

'Yes, I am staying in New York tonight, and em, well, dinner would be lovely, thanks, Donal.'

'Great!' he replied, the mention of his name registering with a smile. 'I'll even change my trousers for the occasion.'

'Thanks! Well, I'm sure I'll see you again before the end of the flight, so we can make arrangements later,' Madeleine said, suddenly excited at the prospect of going out with him.

'Is everything all right, sir?' asked the senior hostess who had come up the aisle to where she was standing.

'Absolutely wonderful, thanks,' Donal replied, ignoring her tone. 'I've always said that Aer Lingus have the best hostesses,' he finished, winking at Madeleine.

Positively simpering at his unexpected reply, the senior hostess smiled ingratiatingly at Donal and retreated back into economy class.

'I really should get back to work,' Madeleine giggled, nodding towards her trolley. 'There'll be other people waiting to have coffee spilt over them.'

'Well, I wouldn't want to keep you from that!' he said, looking down at the damp patch on his trousers.

Unlocking her trolley, Madeleine just smiled her goodbye, and hurried on up the aisle. Her insides were tingling and her cheeks had acquired a rosy glow of expectation. She could hardly wait for the plane to land so she could get ready for dinner in New York with this handsome stranger.

* * *

A few hours later, Madeleine and Donal were sitting in Café des Artistes lost in conversation. Madeleine felt as if they had known each other for years. Remembering how easy it had been to talk

87

to him at the Wexford Opera Festival, she slipped effortlessly back to where they had left off three years previously. Donal told her about his job and his new consultancy and she spoke about friends and work. They found that they had so much in common that their words tumbled over each other, keen to agree or add something unsaid. With wine and conversation flowing, the evening seemed to pass in a wonderful haze of laughter and intimacy, and although she should have been jetlagged, Madeleine had never felt more awake.

As they finally finished their seemingly endless glasses of wine, Donal asked Madeleine if she would like to go and see Bobby Short play in the Carlyle. Madeleine didn't need to be asked twice. She was having an incredible evening, and was loath for it to end. She couldn't help but notice, though, the occasional mention of someone called Judith in his conversation. Hoping that it was Donal's sister, she tried not to think too much about it, but as they talked on, her curiosity couldn't help but make her ask him who she was.

'Oh, em... Judith's father helped me to get my own consultancy in Dublin when I came back from studying in the States. And, well, we've, ah, sort of been going out for a while.' Donal waited anxiously for her reaction.

Madeleine was sorry she'd asked. They had been having such a wonderful time that she couldn't believe what she was now hearing. As Donal continued talking, though, the events of the Wexford Opera Festival all began to make sense. It was actually Judith who was interested in opera, which was why he had been there at all. It turned out that Judith had been unwell on the night that Madeleine first met Donal, which explained her absence – and Donal's mysterious departure without so much as a kiss.

Madeleine couldn't help noticing that he didn't speak very lovingly about Judith. She wasn't sure, though, whether or not that was just her hopeful imagination reading too much into what he was, or rather what he wasn't, saying.

'You see,' he went on, 'Judith and I have been going out for about four years now, and somewhere along the line, it just became impossible to get out of. First, it was little things, like she would lend me some money to pay for textbooks when I was studying. Then when her mother was sick, she seemed to become so dependent on me that it would've been callous to leave, and now that her father has pulled a few strings to get me my own consultancy, it's like I owe her more than I ever have.'

Madeleine could sense the desperation in his voice, and found that she couldn't stay angry at him for long. It was clear that he didn't love Judith, but a sense of duty and guilt and probably cowardice, she thought, had kept him bound to her.

'I know that it's wrong,' he continued, 'to be with somebody when you don't love them any more... but it won't be for long.'

Donal's last words hung in the air between them. They looked at each other with the realisation that this wasn't going to be a once-off fling for either of them, and in the candle-lit silence that surrounded them, Donal tentatively put his hand over Madeleine's. In the short time they had spent together, they had quickly become entranced with one another, and were oblivious to everything that wasn't encompassed in their own little world. Waiters passed, and people came and went, but all Donal was aware of was the beautiful woman in front of him, whose eyes were responding to the warmth and attraction in his own. Madeleine was equally taken by the person who sat before her. She had found in Donal someone who shared everything that was special to her: interests, sense of humour, morals and values had all been laid bare over the course of the evening, and there was nothing that they hadn't agreed on.

Later that night, after two hours of ethereal jazz, Donal walked Madeleine back to her hotel. As they stood by the steps to the entrance, it seemed to Madeleine the most natural thing in the world to put her arms around him and kiss him. He responded readily, and, lifting his hand up to cup her face, they kissed tenderly and full of the promise of seeing each other again. Standing so tantalisingly close to each him, Madeleine wondered whether or not she should ask Donal up for a euphemistic cup of coffee. She knew that he wasn't likely to refuse her, but somehow, knowing about his relationship with Judith, however meaningless it might be, it didn't seem appropriate to invite him up. With a similar conflict also running through Donal's mind, he decided that it would be best just to ask for her number.

After saying goodbye, Madeleine walked up the steps into the lobby of the hotel with a warm feeling in her stomach. As well as her telephone number, she had also given him her roster for the next couple of weeks, and with a quiet but deep-rooted confidence, she knew he would call.

* * *

What followed turned out to be a magical time for them both. Donal woke her every morning with a telephone call, no matter where in the world she was, and as soon as she flew home, he came straight over. He was also the first person Madeleine had ever had sex with, and as time went by, their lovemaking became more and more intense. She had found it hard to admit to him the first time that she was scared, but intuitively, and gently, he had made her feel beautiful and perfect, and with ever-increasing amounts of enjoyable practice, he led her to a whole world of wonderful places. It was with him that she experienced her first orgasm, and with him that she first went skinny-dipping. For Madeleine, it was with Donal that she first knew life could be so amazing.

The only fly in the ointment was Judith. Donal had promised that he would finish with her, but he kept telling Madeleine that the time had to be right. Madeleine, although never having been in the situation herself, knew that there would be no right time for breaking up, and encouraged Donal to get it over with. At first, she had been supportive, allowing him the space to find the best way to do it himself, but as time went by, she grew impatient and began to feel that sharing him was becoming too much the norm.

One evening, after having dinner in a small restaurant in Wicklow, they sat in Donal's car outside Madeleine's house, saying goodbye. Suddenly, she felt uncontrollably angry, and the hurt of being constantly hidden that she had been bottling up inside, bubbled to the surface.

'When is all this secrecy going to end? I want to be able to go out with you in public, Donal, you know? Nightclubs, bars, even just a walk around town. I'm fed up with this, with the constant worry of "Judith finding out" and tiptoeing around like we've something to be ashamed of.'

Donal was silent. He knew that Madeleine was right, but couldn't bring himself to say out loud that he was scared of the consequences of a split with Judith. He had wanted to become established as a consultant on his own before he broke up with her, so that he wouldn't have to be reliant on her dad passing clients his way. He recognised, though, that Madeleine was too important to him to let go of because of his cowardice, and struggled to come up with a compromise that might appease the situation.

'Mad, you know that I love you. Judith means nothing to me, but I just can't risk the consultancy yet. She sort of has me by the balls here, can't you see that?'

'I see this for what it is, Donal. You're too scared to do anything about this situation, so I'll tell you what. I'll make the decision for you. I'm giving you a deadline, not to be unfair, but to try and sort this out once and for all. Finish with Judith by my birthday on the third of May, or else it has to be over between us.'

Tension filled the car as Donal stared numbly out the window, and Madeleine reached into her bag for a tissue. She knew she was being harsh, but she'd had enough. Besides, she was giving him a couple of weeks to do it. They had planned to go to London for her birthday, where Donal had promised to take her to the famous Ronnie Scott's. Madeleine wanted to be able to relax fully and enjoy the holiday, but if the weight of their current arrangement was still hanging over their heads, she knew that her enjoyment would be marred.

'I *will* do the right thing, I promise,' Donal said, turning around to face her. 'I can't be without you, Mad, I just can't.'

As she noticed that his eyes had filled up with heavy tears too, Madeleine reached her hand up to hold his face and kissed him. Believing that the tangled mess of their relationship was eventually unravelling, Madeleine was totally unaware of just how much she would live to regret asking him to do the right thing.

# CHAPTER SIX

JUDITH STOOD IN THE STUDY WITH ONE HAND ON HER HIP and the other holding the telephone receiver against her ear. Up early, she had decided to call the caterers to make sure everything was running smoothly for the barbecue before she went to work.

'Yes, obviously I know that the forecast is good for the twenty-sixth, but you don't think I'd be so disorganised as to leave anything to chance, do you? Rain is hardly an unusual phenomenon in this country, Mr Ryan, so I want you to have alternative arrangements made, just in case.'

The silence from the other end of the phone went unnoticed by Judith.

'So, if by any chance there is a shower,' she continued, 'we're going to need marquees, and some sort of ground covering as well – matching, obviously. Is all of this clear?'

'Crystal,' came the curt reply down the line.

Satisfied that everything was in order, Judith hung up the phone, and smiled to herself. Everything was going perfectly. Food, caterers, music, venue and invitations were all sorted, and with her outfit already back from the dry-cleaners, there were only one or two minor things left for her to do before the party. Judith was leaving nothing to chance. She was a perfectionist at the best of times, but with an opportunity to shine at Redcliff, which might improve her chances of becoming lady captain, she was going to make sure everything ran like clockwork. She wasn't going to have some caterer ruin things for her just because he hadn't thought of the possibility of rain, so if another phone call was what he needed, then another phone call was what he'd get. Whether or not these people liked her was of no importance to Judith. She paid them to work for her, and that was all anybody needed to remember. Money made things happen, she believed; small talk didn't.

The only thing Judith had any concern about was whether or not the evening would secure her enough votes from the other members to become Redcliff's next lady captain. She had handwritten every invitation, to add a personal touch, and would make sure that she got to talk to all the guests on the night. Not an appealing prospect, she thought to herself, but necessary all the same.

Picking up her memo pad from the desk, Judith crossed off 'Check with caterer re alternative arrangement', and noticed that next on the list was a reminder to get something for Donal's birthday. She had almost forgotten about it. A subscription to *The Golfer* would be OK, she thought to herself. It was appropriate, easy to find, and if he told anyone about it at the party, they would think it was suitably thoughtful. 'Yes,' she decided, 'that'll do fine, and I can get Carol to organise it when I get into the office.'

Judith was still thinking about the party as she went upstairs to her bedroom and took her navy suit jacket from the wardrobe. Her fingers automatically ran down the crisp cotton of the white Gucci blouse she planned to wear with it. She knew she would look fabulous in it for the barbecue and, if she matched it with a perfect-fitting pair of Valentino jeans and some well-chosen pieces of expensive jewellery, she would be a picture of under-stated elegance.

After she called goodbye to Donal, who was still in the shower, Judith went downstairs and picked up the keys to her silver Mercedes. As usual, she checked her reflection in the hall mirror and, happy with her immaculate appearance and faultless organisation, Judith left the house with more than her usual air of self-satisfied confidence.

* * *

'Ian, darling, I did tell you about the barbecue for Captain Donal next Saturday, didn't I?' Linda asked as they cleared the table together after dinner.

'No, I don't think so, love. I don't remember you saying anything about it. I've already arranged to play bridge that night, though,' Ian replied with an apologetic smile as he folded the mats. 'It's a shame. Donal's a nice guy, but I really couldn't let the others down.'

Disappointed, and a little confused, Linda stopped loading the dishwasher and looked over at him.

'But I'm sure I told you about it,' she said. 'I even remember where we were at the time. It was because we had just driven past Judith's office and I said wasn't she so good to be throwing a birthday party for Donal. You don't remember?'

'Well, if you did, I mustn't have heard you, then, because I write everything down in my diary – you know what my memory's like! – and when I arranged bridge with the others, there was nothing down for Saturday.' Ian looked at her crestfallen face. 'Oh, love, you don't need me there anyway. Sure, I wouldn't know half of the people at it, and you'd be talking to everyone, with me just standing there mute beside you. I always feel like a bit of a spare at these things.'

'I know that,' Linda said, rinsing a plate under the tap, 'but I like having you with me.'

The discussion was cut short as Ian glanced up at the clock and threw the last mat into the drawer.

'The programme Jean is working on is starting in a couple of minutes. We should go in to watch it. Oh, I hope she's OK, she was so nervous about it last night.'

Ian rushed into the living room and flicked on the television.

'Apparently the director is a bit of a nightmare to work with on the live shows,' he called out from the other room, 'so I hope Jean doesn't get too stressed out about it.'

Linda heard Ian continuing to talk to her, but found she was unable to say anything back. Finally putting the plate into the dishwasher, she peered in to see Ian settling back into his armchair and turning up the volume as the opening credits flashed up on screen. Linda was aware of the same uncomfortable feeling settling over her as she had felt in Redcliff the previous Tuesday. When she had asked Ian about the restaurant, he told her that he had never been there.

'Nessa must have just seen someone who looked like me,' he had said, laughing it off. Much as Linda wanted to believe him, she couldn't share his nonchalance about the situation. And now this. She was sure that she had told him about Donal's party. She began to feel worried that something was going on that he didn't want her to know about. She knew it annoyed him that she had to spend so much time in Redcliff, but he had seemed so genuinely pleased for her when she had become lady captain. Surely he didn't resent the fact that she had to spend so much time at the golf club? Once again, Linda wished that Ian played golf as well, so they could be up there together.

Interrupting her thoughts, Linda heard the salsa tune of Ian's mobile ringing on the kitchen counter. She looked into the living room to see if he had heard it, but he was oblivious to everything except the television, so she went to answer it herself. As she picked up the phone, Linda stood frozen, looking at the name 'Denise' flashing on the screen.

Who the hell is Denise? she wondered, as all her worst fears came rushing to the forefront of her mind. Obviously someone who called him often enough to be in his phone book, she thought to herself as the mobile stopped its piercing ring. Miraculously, Ian remained seated in his armchair watching TV, ignorant of Linda's drama unfolding in the kitchen.

Still standing with the phone in her hand, she tried desperately to remember whether he had ever mentioned a Denise before. She was sure he hadn't. She knew that she would have remembered if he had mentioned her.

Was Ian having an affair? She could hardly bear even to think about it. And yet, here in her hand, was something that could indicate quite conclusively that he was. As much as she wanted to, Linda couldn't forget about the restaurant, and the other arrangements he had made on the night of Donal's party, and with tears stinging the back of her eyes, she wondered if maybe she had been too caught up with Redcliff to notice the cracks forming in her own marriage.

Linda's mind was reeling as she went into the living room. She decided, however, that she wouldn't say anything about the call, at least not until she had stopped panicking and gathered her thoughts a little. Ian was still totally engrossed in the programme when she sat down on the couch. Although Linda sat looking at the screen, she couldn't take in any of it, and behind her vacant, staring expression, thoughts raced through her head. She remembered once reading an article about the signs you were meant to look out for if you suspected your partner was having an affair. It hadn't occurred to her then that she would ever have to watch out for them herself.

'Well, that was terrific!' said the object of all her speculation. 'What did you think of it?'

Linda realised that she hadn't taken in any of the programme.

'Oh, yeah, really good,' she answered lamely, aware that she was somewhat lacking in enthusiasm.

Ian hardly seemed to notice, though. Standing up from the armchair, he yawned loudly, stretched and finally announced that he was off to bed. 'If you're going to stay down here reading, love, would you mind locking up?' he asked and, without waiting for an answer, he gave her an affectionate pat on the shoulder.

After Ian had left the room, Linda sat in the semi-darkness, blindly watching the animated images flicker across the screen. A pat on the shoulder. How long had he been doing that, she wondered to herself. It was hardly the most affectionate gesture in the world. Maybe he was saving those for Denise, she thought, as she tried to fight the tears that had begun to fall down her cheeks. Turning off the light beside her, Linda sat in the darkness listening to Ian's footsteps go up the stairs and prayed that this was all just one big misunderstanding.

* * *

Madeleine settled back to read her book, though the gentle clacking of the wheels on the train track threatened to send her to sleep. Looking out the window at the countryside flying past her in a blur, she looked forward to the fried breakfast that was due to arrive at any minute. She really did love going away for the weekend, and had already decided that her holiday was going to begin the minute she got on the train, starting with the large Irish breakfast that she rarely allowed herself at home.

As a roasting hot plate of mouth-watering sausages and crisp rashers arrived, Madeleine wondered to herself how the weekend with Thomas would go. This would be the longest amount of time they had ever spent together, and Madeleine couldn't help feeling slightly anxious about how it would be. Piercing her fork into the fried egg and watching the yellow centre tantalisingly ooze out onto the plate, she decided that she was worrying unnecessarily. They would take it one day at a time and deal with any problems, if any, as they arose. Besides, she thought to herself, she and Thomas got on brilliantly together and she couldn't remember a single awkward silence between them at any stage during the last two months. What she tried not to think about, however, as she savoured the food, was that her apprehension was caused not by the prospect of awkward conversation, but rather about how the sex would be.

As the train whizzed faster through the lush green fields around her, Madeleine found herself thinking about Donal and his upcoming party. Part of her wanted to stay away. She had realised after seeing him at the airport that it wouldn't take much for her to fall in love with him again and knew that the only thing to do was to avoid situations where they might see each other. She couldn't stay away, though; she didn't have the will power to deny her curiosity, and so not going just wasn't an option.

'It'll be fine, Thomas will be with me,' she thought to herself, reasoning that he would act as a safeguard against any flirtation with Donal. This was exactly what worried Madeleine, though. She was troubled by the fact that Donal's reintroduction into her life was taking from what should be the most exciting part of her new relationship. What made things worse was that she really did like Thomas, and felt bad about the emotions that raced through her every time she saw or even thought about Donal.

## April 1992

She would never forget a single moment of that day. As usual, Madeleine's morning had been brightened by her habitual wake-up call from Donal. They chatted like they always did, except that, this time, Madeleine's voice was brimming with the excitement of their upcoming trip to London. She was on top of the world, knowing that, by then, she would no longer have Judith to worry about, and Donal had promised her that it would be her best birthday ever. He had teased her with hints of the plans he had made and insinuations about where they would be staying, but he never gave much away, leaving his sentences tantalisingly half-finished. Madeleine had played along willingly. In truth, she didn't care where he took her, or what they did. All that mattered to her was that they would be together, for once without the constant feeling that they should be looking over their shoulders for fear of being spotted.

Madeleine had long ago stopped asking Donal why everything had to be so difficult, and why he couldn't just have ended his relationship with Judith years ago. She knew that it was much more complicated than that. It was Judith's father who was at the root of Donal's concern, and extricating himself from his clutches was a far riskier business than just getting away from Judith. Without fully realising it, over the course of his relationship with her, Donal had become more and more embroiled in a tangled web of debt. It didn't occur to him in the beginning to ask Judith where she got the money to buy him expensive textbooks, and even meals. As her small gifts expanded to a new set of golf clubs and trips away, however, Donal began to get a little anxious, and slightly annoyed that Judith was always the one to foot the bill. One evening, Judith explained, indifferently, that it was no big mystery – she just had a very wealthy father, who was an extremely affluent and highly influential surgeon. Before long, Donal found himself wondering what an alliance with such a prominent man could do for his career, and within weeks of intimating this question to Judith, all the right strings had been pulled and he was happily set up with a consultancy of his own and a waiting-room full of patients.

The only downside of the arrangement, as far as Donal was concerned, was the knowledge that he was now more indebted than ever. Judith's father took any slight against his daughter as a personal insult to himself, and Donal knew that breaking up with her could mean losing everything he had gained over the last four years. Not only would the break-up have to be well-timed, it would also have to be well-planned and executed in such a way that Donal wouldn't come out looking like the bad guy. An unlikely task, he knew, but not impossible – he would just have to bide his time.

* * *

Sitting watching television, eating a leisurely lunch in the front room, Madeleine was surprised to see Donal coming up the driveway that afternoon. She hadn't expected to see him until later on. She knew, though, as soon as she saw his reluctant gait and his head hung low, that something was wrong. Instead of his usual cheerful demeanour and happy expression, his face was clouded with contemplation. His tie had also been roughly loosened, and his tousled hair looked as if his hands had run through it a thousand times.

'What's wrong?' Madeleine asked as soon as she opened the door, reaching out to take his hands and lead him into the hallway.

'Everything,' he replied, unable to meet Madeleine's concerned gaze and freeing his hands from hers to knot them anxiously together. 'I've been driving around for the last hour hoping to figure things out myself, but I couldn't... I couldn't put it off any longer.'

Madeleine felt her heart beat faster and louder and, seized with a dread that her calm exterior disguised, she quietly asked him the question she knew she didn't want the answer to. 'What do you mean, Donal? What couldn't you put off?'

Although her voice was steady, Madeleine's eyes revealed the panic she was trying to control, and when Donal looked up to her face, he saw there a despondency that mirrored his own.

'I realised I couldn't put off what I need to tell you,' he said as they went into the living room, sitting down uneasily on the edge of the couch. He was desperately scrambling through his thoughts to find the words that would hurt her the least. He knew, however, that nothing would be able to soften the pain that his news would bring.

'It's Judith, isn't it?' Madeleine said, as Donal stood up again and began to pace the floor restlessly. 'Did you tell her it was over?' she asked, momentary hope illuminating her worried face.

'I tried to,' Donal replied eventually. His quiet answer came just as he stopped his pacing and stood by the empty fireplace. 'You see, I met her for lunch today,' he started, taking a deep breath in preparation for what he had to say, 'and I explained to her that I had met someone else. And not just that I had met someone else, but that I had fallen in love with someone else, and so couldn't be with her any more. But then – she said it – and it sort of put an end to everything I needed to say.'

'Said what?' Madeleine asked, apprehension lowering her voice to a barely audible whisper. Her fingers had started to tear frantically at a loose thread on the arm of the couch, but all the while, she kept her teary stare focused on Donal.

'She told me that she had been waiting for the right time to tell me the good news,' he said shakily, returning Madeleine's look and willing himself not to cry, 'and that although there didn't seem to be a right time to say it now, it was still good news to her – she's pregnant.'

'Pregnant!' gasped Madeleine, almost choking on the tears that had begun to fall freely down her cheeks. 'But how can she be pregnant?'

'It was months ago, Mad,' Donal said fretfully, coming to sit back down beside her, 'she's nearly three months gone, and it just happened stupidly one night after we had had an argument and I was drinking. And then Judith got really annoyed, listing off everything she'd done for me, and started saying that I was a useless boyfriend, that we hadn't slept together in months, and that…' Donal looked up in the hope of finding some understanding written on Madeleine's face, but all he saw was hurt and heartbreaking disbelief.

'Anyway, apparently she had food poisoning the next day and well, the Pill didn't, you know, it...' Donal trailed off, unable to find a way of making what he had to say any easier.

'What is she going to do about it?' Madeleine asked, with sickening anticipation, looking into her lap.

'She's told her father already, and he's over the moon at the thought of his first grandchild. She's also told him that we're going to get married.'

As Donal's final words lingered like an echo in the silent room, an unbearable feeling of helplessness descended on Madeleine.

'I have to do the right thing, Mad. You see that, don't you?' he pleaded.

'No, I don't see that!' she shouted back, sobs rising from within her. Her shaking body conveyed all the sadness she couldn't find the words to express, and the hotly erupting tears pierced Donal's heart until he could no longer deny his own anguish.

'I'm so, so sorry, Mad,' he cried, taking up her hand. 'I just love you so much, but what can I do? I can't ignore the fact that I'm about to become a father. I have to do the right thing. What sort of person would I be if I ran off and left her now?'

'But what about me, Donal? What about leaving me?' Madeleine asked angrily, unable to accept the injustice of being left out of his decision. 'What am I supposed to do now?' she asked after a few moments, her voice weakened with grief.

Donal turned to look directly at Madeleine and cupped her face in his hands. 'You'll get over me, Mad. You'll find someone else to love, who's going to love you back as much as I do, and you'll forget all of this.'

'How can you say such a thing?' Madeleine asked, appalled at the idea of ever being with another man.

'Because I have to. Because if my life has to be tangled up with Judith's, then the only compensation I can think of is that you might find somebody else. It'll take time, Mad, but you will, and you'll be happy.'

Unable to say anything, Madeleine threw her arms around Donal, hoping that it would convince him, more than any words could, to stay. Answering her embrace, he pulled her tightly towards him and kissed her tears as they spilled down her cheeks.

'Goodbye, Mad. I love you,' he whispered, as he released her and stood up.

Leaving Madeleine convulsed with tears on the couch, he opened the door, and wordlessly left.

She didn't know how long she sat there after he had gone. Feeling as if her well of tears would surely dry up sooner or later, Madeleine cried passionately until eventually she sat, exhausted, in silence. Until now, heartbreak had seemed like a cliché to her. It was a word that was thrown around by actors and songwriters, a word that had only ever existed for her in a two-dimensional capacity on the page or the screen. Madeleine felt now the full force of what it really meant. She saw that heartbreak's foreboding reached further than just the realms of romance. It stretched its lonely claws out to steal her best friend with whom she shared experiences and shared jokes. It took away the intimacy of happiness and the comfort in sadness – and, like never before, his was the comfort that Madeleine now needed most. She longed for Donal to come back and make everything all right again, to tell her that he had been a fool to say what he had said. With fresh tears, she realised that there would be no more morning phone calls, no more sex and the magnificent feel of his body warm against hers. No more of anything that made life so wonderful. She simply couldn't contemplate living without him, and yet, somehow, that was the only option available to her. Stirring herself out of her trance, Madeleine reached out to pick up the phone. She had to talk to Kay.

* * *

A short time later, Kay was sitting opposite Madeleine at the kitchen table, unsure of what to say. They had been over and over what had happened more than a dozen times, but still there didn't seem to be anything positive to be gleaned from it. Whatever way they approached it, and whatever angle they looked at it from, the outcome was always the same – Donal was going to marry Judith, and nothing, it seemed, was going to change that.

'I'm so sorry, Madeleine. I feel so helpless. I just wish there was something I could say to make it better,' said a despondent Kay. She couldn't bear to see her friend so totally dejected. 'Will I make you a cup of tea?' she asked eventually, knowing it was a lame sort of substitute for Donal, but perhaps it was better than sitting there and offering her friend nothing.

'No, thanks. I wouldn't mind some of Mum's brandy, though,' Madeleine replied, looking at Kay though swollen eyes.

Throwing another tissue into the growing mound in the wastepaper basket, Madeleine got up and went over to the cabinet to find the bottle of Hennessey.

'Do you want some?' she asked, as she brought the bottle back to the coffee table.

'Well, I can't have you drinking on your own, now, can I? I'll go and get something to put it in,' Kay said, thankful at last for something useful to do.

'Jesus, Kay, what am I going to do without him?' Madeleine said as Kay returned with the glasses. 'I love him so much and I know that he still loves me. It's all that bitch's fault,' she finished, as her shaking hands finally opened the cap on the bottle and she poured two generous measures of the amber liquid into the tumblers.

'Why does he have to be such a nice guy, eh?'

Kay wasn't so sure.

'I mean, why couldn't he be more of a bastard so that he wouldn't feel the need to "stand by her", or whatever his bullshit reason is for staying with her?'

For a moment, Kay wondered whether or not her friend had already partaken of the brandy, but then reckoned that it was just a level of hurt and anger she had never seen in Madeleine before that provoked such a response. She didn't think she'd ever seen Madeleine so distraught. Once again, Kay found herself with nothing constructive or helpful to say. She knew that if she did open her mouth, she would only criticise Donal – something she knew Madeleine wouldn't want to hear. Instead, she put one arm around her friend's shoulders and raised her glass with the other. As Madeleine did the same, it occurred to them that there didn't seem to be anything worth toasting, and so they just threw the potent brandy down their throats and grimaced as the hard liquor slid burningly down into their stomachs.

This was the scene that greeted Mrs O'Connell when she returned from her shopping later that afternoon.

'A bit early in the afternoon for the booze, isn't it, girls?' she asked, her amusement tinged slightly with concern at the nearly empty brandy bottle. 'Is it a special celebration?'

Almost as soon as this question was out, she noticed the red eyes and blotchy skin of her daughter, and the slightly awkward look on Kay's face, and realised that something was very wrong.

'What happened?' she asked, suddenly panicking at what could be so serious as to have Madeleine drinking and in tears in the middle of the afternoon.

'Donal was here earlier on, and it's all over between us,' Madeleine said, starting to cry again.

'But... but... I thought everything was going so well between the two of you? You were so happy... And London, what about London?'

'I think, Mrs O'Connell,' said Kay, when Madeleine didn't seem able to answer, 'that Donal has quite a lot to deal with at the minute, and he just thinks that he'll be able to cope better on his own.'

'But, dealing... coping with what? I mean, how much could he have to sort out?' she asked with mild contempt in her voice.

'Another girlfriend,' Madeleine retorted, 'who's pregnant.'

She knew that this was the sort of sentence that she would never be able to take back, a dangerous thing when it came to her mother. She thought, however, that the few seconds' silence the remark would cause would be worth the grudge her mother would hold against Donal as a result. She was upset enough as it was and she couldn't settle her mother's questions now as well as her own.

Madeleine wanted to leave it at that, but knowing that her comment would inspire a whole new barrage of questions, thought it better to deal with them now rather than confront them later. So she continued: 'You see, Mum, I didn't tell you before, but when I met Donal, he was going out with someone else, and after he waited for the right time to break it off with her, which happened to be today, she told him that she is going to have his baby. Unfortunately, it would seem that Donal feels some sort of moral obligation to her, more so than to me, so we've broken up.'

'Well, I must say,' Mrs O'Connell started, 'I don't think much of...' but Madeleine cut her short.

'Mum, whatever the end of that sentence was, I don't think it was going to help, so please, unless you're going to say something that doesn't incriminate Donal, don't say anything at all. Come on, Kay, we're going for a walk.'

With an apologetic look in Mrs O'Connell's direction, Kay got up from her chair, grabbed her coat from the bottom of the stairs, and followed Madeleine out the door.

'I'm sorry, Kay, I just couldn't sit there and listen to her, knowing she was going to pass judgement on Donal and this whole messy situation,' Madeleine confided as they walked away from the house. 'Besides, I feel I need some fresh air. That brandy went straight to my head.'

'You know I don't mind, and my head could do with the fresh air as well. It's not often I'm downing brandy at three o'clock in the afternoon,' Kay said, smiling at Madeleine. 'Come on, let's go to the park.'

Strolling along the path through the lush grass and fresh spring flowers, Madeleine was oblivious to everything except the number of couples walking past them, hand in hand. She was sure there were more of them than usual, and after the day she'd had, it felt like a direct slap in the face. She didn't notice the children playing in the playground or the people on their breaks from work, stretched out in the sunshine on the grassy banks, engrossed in their books. All she saw was that everyone else's irritatingly happy lives seemed to be going on as normal, while her whole world was crumbling to pieces.

Every so often, the sound of a car horn or a dog barking would momentarily distract Madeleine, and for that second, she could almost forget about her and Donal. This respite was never long, though, and after each fleeting reprieve came a fall back to reality, each time harder than the last. Acutely aware of her friend's grief, Kay felt more and more helpless, and found that the only comfort she could offer was to listen, as Madeleine tried to work through the questions that were plaguing her.

Eventually, after hours of wandering through parks and streets, Madeleine and Kay found themselves outside the local pub.

'Come on, you, you haven't eaten a thing all day. It's bad enough drinking brandy in the middle of the afternoon, but drinking on an empty stomach will have you feeling worse in the morning than you already do.'

At this, Madeleine just smiled her appreciation at Kay. She was so tired, and drained from all the emotion of the day, that it was nice to have someone make the decisions for her.

Ten minutes later, with cups of tea and toasted ham and cheese sandwiches in front of them, Madeleine began to think about going home again.

'Thank God I'm working early in the morning,' she said. 'I love Mum, but I really couldn't handle having to explain everything to her at the minute.'

'You do know she means well, though,' Kay said.

'Oh, I know you're right, but I just need to give it a few more days before I can tackle the questions. Anyway, it's not like I'll be avoiding her deliberately. I'd already arranged to be picked up at four thirty in the morning for work.'

'Well, you make sure that you ring me as soon as you get home, or earlier if you like. I'll have my phone on all day,' Kay said. Taking her hand out of Madeleine's, she took a bite of her sandwich.

As they said goodbye outside the pub, Kay hugged Madeleine tightly, and found herself crying too as she felt her friend's body silently sobbing into her shoulder.

'It'll be OK, Madeleine. I know it's not what you want to hear at the minute,' she said quietly, 'but with a bit of time, this does get better.'

'Hopefully,' Madeleine whispered, as she sniffled into her tissue. She really doubted that it would, but not wanting Kay to feel guilty about leaving her, she mustered up a weak smile and just hugged her again.

'Thanks, Kay, I don't know how I would've got through today if you hadn't been there.'

'You don't need to thank me, you know that. And just remember, any time you need to talk, I'm only five minutes way.'

As Madeleine watched Kay walk down the road, she felt unutterably lonely. She didn't know how she was going to get through the next few days without Donal, never mind a whole lifetime. She wanted with every fibre of her being to be back with him again, but knew that what she wanted had no bearing on his decision. Standing on the footpath as people pushed impatiently past her, Madeleine realised that without Donal, nothing really mattered any more.

## *June 2002*

Madeleine was jolted out of her reverie as the train pulled into Limerick station. Gathering together her things that were strewn across the table – magazines, sunglasses, bottle of water – she put everything back into her bag, picked up her coat from the seat beside her and walked to the door at the end of the carriage. After only a brief scan of the platform, Madeleine spotted Thomas almost immediately as he stood smiling at her like a child on Christmas morning. She felt quite overwhelmed by his pleasure at seeing her, and realised, as she took in his appearance, that she felt the same way herself. Stepping onto the platform, Madeleine ran over to where Thomas stood and, putting her bag down, she threw her arms around him.

'God, it's great to see you, Madeleine. You look incredible.' He beamed as she stood back from him and modestly bowed in a mock curtsey.

'And you're looking quite handsome yourself, Mr Killeen,' she answered and reached up to give him a kiss. To her surprise, Thomas passionately kissed her back and, lifting her up, twirled her around.

'Well, what was that for?' Madeleine asked after he had put her down, smiling as she caught her breath.

'For being you, and for coming down – you wouldn't believe how mind-numbingly boring this conference has been.'

'Oh, so I'm boredom relief, am I?' she said flirtatiously, raising an eyebrow.

'I wouldn't underestimate the position, Madeleine, it's a very skilled and important job,' he answered, winking at her. Taking her case, he led her over to his car.

'I thought we could drive as far as Ennis tonight if that was OK with you?' he suggested as he unlocked the doors. 'We're booked into the Old Ground Hotel there, and I had thought it might be nice to explore a bit more of Clare tomorrow and Sunday – the weather's perfect for it.'

Sitting back into the comfort of Thomas's car, Madeleine clicked in her seatbelt and reclined the back of her chair.

'It all sounds good to me,' she replied, not really bothered about where they stayed. She trusted Thomas's judgement, and was really quite happy to be driven to whatever destination he had planned.

As they drove through the rugged landscape of lilac heathers and slate-grey rocks, Madeleine felt deliciously relaxed. Conversation between her and Thomas flowed effortlessly. They chatted about the conference and the news in Dublin he had missed in the few days he'd been gone, until they reached Ennis. Thomas navigated his way to the hotel, somewhat flustered in the dusk light, trying to find the signposts.

'You're sure you wouldn't like me to get the map out?' Madeleine asked, half teasing Thomas as she took in the look of concentration on his face, half concerned that they were actually lost.

Before Thomas had time to reply, though, the hotel loomed large in front of them as they drove around a sharp bend in the road.

'Doesn't look like we'll need it,' he said, leaning over to kiss her on the cheek, his eyes twinkling with self-satisfaction.

* * *

As soon as she opened the door to their bedroom, Madeleine was struck by the beauty of the Georgian décor that greeted her. A large four-poster bed stood proudly in the centre of the room, covered with an opulent gold and blue eiderdown quilt. Madeleine went over to run her hands down the beautiful design of its raised fabric and noticed the same brocade motif repeated in the lustrous curtains. She felt as if she had been transported onto the set of a Disney film as she saw the spiralling candle-sticks and hand mirrors on the dressing table.

'Oh, Thomas, it's beautiful,' she exclaimed, running around to the other side of the bed, where he stood looking at her.

'I'm glad you like it,' he said, smiling. 'Worth getting lost for?'

'I'm surprised you admit it!' Madeleine answered, but before Thomas was given the chance to reply, she slid her hands around his waist and kissed him. Her stomach was fluttering with nerves as she became aware that this could finally be the moment that they would make love, but just as she was warming to the idea of trying out the magnificent bed, Thomas pulled away.

'Why don't we go and check out the restaurant?' he said, picking up the key from the bedside table.

'Eh, the restaurant? Sure...' Madeleine sat down on the bed, baffled as to why Thomas had chosen to investigate the hotel instead of investigating her, and felt a little offended at his preference. This certainly wasn't the way she had envisaged it. Thomas seemed to be in no rush to get her into bed.

Deciding, however, that she wouldn't say anything because it was only their first night, Madeleine reluctantly got up, and she was soon ensconced in the bar with a vodka and tonic. Sipping his glass of beer, Thomas talked about his plans for the weekend, unaware of the slightly distracted look in Madeleine's eyes. He seemed totally oblivious to her disappointment, but as the evening wore on, she slowly forgot about the earlier rebuff and began to enjoy herself more and more. Her excitement grew as they discussed what they would do over the weekend, and with memories flooding back of her dad telling her how fabulous the golf courses were, Madeleine readily agreed to going to Lahinch the following day.

After another drink in the lounge, Thomas and Madeleine moved into the candlelit restaurant. They were seated in a private alcove where the sounds of a string quartet and delicious smells floated around them, enhancing Madeleine's amorous mood. But Thomas followed her order of red wine with a mineral water. She didn't like the idea of drinking on her own while he remained totally sober. She hadn't exactly planned on falling out of the restaurant drunk, but there was no denying that nerves could be calmed by alcohol; and besides, it could help to get things started in the bedroom. As the bottle of sparkling Ballygowan was placed in front of Thomas, it occurred to Madeleine that the bedroom could in fact be his reason for ordering the water. She hadn't thought that, while alcohol would settle her own nerves, it might have too much of a relaxing influence on Thomas.

It's kind of sweet, I suppose, she thought to herself, softening a little as she watched him tentatively sipping his water. I've been so busy thinking about myself that I never really considered how worried he might be.

Despite Madeleine's initial reservations about dinner, by the time the dessert plates were being cleared, she was thoroughly enjoying herself. Thomas had proven to be his usual funny and charming self, and Madeleine didn't quite know what she had been so worried about earlier on. They chatted incessantly and flirted openly, and when Madeleine had finished the last of her wine, they were in silent mutual agreement that the digestif would be taken upstairs.

To Madeleine's relief, Thomas was showing none of his previous reticence as they left the restaurant and made their way upstairs, slipping his arm around her waist and nuzzling her neck as she unlocked the door to their bedroom. Before she had closed it again behind her, Thomas had already started to unbutton her blouse. His smooth, tanned hands circled her waist as she allowed herself to succumb to his gentle touch. Before long, their hands began to find each other with the urgency of anticipation. Searching fingers travelled contours of exposed skin as they stumbled onto the bed, their limbs entwined. Madeleine held Thomas away for just a second to admire his lithe, athletic body, while he relished the softness of her skin and the faint perfume of her hair.

As Thomas cupped her towards him, desire raced through her body until, seconds later, he was inside her. Moving together sensuously in the light cast over them by a single lamp, Madeleine was filled with a sensation of how right it all felt. The guilt she had feared, and the anxiety she had dwelt on, evaporated as Thomas moaned in pleasure above her. Contentment and desire were soon dissipated, however, as Madeleine became aware of his quickening pace, until, seconds later, he lay heavily over her, spent.

'I'm sorry, Madeleine,' he whispered, his voice hazy with satisfaction. 'I'll last longer the next time. I was just looking forward to being with you so much that I got a bit too excited.'

'It's OK,' she replied, rubbing his head. 'I suppose it's a compliment, in a way.'

She had barely finished her sentence when Thomas sleepily climbed under the covers and rolled over in the bed.

'I'm still listening,' he muttered into the pillow, lazily reaching one hand behind him to half-heartedly caress Madeleine's thigh. 'I think I'm just more tired after the conference than I thought I was.'

Madeleine was about to answer when she heard the sound of heavy breathing. She couldn't believe he had fallen asleep so quickly, especially when she was still so awake. As she lay there, questions filled her thoughts. Why hadn't he made a move before now? she wondered. She had initially thought that perhaps there was something wrong, whether with her or with him, but clearly this wasn't the case. Baffled, Madeleine fell asleep shortly afterwards, with niggling doubts still swirling around her head.

* * *

The following morning, Madeleine woke up slightly disorientated. She had become so used to sleeping on her own that it took her a few seconds to work out who the figure sharing her duvet was. Light and recognition filtered in between her opening eyelashes, as she became aware of Thomas, propped up on one elbow, looking at her.

'Morning,' he said, smiling, reaching across to give her a kiss. 'You know, you're even more beautiful when you're asleep.'

Madeleine's voice croaked with morning sleepiness as she tried to tell him not to be so silly. She was quite aware that her hair would have turned into a fuzzy mess while she was asleep, not to mention the fact that she could feel the indent of a pillow crease etched across her cheek. Still, she appreciated his admiration of her tousled look. It had been quite some time since someone had found her attractive at nine o'clock in the morning.

'So, what do you fancy for breakfast, then? We could have it up here, or go down and eat in the conservatory – it's a really beautiful day outside.'

Thomas's last comment made it clear to Madeleine that breakfast in bed was not on his agenda. She had thought that a little morning sex would be the perfect way to wake up, but she was obviously going to have to forget about that idea now.

'Em, I suppose the conservatory sounds nice,' she said, hoping her slight hesitation would persuade him otherwise.

'Great!' he replied instead. 'I'll just hop in the shower, and then wait for you downstairs. I could have the breakfast ordered for you when you come down.'

'Oh, OK,' Madeleine said, a little taken aback, unsure how to interpret his enthusiasm to leave the bedroom.

As Thomas whistled to himself in the shower, Madeleine decided that maybe he was right. She could feel the warm intensity of a single ray of sun, shining into the bedroom through a small slit in the heavy curtains, and imagined how glorious the weather would be outside. Despite the allure of beautiful sunshine, however, Madeleine was still a bit irked about his unwillingness to stay with her in the bedroom. After all, this was the first time they'd been away together, the first time they'd woken up together, and a little morning sex, Madeleine reckoned, was not too unusual a request to have.

* * *

The day that unfolded before them turned out to be more perfect than Madeleine could have imagined. They drove to Lahinch in the balmy sunshine, settling eventually on a vast, golden beach to have a lunchtime picnic. Madeleine found that she was more relaxed than she had been in months, but wasn't sure whether it was Thomas's easy company or the sea air that was freshening her spirits and releasing her tension. She revelled in the bliss of having nothing to do, and no one but herself and Thomas to think about. As the tide crashed against the shore, they lounged back on grassy banks, watching the waves buoyantly support tiny surfers further out. Madeleine felt herself laughing like she hadn't done in months, as she and Thomas chased each other through the camouflage of marram grass, until finally they lay exhausted in the sheltered snug of the sand dunes, hidden from passers-by as they kissed. Reluctant to leave their sandy haven, it was some time before Thomas eventually convinced Madeleine that they should. His tempting arguments of more wonderful places played on Madeleine's curiosity, until, with a last look at the frothy waves and blond beach, she got back into the car.

A short drive later, their conversation was drawn to a sudden halt, as, driving over a rise in the road, the impressive Cliffs of Moher were revealed in front of them. In the softness of the afternoon light, the cliffs appeared to Madeleine to have been dipped into an indigo bath. She found herself speechless in front of the awesome chasm in the landscape, and as she watched tiny birds dive and swoop over the edge, she realised that there was no other place in the world she would rather be. With Thomas standing behind her, protecting her from the cutting wind slicing in from the sea, Madeleine snuggled in under his coat, wrapped her arms tightly around his waist and kissed him.

'I'm having a wonderful time,' she said, as he looked at her, slightly baffled at what he had done to deserve such a kiss.

'And we're only half way through,' he answered, taking her hand, and walking away from the edge, 'I get to have you all to myself for at least another twenty-four hours before I share you with anyone else.'

He curled his fingers around hers, and Madeleine responded by tightening her own grip, smiling to herself as they walked back to the car. With nothing but a lovely meal and the promise of thrilling night ahead of her, she knew that life didn't get much better than this.

* * *

Later that evening, back in the hotel, Madeleine and Thomas made love. It was slow and intense and, much to Madeleine's relief, lasted longer than the previous night. Surrounded by riffs of Duke Ellington playing around them in the candlelight, Thomas gently caressed her breasts, beginning to kiss them as his hands smoothly ran over her flat stomach. Lying back against the plush pillows, Madeleine was silent as Thomas explored her with roaming fingers, arching her body closer to him as he teased her with his tongue. Madeleine noticed that each time she reached out to hold him, or reciprocate his touch, he pulled away, preferring to dedicate his attention to her. At last, as he moved up to kiss her voluptuous breasts, in one smooth movement he slid his hands beneath the silky small of her back and entered her. Madeleine felt the thrill she had been so expectantly waiting for the night before, and called out his name as their rhythm became faster and hungrier. He ran his tongue tantalisingly up the side of her neck until she could feel the warmth of his mouth circling behind her ear and was overwhelmed with the pleasurable sensation of his weight above her. Sitting up so that their bodies moved together in one motion, Madeleine reached a powerful climax, sensing Thomas's release too as she held him tighter, her hands clasping his thighs.

Afterwards, as they lay back on the coolness of the sheets, Madeleine smiled over at Thomas.

'It's been a long time,' she said, snuggling in to him.

'And more to come,' he answered, deciding to ignore the worry that was beginning to creep in. He had enough tablets to get through the rest of the weekend, but there would be no avoiding having to look for a long-term solution once he got home. Looking at Madeleine, already asleep, he held her tightly beside him. It was now his turn to lie awake in the dark, alone with his thoughts, pondering the many questions swirling around his head.

# CHAPTER SEVEN

'WELL, AT LEAST THE WEATHERMAN GOT IT RIGHT,' JUDITH thought to herself as she looked out the window at the pale blue, cloudless sky. Eight o'clock had been printed on the invitations, but she didn't really expect that people would start arriving until nine. Still, she would go down to the golf club herself for seven to make sure everything was properly organised. She had already been down early that morning to check that the flowers were delivered, and, as expected, everything was carefully stored in the ladies' locker room and ready for display. Grudgingly, she had allowed the house and plants sub-committee to arrange the magnificent bouquets of tiger lilies around Redcliff for the party. She knew that treading on the wrong people's toes would be just the thing to prevent her from becoming lady captain. So, with a superficial smile, she had agreed to let the golf club handle the decoration. Besides, they had been only too happy to help out 'in any way they could for Captain Donal', and they had also promised to take care of the balloons and the Happy Birthday banner. A few less things for her to worry about, she supposed.

As she prepared her lunch, Judith wondered idly where the birthday boy was. She knew he had been playing in a four-ball that morning, but was sure he would have been home by now. Carefully layering her wholewheat bread with crisp iceberg lettuce and cherry tomatoes, Judith tried to calculate mentally how long he had been playing with the group on Saturdays. She had thought when they married first that she would be able to rid him of that infernally boring group of men, but his resolve on the matter had proven to be stronger than hers. Something about being friends for years, she remembered him telling her once, but as far as she could see, they were just a bunch of unambitious guys with nothing in particular to offer Donal. Every so often, he ventured to suggest that they have Ray Barnes, one of his closest friends in the group, and his wife Betty over for dinner, but Judith had always managed to extricate herself from the arrangement. She smirked as she thought back on the times a 'client' had rung her at the really very inconvenient time of an hour before her guests were due to arrive.

Guilt was not something that ever featured in Judith's mind. Early on in her relationship with Donal, she had put in the requisite time with his friends, but she saw no need to do it now. After all, if he wanted them to have mutual friends, all he had to do was take his pick from the wealth of influential people in Redcliff, instead of scraping the bottom of the barrel, as she saw it, with the Barneses. 'I mean, for goodness' sake,' she muttered to herself, 'Betty's still a receptionist in that hospital and she's been there for years.' Her contempt was obvious as she curled her upper lip in disdain.

It occurred to her that the Barneses would most likely be at the party later on. She had formally written out all the invitations herself, but she knew that Donal had mentioned it to a couple of extra people as well. It really did infuriate her the way he could be so laid-back about plans that she was trying to keep a tight rein on. But, as the hostess, she wouldn't be expected to talk for very long to any stragglers Donal brought with him.

Anyway, Judith had a hair appointment in half an hour, and was treating herself to a manicure as well, and so, looking forward to an afternoon of pampering, she decided not to dwell any more on arrangements for the party until at least seven o'clock that evening.

*  *  *

As she was getting ready, Linda wished once again that Ian was coming to Redcliff with her. He had just left the house to go to bridge, and she could still smell his aftershave lingering in the bedroom. Running a comb through her blonde hair, Linda's actions became heavier and slower as her distracted mind ran forward to the next few hours. People were going to ask her where he was and she didn't know if she trusted herself to answer them convincingly. She had bumped into Eileen O'Flaherty at the butcher's yesterday, the wife of Harold, a member of Ian's bridge foursome, and their conversation had cast some doubt over what Ian had told her. It turned out that Eileen was buying food supplies for when her daughter, son-in-law and two grandchildren came to visit from the States at the weekend. Apparently it had been quite some time since they had been over, and Eileen's enthusiasm and joy at the prospect of seeing them was more than obvious. Seeing the smile on her face as she chattered on, picking up a large bag of lamb chops from the counter, Linda decided against asking whether or not Harold would be going to bridge on Saturday. The question sounded ridiculous even to her.

Putting down her comb and staring blankly at the array of lipsticks and eye shadows lying on the dressing table, Linda felt miserable. She hadn't mentioned anything to Ian when she got home that evening, and since then, the questions that had arisen from her conversation with Eileen had consumed her thoughts. If

Harold wasn't there, then who was Ian playing bridge with? They had played in the foursome for as long as Linda could remember, cancelling when one of them couldn't make it, and it seemed implausible that they would change that arrangement now. Despite the unlikelihood of someone else taking Harold's place, Linda desperately clutched onto the idea to try and take her mind off other possible alternatives – alternatives that were becoming increasingly hard to ignore. Last week's unfamiliar feeling of anxiety had turned into a horrible and persistent concern, and she found herself watching every little thing Ian said in the hope that he might, subconsciously, give something away.

Linda felt that what should have been the best year of her life was turning into the worst. It had started so well when she became lady captain, but now it just seemed that all of her happiness and the confidence she had in her relationship were shattering before her eyes. Previously, she had juggled her roles as headmistress, mother, wife and friend, as well as spending time on all the Redcliff committees. Since she had retired, though, the hectic pace she was so used to had quietened; with Jean old enough to look after herself and no job to attend to every day, Linda had been enjoying a wonderful new sense of freedom. It seemed, however, that just as she had reached the top, with time to devote to Redcliff, Ian and their relationship, it was all about to go horribly wrong. And what worried Linda most was that it might now be too late to fix it.

* * *

Kay kissed the children goodnight and smiled brightly at Claudette as she waved goodbye, closing the hall door behind her. Inside, her feelings were bordering on dread, however, as she thought back on the conversation she had had with Ed earlier on that day. Initially, he had planned to watch a match down at the rugby club and come home in time to drive to the party with her. Plans had changed, however, when he called late that afternoon, and with a slight slur in his voice, told her it would be easier if she just picked him up on the way. He explained that some friends he hadn't seen in a while had unexpectedly turned up and so he was going to stay for a few drinks with them. It was no problem, he assured her, she could just drop him down in the morning to pick up his own car. Kay didn't appreciate the way he assumed that she would be free to take him back in the morning, but there were bigger things to worry about, namely the fact that it had been over two hours since the match had ended, and she was afraid to think about how much Ed would already have had to drink.

'Please, God, don't let him be drunk when I get there,' she prayed silently as she drove along the lush green winding road. It was one thing trying to deal with him on her own, but the thought of having to cope with his aggressive, drunken behaviour in front of the likes of Judith didn't even bear thinking about. She would be mortified if he let her down.

'At least Madeleine and Thomas will be there,' she thought to herself, as she pulled up outside the rugby club. A little extra backup might be just what she needed if Ed started to get abusive. For a second, Kay contemplated not going at all, but it was too late for that – she had already told people she would be there. Besides, she thought, Madeleine was probably going to need some support herself. This was the first time she would ever have seen Donal and Judith together, and Thomas or no Thomas, Kay knew how hard it was going to be for her.

Tentatively opening the door into the bar, Kay was greeted by a semi–circle of backs. The hands of the owners of the backs were cushioning pints on the counter in front of them.

'Kay!' Ed shouted, lifting up his arm to motion her over, bringing the din of voices discussing the match to a halt as they all turned around to see who had arrived.

As she walked over to where he was sitting, she noticed the slightly glazed look in his eyes, confirming what she had already fearfully anticipated.

'What are you having?' he boomed, unaware of the deafening silence Kay's scowl had caused to descend on the group.

'Nothing, thanks, we're already late, Ed, and anyway, I'm driving,' she answered coldly.

'Ah, don't be so uptight, why don't you just have a drink?' he asked scornfully, much to Kay's embarrassment.

The last thing she wanted was to have an argument in front of his friends, so, leaning in closer to him, she whispered so that only he could hear: 'I'll wait in the car, Ed. Don't be long.'

Half an hour later, Ed sloppily wove his way around the other cars outside the club and sat in beside an irate Kay. She knew how pointless it was to get angry with him, especially in this state, so she started up the engine without saying a word. As they drove off towards Redcliff with Ed dozing in the passenger seat, Kay wished that she was going anywhere but to a party, and with anyone but her husband.

* * *

Mike was humming to himself as he stepped out of the shower.

'I really did have a great score this morning,' he told Catriona, for the fifth time, 'and I'm dying to get back to Redcliff to hear the results. I may even have lost a shot and you know what that means, Cat? Single figures!'

Catriona gave him her best enthusiastic face, while behind it she thought about what she was going to wear. She knew how much winning meant to Mike, but she had exhausted all her support by the third reminder of how well he had played. Much as she wanted to share in his zeal for golf, she just couldn't continue to get excited about the same game over and over again. She had found it difficult enough to muster any excitement the first time she was told about it.

Just as she had finished getting undressed for her shower, Mike surprised her by coming into the bathroom and kissing her passionately. For a moment, Catriona thought that he might be in the mood for a quickie before they left for the party, but any passionate notions she had were quickly dashed, when Mike went back into the bedroom to find his shirt.

'Hurry up with your shower,' he called to her, as she stood, naked, and slightly disappointed, holding onto the shower curtain. 'We don't want to waste any time getting to Redcliff.'

Catriona found it remarkable how golf seemed to be like a drug for Mike. He was obsessed with it, and she almost felt jealous that he sometimes seemed to have a better relationship with it than he did with her. After all, why else would he choose to go up to Redcliff early instead of having sex with her?

Feeling a little dejected, she stood in under the hot jets of water, and let the streams cascade down over her body. She didn't care if he was in a rush, she had had a busy day herself in work – which he had yet to ask her about – and so she was going to indulge herself in a few moments of relaxation in the steamy shower.

Hearing Mike's voice bellowing at her from the kitchen to hurry up, Catriona turned off the water, quickly dried herself and opened up the wardrobe to decide what to wear. She knew that everyone would probably be dressed up to the nines at the party, so she had better do the same. Some of the women in Redcliff managed to look sophisticated and stunning when they were just out for a round of golf, so she could only imagine how glamorous they would be tonight with a celebration to dress for. Flicking through rows of unsuitable clothes, Catriona remembered the red dress she had bought in Spain the previous year with the girls. Mike hadn't seen it either, so at least it might look as if she had bought something new for the occasion. Besides, it was the most stylish thing she owned, she supposed. Slightly reluctantly, she pulled it on over her damp skin.

Thinking that she must have put on a bit of weight since her last holiday, Catriona became flustered as she straightened the short, glittery dress over her bum and adjusted the straps.

'God, was it really this tight last year?' she muttered to herself, bending down to root through her shoes to find a pair that matched her dress. Settling on an extremely high pair of red sandals, she heard Mike once again shouting at her from the other room. After tightening the strap, she stood up, a little shakily, and hastily put on her makeup in the bathroom. Standing in front of the fogged-up mirror, she could barely see what she was doing, but she didn't have time to put in her contacts, so she just hoped that the end result would be presentable. Anyway, Mike liked her glasses, she thought to herself, as she snatched them up from the bedside locker, and, grabbing her coat with one hand, she clutched a bracelet and some rings from the dressing table in the other and rushed out of the apartment to Mike who was already sitting waiting for her in the car.

* * *

The barbecue was in full swing by the time Madeleine and Thomas got there. Jazz filtered through the warm air as they walked down the steps to mingle with the rest of the guests already sipping drinks outside. Knowing that she would have to face both Donal and Judith at the party, Madeleine had spent an extra hour getting ready. The effect, she knew, was stunning. Her hair hung loosely over her shoulders and the blonde highlights shimmered in the mellow evening sun. Her skin, lightly bronzed from their weekend away, looked amazing beneath the tiny straps of her pale blue top and she couldn't help but notice Thomas' reaction to the figure-hugging pencil-slim skirt she had chosen to wear. Its silken material emphasised her curves as she moved in the low, dusky light, and she was aware of the attention she attracted as she walked sveltely through the crowd towards the clubhouse.

Thomas, feeling slightly awkward amongst so many people he didn't know, put his arm reassuringly around Madeleine's slender shoulders. He had been delighted to go to the party with her, but couldn't help feeling somewhat inadequate as he looked around at the glamorous gathering he was about to join. Sensing his tension, Madeleine looked up at him and gave him a kiss.

'It'll be all right, you know, they're nice people, honestly. Well, the ones I've met so far,' she said, giggling, as they passed a rather sombre-looking group of people discussing swing technique. 'And if it's too boring for you, we can just leave!' she whispered, out of their earshot.

* * *

Standing talking with the club president, Donal found himself tuning out of the conversation. It hadn't even crossed his mind that she might bring someone with her, and as he watched Madeleine disappear into the clubhouse with Thomas, he felt his hand begin to shake ever so slightly. They had been laughing together and, worse still, he had his arm around her, he noticed, as a pounding sensation began to tighten in his chest. Excusing himself from the club president's company, Donal put down his glass on a nearby table, and hurried to follow them inside.

'Madeleine, I'm glad you made it! It's lovely to see you,' he said as he caught up, feigning coincidence at bumping into them.

'Donal, hi!' she responded, brushing his cheek with a kiss. She hadn't seen him arrive, and her voice held a slightly frenzied tone of surprise. 'Thomas, this is Donal O'Sullivan... an old friend,' Madeleine continued, feeling her pulse race as the two men looked at each other.

'Pleasure to meet you,' Thomas answered, extending his hand. Madeleine had never mentioned Donal to him before, and she couldn't help but notice the look of confusion that crossed his eyes as he too perceived the tension that lingered in their small group.

'And Donal, this is Thomas Killeen,' Madeleine introduced, putting her arm gently around his waist. Immediately, she saw the hurt that flickered in Donal's eyes as he took in this intimate gesture, and for a moment she considered taking her arm away.

Don't be so stupid, Madeleine, she chided herself, willing away the urge to soften his pain. After all, he was the one who had made being together impossible, not her.

For a few minutes more, Madeleine, Thomas and Donal chatted together with ostensible ease. Of the three, however, only Thomas's conversation was genuine. He spoke eagerly about the decoration of the clubhouse and the impressive turnout, oblivious to the inner turmoil of his companions. Eventually Donal excused himself to join another group of guests, and Madeleine anxiously led Thomas away to find a drink.

She had been so preoccupied with her own thoughts that she had never stopped to think about how Donal might feel about her living in Ireland again. It was obvious, however, that meeting was as difficult for him as it was for her. While Thomas had been chatting, Madeleine watched Donal as he wrung his hands together, wiping them on his trousers to cool the clammy feeling of stress in his palms. She was also sure that her own appearance had been ruffled by his arrival. Thomas, unaware at the significance of what he was saying, mentioned at one point how beautiful the weather had been while they were away the previous weekend. Just as he was finishing his sentence, Donal shifted his weight onto his other foot and looked awkwardly around him. Clearly the idea of Thomas and Madeleine away together was more than he could cope with, and within seconds, he had politely told them he had just seen somebody he needed to speak to. It was the first time Madeleine had ever witnessed jealousy in him, and she was shocked at the difference between how he spoke to her alone, and how he had reacted when Thomas was there.

With a drink in her hand and feeling slight calmer, Madeleine spotted Kay and Ed in the far corner. Even from the other side of the room, she could see that Ed had already been drinking and her heart went out to Kay as she stood nervously beside him, hoping no one would see them. Her normally happy face was overshadowed with worry, and Madeleine hastened her step towards them to lend her some support. If the past was anything to go by, Ed was likely to say or do something to embarrass his wife in his drunken state, and she knew that Kay would spend the whole night in fear of it happening. Still, she thought, maybe she wasn't giving him enough credit, and if his behaviour did take a turn for the worse, they would just deal with it when it happened. Until then, Madeleine was determined to enjoy herself. She had met Donal, with Thomas, and it had been fine. She didn't want to relax too much, though, as she knew the introductions weren't quite over. The night had only just begun, and Madeleine had yet to meet her hostess.

* * *

Donal wasn't the only one who noticed Madeleine and Thomas when they came in. Judith, struck by the attractiveness of the couple as they walked towards the clubhouse from the car, was further intrigued as she watched her husband rush over to chat to them. She was soon shocked at Donal, one of the most laid-back people she knew, as he stood decidedly uncomfortable in the group, shifting from one foot to another as if aching to leave them. She had never seen him like this before. He was usually the life and soul of every party, or the person to count on in a crisis, but now, standing only a couple of feet away from her, he was positively sweating with stress. Moving closer to get a better look, Judith turned her attention to the couple he was talking to. She knew she had seen the girl a few days ago in the ladies' locker room, but she couldn't shake the feeling that she recognised her from somewhere else too. Judith tried to remember why she looked so familiar, but before she had the chance to figure it out, the trio broke up and went their separate ways.

'Never mind, it'll come to me,' she thought to herself, going outside to check on how the caterers were doing. She would ask Donal about it later.

As most of the guests had already arrived and were beginning to wonder about the food that lay temptingly under pristine white napkins, Judith nodded at the waiting staff to bring out the plates. Trestle tables had been set up outside the clubhouse, and these were covered with salads, breads, raw vegetables and dips, and aromatic smells of Cajun chicken and juicy steaks were starting to waft over from the barbecue. Everything was going perfectly, Judith decided, as she watched the band bring their instruments onto the stage in the clubhouse. The drinks were flowing freely, food was on its way and, with the music about to start playing, it was all running completely according to plan. All she needed to concentrate on now was chitchat with the members, after which, Judith reckoned, she would be picking up votes faster than Donal would be collecting birthday wishes.

\* \* \*

'Don't tell me whad I can't have, juz' get me another dhrink, Kay,' Ed slurred, holding his hand up as if wondering what the big deal was.

'I'm not getting you any more, Ed. I told you, you've had enough,' Kay replied, hushing her voice down to a whisper to try and deflect the attention that Ed was attracting. Madeleine and Thomas had only been standing with them for five minutes when an argument had started about how much drink Ed had taken. It was obvious from the smell of alcohol encircling him that he had already had more than enough, but with a free bar, and darkness yet to descend for the evening, he was in no mood to cut the party short.

130

'What about some food, Ed, I could get you something from the barbecue?' Kay pleaded, helplessly looking at Madeleine, hoping she might to come up with a suggestion that would make him stop.

'Well, iv you can bloodhy go to the barbecue, there'z nothin' stoppin' ye from pickin' me up a beer on the way back now, ish there?' Ed asked her with a vindictive look.

Kay, mortified, stared at him in exasperation. He was impossible to deal with when he got like this, and the louder he got, the more she became aware of people looking over to see what all the commotion was about.

'Why don't you and I go out to grab a beer and get something to eat while the women stay chatting in here for a while?' Thomas suggested, hoping that the 'boys together' approach might work more successfully than Kay's entreaties. To everyone's surprise, Ed rose unsteadily from his feet in agreement with Thomas.

'Good plan, Tom,' he said, his eyelids drooping sleepily as he tried to focus on his new friend, 'iz all bullshit in here anyway, lez go out an' gedda pint.'

As they watched Ed zig-zag uncertainly through the guests, with Thomas inches behind, trying to support his elbow to lead him towards the door, Madeleine and Kay stood for a moment without saying a word.

Eventually, it was Madeleine who broke the silence. 'I never realised how bad things had got...' she said, unsure, once the words were out, what to say next.

'Well, at least that means I've done a pretty good job of hiding it, then,' Kay answered with a weak smile.

'But you know you don't have to hide this from me!' Madeleine exclaimed, thinking back on all the times Kay had supported her in the past.

'Oh, I'm sorry, I think I just thought that if I didn't tell anyone about it, it would go away. And I'm so mad at him

131

today,' she began to explain. 'You see, he went to watch a rugby match earlier. The plan was that he would come home to get changed and then go on to the party with me. I ended up having to collect him, though, because he'd had too many beers to drive the car home, and he hasn't stopped drinking since he got here either. I don't know what I'm going to do,' she finished, looking at Madeleine hopelessly.

'Oh, Kay, I really don't know what to say. At least for tonight, though, perhaps Thomas taking him outside to get some fresh air and something to eat might sober him up a bit?'

'Yeah, maybe you're right. Honestly, it's worse than trying to look after the kids,' she said with a laugh, allowing herself a moment of light reprieve from the weight of concern she usually carried around with her. 'But at least I can punish *them* if they misbehave!'

Just then, they both heard a loud crash coming from the lawn, and after a quick glance at Madeleine, Kay rushed outside, visions of disaster looming in her thoughts.

The scene that they were confronted with was worse than either of them had expected. Dazed, and clearly inebriated, Ed sat amidst a fallen avalanche of broken glass. Behind him, an overturned table lay on its side spilling forth a twinkling sea of tiny crystals, the pitiful remains of a once impressive tower of champagne glasses.

'He was heading towards the drinks table, but somehow lost his footing and grabbed onto the tablecloth to steady himself,' Thomas explained apologetically to Kay and the growing crowd of onlookers gathering around them.

'Stchupid fuckin' glashes, Kay, in the way, the table was... stchupid fuckin' table gettin' in the... bloodhy way,' Ed offered, fumbling with his clothes as he tried to remove the shards of glass that had splintered all over him.

Kay wasn't interested in hearing his excuses, though; in fact, with a growing number of questioning guests looking from Ed to her, she needed to think up some of her own. Helping Thomas lift Ed up from the toppled tower of champagne flutes, Kay smudged some of the blood on his hand to make it look worse than it was. She knew that the only thing to do now was to get him out of the party, the sooner the better. Feigning concern at his injuries from the fall, Kay insisted that she take him to their GP to have the cuts looked at. Madeleine, unable to think of anything to ease her friend's troubles, just stood with a defiant look on her face, glaring at anyone who dared to judge Kay for the behaviour of her husband. Eventually, with Ed securely propped up by her side, Kay smiled her thanks at Thomas, hugged Madeleine, and walked off in the direction of the car. Alone, she was suddenly flooded with the shame of what had just happened. How could she show her face in Redcliff after this? One thing she was quite sure of, however, was that this kind of life simply could not go on. She had put up with a lot from Ed, but this was the last straw. Whatever residual feelings she had for him had disintegrated with the splintered glass, and from now on, he was on his own.

* * *

As the crowd dispersed, Madeleine and Thomas remained where they were, discreetly apologising to the catering staff for Ed ruining the champagne display. Madeleine almost felt responsible herself for the disaster, as guest after guest walked past them with an accusatory glance. At least Judith hadn't seen the fiasco, she thought, furtively looking around her for any signs of her hostess. However bad she was feeling, though, Madeleine couldn't even begin to imagine what Kay must be going through. She had no idea that Ed had become so unmanageable. Resolving to call Kay first thing in the morning, Madeleine decided to try to put the whole catastrophe behind her and enjoy what was left of the party. Retrieving her glass of wine, she silently prayed that the rest of the night would go smoothly, and, linking her arm through Thomas's, she walked back inside with him, away from the mess.

Just as they were about to go into the clubhouse, Madeleine heard her name being called from across the lawn. Turning around, she found herself looking into a wonderfully familiar face.

'Betty! God, you haven't changed a bit,' she said, hugging the woman in front of her warmly.

'And as for you... well, you're still as gorgeous as you ever were! How've you been?' Betty asked, standing back at arm's length to get a good look.

'Great, thanks,' Madeleine replied, still smiling. 'I'm just back from New York, actually, and with no job to speak of, I've become a lady of leisure, so no complaints, really!'

'Well, lucky for some,' Betty replied, 'though I can't say I have it too hard either. That is, of course,' she whispered quietly, 'unless you count spending the entire evening trying to avoid "the bitch" as a hardship.'

Madeleine laughed. She had always been grateful to Betty for disliking Judith. She knew it was probably childish, but it meant a lot to her to know that not everyone thought that Donal had made the right decision.

It had been a long time since the two women had seen each other, and their meeting now rekindled memories that had lain dormant for years. While Madeleine had been with Donal, they had gone out with Ray and Betty Barnes almost every week-end, and she couldn't remember a single occasion when they hadn't enjoyed themselves. Since the break-up, however, and Madeleine's decision to go to New York, she and Betty had fallen out of touch. Somehow, it hadn't seemed appropriate to keep in contact with Donal's friends.

Noticing Thomas looking slightly uneasy, Madeleine apologised for not introducing them.

'I'm sorry, Thomas, this is Betty Barnes, an old friend of mine, and Betty, this is Thomas, a new one!'

Catching the obvious insinuation, Betty winked at Madeleine and shook Thomas's hand enthusiastically. 'You'll have to come inside to see Ray as well, he'll be delighted to see you,' Betty said, looking again at Madeleine. 'Apart from anything else, my talking to the two of you will make a nice change from being ostracised from everyone else's conversation because I don't play golf. A crime in this place, as far as I can tell.'

'Well, in that case, I'd better not stray far from you either,' Thomas added, relieved that he wasn't the only interloper at the party. 'I've never picked up a golf club in my life!'

A few minutes later, Madeleine, Thomas and Betty had found Ray on his way back from the barbecue. Getting another drink from the bar, they settled themselves in a corner away from the music to catch up properly. Tucked away in their quiet recess and immersed in reminiscent conversation, no one noticed Judith as she stood close by, watching the group as they laughed and joked together. She had been watching them discreetly since they had come inside, trying to allay her frustration and remember why the blonde girl looked so familiar. She was loath to go up and introduce herself, knowing that it would mean having to make small talk with the Barneses, but her unsatisfied curiosity was becoming so frustrating that she just didn't see any other way.

It suddenly dawned on Judith why identifying her had been so difficult. She had been racking her brain to find some occasion where they might have met, but this had been her mistake. The reason why she was having so much difficulty, Judith realised, was because this elusive beauty was not someone she had ever met before. No, she thought to herself, watching Madeleine throw her head back in laughter at something Betty had said, Judith might never have seen her in person before, but she had seen that face smile out at her from a photograph. One day, a couple of years ago, she had been clearing out some files in their study at home and, replacing a folder up on a high shelf, she had noticed something falling out and flittering to the floor. Reaching down to pick it up, Judith realised that it was an old Polaroid of Donal, with friends. Looking a little more closely at the picture, she also recognised Ray and Betty Barnes, laughing in the sunshine at some unseen photographer's joke, but she had never before come across the fourth person in the group. Standing there, with her arm entwined around Donal's waist, was an exceptionally pretty young girl, smiling as if she hadn't a care in the world. As she stared at the picture, it suddenly occurred to Judith that this girl, at whom Donal was looking so lovingly, was the girl he had wanted to leave her for. Taking in every minute detail, from her hair and clothes, to the expression on her face and her body language, Judith began to feel anger well up in her. Donal had never looked so adoringly at her, nor had he ever looked so happy, and in an uncharacteristic fit of jealousy, she tore up the picture and threw it in the wastepaper basket. After standing for a few minutes in the quiet study, Judith soon regained her composure. After all, she thought, Donal had chosen her, hadn't he?

She remembered how shocked she had been that day when he had tried to break up with her, and not only shocked, but incredulous that he would be so stupid. Didn't he know that his practice would collapse without the support of her father, not to mention the idiocy of throwing away all the money that Judith was sure to inherit? No, she decided, she was right to have done what she did. Who knew when his love for this girl would diminish? Judith's money, on the other hand, wasn't going any-where. She would be able to back him financially for as long as he needed, while his reputation as a fine consultant would lend her own business a certain degree of prestige. She believed it then, and she believed it now – telling Donal that she was pregnant had been best for everyone. After all, no one ever had to know that she had lied, and at the end of the day, she had really done him a favour. What did surprise Judith slightly was how well her plan had worked out. As she suspected, Donal's conscience wouldn't allow him to abandon her, but the way he reacted when she 'lost the baby' was an added bonus. He never once questioned her beyond what she was willing to tell him, a real blessing, considering how easily he could have found out the truth, and it had only taken a smattering of superficial tears to make him promise her that he would never mention the subject again.

After they got married, Donal never mentioned the other girl. They got on with life, as they always had, and achieved the kind of success that Judith dreamed of. As for other women, it was never something she worried about. She suspected, although she didn't like to dwell on it, that it had taken him so long to get over the beautiful blonde, that he would never even contemplate falling in love like that again. The problem of his being unfaithful, therefore, simply hadn't been an issue. That was, until now.

Letting her curiosity get the better of her, Judith resolved to go over to the group to get an introduction. At least that way, she would be able to find out what the story was with the handsome, dark-haired man who stood beside her. They probably weren't married – there was no ring – but they might at least be living together. Judith didn't recognise the feeling of insecurity as it crept up on her, but she was in no doubt that a little assertion of her own status as Donal's wife wouldn't do any harm. Donal had very nearly been snatched away from her before by this woman, and she had no intention of letting it get so far a second time.

Fixing a smile on her face, Judith left her vantage point from behind a giant vase of tiger lilies and approached the group. Totally unaware of her close scrutiny, they were taken by surprise when, cutting in on their conversation, she positioned herself in the centre of their circle and stood for a moment, smiling benignly at her guests.

'Betty, darling, don't you just look superb! I'm delighted you could make it,' Judith started, her voice dripping with false admiration. 'And Ray, God, it's been too long,' she said, kissing the air over his cheek. 'I'm just *so* happy you could both make it tonight, and I know how absolutely thrilled Donal will be to see you.'

Dumbfounded, Betty looked at Ray on the off chance that he might have some clue as to why Judith's behaviour had made such a suspicious U-turn from her usual apathy towards them.

'Old friends really are the best aren't they?' she continued, turning to face Madeleine. With her smile painfully fixed from cheek to cheek, she stretched her hand out and, with a barely discernible glance over Madeleine's outfit, introduced herself.

'Hello. I don't believe we've met before. I'm Judith O'Sullivan, Donal's wife. You're very welcome to the party.'

Although the introduction was aimed at both Madeleine and Thomas, it was only Madeleine who felt the huge significance of Judith's cold stare as she told them her name. For a moment, she found herself speechless, and willed her mouth to say anything to relieve the deafening silence pounding in her ears. Eventually, she managed to whisper her thanks, and as an almost inaudible afterthought, her name.

Thomas, completely oblivious to the history that connected the two women, chatted amiably to Judith, congratulating her on the wonderful party and fabulous food.

'You even took care of the weather!' he said, glancing outside at the mellow evening light still illuminating the lawn.

'Oh, thank you, you're too kind,' she replied with ingratiating modesty. 'Of course, a party is only as good as its guests, so really, once the food is out and the music's playing, my work is done.'

'Nothing left then but to enjoy yourself,' Thomas pointed out, as Betty looked quizzically at Madeleine, still suspicious of the uncharacteristic friendliness.

'So, tell me, Madeleine, what is it that you do?' Judith asked, changing the subject. Small talk about party organisation was hardly going to enlighten her significantly on the opposition standing before her, she thought to herself, hoping that Thomas would stay quiet. She needed to find out why Madeleine was back, and exactly how long she would be back for.

'I'm not actually working at the minute, I'm only recently home from New York,' Madeleine replied, her assertiveness somewhat recovered, and her voice in working order again.

'I *see*...' Judith said, satisfaction flickering in her eyes, 'it must be so nice to be able to pop home on a holiday like that.'

'Oh, it's not a holiday,' Madeleine answered, relishing the sight of discomfort beginning to bubble under Judith's cool exterior. 'No,' she continued, 'I'm home for, well, the foreseeable future I suppose. And I just can't wait to get up to Redcliff more often, make up for lost time, you know. I've always loved the course.'

As Judith's mouth ever so slightly gaped open, Madeleine fought the urge to think of something else that might rattle her insecurities about Donal's past. It was obvious that Judith knew exactly who she was, but what neither of them had reckoned on was that Madeleine was turning out to be the one with the upper hand.

Betty, enjoying the confrontation, was certainly not going to say anything to stop it. She was delighted to see Judith squirming at last. Feeling yet another nudge from Ray urging her to try and change the subject, however, she turned to Thomas and, with a discreet cough, enquired as to what he did for a living. From the look that Judith shot at her, Betty wasn't sure if she was annoyed that her inquisition had been cut short, or if she appreciated a way out of the awkward spotlight she had created for herself. Either way, the new direction of conversation held no appeal for Judith, and minutes later, she made her excuses and left.

As she walked away, the two men took long gulps of their drinks, thankful that the tension had passed. Madeleine looked at Betty and smiled. She had thought about this moment for the last ten years. Much to her relief, Judith had been the one to walk away. It hadn't been half as bad as she thought it would be either, Madeleine thought to herself as her adrenalin slowed down. The end of Judith's interrogation may only have been a minor relief to everyone else, but for her, it was nothing short of a major victory.

*  *  *

On arrival at the golf club, Mike, with Catriona in tow, headed straight for the notice board. The results had just been pinned up and, scrolling down through the list of names, Mike frantically searched for his own. Meanwhile, Catriona stood apprehensively behind him, praying that he would find his score so that they could just enjoy the party. He had talked animatedly in the car about losing a shot from his handicap, and Catriona hadn't seen him so excited since his birthday two years ago when she had bought him an electric caddy.

As he turned around, Mike's thunderous expression showed traces of incredulity as he asked her to check the board for him. He couldn't see his name. Catriona held her breath as she too cast her eye down the list, but, failing to find it, she bit her lip and turned to face him.

'I can't see it, Mike,' she said, furrowing her brow. There was no chance of their having a good night now.

'No, it's not there, is it?' he replied, in a quiet voice. Catriona got the horrible feeling that his placid reaction was just the calm before the storm, and unsure whether to try and comfort him, or run away, she just stood there, hoping that there was another notice board somewhere, with another set of names on it.

To her relief, Mike wasn't totally dejected. Apparently there was a computer printout which automatically regulated new handicaps. With bated breath, Catriona remained fixed in her position beside the notice board, and waited for Mike to check it and discover the mistake. Her fears were confirmed, however, when he came back to her again, with an expression on his face even more incensed than before.

'Well, someone's obviously made a mistake!' he exploded, looking at Catriona as if hoping that she might tell him what could have gone wrong.

'I mean, look at this,' he went on, reading from the winners on the board, 'Gerald Murphy – winner in class one with sixty-six strokes. I only had a sixty-three, for God's sake, how the hell am I not up there?'

Catriona didn't know why he wasn't up there either, but, still unsure as to how the competition worked, she shied away from offering any words of encouragement in case what she did say was wrong. It certainly seemed to her that Mike should have won, but when it came to golf, she could never really be certain.

Just as Catriona was searching for something appropriate to say, John Sweeney, the competitions secretary walked past.

'John, there you are, I was just about to go looking for you,' Mike called out, interrupting John's stride toward the bar.

'Oh, yes, I'd been meaning to speak to you too, actually. Quite a mix-up today, eh?' he said, looking slightly bashful.

'Mix-up? Why isn't my name on the notice board?' Mike asked carefully, hoping in his confusion that the whole situation could be easily rectified.

'Well, not so much of a mix-up really as… well, there's no other way to say it: you didn't sign your card after today's round. I'm sorry, Mike, but it means that your score doesn't count.'

For a moment, Mike stood still, digesting the information. Catriona could see that his smouldering anger was only barely being contained.

'But of course I signed my card, John, I always do,' he replied slowly. He wasn't going to give up that easily.

'Again, Mike, I'm really sorry, but I can show you the card if you want, and rules are rules. Look, better luck next time, you're bound to have as good a round again.'

As the competitions secretary walked off, Mike sat down heavily on a nearby chair, looking disconsolate. Realising that there really wasn't much she could do for him, Catriona went off to put her coat in the locker room, thinking that it mightn't be a bad idea to let him cool down on his own for a bit.

As she walked precariously back across the tiled floor in her high heels, Mike raised his eyes from his lap, and looked at her. Seeing Catriona for the first time without her coat on, Mike's expression changed from one of dejection to shock.

'Where on earth did you get that dress from?' he asked incredulously, staring at the way the sequins sparkled as she moved. 'God, this is Redcliff, Cat, not a nightclub in Ibiza.'

Catriona froze in her tracks, shocked and embarrassed at his harsh words and her own obvious faux pas.

This is his fault for rushing me out of the apartment, she thought to herself in the split second it took her to turn on her heels and run to the ladies' toilet where she locked herself in and burst into tears. Nothing ever went right in this god-forsaken golf club she decided, as tears ran down her cheeks and dropped into her scarlet lap. The game was difficult, the rules were impossible, and now, it seemed, she couldn't even get the dress code right.

\* \* \*

Marie was having the time of her life. The food was delicious, the company was entertaining and with a taxi organised to pick her up later, the gin and tonics were in plentiful supply. She knew that any party of Judith's would be extravagantly generous, but the best thing about it was that with so many guests milling around, she wouldn't be expected to chat with her hostess for very long. Besides, she had far more important things to think about. Ciaran, for example, had been catching her eye all night, and she was counting down the minutes until they could grab a few moments together for a quick shag.

Sneaking another look at him serving behind the bar, Marie noticed a small, red-haired girl flirting with him while she paid for her drink. She wasn't getting very far, Marie thought, watching as the girl chatted on, oblivious to her inattentive audience. Ciaran clearly had other things on his mind, like sex with *her*. Sauntering over to lean seductively against the counter, Marie patiently applied some lipstick, and waited for Ciaran to make his way down to where she stood.

'I'll be on my break at about half past ten,' he said, reaching over to get an empty glass beside her. 'It should be dark by then.' Looking around to make sure that no other bar staff were within earshot, he added quietly, 'See you then at the back of the men's tee box on the fourteenth.'

Simply nodding her agreement as other guests came up to order their drinks, Marie walked away from the bar to join another conversation. She wasn't sure whether it was the thrill of anticipation of having sex out on the golf course that was sending shivers down her spine, or the fact that no one knew about her kinky exploits with the barman that excited her. Either way, she reckoned, it was all adding up to make one of the best parties she'd been to in a long time.

\* \* \*

As Linda rinsed her hands under the warm running water, she became aware of sniffling sounds coming from one of the cubicles. Turning off the tap, she stood for a moment, trying to sieve through the noises of the party outside to see if she could hear the quiet crying again. A few minutes later, the cubicle door tentatively opened, and with her eyes cast down to the floor in the hope that she could make it unobtrusively to the mirror, out stepped Catriona.

'Hello... it's Catriona, isn't it? You're Mike's girlfriend?' Linda asked, trying to look sympathetic as she took in the miserable state of her companion. A charcoal black waterfall of smudged eyeliner and mascara had streaked down her cheeks with the falling tears, and her tight red dress had risen up towards her thighs from sitting down for so long.

Catriona, on the other hand, aware of what she must look like, and unable to think of any way of avoiding such a direct question, just stood outside the cubicle staring blankly at Linda like a dazed rabbit. The evening was bad enough now that Mike knew he hadn't won the competition, the last thing she needed was to make small talk with a well-meaning golf enthusiast while she was looking like she had been dragged through a bush backwards.

'Eh, that's right,' she stuttered eventually, realising that she would have to answer the question sooner or later.

'I'm sorry, I just couldn't help overhearing that you were crying. Is everything OK?' Linda enquired, walking over to where Catriona stood. 'I'm Linda, by the way, is there anything I can do for you?'

'Oh, no, thank you. Everything's grand really, I'm just sort of, well, taking a break from the party.' Catriona knew how pathetic she sounded, but was afraid that she might sound even stupider if she told the truth. She wasn't sure how much a member of Redcliff would really want to hear her views on how awful she thought everything about the club was.

'You're sure? I really would be happy to help in any way I could...' Linda trailed off. She didn't want to push it too much.

To her surprise, however, Catriona looked up and took a deep breath.

'Unless you can turn me into someone who can actually play golf, then I'm not sure that there's very much you can do for me,' she said with a hopeless smile. 'Thanks anyway, though.'

When Linda didn't say anything in response, Catriona stood awkwardly for a second, until, deciding that it couldn't do any harm to get a little bit off her chest, found herself explaining everything that had gone wrong. Starting with her innate inability to play golf and how she couldn't master even the simplest of shots, Catriona poured out all of her problems right up to the part about Mike's disappointment over the competition results and his dislike of her outfit. Finally she told Linda how it seemed to her that joining Redcliff looked more and more like a huge mistake with every day that went by.

'Do you know,' she said, fighting the tears that were threatening to fall again, 'that you're the only person I've really talked to since I came up here? People don't seem to have that much time for the more "handicapped" players.'

Linda laughed at the pun, and put her hand around Catriona's shoulders.

'Things do get easier, you know,' she said, handing over a tissue. 'I had some awful experiences when I arrived here first as well. I remember one morning coming up for a round, only I hadn't realised that I was meant to have put my name down on a time sheet. By the time I'd figured it out and asked somebody what I was meant to do about it, I was told that I couldn't play at all. I remember being absolutely mortified, getting back into my car, hoping that no one would realise that I'd come up and gone home again without so much as taking a club out of my bag.'

'That sounds familiar,' Catriona said smiling, finally able to see some humour in her rumble debacle.

'And that wasn't all,' Linda continued, glad that she had been able to elicit a smile from Catriona through the tears. 'I was only quite recently married – a time when everything had to be on a tight budget – and because I ended up getting stuck in awful traffic on the way home, I had to pay the babysitter for the whole morning. No golf, public humiliation, and I had to pay for the pleasure too! But the thing is, I persevered with it, got to know the people – we're really quite nice, you know – and look at me now, I'm lady captain.'

Catriona gasped as she realised who her confidante was.

'Oh, God, sorry, I would never have complained to you if I'd known who you were!'

'Don't be ridiculous. I mean, surely I should be the first person to talk to, seeing as I could probably do something about helping you?' Linda reasoned. 'Listen, why don't you play with me in the Scotch foursomes? With my long drives and your high handicap, we'll be unbeatable! I really think you might like it if you gave it another chance,' she said, hopeful that Catriona would say yes.

Feeling slightly more positive about the whole situation, and deciding that she had nothing to lose, Catriona agreed to play. Linda waited for her as she fixed her makeup, and with a quick hug, they walked back out to the party together. Just before they went into the lounge, Linda gave one final piece of advice.

'I hope you don't mind me saying this, but it seems to me that Mike is what you're most worried about. You shouldn't have to feel like you're playing golf for him you know. Play it for yourself, and remember that at the end of the day, you don't have to know a thing about the game to be able to give him your support. Trust me, he may have made some harsh comments earlier on when he was upset, but he does love you, and he'll want you to be there for him.'

Realising that Linda was probably right, Catriona resolved to try to remember what she said when she went back out to Mike. As she opened the door, the sound of the band greeted them with loud jazz and for once, the throngs of people and even

Redcliff itself didn't seem so formidable. Walking into the crowded room, Catriona decided that maybe things were beginning to look up.

* * *

At ten twenty-five, Marie stole out of the clubhouse unnoticed and walked silently across the manicured grass of the golf course. Within minutes, under the cover of the twilight sky, she had made her way through the dense trees, past fairways and putting greens, to the tee box on the fourteenth, where she found Ciaran already there waiting for her.

'I don't have much time,' he said, as he came over and kissed her. 'It's mad up there today, so I have to be back in fifteen.'

'We'd better hurry up, then,' Marie teased as she undid the clasp on his belt and put her cool hand down his trousers. She smiled as she felt the firmness of his erection, and, pulling up her skirt, his own inquisitive fingers searched her body eagerly. Before she had left the clubhouse, Marie had quickly gone into the ladies' bathroom to take off her thong and put it into her handbag. If time was of the essence, she thought, there was no point in putting unnecessary obstacles in the way. Now, as Ciaran made the discovery, she was delighted she had done it. Apart from her own thrill of walking in the cool evening air with nothing on beneath her skirt, he was obviously enjoying her foresight in taking it off.

'That's such a turn on,' he said, as he caressed his fingers in and out of her with increasing desire.

She could feel him getting harder and harder with her every touch. Moving her legs apart, Marie was just about to take him in, when suddenly, he turned her around and pushed her up against the tree behind them. Ciaran reached one hand to cup her breast, and within seconds he was in her. Marie gasped with pleasure as she felt him enter her, and thrilling sensations shot up through her body as he thrust hungrily. She strained against his body to savour him more deeply, and as her arousal mounted and mounted until she felt she could take it no longer, she exploded in a dramatic climax, vaguely aware of Ciaran tightening his grip around her waist and muttering 'Oh God!' as seconds later, he too, came inside her.

'Fuck me!' Ciaran panted, taking out a cigarette, while Marie leant against the tree, wallowing for a moment in orgasmic ecstasy, throbbing echoes of pleasure continuing to shiver through her.

'I'd better go,' he said as he lit up, 'they'll start wondering where I am if I'm not back soon.'

'Well, we should probably walk back separately,' Marie replied smiling, 'though I'd like to point out, for the record, that this is definitely something that we should get more practice at!'

'Yeah,' Ciaran answered with a cheeky grin, 'maybe we could try out each of the tee boxes. You'd never know, one might be better than the other.'

Laughing, Marie straightened her skirt and adjusted her top, kissed him a quick goodbye and, feeling a playful slap on her bum as she walked away, turned around briefly to face him.

'You'd be lucky,' she said flirtatiously, blowing a kiss at him, and turned around again to walk back to the party, smiling as she heard his lascivious reply float across the evening air.

A short while later, Marie was sitting at a table with Nessa, the first person she had met on her arrival back at the clubhouse. They were deep in conversation when James, Nessa's husband, returned with a fresh round of drinks, and as he sat down on his stool, Marie took out the post-sex cigarette she had been so looking forward to. She didn't know who got the biggest shock, however, when her red and black lace thong fell out of her handbag and landed on the table between her companions' Chardonnay and pint of Guinness. There was a moment of stunned silence as Marie desperately tried to think up an excuse.

'Well, as my mother always used to say,' she started, with a frenetic smile, picking the offending article off the table, "always carry a pair and a spare"!' The look on Nessa and James's faces told Marie that they weren't quite convinced.

'It's terrible, but I've this awful fear of being taken into hospital after an accident with no clean underwear, it's desperate isn't it?' Marie continued, aware that with every word that came out of her mouth, she was digging a bigger and bigger hole for herself.

'Eh, yes, desperate,' Nessa agreed, hesitantly, looking at her husband in the hope that he might have a more constructive answer for Marie and her thong.

'Oh, em, certainly,' James coughed, 'you never know when you'll need them, do you?'

'So true,' Marie said with a smile, taking a long drag on her cigarette.

'Right, well, I'll leave you two together, shall I?' she asked, standing up, guessing it was probably better to find another conversation elsewhere. 'Oh, and James, thanks again for the drink.'

Walking away, Marie couldn't help but laugh. She knew that neither of them had bought the story about her mother, but reckoned that her breezy encounter on the golf course more than made up for any embarrassment caused by her renegade thong. And given the choice, Marie thought, as she stubbed out her cigarette with the point of her stiletto, she'd do it all again in a second.

* * *

Later that evening, as the light grew darker and the band slowed down their music so that mellow licks of jazz circled the couples on the floor, Madeleine danced slowly in Thomas's tight embrace. In the wordless calm of the tune, she thought back over the night and tried to figure out what she was feeling. What was beginning to really worry her was how little control she was proving to have over the situation she was now in. Against her will, the emotions that she had stored away for so many years were resurfacing, and she was more confused than ever. What was also distressing to her was the fact that she really did like Thomas, and so with every thought she had for her past love, she felt like she was being unfaithful to the man who adored her now. While a saxophone solo played softly in the background, Madeleine looked over to see Donal dancing with Judith, smiling together as if they were sharing some intimate joke, and she felt as if a knife was twisting in her heart. Despite the pain of seeing them together, though, Madeleine knew she could be under no illusion. Donal was married now, and no matter how much she wished it wasn't so, there was nothing she could do to change it. They simply couldn't be together anymore.

Tired of struggling with the turmoil of her emotions, Madeleine nestled closer in to Thomas, and tried to empty her mind of everything but the music. Unaware that they were being watched from the other side of the room, however, she was oblivious to the reaction that Thomas's answering hug was causing. While a satisfied smile crossed Judith's face, Donal closed his eyes against her tactile intimacy with another man, and tried to hide his inner anguish. He couldn't deny that since Madeleine's return to Ireland, he was more confused than ever, and as he danced on with Judith, he too was troubled by unsettling thoughts.

# CHAPTER EIGHT

DRIVING ALONG THE COAST ROAD ON THE FOLLOWING Monday, Madeleine glanced out at the sun sparkling on the sea. Perfect weather for golf. Convincing herself that she had finished all her errands anyway, and swayed by the knowledge that her clubs and golf gear were already in the boot, she made a quick U-turn on the road and headed off in the direction of the Redcliff.

Since her return from the States, she had been nervous about going up there, afraid that she might run into Judith if she did. After the party, however, meeting her didn't seem quite so daunting any more, and so, hardly giving her a second thought, Madeleine happily planned her round. She could play two balls instead of one, she thought to herself, as she began to imagine the blissful solitude of sauntering around the course on her own. Putting her foot on the accelerator, she sped up Redcliff's leafy driveway in anticipation of a relaxing afternoon.

An hour later, caught up on practising her putting on the seventh green, Madeleine was unaware of a man walking silently towards her and stopping at the far side of the bunker as she took her shot.

'That's what I like to see – dedication,' said a familiar voice, as her ball sloped down the velvet grass and disappeared into the hollow pot in the centre of the green. Startled, Madeleine turned around to see Donal smiling at her from the shade of the evergreens. Stepping out into the sunlight, he walked across to where Madeleine was standing.

'I... I never saw you coming up,' she said, hoping she looked OK. She didn't know how long he had been standing there. 'Were you waiting for me to let you through?'

'When was the last time you ever had to let me through, Mad?' he replied, leaning nonchalantly on his putter. 'You're too good for that. No, I actually saw you from the fifth and decided to forgo a hole to catch up. I hope you don't mind?'

'No, not at all,' Madeleine answered, pleased and slightly surprised that he had been so keen to come over to her. 'Would you like to join me? But I must admit I'm quite rusty.'

'Not from what I just saw. In fact, judging by the way I've been struggling to keep up with you, I'd say you're quite the opposite.'

'You flatter me,' Madeleine replied, delighted that he had obviously been watching her for some time. 'But certainly, if you want to, you're more than welcome to play with me. I wouldn't have thought our captain would need all this extra practice though,' she teased, knowing how he would hate her insinuation that he wasn't playing well.

'This isn't practice, Mad. I'm just doing my duty as club captain by socialising with the members out in the field,' he said, as she looked disbelievingly at him, picking up the pin and putting it back into the hole. 'Apart from which,' he admitted, 'I hardly ever get to play these days, with all the meetings I have to attend up here, so it's nice to get out when it's quiet.'

'That sounds more like it,' she smiled at him, an idea springing to mind. 'Well, seeing as we're both a little out of practice, why don't we put a bet on the last couple of holes – loser buys the drinks?'

'Sounds good to me,' he replied, confidently dropping his club back into his bag, 'but you'd better start counting your change now – I'm in good form today.'

'Oh, are you?' said Madeleine. 'Well, we'll see about that. You saw how I putted that last ball, and I'm only getting started.'

As they walked towards the tee box on the eighth, Madeleine felt like she was ten years younger. It was amazing how easily they fell into the roles they used to inhabit, and for a few moments, Madeleine managed to forget about everything they had been through. The silences they fell so comfortably into seemed as natural as the conversations they had as they walked the fairways, and sunny hours flew by in a wonderful haze of companionship. Relaxed as their conversation was, however, Madeleine was aware of the physical tension that remained between them. She had felt Donal drink in her every move as she walked up to take her shots, and she was also captivated by the muscles in his arms and back as he drove powerfully off the tees.

Madeleine was one shot behind as they reached the eighteenth green, but with Donal in a bunker, it looked like Madeleine would still win. If she was honest, though, she didn't really mind. All she could think about was the fact that they were to have a drink together after the game. For some reason, despite having been in his company all afternoon, Madeleine was suddenly nervous at the thought of sitting down in the bar with him. There would be no golfing distractions to take the focus off them, or comments on how well the other was playing. Instead, sitting beside one another, and without golf scores to keep track of, it would just be two drinks, a table and their past between them.

Donal chipped his ball out of the bunker, and Madeleine was eventually forced to concede defeat as it rolled smoothly down the green's gentle contour and dropped into the hole.

'Well done... I suppose,' she called over to him begrudgingly, as he swung his golf club up in the air victoriously, its metal head glinting in the afternoon sunlight.

'Ha, ha!' he said, walking over to her. 'I *told* you I was in good form!'

'Didn't your mother ever teach you not to gloat?' Madeleine replied, feigning annoyance at losing.

'Ah, ever gracious in defeat, Mad,' Donal added with a smile, nudging her elbow.

'Only to you, Don,' she answered, laughing at the memory of the many times they had ended up competing with each other over what started as a friendly game on a Sunday afternoon.

'So, drinks are on you then... great,' Donal said, as they walked towards the clubhouse.

'Looks like it,' Madeleine called out as they walked their separate ways. 'Just let me just drop my clubs back to the car, and I'll see you upstairs shortly.'

Searching through her bag to find her keys, Madeleine was glad that he had gone inside. She needed some time to gather her thoughts before she went back in. It had been a long time since they had been for a drink together. Thinking ahead, Madeleine decided that it might actually be the best thing for her. She didn't know whether it was nerves or excitement fluttering in her stomach, but either way, a glass of wine would be exactly what she needed to settle her down.

Some time later, having showered and changed, Madeleine and Donal were sitting in the lounge with their drinks. To Madeleine's relief, the intimacy of the small bar table did nothing to stilt their conversation, and it was only the other Redcliff members coming over to talk to Donal that punctuated the steady flow of discussion. They spoke about upcoming competitions and exchanged golfing tips, but for the first hour, they managed to successfully skirt around every issue that might give anything personal away. As if by silent mutual agreement, neither Judith nor Thomas was mentioned, and even the topic of the barbecue was tactfully avoided.

Just as Donal was in the middle of asking Madeleine if she would like another drink, he stopped himself, and thought for a second.

'Actually... did you have any plans for eating?' he asked, fiddling with the beer mat in front of him. 'It's just that I was thinking of having a steak here. I'm not expected home for dinner. And sure, you could look at it as a sort of consolation prize for not winning earlier,' he added, with a hopeful smile.

'Well, there's no need to rub it in,' Madeleine said, 'but I suppose a steak does sound nice. All right, then,' she agreed, settling back in her chair, as if confirming that she would stay.

While Donal went off in search of some menus, Madeleine took the opportunity to quickly check her make-up. Flipping open the mirror, and running some cream powder over her porcelain skin, she saw that her cheeks were slightly flushed, and her lips seemed to be fixed in a smile. She couldn't remember the last time she had laughed so much, not even with Thomas, she thought to herself, as she watched Donal walking back to the table.

'I don't know why I even bother to get a menu any more, considering I know it backwards at this stage,' Donal remarked, as Madeleine discreetly put the compact back into her bag. 'It's what being captain does to you. I'm beginning to feel like I live up here.'

It was on the tip of Madeleine's tongue to tell him that it was probably preferable to being at home with Judith, but she was afraid it would ruin their dinner. And after enjoying such a lovely day so far, she didn't want to do anything to jeopardise it now.

The evening light was fading as they finished their meal, and the last of the golfers had come in from the course. Looking at her watch, Madeleine couldn't believe that it was ten o'clock already. They had been sitting there for almost three hours.

'Can you believe the time?' she asked, astonished, as Donal swallowed the last of his drink, 'I could've sworn it was only about eight!'

'Ah, but remember how time flies when...' Donal paused as the end of their old phrase lingered unspoken.

Madeleine ached to hear him finish it, to hear, 'when you're with the one you love', but instead, he cast his eyes down to the table, and finished it quietly.

'...when you're having fun.'

Nothing was said until the barman came over to give Donal his change, interrupting the moment of longing that passed between them.

'I should probably get going,' Madeleine said as she stood up.

'Of course, yes, me too,' Donal answered, hastily throwing his napkin on the table and helping her with her coat.

After walking Madeleine to her car, Donal waited while she opened the door and sat in.

'I've really had a wonderful time today, Don, thanks,' she said looking up at him. Having sat in the sun all day, the car now felt stuffy and warm, and Madeleine shifted uneasily in the balmy heat, unsure of how to say goodbye. Then, unexpectedly, Donal squatted down and, without a word, leaned in to kiss her. As his lips softly touched hers, little electrifying shivers tingled down her spine. She could smell his subtle aftershave and the heat on his skin, and she revelled in the moment she had tried not to think about all day. One by one, seconds of intensity replaced years of missing him, and as they kissed, protected by the cloak of evening's dwindling light, Madeleine reached out to hold him.

\* \* \*

'You what?' Kay shrieked down the phone. 'After everything he put you through the last time, how could you, Madeleine?'

'It was just a kiss, Kay. It isn't like I hopped into bed with him.'

'*Just a kiss?*' came the shrill voice down the line. 'I can't believe you – it took you years to get over Donal. Do you not think that your "just a kiss" is going to set you back all over again?'

'God, I'm sorry I told you, Kay. You're making too big a deal out of all of this,' Madeleine retorted.

'I'm not the one making a big deal out of it. I'm not the one who kissed Donal O'Sullivan. You are. I mean, what the hell were you thinking?' Kay asked.

Madeleine initially phoned Kay to make sure that everything was all right. She hadn't turned up for golf that morning, and, unable to remember a time when Kay had ever missed ladies' day, Madeleine had been slightly concerned. It turned out that Claudette had a stomach ache and was unable to mind the children, but Madeleine couldn't help wondering if Kay just hadn't come up because she was too embarrassed about Ed's behaviour at the weekend.

'And in the car park, for God's sake, in full view of the clubhouse. Just imagine if Judith had come along. And what about Thomas?' Kay continued. She was asking so many questions, so quickly, that she was almost tripping over her words, and Madeleine, grateful for small mercies, was barely able to interrupt her onslaught to get enough time to answer them.

'I really think you're over-reacting to this, Kay. As I said, it was only a kiss, and a short one at that.'

There was silence on the phone as both women considered what to say next. Eventually, Kay spoke up.

'Well, don't come crying to me if you go and take this any further, and end up getting hurt all over again.'

Madeleine knew that Kay's anger was born out of concern for her, but she couldn't help feeling slighted by her reaction. She was all too aware herself of the risks involved, for everyone, but she somehow hadn't expected this from Kay. If anything, after losing the only great love of her own life, Madeleine had thought that she might even be mildly supportive. She couldn't have been more wrong. Kay sounded angrier than Madeleine had heard her in years, and Madeleine couldn't understand why she was taking it quite so badly.

'Kay, let's just leave it. It's not worth us having a row about,' Madeleine replied, her own temper beginning to fray, 'and anyway, I'm meeting Thomas in a few minutes, so I really have to go. I'll talk to you tomorrow.'

After she replaced the receiver on the hook, Madeleine sat in silence for a few minutes. She wasn't actually meeting Thomas at all, but she needed an excuse to get off the phone. What annoyed her most was the fact that she knew Kay was probably right. In getting involved with Donal again, she was treading on thin ice, and with Judith and Thomas now in the picture, it was more dangerous than ever. Not only had her conscience erased all thoughts of Judith when she was with Donal, but Thomas was also forgotten in the few minutes that Donal's lips had tenderly kissed hers. For the first time since it happened, Madeleine really considered the consequences of their actions, and as she sat alone, she became genuinely scared of what she was getting herself into. What frightened her more, however, was that she didn't know if she could stop herself now, even if she wanted to. Breaking her train of thought and the silence of the quiet apartment, Madeleine's phone rang again.

'It's OK, I accept your apology for over-reacting, let's just forget about it,' she said as she picked up the receiver. She knew Kay would feel bad about their argument and ring back.

'Well, I wouldn't exactly say I over-reacted, but then, you seemed to give as good as you got, too,' came the reply.

'How did you get my number?' Madeleine asked, thrown by the unexpected voice.

'Captain's privilege,' Donal answered. 'I just called the office at Redcliff and told them I needed to talk to you about an upcoming team event. Good, eh?'

'Conniving, I'd say,' Madeleine said flirtatiously. She could hear him smiling.

With preliminaries out of the way, Donal's voice softened. 'So how are you? Did you get home all right last night?' he asked cautiously.

'Oh, yes, fine thanks,' Madeleilne replied, surprised that he had gone to the trouble of finding her number, let alone actually calling.

An awkward silence followed, as they both contemplated the significance of the phone call. Madeleine knew that they were on the brink of something big, and that they should pull back before it went too far, but she felt powerless to stop herself.

'Can I come over?' Donal asked carefully. The hesitation in his voice told Madeleine that he too had registered the danger of their situation, but, like her, he was unable to put an end to it.

'No, eh, that's not such a good idea,' she replied. Much as she wanted to see him, she just couldn't risk Thomas seeing them together. She didn't know what she was doing herself, let alone having to try and explain it all to someone else.

'We could go for a drink, though. I'm free now, if you like,' Madeleine added quickly. She could explain the difficulties of meeting in her place to him then.

'Great,' he said, clearly delighted at her acceptance. 'How about Kehoe's in half an hour?'

'Perfect, see you then,' Madeleine said, and hung up the phone.

Unaware of the smile that had crept across her face, she went into her bedroom to change. Apart from wanting to look her best, she knew that the distraction of finding an appropriate outfit would occupy her thoughts for a while. At least that way she wouldn't have to try and answer the questions that were saturating her own thoughts. What she was doing was wrong, she knew that, but for the first time in years, Madeleine felt truly, deliriously happy. She was equally aware, however, that she would have to keep it all to herself. This was one drink that her mother, Kay and the rest of the world, could know nothing about.

Madeleine was already sitting at a table when Donal came into the bar. She spotted him immediately as he opened the door and furtively glanced around to find her. Dressed in a pair of pale blue jeans and a white tee-shirt, his casual appearance was at odds with the expression of anticipation on his face. His anxiety eased, however, when he sat down beside Madeleine and ordered a drink.

'Hi, you look really great,' he said, as the lounge girl walked away with his order.

'Thanks,' she replied coyly. With Donal next to her, the reality of what they were doing suddenly became clear to Madeleine. As she took in the slight tan across his cheeks, and the smell of freshly cut grass and cologne on his clothes, Madeleine realised that she was already in too far. The euphoric feeling she got just by being close to him reminded her, more powerfully than anything else, of how she used to feel when they were together. She had forgotten the little things, like how he rubbed his right temple with his thumb when he was concentrating, or how he tapped his hand on his knee when he was nervous. And as she watched every familiar flick of his hair and change of expression, Madeleine knew that she was falling in love with him all over again.

Nervous at their silence, Donal started talking first.

'So, did you just not want me to come over to your place, or…' he started, not wanting to guess what the problem might be.

'No, it's not that, it just, well, Thomas – you remember, from the party?'

160

Donal sombrely nodded his recollection.

'Well, he lives in the apartment above mine, that's how we met, and I just couldn't risk him seeing you there,' Madeleine said, the guilt she was feeling evident in the shake in her voice. 'You see, we've been seeing each other for a few months now, and, well, you know...'

Donal did know. He knew as well as Madeleine that what they were doing was bordering on having an affair, but like her, was loath to say it out loud. If it was said, then it was real, and for the moment, neither of them wanted their feelings leaked to the outside world.

'Does he know about us?' Donal asked. 'I mean, that we used to go out with each other?'

'No,' Madeleine said, looking into his eyes, 'he doesn't know about any of it. He doesn't know that you broke my heart, or that I left the country to try to get over you, or that it's taken me years to get used to not making you my first thought of the day, even though I married another man. Tell me, how I could tell him about any of that, Donal?'

Donal looked at her and lifted his hand to wipe away the tear that had escaped down Madeleine's cheek. She had been determined to control the emotions that had been forcing themselves out since they had met, but speaking honestly to him for the first time in years, she couldn't help herself.

'Oh, Mad, if you knew what I've been through...' he said, resting his hand on his leg again, aware that they were in a public place. Just as it had been before, they couldn't risk the danger of being seen. 'Surely you can't think that I've been happy? That I don't constantly blame Judith for the way things turned out? I wanted to spend the rest of my life with you, Mad. You know that. But I couldn't abandon Judith when she got pregnant; you do understand, don't you?'

Madeleine's mind was swirling. She didn't know what she should think any more. Everything she was feeling seemed so poorly timed, redundant, like finding a winning lottery ticket too late. It didn't matter what they felt for each other now, did it? There were other people to consider and, like the last time, Madeleine was just going to have to get used to the idea of being without him.

'And then, after everything, she miscarried...' Madeleine said before she could stop herself. Aware that she had touched on a nerve, however, she was immediately sorry she'd mentioned it, and looked apologetically over at him. 'I'm sorry, Don, I shouldn't have...'

'No, don't worry, it's what we've both been thinking, isn't it? I mean, after all, it was the only thing stopping us from being together, and then just six weeks after the wedding, it seemed that it was all for nothing.'

'How did you feel?' Madeleine asked, quietly.

When she herself found out that Judith had miscarried, she had cried for weeks. It was as if it had all been one cruel joke. By that time, though, Donal was already married, and there was nothing she could do about it.

'How do you think?' he asked her, a moment of anger flickering through his blue eyes. 'Instead of believing that I would spend the rest of my life with you, I was married to Judith. There was no baby, and as far as I was concerned, no chance of my ever being as happy as I was when we were together. None of this has been easy for me either.'

Madeleine didn't say anything. She wanted with all of her heart to believe what he was saying, but she had also learnt through past experience that believing him didn't always work out for the best. Hadn't he promised her before that he would do what was right? But then, she supposed, how could he have known that it just wouldn't be what was right for her?

'Mad, what I have is an empty life. It looks pretty from the outside, but all it's filled with is superficial dinner parties and a tolerable relationship with a trophy wife,' he said, desperately trying to convince her that without their relationship, his life was incomplete.

'Why did you never have any more children?' Madeleine asked. She doubted whether or not she would ever get the chance to ask him these questions so candidly again, so, hiding the emotion in her voice, she probed him for the answers she had been struggling with for years.

'Well, we tried, but without much luck. Judith went for all sorts of tests, and visited doctors all over the country, but all it ever came down to was unexplained infertility,' Donal said, unable to hide a slight tone of bitterness.

'And what about you?' Madeleine questioned. Donal's response was a quiet stare at his drink.

'No, everything's fine with me,' he said eventually, looking at her. 'We both went for fertility tests a couple of months after it happened, but apparently there was nothing wrong with either of us. Judith seemed to take it the hardest. I suppose I had numbed my emotions to a certain degree by that stage, and then, after a while, she started insisting that she go to her doctor's visits alone. She was so determined to find out the cause of the problem that I think she was frustrated when the answer turned out to be more elusive than she'd expected it to be. She ended up going to see as many specialists as she could find. What about you, though?' Donal asked, growing weary at even the memory of his first few months of marriage. 'Were children ever on the cards for yourself and Kevin?'

Madeleine took a deep, silent breath. She didn't like talking to Donal about her life in New York.

'Yes,' she said, 'they were, but I suppose we both thought that we had loads of time for all that sort of stuff. My career was beginning to take off, and he was doing really well himself, so we figured that we'd just dedicate another couple of years to work and then start having children. In hindsight, it was probably for the best,' Madeleine reflected. 'I can't imagine how a child would cope with losing a father like that, and then being uprooted and brought back to Ireland. No, it's definitely better the way it is.'

The air was thick with the unintended double meaning of Madeleine's last words. Neither of them really knew if what they were doing now was better than the way it was before, but with two relationships at risk, they were at least hoping that they were doing the right thing.

'Come on, let's get out of here,' Donal said, hoping that the fresh breeze outside would ease the emotional tension that was building between them.

Standing together in the exposed car park, Madeleine was suddenly aware of how easily they could be spotted. On edge, she walked quickly over to her car, and looked questioningly at Donal, hoping that he had a plan in mind.

'Do you want to just follow me?' he asked, equally nervous about being seen.

With a nod, Madeleine closed her door and switched on the engine. Somehow, the safety of being inside the quiet car restored her confidence, and she thought she might go with him. Pulling out onto the road, she followed close behind him.

Driving out of town and along the Coast Road, they eventually arrived at Dollymount Strand. Parking beside Donal's black BMW, Madeleine reached behind her to grab a sweater from the back seat, and, pulling it on quickly over her head, she got out of the car. Donal was already waiting for her, and they immediately fell into step together, setting off for the beach with their heads bent down against the wind.

The evening sun was low in the sky and the small waves beat steadily against the shore as they ambled along, while seagulls battled the breeze above them. Having encountered no one for miles, Donal slipped his fingers tentatively through Madeleine's and, though she had been expecting it, the soft warm feeling of his palm startled her. Its familiarity was at once comforting and alarming, but despite the warning bells sounding in her head, she tightened her grip.

After a while, Madeleine realised that they had made their way towards the sand dunes and, stopping for a moment in their shelter, Donal pulled her towards him.

'Oh, Mad, it's been such a long time. I've been so lonely without you,' he said, desperately searching her eyes to find some reciprocation of feeling. 'If you can tell me that you have found anyone else that understands you like I do, then I'll believe that we're not meant to be together,' he continued, 'but if, like me, no one's even come close to giving you what we have, then promise me you'll at least consider giving this a second chance?'

Madeleine couldn't help but notice that he had spoken about them in the present, that he had said 'what we *have* together', instead of talking about what they *had*. She knew then that, after all the years, nothing had changed for him either and, lost for words, she kissed him passionately, secretly wishing that they could stay tucked in their sandy niche away from reality forever.

Finally, she pulled herself away from him. Much as Madeleine wanted to escape the truth of the situation they were in, she knew that they would have to go home, separately, sooner or later. And when that happened, she would be left once again with her conscience to deal with.

'No, Donal, no, sorry, I can't,' she said, stepping back, lowering her eyes from his pained expression. 'You have to see that everything has changed,' she pleaded. 'You're still married, how can I... how can *you* forget that?'

'You're right, Mad, you're absolutely right, but I can't stop now. I don't know what's around the next corner, but I'm hoping that, however my future's mapped out, you're in it too.'

'But Judith?' Madeleine replied. Her ideals had been too romantic before, and she knew now that she had to face up to what she hadn't wanted to face before.

'I don't know,' Donal said, reaching towards her and taking her hands in his. 'But, just, please don't write this off, Madeleine. Give me some hope that we can work this out.'

'Hope is one thing, Donal, but the reality of sharing you with another woman is quite another,' she said, not quite as confidently as she would have liked.

Madeleine could feel her fleeting resolve to take a hard line with him weakening. She felt exactly as he did. Neither of them knew what their futures held, but one thing she was certain of was that she wanted more than anything in the world to be with him again.

'I'm not saying this is the end, Don. I'm just saying that it can't be like last time. And if you can find a way to make it possible, then I'll be with you all the way...'

'A bit of time, that's all it'll take,' Donal promised, a little shakily. The magnitude of his pact was weighing heavily on him as he considered how he would go about doing what he had meant to finish years ago.

'And Thomas?' he asked, aware that his was not the only difficult job.

'I don't want to sound hard, Donal, but I gave up everything for you the last time, and I was left with nothing. I can't do that again. I like Thomas, and I'm not going to end anything, especially if it means hurting him, until you've shown me that you're serious about us.'

Madeleine's brow was almost sweating with anxiety. She had never been in such a difficult position before, and making it worse was the fact that, whatever happened, someone was going to get hurt. This time, however, she knew that she had to think about herself.

Walking back to their cars in the cool evening air, the intimacy of their conversation was interrupted by the sound of two women deep in discussion, coming towards them. Madeleine quickly dropped Donal's hand, and the momentary fright she felt just thinking about them getting caught reassured her that she was doing the right thing. She was not going to sneak around pretending anymore. If he wanted to be with her, then it would have to be her alone.

'I'm not going to sleep with you either, Don, not until all this is sorted. We're in a messy enough situation, and I'm not adding that to the equation.'

Donal smiled at her candour. 'You always were a straight talker,' he laughed, 'but you're right. I know we can't,' he finished, more seriously.

Back in the car park, Donal looked around to make sure there was no one else there and, satisfied that they were alone, he slipped his arms around Madeleine's waist and kissed her.

'This is all going to be all right, you know,' he whispered into her ear.

'I hope so,' Madeleine replied, looking up at him. 'I hope so.'

With that, she walked over to her car, opened the door and sat in.

She could see Donal mouthing 'I'll call you' through the closed window, and she smiled. Despite the knowledge that this was one situation she probably shouldn't be getting into, Madeleine felt that it was the best thing she had done in years.

\* \* \*

Marie sat in the passenger seat of her son's Audi A3 as they sped along the motorway. The warm caramel interior of the car was making her feel hotter, as the sun beat down on her through the open sunroof. She was feeling anxious enough already, but in the sticky mid-day heat, her concerns about the day that lay ahead were multiplying with each passing mile.

'John, please say something that will reassure me that everything is going to be fine today,' she asked him as he sang along with the radio, totally unconcerned. 'I mean, I don't usually enjoy weddings at the best of times, but I'm dreading this one,' she continued, trying to elicit some empathy from her son. 'Oh, for goodness' sake, John, aren't you even remotely worried about your brother's behaviour?' she cried out in exasperation.

'Mum, relax, would you? Eugene will be grand,' he replied distractedly. He was trying to read the road signs.

'Weddings are awful occasions anyway,' Marie went on, annoyed that he didn't seem to be taking her seriously. 'You have to sit at a table with a bunch of people who you wouldn't choose to socialise with in a month of Sundays; cringe through the best man's speech as he uses every inappropriate phrase under the sun; and keep an eye on the father of the bride in the hope that he might stay sober long enough to string together a few decent sentences about his daughter,' she finished, running out of breath.

'Well, I don't really mind, it's easy to score at weddings,' John replied in his usual insouciant manner. He had taken the day off college to be at his cousin's wedding, so for him, it was more of a holiday than a dreaded encounter with the family firing squad. With so many snide siblings congregated in the same place, however, Marie knew that she would be in for an almighty interrogation.

'And I can just imagine all the nasty comments that will be made about your father,' she went on, by now oblivious to her indifferent audience. 'There'll be all sorts of "And how *is* Billy's *partner* these days?" and "Gosh, it must just be so lonely up there in that big house all on your own." I should just tell them about my sex life – that'd shut them up.'

John turned his head to look at his mother and raised an eyebrow. 'Mum, please, you're more embarrassing than Eugene,' he complained.

He knew all about his mother's new-found sense of freedom, but had no desire to witness her boast about it. The rest of the family thought they were all weird enough as it was.

'Ah, so you do agree then that Eugene is going to create a scene?' Marie asked, delighted that he had admitted it.

'I never said that, all I meant was...'

'No, it's too late, you've said it now. I knew I was right!'

'I'm not even getting into this,' John said wearily, turning into the church car park. 'He's entitled to bring anyone he wants.'

'Holy Family indeed,' Marie muttered, as she read the sign above the entrance. 'Holy show more likely.'

Stepping out of the car, she straightened what was, for her, a very reserved black and white dress which she had bought earlier that week. She had also worn the matching jacket in the hope that if she at least made the effort to look understated, then she might blend in with the crowd and avoid some of her family. Just to feel a bit more normal, however, Marie had put on the sexiest black underwear she could find, and her signature hold-up stockings. She might have to look like a middle-aged conservative, she had thought to herself that morning, but she didn't have to feel like one as well.

The smell of fresh lilies and polished wood greeted them as they entered the church. Related to the bride, they were ushered to a pew on the left and seated beside an austere-looking couple whom Marie didn't recognise. People who hadn't seen each other for ages chatted animatedly as the organ played softly in the background, and those who weren't catching up with friends were looking around at the other guests to inspect their outfits. Whispered observations were exchanged beneath the brims of large hats, and plumes of feathers flew on top of extravagant hair-pieces as gossip was passed down the pews. Marie's trite neighbour was exceptional only in the amount of perfume she wore, and snubbed her attempt at polite conversation with a tight smile. Marie couldn't wait for the day to end. John, already looking around for pretty young friends of the bride, was proving to be no ally in her time of discomfort, and just when she thought she would be all right, so long as she didn't draw attention to herself, she heard a commotion bustling up the aisle. Quickly straining her ear in the hope that the organist had started to play the Wedding March, Marie suspected the worst as she realised that it wasn't the bride making her entrance. Turning around, she saw Eugene walking dramatically up the aisle with his arm entwined around Ken's, smiling beatifically at all of his inquisitive onlookers. They wore matching suits of white linen, complete with green carnations in their buttonholes, and were veritably wallowing in the attention their appearance was attracting. Marie, praying that they would just sit into their seats and stay quiet, nearly died as Ken bent down to smell the flowers tied to the end of their pew, remarking to anyone who would listen that they were 'simply divine'. In that moment, Marie was so embarrassed that she would have been prepared to take a vow of celibacy if only they would disappear back to wherever they came from. She was under no illusion, however, that her son had anything of the sort in mind, and so resigned herself to a day of continuous mortification. Questions about Billy were turning out to be the least of her worries.

'Hiya, Ma,' Eugene said, as he sat in beside her, 'you remember Ken, don't you?'

'Yes, of course, how could I forget?' Marie answered with a forced smile.

'Ken, this is my older brother, John.'

The introductions were cut short, however, with the arrival of the bride, who thankfully distracted everyone's gaze from Marie's pew to the front door. She looked absolutely radiant in a simply cut ivory dress, and with one hand nervously clutching a small bouquet of pale pink roses. Her other arm was held supportively by her father. As Marie watched Charles proudly walk his daughter up the aisle, she noticed him glance briefly over at her, and was sure that, in that second, she could see him mentally clock up the tirade of questions he would have for her about Eugene later.

As the ceremony started, Marie tried to relax and enjoy the service. The music was beautiful, the service was emotional and everything was running smoothly as the couple said their vows and exchanged rings. Knowing it was too good to be true, however, and that something had to go wrong sooner or later, Marie wasn't surprised at what happened when the priest enjoined the congregation to give each other the sign of the peace. While everyone around them turned to shake their neighbours' hands, Ken and Eugene, deciding that a kiss would be far more sincere, wrapped their arms around one another in a clinch that put the bride and groom to shame. Marie heard a sharp intake of breath from behind her as her son and his lover came up for air, but decided that she wasn't even going to turn to see who it was. She might as well save herself the apology she thought. She had only been there forty-five minutes and was quite sure that, before the day was out, she would have plenty more opportunities to explain Eugene's behaviour. He gave her a wink as she looked over at him, and then he sat back down. It seemed that he had his own agenda for the day, one that was more concerned with shocking his straight-laced cousins than protecting his mother's sanity.

A strong gin was what she needed, Marie thought to herself, as she sat listening to the organist playing the final hymn, or, rather, a couple of gins. Still, she reasoned, only an hour or so until the reception, where she might be able to hide in some corner by the bar. It was just a pity that the calibre of staff in the hotel probably wouldn't be quite up to the standard of the bar staff in Redcliff.

But, then, tomorrow is Tuesday, Marie remembered as the newly married couple walked back down the aisle, and if anybody will be able to make me forget this miserable wedding, Ciaran will.

A few hours later, in spite of her numerous misgivings, Marie actually found that she was enjoying herself. As anticipated, the after-dinner speeches were incredibly boring, but once the dancing started, and the gins had taken the edge of her uneasiness, she relaxed enough to be able to sit back and watch proudly as her sons kept her entertained. Since they had arrived, she had seen John make his way around the room chatting up every girl he could find, and Eugene had caused endless amusement out on the dance floor. Marie had also had her first real conversation with Ken. The matching linen suits had apparently been his idea, but, as he explained to Marie, 'The kiss,' he whispered closely, his hand on her knee, 'was all Genie's idea. He's such a *brat* isn't he?'

Marie discovered that it was, in fact, extremely hard to dislike Ken. His running commentary on the other guests had her laughing for hours, and their conversation was only interrupted when Charles, walking over to where they were sitting, stood in front of them and coughed.

'Marie,' he said, beaming an intoxicated smile, 'I, em... I, ah...'

'Oh, sorry, excuse *me*,' Ken apologised, taking the hint. 'Marie, I'll talk to you later,' he finished, winking at her as he mimicked Charles, walking away.

'What can I do for you, Charles?' Marie asked, a little annoyed that, of all people to break up a good conversation, it had to be her brother-in-law.

'I was just, eh, just wondering if, em, ah... you'd, well... if you'd like to dance?'

Marie was shocked. Charles had had difficulty in the past asking her if she could pass him the salt at the dinner table, so she could hardly fathom his request that she go out on the dance floor with him.

'Oh, OK. Yes, I suppose so,' she answered, reluctantly getting up from her chair, unable to think of a plausible reason to refuse him.

As he led her to the centre of the floor, into the middle of all the other couples, she saw her sister arguing with the hotel manager and wondered what she would make of the two of them dancing. As they moved stiffly to the music, Marie became suddenly aware of a sweaty hand moving nervously across her bottom.

'That's what you are, Marie, unforgettable.'

Marie was stunned. 'What? And, sorry, but get your dirty little hand off my ass,' she said, not planning to make a scene, but quite prepared to if she had to.

It dawned on her that 'Unforgettable' was the song they were dancing to. She couldn't believe it. Of all the people to be flirting with her, she couldn't believe it was Charles. Holier-than-thou, married-to-her-sister Charles. She was stunned further as she felt his fingers graze the side of her breast.

'You have such lovely...' he started, becoming braver in his exploration, but Marie cut him short.

'Don't you even dare, you little pervert,' she said, raising her voice, 'and you'd better listen very carefully, because you only get to hear this once. If you ever touch me like that again, I swear I'll smack that squat head of yours right off your lecherous little body. Got it?'

She stood in the middle of the dance floor waiting for his answer. The band, who were not-so-subtly trying to listen while at the same time continuing to play, were beginning to sound like a cassette player in need of new batteries. The bride also stood aghast with her new husband and Marie's sister in front of them. Too embarrassed to say anything, and aware of the attention of the whole wedding party, especially his wife, Charles stood mute.

'Just because I'm separated doesn't mean that you're doing me a favour by touching me up with your greasy little mitts,' Marie started, standing back with her hands on her hips. 'And if you must know, I have a *fabulous* sex life, a concept I'm quite sure you're not familiar with.'

Marie was on a roll. She had put up with their condescension and their reproachful comments ever since she and Billy had split up, and it felt wonderful to give them back a taste of their own medicine, albeit in a slightly more public arena. Their opinions about homosexuality, not to mention what they thought of Marie's social life, had been kept no secret, and now, Marie reckoned, it was about time to point out a few of their own flaws.

As Charles stood frozen on the dance floor, the rest of the guests parted like the Red Sea to let Marie past.

'John, Eugene, Ken, I think it's probably time we left,' she said gleefully, picking up her handbag and collecting her coat. For the first time that day, neither of her sons could think anything to say to their mother. Instead, the sound of Ken clapping on his own and shouting out a triumphant 'bravo' accompanied Marie as they all followed her out the door.

Sitting in John's car again, Marie couldn't believe what had just happened. It was at times like this that she really began to think there was a God. Ken had proven to be wonderful company, she had finally told her sister's family what she really thought of them, and, above all, she thought with excitement, tomorrow was Tuesday.

* * *

Ed woke up with a thundering headache and a throbbing wrist. Lifting his head up just a fraction off the pillow, enough to afford him a view of the injured hand, he tried to recollect why he might be covered with Band Aids. All he could remember was Kay being in a bad mood with him, and for some reason, he was sure he had been picking bits of glass off himself. Somewhere in between the rugby club and Redcliff, he seemed to have blacked out, and his memory was just a blur of broken images and strange faces. Pulling the duvet up over his head, he tried to think what day it was. He knew that it couldn't be a work day. If it was, Kay would have shouted at him by now, which meant that it had to be the weekend. Sunday! Yes, that must be it, he thought, as he continued trying to piece together the events of the previous evening. He remembered now that he had been at the Saturday game in the rugby club and that Kay had picked him up to go to the party. He mustn't forget to pick up his car, he noted to himself, vaguely wondering whether there would be another match on today. Yes, he decided, he would deal with that just as soon as he could get out of bed.

Donald's… or Darragh's?… birthday, wasn't it? One of those golfy types anyway, he thought to himself, reaching one warm arm out into the cool air in the hope that there might be a glass of water on the bedside table. His hand searched aimlessly about for a couple of seconds before he realised that there was no bedside table. With huge effort, he looked out from under the sheets to find that he was in the spare room.

'Kay must've been really pissed off,' he laughed, oblivious to the fact that he had spent most of his drunken nights in there recently. The ripple of his quiet laughter resounded through his pounding head until, reluctantly, he decided he could survive no longer without water.

With a deep sigh, Ed lifted his feet heavily out of the bed and ran his hands over his unshaven face. The movements of his body were turning large, nauseating waves over in his stomach, and it was a few moments before he gathered enough momentum to stand up and make it to the landing. Leaning against the wooden banisters, he looked down the stairs, and mentally prepared himself to speak. His tongue felt dry and sour, and at that moment, trying to form any coherent sentences seemed entirely unnatural. His voice croaked hoarsely on his first attempt, unsettling the contents of his stomach as he coughed to clear his throat.

'Kaaayy,' he hollered in his gravelly voice at the empty hall beneath him. 'Kay, get me some Paracetamol would you? I'm dying up here.'

Not waiting for an answer, he shuffled back to the bedroom and crawled in under the covers again. He dosed fitfully for what seemed like hours and eventually began to wonder what was taking Kay so long with his tablets. As Ed's mind mulled over what his wife could be doing in the kitchen that was taking so long, he began to think about what else she could rustle up for him. Tea and toast were beginning to sound appealing, even to his unsettled stomach, and, rousing himself once more out of his feather duvet cocoon, he decided to go down to the kitchen to investigate.

The first thing Ed noticed when he finally reached the bottom of the stairs was that the house was unnaturally quiet. There were no children watching garish cartoons, nor was there the sound of the radio reciting this weekend's top twenty countdown. In fact, the only movement stirring in the house was the net curtain in the living room swaying gently from the breeze blowing in the open window. Squinting irritatedly at the sunlight streaming into the room, Ed tried to figure out if he had been told where everybody would be this morning. Even the au pair was gone, he thought to himself, totally baffled. Either way, he decided, it was probably better that they were out. He couldn't imagine what the children and their Sunday morning television would do to his already thumping headache.

Settling himself on a stool at the kitchen counter, Ed contemplated what he would like to eat or, more accurately, what he would be able to rustle up. The sounds churning inside him were convincing him that perhaps food wasn't such a good idea and, eyeing the Tabasco through the glass of the cupboard door, he settled on making a Bloody Mary. As he poured the thick tomato juice into a tall glass, Ed thought ahead to the rest of the day. Deciding that Kay and the kids might not be home for hours yet, he picked up the phone and dialled the number of the first taxi company he could find in the Golden Pages. With the ice rattling around in the glass of his Bloody Mary in one hand, he held the receiver in the other, and arranged with the receptionist to be taken back to the rugby club. He would collect the car himself.

As he waited for the cab to arrive, Ed glimpsed himself in the hall mirror, and was mildly surprised at how awful his appearance was. Dressed in a faded old tracksuit, the stubble on his face looked dark and patchy, and the puffy bags under his eyes seemed almost to reach his cheeks. At least he felt marginally better than he looked, he thought to himself, as he saw the cab pulling up in the driveway. It really was better that Kay was out. He could imagine the lecture already. The nagging about being so hung-over in front of the children would last for at least ten minutes, not to mention how she would go on about him embarrassing her in front of her friends. God, no, that was far more than he could handle, he thought, relief sweeping through him as he locked the door behind him.

When Ed reached the rugby club, he noticed the parked car of a friend. Figuring that it would be rude to leave without saying hello, he decided to delay going home for an extra five minutes. Walking into the club, he immediately saw Tony with his back to him, reading the Sunday papers with a pint of Guinness. It turned out that he had opted out of going to Mass and, instead, had chosen to go for a quick drink while he waited for his wife to come out. After a half an hour of reminiscent talk about yesterday's game, Tony folded up his papers and excused himself. Mass was over, he explained, and if he didn't go now, he'd be 'in big trouble with the missus'. Ed thought fleetingly about his own missus, but, deciding that there would be no way she could be home already, ordered himself one more pint. Combined with the alcohol still coursing through his veins from the day before, his early morning Guinnesses were successfully numbing the sensation of his headache. He was beginning to feel better already. With no one else to keep him company, however,

Ed said goodbye to the barman with a slight slur, and went out to his car.

Opening up the windows and turning on the radio as soon as he got in, he swerved out of the car park and drove onto the main road. Thinking about what he would do when he got home, Ed failed to see the young child running across the road to the church ahead of his parents. He barely managed to register the screams as he realised what had just happened, and, as people ran towards the little boy, confused, he stepped out of his car. He registered the sight of the listless body on the road with a paralysed sense of detachment and, as the frantic scene played out in front of him, all Ed could think was that his hand was sore again.

\* \* \*

Depressed and scared, Kay set off for the hospital. Her mind ran over, again and again, the conversation she had had with the policeman, envisaging him as he stood in the hallway explaining with a grave face what Ed had done. She had had such a lovel;y morning in the park with the kids but now, alone in her car, Kay cried as the enormity of the situation slowly sunk in. She silently cursed her husband as she imagined what the parents of the little boy must now be going through. When she reached St Vincent's, she was shown up to Ed's room, where she found him looking pitiful in a neck brace and with a bandaged arm. She could see the Band Aids she had put on him the night before, and wished that a few splinters in his hand were all she had to worry about.

'Kay, I'm so sorry,' he said, looking pleadingly at her. Tears were streaming down his face. 'Kay, please,' he continued beseechingly. 'Kay, say something. I'm sorry, I really am.'

Kay looked at him in disgust. Although she had gone over the things she would say to him when she got there, now that they were facing each other, she found that she couldn't utter a word.

The monotonous beeping of the monitor beside Ed's bed measured the minutes that she didn't respond.

'I need to speak to a doctor,' she said eventually, turning to walk out the door. She could hear Ed calling after her, crying, as she continued on down the corridor, but she was so furious with him, and so incredibly sad, that she blocked out the sound of his pleas.

After speaking with the consultant, Kay realised that Ed now had a long, hard road in front of him. The child that had been hit was still in hospital, unconscious, and Ed would most certainly be charged. The question now, Kay wondered, was whether she had the energy, or the desire, to travel it with him. Until she figured out what she was going to do, however, she decided that she wouldn't say a word to anyone else just yet – the kids, Ed's parents, or even Madeleine. Things were serious this time, and Kay needed some time to think on her own before she faced the inevitable line of questioning from everyone else.

# CHAPTER NINE

CATRIONA ARRIVED FIFTEEN MINUTES EARLY FOR HER SIX o'clock shift at the restaurant to find her boss looking decidedly stressed as he scrolled through names in his black phone book. Unaware that she had come in, he continued to mutter to himself in a manner that was beginning to concern her.

'Em, Gerald, is there anything I can help you with?' she asked, startling him out of his concentration.

'Ah, Catriona, hello,' he answered, looking up from the age-worn pages in front of him. 'No, unfortunately, I don't think there is. You see, Marcel called in sick an hour ago and – typical – every other chef that I've ever worked with in the past seems to be busy tonight.'

Gerald's state of panic was mounting as he flicked closer to 'Z' in the phonebook, realising that the chances of finding a suitable replacement were growing slimmer with every passing page.

'I just don't know what I'm going to do,' he said eventually. Tiny beads of sweat were forming on his forehead in the cool kitchen, and as he looked expectantly at Catriona, he wrung his clammy hands together to the sound of the clock on the wall fast ticking towards opening time.

'I mean, I know it's only a Monday night, but there are still a lot of bookings and we'll never be able to cook for the customers if no bloody chef turns up.'

Before Catriona had time to answer, the door swung open, and in came Anne, Gerald's wife and co-owner of the restaurant.

'Well, no luck with me either,' she said, acknowledging Catriona's presence with a weak smile. 'I've tried all the agencies in Dublin and I've been given the same answer from everyone – we've left it too late to get any chef to cook for this evening's dinner menu.'

'What the hell are we going to do?' Gerald said despondently, putting his head in his hands.

'I could do it,' Catriona said quietly, to which both Anne and Gerald looked up in surprise. 'I mean,' she continued, 'I've been working with Marcel for months now, and I've tried most of his recipes at home anyway.'

'Are you sure about this?' Gerald asked, hardly daring to hope. 'You'd be able to manage on your own?'

Catriona was afraid that she might begin to doubt herself too if she hesitated, and so, straightening herself up, she spoke confidently.

'Absolutely,' she said with a smile, 'as long as we take the soufflé and Marcel's famous lobster thermidor off the menu, I'll be fine – I don't want to push my luck.'

'That's settled, then,' Anne said, clearly delighted, despite the reservations of her husband. 'Gerald and I do your tables, and you, Catriona, will be head chef for the night.'

For the next six hours, Catriona worked harder than she had ever worked before. Apart from calling out the names of dishes that were ready to be served, she was silent. It took all her concentration to time the courses correctly, and she moved quietly around the kitchen in a state of controlled panic. Pans of soups and sauces bubbled continuously, being stirred and tasted in turn before they were poured into bowls or over succulent meats. Salads were tossed gently in dressings and powdered chocolate was delicately sprinkled over mousses in a carefully measured dance to serve each customer on time. And as Gerald and Anne rushed out of the kitchen with each dish, Catriona felt a little bit more confident that she had, at last, found something she was really good at. Reports congratulating the chef had been coming in all night, and the earlier doubts Gerald had had about her abilities evaporated the moment he stepped out to the first table with delectable starter plates of salmon parcels and goat's cheese salads. By the end of the night, Catriona was exhausted and sweating and she had burnt the tips of her fingers several times, but in spite of her fatigue, she had never felt happier.

After the last customer had left the restaurant, Gerald and Anne came in to find Catriona leaning against the large chrome fridge with her eyes shut.

'Do you think you could stay awake long enough to share in a little glass of this?' Gerald asked, holding up a bottle of champagne.

'I think I probably could!' she answered, smiling through her yawn. 'But I should warn you, I might need carrying home after it. I feel like I could sleep standing up as it is!'

For the first time since she had arrived to work, Catriona was able to sit down and relax, and as sparkling champagne frothed up in the glasses, she wondered if she'd be given the opportunity to do it all again. Judging by the praise she had received, she had done a good job, but Marcel was excellent, and Catriona knew it would take more than standing in for one night to really be taken seriously as a chef.

Later on, as Catriona climbed into bed beside Mike, she contemplated waking him up to tell him about her night. Despite her tiredness, adrenalin was still rushing through her veins, and her mind was only beginning to unwind after the quick pace she had been working at in the kitchen. He was sleeping peacefully, however, and she knew that he had an early start in the morning, so she decided against it.

Snuggling in under the cover, a terrible thought suddenly struck Catriona. Tomorrow was Tuesday, and Mike would more than likely offer to drop her up to Redcliff on his way to work. The confidence and satisfaction she had been feeling all night quickly disintegrated as she imagined herself playing golf. Worse still, Catriona remembered that she had agreed to play with Linda. However embarrassed she usually felt at the golf club, tomorrow she would have an audience. And not just any audience, she thought with dread, but the lady captain of the club, under whose watchful eye her shameful lack of talent would be more evident than ever.

\* \* \*

At ten o'clock, Thomas sat, freshly shaven, immaculately dressed and extremely nervous, in the waiting room. After he'd sat alone for a few minutes, a polite receptionist came in to tell him that Dr O'Sullivan was ready to see him. He followed her into the adjoining room. As the two men shook hands, both were aware that they had met before, but unlike Donal, Thomas couldn't quite work out where it had been.

'Didn't we meet at Redcliff just last weekend? My birthday, you came up with Madeleine O'Connell I think?' Donal said, sitting behind his desk in the large comfortable leather chair.

'Oh, of course,' Thomas replied, glad to have made the connection. 'I knew I recognised your face. Yes, we had a great night, thanks.'

'Indeed, it's a small world,' Donal agreed, starting a new file for Thomas. 'Look, just before we begin, if this makes talking to me difficult in any way, I'd be more than happy to refer you to someone else. I mean,' he continued, 'obviously everything you say will be absolutely confidential, but if you'd rather...'

'No, no,' Thomas interrupted, 'it's really OK, thanks. Besides, if I leave seeing a consultant any longer, I may leave it altogether... I'm not the biggest fan of doctors – no offence.'

'None taken,' Donal answered with a smile. 'I can understand the lack of appeal. Still, this shouldn't take too long today, just a quick examination and a couple of tests. If it's all right with you, though, I'm going to ask a couple of questions first.'

'Sure, fire away,' Thomas replied, a little of his earlier anxiety creeping back in, 'but... eh, can I just say that Madeleine doesn't know about any of this, so...'

'Don't worry,' Donal reassured him. 'This is strictly between the two of us. Now,' he continued in a more serious tone, 'your doctor tells me that you're having trouble with erections, which is of course attributable to the diabetes, but she mentioned that Viagra has been effective?'

'Yes,' Thomas agreed, still not totally comfortable with the topic of conversation. 'As you can imagine, it's not exactly convenient, or conducive to, eh, spontaneity.'

Donal tried to block out the pain wrenching in his chest, caused by the thought of Madeleine having sex with Thomas, and simply nodded.

'You see, we were away a couple of weekends ago and, while the Viagra was great, I couldn't drink on it, or eat very large meals, so I was hoping that there might be some other solution.'

Thomas was more than just hoping. The weekend in the west was over two weeks ago, and by now he had used up the last of the pills, which meant they had only had sex twice since they had been home. He knew Madeleine suspected something was wrong, but he was praying that after his meeting with the consultant, it would all be fixed and he wouldn't need to explain anything.

'As it happens, there is a new drug on the market, called Cialis, which I could perhaps prescribe for you on your next visit, but in the meantime, I'd like to determine the exact cause of what you've been experiencing.' Donal was struggling to

184

control his voice as he became increasingly convinced that Thomas would be able to tell that he and Madeleine were more than old friends. In an effort to control his paranoia, he decided to stick to purely medical topics. 'Your doctor also told me that you are having problems with the frequency of urination, and, what she was more concerned about, the fact that you have had some blood in your urine?'

'Oh, em, yes,' Thomas agreed, rather shamefacedly. Having delayed so long in seeing a consultant somehow seemed quite stupid now that he was confronted so directly with his symptoms. 'You see, I thought for a while there that it had cleared up, which is why I kept putting off coming to see you, but now I have some back pain as well, and I wasn't sure if the two were related.'

'Can I ask you how many cigarettes you smoke a day?' Donal asked, looking up expectantly from the file.

'About twenty,' mumbled Thomas, 'but I'm cutting down,' he added feebly.

Donal frowned in disapproval. 'Well,' he sighed, 'I know you probably don't need to hear it from me, but you really should cut them out altogether.'

When Thomas simply nodded his agreement, Donal got up from his chair, and indicated a discreetly drawn curtain in a corner of the room. 'Right, well, I'll leave that in your hands anyway, but for now, we can just concentrate on the more immediate issue. Could you go behind the curtain and remove your trousers please? I'll be in then in a minute to examine you.'

Several blood tests and a physical examination later, Thomas left the surgery feeling relieved. He had made another appointment with the receptionist to discuss his results with Donal when they came back, and decided that, until then, he would try to forget about it. After having had it hanging over him for so long, Thomas now felt good that he had shared his problems and was happy to have passed the worry into someone

185

else's hands. If nothing else, he thought, there was always that new drug Donal had spoken about, which would mean he wouldn't have to rely on Viagra. At least that way, sex wouldn't have to be so premeditated, he thought, as he took his keys out of his pocket. Feeling less stressed than he had in a long time, Thomas walked back to his car, looking forward to his next visit and a new prescription. He really didn't know why he had put off seeing the consultant for so long.

Donal sat at his desk for a long time after Thomas left. He was now faced with a problem he had never encountered before and was quite sure that he couldn't talk to any of his colleagues about it. He could just imagine it, explaining how he wanted to cheat on his wife with the girlfriend of one of his patients. Yes, he thought, tapping his pencil on the table, that would go down well. Ethically, he didn't have a problem, there was no confidentiality being breached, but Donal was worried it might all be a little too close for comfort. He had planned to call Madeleine later on that morning, but felt he couldn't, now that he had met Thomas. However bad he thought the situation was before, it was ten times worse now. Thomas had proven to be a really nice guy, and he couldn't imagine what might happen if he were to find out about himself and Madeleine. To make matters worse, Donal wasn't happy with the physical examination either, and feared that, whatever the outcome, it wasn't looking good. Buzzing the receptionist to bring in his next patient, he tried to block both Madeleine and Thomas out of his head and concentrate on the simpler task of being a doctor. He had thought that as he got older things would become less complicated, but Donal realised as he filed away Thomas's chart that the mess he was getting tangled up in now was worse than it had ever been.

* * *

Linda eyed Ian speculatively over the breakfast table. She was trying to figure out whether his non-committal answers about bridge that evening were covering up a lie, or if they were simply due to the fact that he didn't know what the arrangements were yet. As she handed him his poached egg on toast, she realised that she had become the obsessed wife she had always been proud of not being. But then, she thought, as she watched him methodically cut his toast into squares, a habit she had never considered annoying until now, she had good reason to be, didn't she? The previous night, plagued by fear and curiosity, she had listened to the messages on Ian's mobile while he was in the shower. She was immediately sorry she had done it. Saved into his phone were two old messages. The first, Linda was relieved to hear, was from a work colleague telling him that a report he had been looking for would be a day late. The second, however, was a female voice, who had clearly nothing to do with work.

'Hi, Ian, Denise here,' the husky voice began. 'Listen, I'm sorry, but I won't be able to make it this evening. My husband's flying in tonight, and there's no way I can get out of picking him up from the airport. I promise I'll make it up to you, though. Are you free next week, same time?'

Linda felt every drop of colour drain from her face as she put the phone down. This was the second time this 'Denise' had come up, and Linda was none the wiser about who she was. She feared, however, that she was beginning to get a good idea.

As she watched Ian stir sugar into his coffee, Linda wondered if she was doing the right thing in going away to Florida. Nessa had wanted to get a group together to go over for a week's sun and golf, as she had an apartment there, and Linda had realised after some thought that it would be the perfect opportunity to get away for a break before they got too far into the season. It really had seemed like such a good idea when she agreed to it, but now, with Denise in the picture, she didn't know if she should leave Ian alone. Wouldn't her absence just be pushing him into another woman's arms? She certainly knew now why he had been so enthusiastic for her to go. Deciding to bring up the subject again to better gauge his reaction, Linda broached the subject carefully.

'I'm not sure now that I'm going to go to Florida with the girls,' she started, buttering her toast.

'Why ever not?' Ian looked up, startled. 'I thought it was all arranged.'

'Well, you'd be on your own in the house for a start. You know that's the week Jean is away with some friends in the country.' Linda knew it was a lame excuse, but she couldn't think of anything better.

Ian raised an eyebrow. 'I'd be on my own in the house?' he questioned, a look of both amusement and slight confusion on his face. 'In all the years we've been married, I'm quite sure it's been safe to leave me on my own.'

Accepting that her point was totally invalid, Linda just shrugged and reluctantly agreed. 'Well, if you're sure you don't mind then...' she trailed off, but Ian had gone back to dissecting his breakfast and the conversation was closed.

Linda felt dreadful. It was as if she was caught in a Catch 22 – if she went to Florida now, she would be leaving Ian and Denise alone together, and if she stayed, he would think she was insane. After all, it was understandable that he considered himself old enough to cope at home without her for a week, she supposed. Deciding that she had lost her appetite, Linda gave up on any attempt at breakfast. She kissed Ian goodbye – he had already begun to read the morning papers – picked up her golf bag in the hall, and went out to the car. As she drove towards Redcliff, she wondered if her imagination was just working overtime. There was a chance that perhaps he wasn't having an affair, that Denise might simply be an acquaintance she had never met before, and that there was a very simple explanation for everything. However, that wasn't terribly convincing, and, unable to come up with any answers, Linda resolved to put it out of her head for the time being. She would spend the morning on the golf course and leave worrying about her husband's supposed infidelity until after she got home again.

'There's nothing like a good game of golf to help me forget about everything else,' she thought to herself, as she drove up Redcliff's driveway. The sun was shining, the company would be great, and now all Linda had to do was act happy.

Stepping out of her car, she noticed that Catriona had already arrived and was standing uncomfortably in the shade of the clubhouse. She was nervously fidgeting with the buttons on her coat and kept her eyes firmly focused on her feet. For a moment, Linda forgot her own troubles as she looked at the poor girl, who stood looking as if she was waiting for a firing squad to come out and shoot her.

'Morning, Catriona. It's beautiful weather for golf, isn't it?' she said, walking up to her.

'My idea of perfect golfing weather is rain,' Catriona admitted, 'but maybe today won't be so bad,' she finished, noticing Linda's frown at her pessimism.

As they walked into the locker room, Linda explained that they would be playing with Marie and Nessa, so she needn't worry, the round would be very laid-back. She also explained the format, but, realising that most of the description was alienating rather than encouraging her partner, she tried a different approach.

'Honestly, it'll be fun out there, trust me,' she said, reassuringly, 'and the great thing about the way we're playing today is that you'll only have to take every second shot, so it won't be half as bad as it would usually be.'

Finally, Catriona cracked a smile. 'Sounds more like my kind of golf,' she said, relaxing slightly.

Marie and Nessa came into the locker room.

'I was just about to explain to Catriona here,' she said to them as they put their bags down, 'that each team marks the other team's cards, to make sure no cheating goes on.'

'Wash out your mouth, Lady Captain,' Marie answered, feigning astonishment. 'I hope you're not insinuating that any Redcliff member would ever actually cheat?'

Ignoring her and Nessa's giggling, Linda went on to explain how they would begin the game. She reckoned that Catriona would probably prefer not to have to drive off on the first tee in front of the clubhouse, and so suggested that she would start first. Catriona's relief was visible. It seemed that with each of Linda's suggestions, the game ahead became a little less daunting for her. Perhaps she would even begin to enjoy the game, Catriona thought.

Linda started by hitting a magnificent drive. Catriona stood back with the others, wishing she didn't have such a tough act to follow. The tiny white ball went soaring through the sky to land with a soft thud, and rolled smoothly through the short, lush grass close to the green. Well, at least she wouldn't have to try and hit it out of a thicket of bushes, Catriona thought, remembering what her rounds were usually like. All she needed to worry about now was to make sure she didn't put it into one herself.

Minutes later, after Nessa's driver sent her first ball flying off the tee and into the small copse of trees to the left of the fairway, Catriona stepped up to take her shot, a little less nervous than she had been. Even if her ball did get lost into the oblivion of the evergreens now, hers would not be the first to end up there, and she silently thanked Nessa for getting off to a bad start. With a gleaming nine iron weighing heavily in her hands, she walked up to where her ball was delicately cushioned in the verdant grass, and contemplated her position. As her audience of three waited in anticipation to see how she would do, Catriona's sweaty palms tried to find a better grip. She closed her eyes, and, swinging the club high into the air, she brought it down again, praying that she wouldn't miss. Hearing a metal pinging sound as her club connected with the ball, she opened her eyes to see a white blur whizzing through the air in the right direction, towards the pin. Elated cheers of congratulation sounded from behind her as the ball plopped down with a slight roll, only inches from the hole.

'Fantastic!' Linda cried, truly delighted for Catriona, and sure that her confidence would be all the stronger for having hit an impressive first shot.

'God, that was bloody great,' Marie echoed. 'Novice, my arse, girls. It looks like we've a bit of a hustler playing with us today!' she added, winking at Catriona.

Catriona, unable to wipe a huge smile from her face, walked back over to where the others were standing and began to explain that it was beginner's luck.

'Don't be silly,' Nessa reprimanded. 'Pure skill is all it is, and it looks like I'm going to have to try and keep my ball out of the bushes from now on if we're to be any sort of competition for the pair of you.'

As the game progressed, the four women chatted and Catriona began to pick up some tips on how she could improve her game. She soon realised that closing her eyes was not always the best tactic, sending two consecutive shots into bunkers; but, learning to laugh at herself rather than castigate herself, she found she was able to enjoy the game. Despite the others' talent, their enthusiasm for her effort was as fulsome as their praise of each other and, for the first time ever, Catriona actually began to feel like she belonged there. Mike's words of advice lingered in the back of her mind as she considered her shots, but as her confidence grew, she began to forget his suggestions in favour of her own judgment.

By the time they had reached the tenth hole, she realised that scrutinising how the others played would be her best education. After watching Nessa sink a long putt from the edge of the ninth green, Catriona went on to mimic her stance on the tenth, with astonishing results. Just by copying exactly how Nessa had struck the ball, Catriona found that her own ball descended gloriously into the hole. Shots like that more than made up for any mistakes she made along the way, she thought, and with such a supportive team around her, Catriona realised that golf wasn't quite as bad as she had thought it was.

While they waited for a group on the eleventh to clear before they teed off, Nessa asked Marie how the wedding had been the day before, knowing how anxious she had been about it. With a brief explanation directed at Catriona as to who had been married, Marie went on to describe the whole fiasco. Given that she had recounted the story several times already, what she launched into was a slightly more colourful version than the actual reality. The arrival of Eugene and Ken to the church in matching outfits ended up sounding like a scene from a pantomime; Marie's episode with Charles on the dance floor appeared to have been a comical assault; and her description of the three men weaving through the reception to follow her out, with Ken clapping at the rear of the trio, had Catriona almost doubled over with laughter. She couldn't believe she was having so much fun on the golf course, and the nervous knot that had been in her stomach at the beginning of the game, she discovered, had entirely vanished. In fact, her opinion of the game and her ability to play it had improved so much over the course of the morning that when Nessa extended the invitation for her to go to Florida with them, and the others encouraged her to accept, it didn't take long for Catriona to agree.

Later that morning, as they walked back to the clubhouse from the eighteenth green, Nessa speculated about who had won.

'Even with my unfortunate incident on the seventh in the lake, I still think, Marie, that we may have won,' she said, trying to make a mental calculation of what their score would be.

Marie looked at her with an arched eyebrow.

'I hate to burst your bubble there, Ness, but after Catriona playing so well with her high handicap, and our dear lady captain in her usual impressive form, I don't think we even came close.'

Hearing such honest praise from somebody so talented, Catriona felt positively ecstatic. She couldn't wait to get home to tell Mike how she had done. Thinking of Mike, she quickly signed her card and handed it over to Linda, who smiled at its significance. They both knew that if it hadn't been for him and the terrible mix-up with forgetting to sign his scorecard, Catriona would never have spoken to her lady captain in the toilets about her miserable experiences in Redcliff. In fact, after their morning on the golf course, Catriona was beginning to look on Linda as something of a saviour. She had her to thank for such an enjoyable round, and for changing her opinion about golf in general, and as they walked back to the clubhouse, Catriona thought she should try to repay her for her kindness in any way she could.

A short time later, sitting in the bar for lunch, Catriona eyed up the unappetising array of sandwiches on their table. With just a little bit of consideration, they could be so much nicer, she thought to herself, imagining wholegrain bread spread with a mouth-watering olive tapenade, rocket and feta cheese or sun-dried tomatoes with brie and salami. Instead, what they got were thin white slices of processed bread with a meagre amount of ham and some cheap cheese. Lack of imagination seemed to extend to the hot counter too, she noticed, as she got the smell of meat slightly burning in the kitchen – burger and chips, sausage and chips, chicken nuggets and chips, and the kitchen's idea of something different seemed to be steak accompanied by home fries.

But what about anyone who doesn't want to eat so unhealthily? Catriona wondered as she saw yet another plate of greasy chips being brought out of the kitchen. Not to mention Nessa, who talked avidly about her new diet while they were on the golf course, and now here she was, tearing open the wrapper on her second Snickers bar as she spoke. Remembering the laughter at her explanation that chocolate was an important way to kick-start a person's metabolism – an obvious requirement to losing weight – Catriona chuckled to herself. Part of the problem, though, she reckoned, was that there just didn't seem to be any appetising low-fat meals on the menu, which surely didn't help the situation.

Catriona began to imagine what she could do if she was in charge of the food and, without realising it, her mind wandered off until she felt Nessa tapping her arm.

'Earth to Catriona!' Nessa called.

Catriona refocused her glazed expression. 'Oh, gosh, sorry! I don't know where I was, I was in a bit of a daze there,' she answered, a little embarrassed in front of her new group of friends.

'Well,' Marie said, picking up where Nessa left off, 'we were just talking about Florida again. We're all delighted you're coming.'

'Yes, about that,' Catriona started, afraid that maybe they hadn't really thought it through properly, 'are you really sure you'd want me there? I mean you don't know me that long, and I'd feel dreadful if I was taking someone else's place.'

'Don't be silly,' Nessa replied. 'The more the merrier, and besides, you needn't worry, I wouldn't have asked if I didn't want you to come.'

'Exactly, and you'll get to see that there's more to Redcliff members than just golf,' Linda continued. 'I, for one, plan to eat everything I shouldn't, swim in the magnificent sunshine every day, and go shopping in a way that I could never justify doing in Dublin. You have to come, it'll be great.'

Convinced, Catriona smiled. 'Well, if you're really sure...'

'Of course we're sure!' the others cried in unison.

'So that's that then,' Nessa added, 'you're coming.'

As conversation flowed around the table, Linda was suddenly depressed by the reality of her own situation. Everything she had said to Catriona about the fun they would have in Florida was true, but she began to worry all over again about what sort of 'fun' Ian would be having at home while she was gone. Although she had managed to stow away all of her fears while she had been out on the course, she felt like she had no choice but to face them now. Suddenly not in the mood for company, Linda excused herself from the group. She would go home and try to figure out what was happening to her marriage and weigh up what the consequences would be of her week in Florida.

# CHAPTER TEN

PRESSING 'END CALL' ON HER MOBILE PHONE, MADELEINE turned up the car radio and thought back over the conversation she had just had with Kay. She couldn't believe how long Kay had waited to tell her about Ed. Last night, calling around to her apartment after dinner, Kay had sobbed as she explained the awful mess her life had become. Ed was now in a rehabilitation centre, as an in-patient being treated for alcoholism; moreover, although the young boy he had knocked over was recovering well, police charges and a possible prison sentence were still looming. Later that evening, after endless cups of coffee and hours of tears, Madeleine had promised, as she hugged her goodbye, that she would ring the next day. Now, however, after the phone call, Madeleine couldn't help worrying about how well Kay was coping. She resolved at least to find something that might help to occupy her mind and distract her from the constant anxiety over Ed's future.

As she continued along the road towards the marina, past little cafés and people out enjoying the sunshine, Madeleine decided she was right to have lied to Kay about where she was going today. During their conversation, Kay had eventually agreed to have a round of golf with Madeleine the following day to get out of the house for a while, and by the time she had hung up the phone, she was almost in good spirits. Telling her about Donal would only have brought Kay down again, Madeleine reasoned, as she tried to convince herself that lying to her best friend was the only thing she could have done.

Donal had rung that morning to say that he couldn't wait to see her again, and Madeleine, both touched by his need to meet and excited by the forbidden nature of their encounters, readily agreed. They had decided to go to the quiet west pier, knowing that with so much still unresolved, they couldn't risk getting caught. Madeleine's stomach was filled with butterflies at even the thought of seeing him again. As she drove towards the bottom of the pier, with her anonymity protected by the shade of the harbour wall, she saw that Donal's car was already there. Driving closer, she could see him leaning against the upturned hull of a weathered boat, squinting in the direction of the road to look out for her, and he waved as he recognised the car.

After she had parked, Madeleine took off her sunglasses, ran her fingers through her hair, and walked over to where he stood smiling.

'You look incredible!' he said as he kissed her cheek. The electricity that sparked between them as he did so was almost tangible, and both of them lingered for just a moment longer than was necessary.

'I hope you don't mind meeting me out here?' he asked. 'It's just that I've been stuck in theatre all morning and I've been dying to get some fresh air.'

'No, not at all, it's beautiful,' Madeleine replied, 'especially when we've weather like this.' She was trying to push the guilt she felt about Thomas to the back of her mind, but with every fibre of her being responding so eagerly to the very presence of Donal, she was finding it extremely difficult to shake the uncomfortable feeling of betrayal.

197

Donal had taken off his tie after leaving work, and the top two buttons of his shirt were hanging loosely open. From underneath the collar, she could see wisps of dark hair on his chest, and Madeleine couldn't help but stare admiringly at the triangle of smooth skin. When Donal had kissed her cheek, his forearms, tanned and strong, had temptingly held hers, and Madeleine's will power not to touch him was only barely maintained by the fact that they were in a public place. Such intensity of feeling scared her, knowing that once she began to experience these sensations, it was difficult to turn back. Unable to fully face that reality, however, Madeleine convinced herself that there was no real harm in what she was doing. After all, it was just two good friends going for a walk together, wasn't it?

They set off on the mossy path with only inches between them, aching to hold each other's hand but knowing how impossible that would be. It seemed that more people than they thought had had the same idea as themselves, and Madeleine became paranoid that they would be spotted on the busy pier by somebody they knew, or worse still, by somebody who knew either Thomas or Judith. Madeleine felt sure that she had 'adulteress' written all over her face, and that the people passing by would somehow know that beneath her carefree exterior, she was having inappropriate thoughts about the married man she was walking with.

By the time they had reached the end of the pier, however, she was beginning to forget the restrictions hanging over them. The sun that beat down on them was tempered by a refreshing sea breeze, and flowing conversation soon smoothed over fears of being seen. They fell as easily into conversation as they always had, and Madeleine's inhibitions about being seen with him were disintegrating as she felt more and more relaxed in his company. In fact, the only concerns left niggling at the back of Madeleine's mind as they turned around to walk back again, were thoughts of Kay and how she could help her.

'What's up, Mad?' Donal asked with concern. 'You seem a bit distracted.'

'Oh, it's nothing really,' she answered. 'It's, well, I was just talking to Kay before I met you, and I really want to think of a way to take her mind off the whole Ed situation. She needs to get out more and try to forget about the sorry mess he's put them in.'

'Well, I don't know if you think this would be good for her or not, but I'm looking for someone to play in the mixed foursomes with me on Sunday. Judith was meant to accompany me, but she's got to go up to Donegal at the weekend to consult with a client. Do you think Kay would be interested?'

'Oh, of course she would, that's brilliant!' Madeleine said, delighted. 'I've been trying to get her to come up to Redcliff myself anyway, and she has to know that there's a certain amount of kudos attached to playing with the captain!' Madeleine joked. 'Why don't you call her tomorrow about it?' she suggested.

Without thinking, she instinctively linked her arm through Donal's and leant into him. She had meant it as a gesture of thanks, but the comfort of his closeness made Madeleine reluctant to let go. At first, she felt him stiffen, but within seconds, forgetting their earlier caution, he put his arm around her too.

'You know, Judith's going to be away for the whole weekend,' Donal whispered, as another couple walked past them.

Madeleine immediately took her arms out from around his and stopped mid-stride.

'I thought we'd been through this, Don. You know how I feel about it,' she said angrily. Madeleine knew that her reaction was unfair, given that she had instigated the contact, but for some reason, hearing his acknowledgement of her intimate action scared her more than she could have imagined. 'God, did it not mean anything to you when I spoke about this the other day?'

she said in a whispered tone, upset at both him for the suggestion and herself for her heated response.

Every bit of guilt that Madeleine had been feeling earlier rushed back as she realised how easy it would be to take Donal up on his offer, and tears of frustration welled up in her eyes. She was trying her best to keep a focus on her resolve to make sure that things were as platonic as possible between them. But if Donal wasn't strong as well, she was afraid that she would crumble under her overwhelming desire.

'I mean, nothing's changed. You know the situation, Donal, how I feel about you and Judith, and nothing can be done about *us*, until you do something about *her*.'

Looking into his abashed face, Madeleine squeezed his hand as a sort of apology for getting so angry. A cloud had drifted over, eclipsing the sun with its hazy cover, and the grey shadow cast over them seemed to emphasise Donal's remorse.

'I'm sorry,' he said, 'you're right,' his voice deep with regret. 'It's just hard not to want to...'

'You don't have to say it, Don, I know,' Madeleine replied sympathetically.

They reached the end of the pier in a deliberative silence. Watching a young boy passing them with a melting ice-cream in his hand, Madeleine suddenly realised how hungry she was. As if reading her mind, Donal raised his eyebrows suggestively in the direction of the Thai restaurant across the road.

To Madeleine's relief, they were shown to a small table in a dimly lit corner towards the back of the restaurant. She was silently grateful, knowing that it was unlikely anyone would spot them there. Vibrantly coloured silk hangings adorned the walls of the small eatery, and candles illuminating tucked-away alcoves were in stark contrast to the sun still shining brightly outside. Shortly after they were seated, plates piled high with delicious chicken satay were put in front of them, and conversation turned to how their mornings had been. Donal, unused to anyone being so interested in his work, talked eagerly about some of his cases, until, suddenly remembering his consultation with Thomas, he went quiet.

'What's wrong?' Madeleine asked, confused as to why he had stopped so abruptly.

'Oh, it's nothing, I just forgot something, left it at work,' he replied. 'My, eh, my schedule for tomorrow.'

He could see that Madeleine wasn't sure that he was telling the truth, so he deflected the questions from himself. 'Have you had any luck yet with finding a job?' he asked, struggling to think of something to say.

'Well, I haven't really been looking, to be honest with you,' Madeleine replied, shrugging her shoulders. 'I've decided to give myself another few months before I make up my mind on what I'm going to do – my old job is still open, if I want it, in New York, so I have to give some thought to whether or not I want to go back.'

Donal's face turned pale and his eyes opened wide in disbelief and fear. 'You never mentioned going back before,' he started, fumbling to find the words to finish his sentence.

'Look, I don't want to upset you,' Madeleine said compassionately, 'but I have to think about what's best for me. I mean, it may never happen, but at the same time, we can't pretend it's not an option.'

Donal was saved a response as the waiter came over with desserts and coffees, and the uncomfortable silence was alleviated by the small talk that surrounded their arrival.

'Let's just forget about it for now, shall we?' Madeleine asked quietly once the waiter had left. 'It's not like it's something that has to be decided today or tomorrow. I've months to think about it, so let's just enjoy what we have now.'

Donal, more than happy to change the subject, took up a spoonful of ice-cream and passed it across the table for Madeleine to try.

'What do you think?' he asked, laughing as she tried to catch the drip that threatened to spill onto her top.

'Gorgeous,' she said, wiping her mouth with the napkin. 'Dessert is always my favourite part of dinner! I often think I'd be happy to forgo the rest of the meal and go straight to the pudding, but then I always realise that the wait just makes it better.'

Donal looked into her eyes and saw that she was no longer talking about the food.

'I was always a fan of starters myself,' he said with a mischievous smile, 'but I know you're right,' he continued in a more serious tone, 'the best things are always worth waiting for.'

Staring at each other across the table, they both savoured the moment of promise and intimacy, knowing that they would shortly be back in the harsh light of day where they would have to drive off in their separate directions. With so many decisions to be made in the near future, Madeleine found it was easier to concentrate on the time that they actually spent together. She didn't know yet if she would go back to the States, but while they were there in the romantic, candlelit atmosphere of the tiny Thai restaurant, she wasn't going to give any thought to anything but the moment.

* * *

'So, will there be anyone interesting there tonight?' Judith asked, apparently directing her question to the window she was staring out of. It was Friday night, and although they were only on their way to the annual Medical Union Benevolent Fund dinner, Donal was already annoyed at her attitude towards the evening. For the past three years, she had declined the invitation to go, always claiming that there was something far more important she needed to do on the night. This year, however, sick of making up excuses for his wife's absence, Donal had given her plenty of notice about the evening so that she wouldn't be able to back out of it.

'I'm not sure who'll be there,' he said as they reached the Radisson. 'It varies from year to year.' He was quietly hoping, however, that she would present a slightly more interested façade when they got inside, whoever they met.

'Well, I don't suppose it matters anyway,' Judith replied in a defeatist tone, just catching Donal's quiet intake of breath as he mentally counted to ten to try and control his growing irritation. 'Medical types are all the same.'

Once they were in the foyer, Donal helped Judith off with her evening coat and couldn't help but admire how well she looked. It wasn't something he was surprised at, though. He knew that however little effort she put into being nice to him, she always glowed in the company of others. Personal feelings were never something Judith would allow to get in the way of letting her public persona down. At one time, Donal knew, he would have been proud to be out with such a glamorous woman, but now, comparing her to Madeleine, he recognised her more clearly for the superficial person that she really was. She was wearing a short black cocktail dress that emphasised her tiny waist and long, shapely legs, and a silk cerise scarf hung delicately over her tanned shoulders. From her sleek, shining hair, right down to the diamond-studded ankle straps on her stilettos, everything about Judith sparkled as she was introduced to some of the guests. Her face, which had, just moments before, been clouded with the anticipation of a boring evening, was now illuminated and friendly as she spoke, and the apathy she had shown earlier to Donal seemed to have disintegrated, to be replaced by a dazzling charm.

They were ushered into a room adjoining the main bar, where pre-dinner cocktails were being served, and spent the next half hour mingling with friends and renewing old acquaintanceships. Judith was charm personified as she moved around with Donal, laughing at just the right moments and complimenting when appropriate, in the knowledge that these people might be of some use to her one day. Eventually, just as Donal was explaining about his work to a visiting senior physician, with Judith standing enraptured by his words beside him, they were asked to take their seats in the dining room. As they set about locating Table F, Donal heard a familiar voice calling him from behind.

'Donal O'Sullivan, how the hell are you?' he heard, as he turned around to see where the booming voice was coming from.

'Frank O'Leary!' he replied, delighted to see his old college friend. 'It must be at least ten years,' he said, shaking the other man's hand warmly.

'Jesus, good to see you, Donal, how've you been keeping?' Frank asked, still smiling at the welcome coincidence of bumping into him.

'Not bad at all, thanks. You know how it is – my own consultancy, new publications on treatment methods in urology. What about yourself?' Donal replied questioningly, patting him on the back. They had been fierce rivals in college, and the need to highlight his successes was as strong now as it had been in med school.

'Well, you know me, O'Sullivan, I don't like to brag, but the US have invited me over to share my paper on recent gynaecological findings with them, which will mean a short break from my private consultancy here, but some things must be done,' he answered, sure that his achievements matched those of his friend.

'And speaking of consultancies,' Donal said, having a vague recollection of hearing about Frank setting up in Dublin, 'I hear you've moved your practice down from Belfast into my territory? It's just as well we specialised in different fields, O'Leary; otherwise you'd have made a wasted trip. I don't think there would've been room for both of us.'

The two men laughed at the pettiness of their competitive natures.

'Well, speaking of my new rooms, it actually seems that I'm to be working with another of your acquaintances – Betty Barnes is moving from the oncology department to work afternoons for me, so I'm sure she'll fill me in on all the gossip I've been missing up in Belfast.'

Donal was about to respond when he became aware of Judith standing uneasily beside him. Coughing to clear his throat of the laughter, he apologised for not introducing her sooner.

'I'm sorry, eh, Frank, you've never met my wife before, have you?' he asked, momentarily thrown by the look on Judith's face.

'Oh, yes, I have actually,' Frank replied with a pleasant smile. 'It's very nice to see you again.'

After a barely discernible flicker of hesitation, Judith regained her former composure, and flashed him a winning smile.

'Of course, I knew I recognised you,' she answered, trying to establish some control over the conversation.

'Frank was one of the specialists I consulted about the infertility,' she explained to Donal. Her tone was direct and suggested that any further questions would be unwelcome. Taking the hint, Frank shifted uncomfortably where he stood, unsure why his saying he had met her had produced such a reaction.

'Anyway, allow me to introduce *my* wife, Vivienne,' he said, putting his arm around the shoulders of a petite, pretty woman who had just returned from the bathroom. 'Viv, this is Donal, an old college friend of mine, and this is Judith who, for her sins, is his wife!'

Donal laughed at the reference to his wilder days in college, and the assumption that Judith was now his long-suffering partner, and happily shook Vivienne's hand. No one noticed, however, as they chatted on, that Judith's expression had become cold and contemplative. She hadn't married Donal 'for her sins' as Frank had said, she thought to herself as she followed them to their table, but rather it was turning out that she had come to this dinner for her sins. She could remember every single moment of her consultation with Frank O'Leary. What Judith hadn't known at the time, however, was how friendly he obviously was with Donal. And now, she realised, she was going to have to make sure that Frank never mentioned anything of the meeting to her husband. With Madeleine back on the scene, she had enough to worry about, but now with this can of worms so close to opening, Judith was experiencing nerves that she had never before known she was capable of feeling.

* * *

After her 'miscarriage', Donal had been quite anxious that they try for another baby as soon as possible. Although it was never said, Judith knew that the only reason he had gone through with the wedding was because she was pregnant, and when she told him she had lost the baby, she knew he needed something else, another child if possible, to validate their marriage. As far as Judith was concerned, however, his request was perfect. Not only had she seen how excited her father had been when she had told him she was pregnant, but more importantly, she also knew that with her first child would come another slice of her inheritance.

For six months, Judith tried to get pregnant, but without success, and when Donal suggested that they see a specialist, she agreed. With initial fertility tests showing no obvious reasons why they couldn't have children, Judith became determined to find out what the problem was, if only to silence Donal's questions and to appease her father's enquiries as to when his first grandchild would be arriving. Judith herself had no real desire to have children quite so quickly, but then, she supposed, it was her lie that had put her into the situation, so she would just have to deal with the questions that had arisen from it.

She had been referred to Frank O'Leary by a friend of a friend, who had seen him herself, and who had sworn to Judith that he was the best there was. With his consultancy up in Belfast, it suited her to travel out of Dublin – the medical circle was very small, and she didn't want anything getting back to Donal that she didn't want to tell him about. She had had an initial consultation with Frank to have blood tests and an ultrasound scan taken. Returning to him for her results the following week, Judith felt confident that her problem, whatever it was, would be easily fixed.

'Well, Judith,' Frank said as he looked at her from behind his desk, 'there are a couple of things that are concerning me about your scan, so if you don't mind, I'll just ask you a few questions.'

'Go right ahead,' she answered, thrown by the presence of a difficulty. She had been so sure that this meeting would solve everything that she hadn't anticipated the possibility that he wouldn't be able to help her.

'There is some scar tissue showing up on your scan which I cannot account for, given your history. This, in turn, is causing a blockage in your Fallopian tubes, which can almost certainly explain your infertility. What I am keen to find out, however, is why such scar tissue is present at all – is there any operation, or anything at all, that you may have forgotten to tell me about?' he asked sympathetically.

Judith eyed him coldly. 'I had an abortion when I was in college. I was very young, and very stupid, and the father of the child – a long-haired art student from Belgium – was very unsuitable.' Judith debated continuing her explanation as she paused for a moment in the still silence of the surgery. When Frank continued to remain quiet, she decided to carry on. 'It wasn't just me, you know. My father's health would have suffered from the shock of it all, and it would've been disastrous for my career,' Judith finished, satisfied that she had said enough.

Frank had seen many women over the years who had had a similar story to tell, but never before had he come across someone so completely devoid of emotion, and so cold in her explanation.

'Well,' he said, gathering his thoughts as to how best to deal with the situation. Clearly, his usual approach of empathy would be wasted on Judith. It seemed that she had come for one thing, and one thing only – an explanation for her infertility – and anything else was superfluous to her needs. 'The abortion would almost certainly account for the scar tissue, which in turn is probably the reason why you've been unable to conceive,' he finished, without any of his usual offerings of advice or counselling.

Judith sat, expressionless, as she heard him tell her that he doubted very much whether she would ever be able to have children. She could tell that he was choosing his words very carefully, and she almost wanted to tell him that he didn't need to be so sensitive, she was in a rush. She wanted to get back to Dublin before the traffic got too bad, and she had certainly thought that she would be finished by now.

Finally, after assuring him that she didn't have any questions, Judith left the consulting rooms, leaving Frank sitting at his desk, marvelling at how she could be so detached about such a revelation. It wasn't so much that she was detached, Judith had thought to herself as she walked back to her car, knowing what sort of impression she had made, but rather that she had had nothing to be attached to in the first place. Children had never really featured in her plans, and, if she was honest, not being able to have any didn't bother her. She would be able to further her career and play golf as much as she wanted without them, and thankfully she would never have the worry of having to get her body back in shape after being pregnant. Judith knew, however, that Donal would be devastated by the news. Driving back that afternoon, she had listened to Rachmaninoff in the car to sober

208

her mood, in preparation for the questions she would undoubtedly face when she got home. The music was powerful and sad, and she was hoping that some of its serious tone might rub off on her, and reflect in the tone of her voice as she broke the news to Donal. One thing Judith was very sure of, however, was that, whatever she told him, it wouldn't be the truth. If he was ever to find out what had really happened, he might well want to leave her in disgust at her behaviour in trapping him into marriage in the first place, and Donal was the one thing Judith had been quite sure, from the very beginning, that she wanted to keep. Speeding along the motorway, she decided that the only way to avoid arousing his curiosity was to act devastated by the news herself, and so, month by month, as her period arrived with monotonous regularity, Judith feigned bitter disappointment that she was not pregnant, again, and again, and again.

Later that evening, as she sat on the couch opposite Donal, she explained how she had been diagnosed with 'unexplained infertility', and that if they kept trying, they might be lucky. She hadn't mentioned Frank's name, and Donal never asked. Watching as he painfully digested the news, Judith smiled inside, knowing that her scheming had won. She thought there was nothing now to burst a hole in the life she had built around her lie, and Judith soon put the whole experience to the back of her mind, satisfied that every issue had been sufficiently dealt with.

Now, though, sitting between her husband and her consultant at dinner, Judith's fears about being discovered began to turn into reality, as the conversation stubbornly refused to budge off the topic of their careers. By the time the band had started playing and digestifs were being served, they had started to marvel at how small the world was, that they should bump into each other at the dinner. But it wasn't until her name was mentioned and the subject of how she had met Frank was once again being broached that Judith began to really panic. She had to ensure that Donal never found out what had been said that day in Frank's surgery, and, a little unexpectedly, she suddenly pushed back her chair and stood up.

'So, Frank, Vivienne here tells me you're a fabulous dancer,' she started, ignoring Vivienne's look of confusion as she tried to remember discussing this particular talent of her husband's. 'In which case,' she continued, avoiding eye contact with Donal, who was equally puzzled by her uncharacteristic outburst, 'you simply must join me on the dance floor for this song, seeing as my own husband has unfortunately been bestowed with two left feet.'

With that, and hardly giving Frank a chance to either accept or decline, she took his hand and led him to the dance floor. The slow music afforded her an intimate conversation with him, and their faces remained only inches from each other. After some perfunctory questions about how work was going for him, Judith looked innocently at Frank as the swing jazz guided their movements, and subtly fluttered her eyelashes in preparation for what she was about to say.

'You know, I never did say anything to Donal about my consultation with you,' she began, lowering her eyes in a vulnerable expression, 'because, you see, if he ever found out the truth, he would be crushed.'

Frank didn't say a word, still confused about why, ten years later, this woman seemed so intent on keeping their meeting a secret.

'I didn't tell you at the time,' Judith continued in a sultry voice, 'but... oh God, I'm sorry, it's just so difficult for me to say this... you see, it wasn't some art student like I said it was, but I became pregnant because I was... I was abused.'

Frank tried to interject with a sympathetic comment, but Judith needed to finish. The song was nearly over.

'And you can understand how it would destroy Donal to find out such a thing,' she went on. 'He was so hurt when he found out we couldn't have children that I simply didn't have the heart to tell him about the abuse – it would kill him.' As the song came to an end, Judith mustered up a tear to glisten in her eye.

'You needn't worry about a thing, I won't mention a word to Donal,' Frank said, ashamed of the opinion he had formed about her so many years previously. She had obviously been through a horrible time, and he was wrong to have so hastily jumped to the conclusions that he had. 'I'm just so sorry that you had to go through it at all, and if you would ever like to talk, my door is always open.'

As the song came to a close, Judith thanked Frank with a grateful smile and walked back with him to the table. They were greeted with inquisitive glances as they sat down, but with her problem dealt with and her secret safe, Judith faced the questioning look from Donal with a blank stare. He, of all people, would never know why she needed to speak to Frank so urgently, and if he asked her about it later, she knew it wouldn't be difficult to fob him off with another little white lie. After all, she thought, their marriage was already a patchwork of deceit and untruths. Settling comfortably back on her chair, Judith took a sip of her expensive Merlot and congratulated herself that she had carried it all off so ingeniously.

\* \* \*

The shrill ringing of the telephone woke Madeleine. Puzzled as to who could be calling so late on a Sunday night, and fumbling to find the switch on her bedside lamp, she eventually picked up the receiver and answered with a sleepy 'hello'.

'Hi, it's me,' came the reply. 'I couldn't sleep.'

Madeleine smiled in spite of being so rudely awakened. 'So you decided that I shouldn't sleep either, did you?' she remarked, sitting up in bed.

'No, no, I was just ringing on the off-chance that you might be awake too. I'd planned on hanging up if you didn't answer.'

'Fat lot of choice I had there! So how did it go today?' Madeleine asked, knowing that today was the day he was playing in the mixed foursomes with Kay.

'Oh, really good, actually. We came third in the end, which I think Kay was pretty chuffed about, and there was no mention of Ed at all while we were out there, which hopefully means that she had a couple of hours' break from thinking about him. What about you, though? Did you get up to anything today?' Donal asked, more interested in finding out about her day than talking about his.

'Well, I hadn't seen Mum in a while, so the two of us went out to Howth for lunch. We ended up going for a walk as well, because the weather was amazing, and I didn't get home till late this afternoon.'

'And tonight?' Donal enquired, wondering if she had seen Thomas.

'Just the usual Sunday night thing,' Madeleine answered, as nonchalantly as she could. 'I met Thomas at about seven and we went for an Indian meal.'

Not allowing himself time to digest the thought of their date, Donal quickly switched the topic of conversation. 'So where are you now?' he asked, his voice sounding mischievous, and his breathing becoming slightly heavier.

'I'm in bed, of course,' Madeleine answered, fiddling with a strand of her tousled blonde hair as she spoke. 'Why, where are you?' she asked as an afterthought. 'It's two o'clock.'

'I'm in bed too, all alone,' he answered. 'What are you wearing?'

Madeleine was both thrown and excited by his unexpected question.

'Maybe you don't remember, Don, but I don't wear anything in bed,' she said softly.

'Oh, I remember all right, I was just wondering if you'd changed.'

The memory of her smooth, naked skin, and her warm and yielding body against his began to turn him on. 'Do you remember how we used to be in bed?' he asked, feeling himself growing harder.

'Uh-huh,' Madeleine agreed, as she thought back on all the nights they had lain with their bodies intertwined. Feeling herself getting more and more aroused as memories of passionate nights flitted through her mind, she reached down to massage herself gently.

'Tell me a time that you particularly remember,' he said, his voice becoming huskier as he sensed her excitement.

Madeleine thought for a moment.

'I remember when I went to meet you in Birmingham, and because I hadn't seen you in almost two weeks, I couldn't get enough of you. We made love when I got to the hotel, and in the shower as I was trying to get ready to go out...'

She could sense Donal smiling.

'... and then when we got back to our room, we had sex for hours and you told me I was going to wear you out,' Madeleine laughed.

'But I loved every minute of it,' Donal interrupted, 'and you didn't see me complaining either when you woke me up later that night by going down on me, did you?' he asked, replicating the movement of Madeleine's hands with his own.

The phone line was quiet as the memory of that night replayed in their minds, and with every quickening breath, they could hear each other gasping with pleasure in their still bedrooms as climax approached.

Madeleine felt as if Donal was sending electrical shivers down the line into her body as she heard him utter the words she had once thought she would never hear from his lips again.

'Oh, God, Mad, I need you,' he whispered in a raspy voice as he came, 'I love you so much.'

His words brought her over the edge to a breathtaking orgasm, and she responded to his avowal.

'I love you, too,' she said, leaning back, exhausted, on her pillow. 'I always will,' she finished quietly.

A fraught silence ensued as they each considered the meaning of what had just happened.

'That was a first for me,' Madeleine said, trying to lighten the mood a little. 'Phone sex is not something I'm sure I've ever thought about before.'

Donal laughed, but just as he was about to answer her, Madeleine cut him off.

'And I don't want to know about you!'

For a few moments, they wallowed in the comfort of each other's company, wishing, however, that there didn't have to be the distance of a phone line between them.

Eventually, Madeleine spoke: 'I think it's time we said goodnight, Don,' she suggested. 'So, sweet dreams, and I hope you can sleep now.'

'Oh, I'll definitely sleep better after that,' he laughed, 'but you know I'll be dreaming of you lying here beside me.'

Madeleine sighed, knowing that his dream, something that she wished for also, was nothing but a fantasy for them both. There was nothing left to say, so she gently hung up the phone.

\* \* \*

Thomas sat in the reception area of Donal's consulting rooms dying for a cigarette to calm his nerves. It had been three weeks since his first visit, and he had received a phone call on Friday morning to say that Dr O'Sullivan wanted him to come in for an appointment as soon as possible to discuss the results of his blood tests. He had tried not to think about it over the weekend, but the phrase 'as soon as possible' kept playing in his head. He hadn't said anything to Madeleine yet about seeing Donal, and Thomas was beginning get the impression that the infrequency of

214

sex was beginning to be a bit of a problem for her. After they had come home from the Indian restaurant last night, he had said goodbye to Madeleine at the door of her apartment without going in. He had run out of Viagra, and didn't want to start anything he couldn't finish. Seeming quite distracted, however, she had said that she had an early start in the morning too, and didn't press him to spend the night with her. Given that she nearly always asked him to stay, Thomas was starting to worry that she was losing interest in him. If only Donal would prescribe him that new drug, Thomas thought to himself as he tapped his foot incessantly on the floor. At least that way, he could be more spontaneous about sex than he was at the minute, and might actually be able to stay in Madeleine's without having to plan it days beforehand.

Breaking his train of thought, the receptionist came in and called Thomas's name. Rubbing his sweating palms on his trousers before he stood up, he followed her into Donal's office and shook his hand as he heard the door close behind him.

'Nice to see you again,' Donal said with a smile, hoping that it hid the guilt he felt at having had phone sex with Thomas's girlfriend the night before, and indicated for him to take a seat.

After a few moments of cursory small-talk, Donal picked up Thomas's file off the desk and his expression became graver.

'I have the results here of your blood tests,' Donal started, a little anxiously, 'and I'm afraid that there are a couple of things showing up which I'm quite concerned about.'

Thomas's reply was a worried stare and a tense silence.

Looking back down at the file, Donal continued: 'What I'd like to do is to take you into hospital and perform some exploratory surgery to see if we can find the cause of the trouble.'

'What do you mean, "exploratory surgery"?' Thomas asked fearfully.

'Well, basically, the blood tests showed that there is some sort of problem with your bladder, and in order to get a clearer

215

picture as to what is happening, I'll need to go in and have a look,' Donal explained. 'You see, while we can assume that this has been the cause of your frequency of urination, it doesn't quite account for your back pain, which is something I'd like to sort out.'

Thomas felt his body go numb as he heard Donal go on to say that he wanted to admit him as soon as possible, and after some ineffective words of reassurance that he should try not to worry, he went out to the receptionist to arrange his admission to St John's hospital the following week.

Thomas sat chain-smoking in his car for a long time after he left Donal's office. Although the window was open, he heard nothing of the passing traffic or the sound of children playing in the schoolyard across the road. Instead, Donal's words were ringing in his ears, and he was frantically trying not to worry about the implications of the 'exploratory surgery'. He had never felt so scared in his life. Unable to talk to Madeleine about it, and unwilling to burden his mother with the worry of it, he sat immersed in a desperate loneliness. What if there was something really wrong with him, he wondered, something that would drastically change his life? And what about his job? He had forgotten to ask Donal how long he would be in hospital for. Adding this as one more thing in his list of unanswered questions, Thomas tried to calculate mentally how long he could financially support himself if he needed to. Although his health insurance would cover the medical expenses, he still had a mortgage to pay, and he was unsure whether the company would keep his job open for him if he was gone for a number of weeks. He buried his head in his hands and felt them tremble. He had never been to hospital in his life, and he was terrified. This wasn't like a broken bone or nasty flu, he thought to himself. Donal had seemed seriously concerned during his consultation, and Thomas felt that there was more to his illness than he had let on.

He picked up and put down his mobile phone innumerable times, and in the end, he decided not to call Madeleine and his mother just yet. He needed a bit more time to let the news sink in, and he would be calmer and in a better position later to come up with something to tell them. Slowly stubbing out the end of his cigarette, he switched on the engine, and drove out of the car park. The radio DJ was dedicating his next song to 'all the lucky people out there in the sun who didn't have to work today', and, feeling more miserable than ever before, Thomas flicked it off just as the sound of the Happy Mondays began to play.

Back in his office, Donal sat gently rocking on his leather chair, pondering what lay ahead for Thomas. Although he knew he had a waiting room full of patients, he didn't move from his contemplative position, staring at the closed file on the desk in front of him. The results of his blood tests had confirmed the worst of Donal's suspicions, and as far as he was concerned, the surgery on Wednesday was to ascertain exactly how bad things were, rather than to examine whether anything was wrong. He had been hoping that after Thomas's physical examination things would be OK, that the blood tests would prove his initial diagnosis wrong, but with the evidence in front of him now, Donal knew that Thomas's future was looking bleak. Thinking to himself who would be there to support him through his illness, Donal wondered whether Madeleine knew yet. As his thoughts turned to the previous night, he couldn't shake the feeling that he was taking advantage of a sick man by meeting with his girlfriend. And the impossible task that Donal faced now was deciding which he would ever be able to let go of – his moral and ethical duty as a doctor, or going after the woman he loved?

\* \* \*

Kay was deep in thought as she walked towards the exit along the quiet, now familiar corridor of Belmont Rehabilitation Centre. Its clinical smell and startlingly white walls had come to represent to her the sterile new life she was about to embark on – an uncertain journey into the future with a sober Ed. The six-week duration of his stay in the centre was fast coming to a close, and Ed would soon be returning home. Having just come from a meeting with his counsellor, Kay thought about how she would cope, living with the new, non-drinking, Ed. The children, of course, were delighted that Daddy was coming home, but Kay couldn't help wondering just how long he would be home for. She had tried phoning the hospital several times to try and find out any news of the little boy's condition, but every time she enquired, they told her that information was only being disclosed to family members. Eventually she had called the garda station and was told briefly about the boy's condition. Kay had cried with relief. She couldn't even begin to imagine how she would feel if such a thing ever happened to one of her own children. However difficult it was to forgive Ed for his behaviour now, she would never have been able to forgive him if the boy had been killed. The Gardaí had also been in touch, and a court date had been set for his hearing. Although the young boy had not been left with any serious injuries, Ed was still facing charges of driving under the influence and dangerous driving, and Kay had been warned to expect a prison sentence. In a way, though, she almost found it easier to think about how the law would treat him than wonder how she herself really felt about what he had done.

Lost in the contemplation of her worries, her head bowed and her forehead creased in thought, Kay never noticed the man who was walking towards her until she had actually bumped into him.

'Oh, gosh, I'm really sorry,' she said, looking up, mortified that she had been so clumsy. The rest of her apology was cut short, however, as she realised who she was standing face to face with. The one person who had occupied her dreams for most of her married life, the man who had been the subject of all of her 'what ifs' in life, was now standing in front of her with an expression of surprise and delight on his face.

'Well, hello Kay,' he said, clearly thrilled at bumping into her.

'Declan, it's, well… it's, you look…'

'And it's great to see you too,' he laughed, as Kay struggled to find her words.

'God, it's just such a surprise,' she replied, giving him a hug.

His embrace was warm and welcoming in return, and for the split second that they held each other, Kay drank in the familiarity of his scent and the feel of his body.

'How've you been?' he asked, looking at her in the same way that he used to, with an intensity that made Kay feel like her legs were melting, and for a minute, she almost forgot about the dark circles under her eyes and her unwashed hair.

'Not bad thanks,' she answered, wondering if she should tell him about Ed, and deciding against it. 'So, eh, what brings you here?' she asked, before realising that he too might be reluctant to share what his business was in Belmont.

'Do you remember my brother Aidan?' Declan started, not seeming to have any qualms about telling her. 'Well, things have been a little rough for him recently, and, instead of asking me for help, he turned to Jack Daniels and ended up in here.'

Kay looked at him sympathetically.

'Oh, he's doing great, though,' Declan added with a reassuring smile, 'and they say he'll be fit to come home in a week or so, so fingers crossed.'

Kay was happy that his situation wasn't too serious, and only wished that her own predicament was as simple.

Suddenly conscious that their conversation sounded loud and animated in the sterile atmosphere of the corridor, Declan whispered the suggestion that they go for a coffee.

'It's just that I'd be afraid we'll be kept here ourselves if we stay chatting for much longer. I'm not sure that they're too keen on excitement in this place,' Declan said, under his breath. 'That is, of course, if you've time for a coffee. I'd really love to catch up.'

Did she have time for a coffee? Was the Pope a Catholic? There was no question in Kay's mind that she wanted to catch up with him, and so, like two errant schoolchildren, they hurried their pace down the corridor, laughing as they passed a severe-looking orderly who frowned as they rushed past.

A short while later, Kay and Declan were seated opposite each other with two large coffees in front of them. They had found a small café just five minutes away from the clinic, and barely noticed the time go by as people came and went. Declan questioned her eagerly about what she had been doing over the years, about how Madeleine was keeping and how her family were. Apart from a brief explanation for why she had been in the Belmont Centre, however, Kay avoided talking about Ed, and instead spoke of her family in terms of her children. She also told Declan that she had followed his career in the papers and the social pages in the magazines, and couldn't resist commenting on the fact that he usually appeared with a glamorous woman on his arm.

'Ah, just a safety in numbers sort of thing,' he laughed, noticing the inquisitive look in her eyes, as if she was wordlessly willing him to confess whether he was with anyone now or not. 'All temporary flings, though,' he said in a softer tone. 'There's been no one special.'

Kay was startled at the relief she felt when she heard this, unaware until that moment of just how much he still meant to her. She would have been crushed to hear that he was seeing someone, or worse still, that he was married. But then, she thought to herself, she was married herself, and that didn't count for much.

Kay studied him as he took a sip from his coffee, unaware of her scrutiny. At six foot one, he looked too big for the small corner they sat in, and his thick black hair, which appeared, as ever, perfectly groomed, fell forward as he bent to wipe the drip that had fallen from his cup onto the table. He had always been very good-looking, Kay thought to herself, as she took in his dark, sallow skin and his striking appearance. And framed within the chiselled features of his face, underneath perfectly shaped black eyebrows, he also had the most incredible smoky green eyes. They were flecked with subtle brown, which Kay knew could be warm and gentle one minute, and intense and emotional the next, and she found herself wishing that they would look that way at her again. Adding to his handsomeness, she thought, was a modesty that suggested he was totally oblivious to the effect his looks had on people, and Kay smiled as he self-consciously brushed the loose strand of hair back from his face.

Accepting an offer of fresh coffees from the waitress, Kay began to ask him how his business was doing. When they were going out together, Declan had worked with an electrical company where he was responsible for their small computer maintenance division. She knew, however, that it hadn't taken long for him to break free from the constraints of the job to become his own boss.

'Everything is still going really well, to be honest,' he explained, 'and I was even able to open another Avocanet office in Cork there last week.'

'That's one thing I've always wondered about, actually,' Kay interrupted. 'Where did you get the name from?'

'Oh, it'd probably sound stupid to you,' he said, looking a bit embarrassed.

'No, no, please, do tell me, I wouldn't have asked if I didn't want to know,' Kay pleaded, now more interested than ever. She was sure from the bashful look on his face that the genesis of the name would intrigue her.

'Well, you remember that day we went to Powerscourt House, because you had wanted to see it,' he asked, 'and ended up staying in that bed-and-breakfast after dinner, down in Avoca?'

221

Kay nodded. How could she forget that day? She had phoned her parents to tell them that she would be spending the night at Madeleine's house, and they had then checked into a room in the B&B, pretending they were married. It was one of the best nights of her life. Declan had told her, for the first time, that he loved her, under the cover of the warm duvet in their cold room, and neither of them had wanted to part company the next day.

'Well, I suppose it just made such an impression on me that, you know, it felt kind of appropriate to immortalise it,' he finished, looking into his cup.

Kay was astonished. She had never heard anything so romantic in her life, and almost felt like pinching herself to make sure that the moment was real.

'Thank you,' she said, quietly and simply, feeling a lump in her throat as she held her breath, trying not to cry. 'That's the nicest thing anyone's ever done for me.'

The owner of the café turned on the lights, and the sudden harsh brightness tipped the balance of their intimate mood back to the reality of the crisp Monday evening that it was. The mellow fading light outside the window appeared dark all of a sudden, and Kay realised with a start that she needed to get home to put Dominic to bed.

'Oh, my goodness,' she exclaimed, looking at her watch. 'I never realised it was so late.' She started to pull on her coat.

Once outside, they walked together back to the car park in the Belmont Centre in a silence that felt oddly comfortable to them both.

'Kay, it's been really, *really* great to see you again,' he said as they reached her car. 'Is there any way, I mean… would you mind if I asked to meet you again?' Declan asked, a little nervously.

Looking at him, as he stood anxiously before her, Kay realised that she was powerless to refuse him. She had thought about him for so long, and wondered so often what would have happened had they stayed together, that the only answer she could give was yes.

'Here's my mobile number,' she replied, ripping a corner of paper from her diary and scribbling down her number on it. 'Give me a call.'

With that, Declan leant down, kissed Kay on the cheek, smiled and said goodbye. As he walked back to his car, like a dark silhouette against the pale blue and lemon of the evening sky, Kay marvelled at how something so good could possibly have come from such an awful situation.

Later that night, after the children were tucked up in bed, Kay phoned Madeleine to tell her about the unbelievable day she just had.

'You'll never guess who I met today in the Belmont Centre?' she said as soon as Madeleine picked up the phone, barely giving her a chance to say 'hello'.

'Who?' Madeleine asked, reciprocating the tone of excitement in Kay's voice.

'Declan McNally!' came the cheerful reply down the line. 'I still can't believe it, I mean, can you? How long has it been since I've lain eyes on *him*?'

Madeleine laughed as the questions continued to trip off Kay's tongue.

'And of all the places in the world, and of all times to meet him... I'm sorry, I know I'm talking too fast, it's just that I still can't believe it!'

'What was he doing there?' Madeleine asked, surprised herself that such a face from Kay's past should turn up again, though she couldn't pretend she wasn't delighted for her. She hadn't heard Kay laugh in weeks, and it was good to see a little sunshine coming into her life. Ed had been nothing but a cloud of trouble and concern for years.

'Well,' she started, slowing her speech a little to make sure that she explained it correctly. 'Apparently, his brother was admitted

223

to the clinic a while ago, and although Declan's been visiting him for ages, unbelievably, today was the first time we've seen each other in there.' Kay paused for a second to think. 'I really can't tell you how good it was to catch up with him.'

Madeleine got the feeling that Kay didn't need her to respond, and so remained quiet until her friend began again in a wistful voice.

'He looks as amazing as ever, and just being with him again Madeleine, I felt, well, I felt so happy.'

'So, how long did you spend together?' Madeleine asked, looking at the hand approaching nine o'clock on her watch, and wondering if Kay had only just come home.

'Oh, I'm not sure. Probably about an hour and a half – I had to come home to put Dominic to bed.'

'And did you talk about Ed at all?' Madeleine asked, curious as to how much Kay would have divulged about the accident.

'You know, we didn't actually talk about him at all. Is it terrible that I avoided even mentioning his name? I mean, I told him briefly why Ed was in the Belmont Centre, but Declan didn't ask anything more after that, and I didn't tell him.'

Thinking that she was in no position herself to preach about the lack of virtue in withholding the truth, Madeleine agreed that Kay was probably wiser to keep the details of Ed's situation to herself for the time being.

'Anyway,' Kay continued, 'we spent most of the time talking about his business, and Holly, Mark and Dominic, oh, and he was asking for you as well.'

Madeleine was touched that Declan had remembered her, and couldn't help but compare his behaviour to the considerable lack of interest, and even politeness, that Ed had extended to her over the years. Although there was no doubt in her mind that Declan was by far the better man, she was still a little concerned that, in her vulnerable state, Kay might leap into something without giving it enough thought. Madeleine also realised, however, that, more than anyone else she knew, Kay deserved some happiness, and so, holding her tongue, she didn't utter a word of warning, doing her best to share in Kay's obvious delight.

'So are you going to see him again?' Madeleine wondered aloud, as Kay finished the description she had given of him with a deep sigh.

'Well, he did ask if we could meet up, and I gave him my mobile number, but I really don't know what I'll do if he calls,' she said a little sheepishly to an entirely unconvinced Madeleine.

'You don't know what you'll do if he calls! Kay, this is me you're talking to – I know you, and I also know that there isn't even the remotest chance that you'd decline an invitation from the lovely Declan McNally if he calls!'

Kay laughed, knowing that what Madeleine was saying was true.

'And actually, I don't even know why I'm saying "if he calls", because we both know it'll be a case of "when he calls". He was always mad about you, Kay, and judging from what you've told me tonight, I'd say he still is.'

Kay smiled at her end of the phone. Her day had been wonderful so far, and now, with Madeleine's blessing, she felt as if everything was going right for a change. She even managed to forget about her guilt and about the problems she was facing with Ed for a few minutes.

'And Kay,' Madeleine said, almost as an afterthought, 'give him my love when you do see him again, will you?'

As she hung up the phone, Kay prayed that Madeleine was right. She had felt exhilarated after seeing Declan, and at a time when even contentment seemed like an unrealistic expectation, it was exactly what she needed to dust away the gloomy cobwebs from her stressful life.

\* \* \*

A short while later, as Madeleine was making herself a cup of coffee, she got a call from Thomas asking if he could drop down for a couple of minutes. Surprised, and pleased with the unexpected visit, she went to open the front door just in time to see him walking down the corridor.

'To what do I owe this pleasure?' she asked, greeting him with a kiss.

'Oh, not much,' he answered with a faint smile, 'just thought I'd pop down.'

'Well, perfect timing, the kettle's boiled and I was about to make myself a cup of coffee – do you fancy one?' she asked as she closed the door behind him.

'Sounds great, thanks,' Thomas replied quietly as he followed her into the kitchen.

They sat on high stools at the small counter. Madeleine dipped a biscuit into her coffee, wondering what had Thomas so on edge. He had hardly said two sentences since he came in, and her initial fear was that, somehow, he had found out about herself and Donal.

'Is everything all right?' she asked with concern. 'You seem a little stressed.'

'I'm sorry, Madeleine, but I can't go to the theatre with you on Wednesday night,' he blurted out.

Madeleine's heart began to beat faster as she became more and more afraid that he had discovered what had been going on with Donal.

'OK,' she replied cautiously, trying to gauge the meaning of his expression, 'that's fine, but, em, can I ask why not?'

'I can't go, because I... well, I... I have to go into hospital,' he said, meeting her stare.

Madeleine put down her mug. Her mind was torn between feeling a sense of relief that her secret was safe, and concern that there was something terribly wrong with Thomas.

'Hospital, but why?' she asked incredulously.

226

Looking slightly embarrassed, Thomas took a second to go over the speech in his head that he had memorised before he had come down.

'It's nothing, really, and I didn't say anything to you before because I didn't want to worry you. The doctor just wants to do a quick operation to sort out a problem with my, em, you know... the waterworks.'

'Oh, Thomas, I'd no idea you were unwell. You should've said something,' Madeleine cried, chastising him with a look of concern that spoke louder than her words. 'So can that be easily fixed then, or will you have to be in hospital for long?'

'I'm sure it's nothing too serious,' he replied, the apprehensive look on his face at odds with the confidence he was trying to instil in his voice. 'I've just been getting a bit of back pain, and Donal wants to check it out.'

'*Donal?*' Madeleine asked, startled.

'Oh, that's right,' Thomas replied with a weak laugh. 'It's such a small world really. Donal O'Sullivan is the urologist I was referred to by my own GP, and I knew as soon as I saw him that I recognised him. I couldn't quite put my finger on who he was, though, until he mentioned he was a friend of yours, and that we had met up in Redcliff.'

Madeleine felt almost paralysed with guilt as Thomas looked innocently at her, completely unaware of the thoughts running through her head. Her internal struggle was beginning to become more than she could handle, and Madeleine was feeling more lost than she had ever been. She really did like Thomas, he was sensitive and attractive, and he made her laugh, and in that moment, she resented Donal for ever putting her in a position where she was given the power to hurt him. It was becoming clearer and clearer to Madeleine that she simply couldn't play with Thomas's heart – she liked him too much for that – and what she needed to do now was make it clear to Donal that he couldn't mess with her all over again, or be a part of her life when they both knew that was impossible.

'Yes, yes, it, em, it really is a small world,' she replied, feeling as if her mind was a million miles away. 'So, what hospital will you be going to?' she asked, trying to change the subject.

'St John's,' Thomas replied, the relief he felt at having shared his problem with someone visible on his face.

'Well, I'll just have to come and visit you with grapes and Lucozade then, won't I?' Madeleine joked, trying to lighten the mood a little. The idea of surgery didn't sound very reassuring to her, but sensing Thomas's anxiety about it, she didn't want to worry him any more than he already was.

Draining his cup of the last of his coffee, Thomas stood up. 'I'd expect no less! Look,' he said apologetically, 'I'm sorry this is such a short visit, but would you mind if I headed off? I think even the idea of hospital and operations is making me tired, and I might just head off to bed.'

'Don't be silly, of course I don't mind,' Madeleine answered, putting her arms around Thomas and giving him a reassuring hug. 'Make sure, though, that you ring me if you need anything at all, and I'll call you tomorrow anyway, just to make sure.'

'Thanks,' he said, grateful that she hadn't quizzed him too much on the exact nature of his illness, 'and I'm sorry again about the theatre.'

'Well, you'll just have to make it up to me when you get out, won't you?' she said, kissing him, 'and I'll be in to the hospital all the time to see you too, so you won't have to worry about being bored.'

As they stood in her doorway saying goodbye, Madeleine gave him a final kiss and watched as Thomas slowly walked up the stairs to his own apartment. Wracked with guilt, she tried to focus on Thomas's recovery, but thoughts of how easy it could have been for him to find out about her and Donal kept creeping into her mind. Not only had it been too close for comfort,

Madeleine thought, but she was also faced with the recognition that there were far more important things than herself to worry about now. Whether it was Thomas's illness that had given her an insight into how strongly she really felt about him, or whether she had just needed something this serious to make her realise how unworkable her situation with Donal was, Madeleine was grateful that at least things were becoming less confused in her own head. However she had behaved with Donal before, and whatever she had envisaged their relationship to be, it was all suddenly very clear. Thomas, the man she knew she should be with, was sick, and neither she nor Donal could abuse his trust any more.

*  *  *

Early the next morning, Kay had a call from Declan.

'It was great to see you yesterday,' he said to a dumbfounded Kay, who couldn't believe he had rung so soon. 'Were the kids all right when you got home?' he asked, sounding genuinely concerned.

'Eh, yes, they were fine, thanks,' she replied, 'and it was good to see you too, Declan.'

Kay didn't know if she should even be talking to him, but convincing herself that the phone call would probably be a once-off, anyway, decided it would be rude if she were to cut the conversation short.

'So,' he continued, 'do you think I could see you again?' Nerves were unsettling the tone of flirtation he was hoping for.

Before giving herself a chance to consider the repercussions of such a decision, Kay found herself agreeing. 'When?' she asked simply, afraid that if she said any more, she would break out in nervous laughter.

'Well, why don't I pick you up this evening and we could go somewhere nice for dinner?' he suggested.

'Tonight?' Kay asked, slightly taken aback. She had somehow thought that she would have more time to prepare for their meeting, and immediately ran a mental scroll through her wardrobe to see what would be suitable to wear. 'Em, yes, I suppose tonight's fine,' she said a little distractedly, looking at her nails. They looked awful, and Kay chided herself that she hadn't had a manicure in months. 'Oh, but, you can't pick me up,' she blurted out, suddenly conscious of what he had said. 'Or rather, what I mean is, I don't think that that would be such a good idea, I couldn't risk the children or Claudette seeing you here. Why don't I meet you in town, say, eight o'clock in Café en Seine, and then we could go for dinner from there?' she suggested. She couldn't even begin to imagine how it would be if one of the children saw Declan arrive to pick her up or, worse still, if Ed heard about her leaving the house with another man – it would be enough to make him start drinking again.

'Of course, sorry, I should've thought of that,' he apologised. 'Town is absolutely fine – I'll see you at eight so.'

Hanging up the phone with a huge smile on her face, Kay felt ten years younger. She hadn't been so excited in years, and the prospect of an actual date was stirring the butterflies in her stomach that she had almost forgotten existed. They had certainly been dormant for as long as she had been married to Ed, and the wonderful, almost unfamiliar feeling of anticipation was making Kay giddy. She skipped up the stairs to decide on an outfit, and, catching sight of herself in the mirror, saw that her usual pallor had changed from that of perennial paleness to a rosy-tinted glow of pleasure.

Sitting amidst an array of clothes covering the surface of her bed, Kay deliberated on what look she should go for. Everything she picked out seemed either too short or too formal, but eventually, looking at an ensemble on a hanger in front of her, Kay settled on the first outfit she had pulled out of the wardrobe. The black trousers were sleek and figure-hugging, and she knew that the pale lemon sleeveless top would show off her golden tan perfectly. The delicate lace detail on the neckline also suggested a hint of romance, but was conservative enough not to give Declan the wrong idea. Kay wasn't exactly sure what kind of idea she *did* want to give him, but knew that a plunging décolletage would send out a message she wasn't ready to give.

The only obstacle in the way of Kay's enthusiastic preparation was the constant interruption to her thoughts of feelings of guilt. Telling herself, however, that she deserved a bit of fun, she put her children's faces and Ed's alcoholism to the back of her mind. Her hope was that if she simply avoided such questions, the struggle in her conscience would disappear, or at the very least, she would be able to forget about her moral conundrum for the evening that lay ahead. As she was leaving, convincing herself that a little untruth wasn't really as bad as a lie, Kay amazed herself at how easily she was able to tell Claudette that she was meeting Madeleine in town for dinner and a few drinks. She got into the taxi after kissing Holly, Mark and Dominic goodbye. With feelings of excitement eclipsing her earlier guilt, Kay sat back, relaxed and looked forward to seeing Declan McNally again.

Café en Seine was buzzing with activity when she got there. Tables of business executives sat next to fashionable twenty-somethings, who chatted beside American tourists, and Kay hoped that she would look inconspicuous amid the mixed crowd. Animated conversation bounced off walls in little alcoves and reverberated along vast, sweeping ceilings, and she felt quite overwhelmed at the sheer size and capacity of the bar. Kay realised how long it had been since she had afforded herself a night out in town. Spotting Declan by the balustrade on the second floor, she was determined she was going to enjoy herself.

Her heart beat faster as she approached his table. As he stood up to greet her, Kay was struck once again by Declan's extreme good looks and easy manner. He kissed her affectionately on the

231

cheek and she sat down next to him, feeling as if she was in a dream, and gave her order to a barmaid, who seemed to appear out of nowhere. Noticing her slightly awestruck appearance, Declan began the conversation, commenting on how busy the bar was.

A little uneasily, Kay laughed. 'I can't say that doesn't suit me, though,' she said, looking around her. 'Hopefully it'll mean no one will take any notice of me.'

'I doubt that,' Declan replied, smiling. 'Nobody could ever miss you, you look stunning.'

'Oh, no,' Kay responded, blushing, 'that's not what I meant, I wasn't trying to...'

'I know you weren't,' Declan assured her, 'but it's true.'

'I'm sorry, I'm so nervous,' she tried to explain, 'but you have to understand that it's been quite some time since I've been on a date, and I shouldn't even be doing it now.'

'Kay, calm down, would you?' Declan laughed. 'You're just meeting an old friend for a few drinks and a bite to eat, so stop worrying and enjoy yourself.'

'You're right,' Kay agreed, composing herself, as the barmaid returned with the drinks. 'I should relax. Here's to old friends,' she toasted him, raising her glass.

Relaxing more and more as time ticked by, Kay was surprised when Declan suggested that they should leave if they wanted to make their dinner reservation. She hadn't realised how long they had been sitting there, and silently hoped that the rest of the night wouldn't pass so quickly. Whatever apprehensions she had been harbouring about the evening, she now wanted to savour every single minute of it.

The restaurant they arrived at was opulently decorated with flowers and satin napkins, and phrases of Mozart floated through the savoury scented air as they were shown to their seats. It seemed that Declan was well known to the maître d', and they were offered complimentary champagne along with their menus.

Kay felt as if she had been loaned someone else's life for the night, and she wasn't sure that she would ever want to give it back. The hours flew by in a beautiful haze of laughter and discussion, and although she knew that the food she was eating was magnificent, she hardly tasted a bite. They shared desserts, and lingered over coffee, and as they swallowed the last of their digestifs, Kay wished that the night didn't have to be over so soon. It also became apparent very quickly that Declan felt the same. As they left the restaurant, he asked if she would be interested in accompanying him to a jazz gig nearby.

Twenty minutes later, they were seated in Vicar Street's dimly lit arena, listening to the melodic riffs of Duke Ellington and Bill Evans gloriously soaring from the players on stage. Kay was both intrigued and shocked to discover the life she had been missing by staying in so many weekends, minding the children and worrying about Ed. Her social life had long since consisted of either the rugby club or the local pub, and she was only now, with resentment, beginning to see how much more there was on offer.

Reality couldn't be warded off for long, however, and when Kay looked at her watch, she realised with a start that it was nearly two o'clock.

'Declan,' she said softly against the background of piano solo, 'I really have to get going. I hate to sound staid, but there's school in the morning,' she added, unable to help herself laughing. She felt like a teenager out past her curfew.

Finishing their drinks and waiting only until 'Mood Indigo' had played out its final bars, they left the left the warm intimacy of the club behind them. As they stood in the cool night air, Declan offered to hail her a taxi, lending her his jacket while she waited, and just as a cab pulled up to the kerb, he turned and put his hands protectively around her shoulders.

'I can't remember having a better night,' he said, looking longingly into her eyes.

'Nor I,' Kay admitted, returning his stare.

Giving him a brief but gentle kiss on the cheek, she handed him back his jacket and got into the taxi. She cast one last look at him as he waved goodbye, and said 'Call me' through the open window as the car pulled away into the hum of traffic. She knew, without looking back, that Declan would still be standing on the path, like he always used to, waiting until the car passed out of his view. Letting her head fall back against the seat, Kay tried not to imagine what could have happened had she not left so suddenly. The whole night had been so magical, however, that she knew she had been right to leave when she did. After all, she still had her own family to go home to, and it was important that she left before she did something she might regret. What worried Kay so much, however, was that she didn't know just how much she would regret it if something had happened, or, what she found even more concerning, if she would regret it at all.

# CHAPTER ELEVEN

THOMAS WAS DOZING WHEN A NURSE POPPED HER HEAD around the door. He felt groggy in the warm, muggy room, and the breeze that she brought in with her stirred the humid air.

'So, how do you feel this morning?' she asked, walking around his bed, efficiently opening windows and fluffing up his pillows.

'Not too bad, thanks, considering,' he answered, smiling weakly at her.

'Well, it's a beautiful day outside,' she said in her matronly voice, 'and the bit of a breeze now will have you feeling better in no time.'

Thomas was oddly comforted by her motherly tone, and was happy, in his sleepy state, to sit back and watch her fuss about the room.

'Mr O'Sullivan is very early doing his rounds this morning because he has to be in theatre at ten, so he'll be in to you now in about five minutes, OK?'

Suddenly, Thomas felt very awake, and sat up straight in the bed. He had had his surgery only yesterday, and for some reason didn't think that he would be speaking to Donal so soon about it. His throat felt dry and, if he'd had a choice in the matter, he would have gladly lit up a cigarette. Knowing, however, that he would never get away with it, Thomas opted for a glass of water instead, and shakily poured it out of the large glass hospital pitcher.

He was still sore from the surgery, and the nurse helped him out of his bed and into the bathroom, where he washed and shaved. While he went about each task with slow and pained movements, he heard another nurse come into the room with his medication. As the two women chatted to each other, Thomas wished that he too could feel the same sense of cheerfulness that the sun outside had obviously inspired in them, but he couldn't bring himself to feel very positive. He had woken up with the horrible feeling that the diagnosis wasn't going to be good, and, jumping to his own conclusions, he had already imagined the worst.

Thomas had just got back into bed, when Donal knocked quietly on the door and came in. The older of the two nurses told him that she would be back to check on him again before lunch, and then, excusing themselves, they both left the room. From the serious look on Donal's face as he sat down, Thomas knew that his own predictions hadn't been too far off the mark. He felt his stomach muscles clench and simply nodded his hello, finding his mouth once again dry, and unable to form any words. When Donal started speaking, Thomas's heart began to hammer in his chest, and he braced himself for the words that he knew he wouldn't want to hear.

'Well,' Donal began, putting the chart down in his lap and looking at Thomas, 'as you know, yesterday's surgery was really about finding out just what exactly is going on inside you. Unfortunately, what we discovered isn't good.'

Thomas could feel his skin becoming clammy, tiny beads of sweat forming on his forehead. He wished Donal would just say that he had made a huge mistake, but from the doctor's intense

236

expression, he knew that his hope was in vain. He was terrified of what he was about to be told.

Taking a deep breath, Donal continued: 'When we went in, we discovered a tumour in your bladder, which is what I had expected I would find. However, it was considerably bigger than I had anticipated, and, unfortunately, it is malignant.'

Thomas felt as if he couldn't breathe. He was taking short, panicked little gasps of air, and his pulse was racing.

'But… malignant?' he asked in a barely audible whisper, his voice choking on the words.

'I know, I'm sorry,' Donal said gently, wishing there was something else he could do to ease the trauma of the news. 'What we need to do now is to treat it very aggressively with radiotherapy, which will hopefully reduce it, and eventually kill it off, so to speak. Over the next six weeks, I'm going to have you attend here as an outpatient so that you can have radiotherapy every day…' Although Donal had broken similar news to hundreds of other patients, he was finding it extremely difficult to remain detached, and was struggling himself to continue talking.

'Look, you're a young, fit man. Hopefully we've caught this in time, and if your attitude is optimistic, then you'll have an even better chance of beating the cancer.'

Donal looked at the ashen face in front of him and watched as Thomas tried to digest what he was hearing. He wished that he would at least say something, but he only continued staring at the bed sheet.

'I know this is a terrible shock for you.' Donal went on talking, both to try and help him accept the news, and also to cover up the horrible silence. 'You'll probably have a million questions for me, so I'll come back to you this afternoon, and answer anything you need to know then. Is that all right with you?'

'Am I going to die?' Thomas asked quietly, finally looking up. All he had heard were the words 'tumour', 'radiotherapy', 'malignant', 'aggressive' and 'cancer' – words that he had thought only described other people's lives, or rather, the precursor to other people's deaths, and so there was really only one question that he needed the answer to.

'Thomas,' Donal replied, leaning a little closer, 'you're in the best hospital for cancer care in the country, and we're going to do everything we can to fight this tumour. What you need to do now, though, is to try and remain as positive as you can so that you're in a better position to beat it. You just have to keep focused on the fact that a lot of people live through these kinds of illnesses to have wonderful lives.'

When Thomas responded with only a nod, Donal stood up and put his chair back against the wall.

'I know you'll probably want some time alone to think about this, so I'll leave you now, but remember, whatever questions you think of, I'll be back this afternoon to answer them as best I can.'

He rested his hand on Thomas's shoulder. 'And if you need anything explained in the meantime, just ask one of the nurses and I'll be back as soon as possible, OK?'

Again, Thomas nodded, without raising his eyes, and Donal left the room in silence.

A few hours later, Madeleine arrived, not with the promised Lucozade and grapes, but with some large sunflowers that she had been unable to resist in the florist's. They had seemed so cheeky and vibrant that she was sure they would cheer Thomas up, and so had bought the biggest bunch that she could find. Madeleine's warm, enthusiastic face appearing above the vivid yellow petals coming through the door was all Thomas needed, however, to trigger the emotions he had been fighting since speaking with Donal, and as she laid the flowers on his locker, he began to cry.

'So, how are you today?' she asked brightly at first, but her face fell when she saw Thomas's grief-stricken expression.

When he couldn't answer her, she put her arms around him, and as they hugged, she could feel his tears wetting her shoulder. Eventually, Madeleine sat up and looked searchingly at him.

'Thomas, what's happened?' she asked, tears stinging her own eyes, 'What's wrong?'

'Oh, Madeleine,' he said pitifully, 'Donal was here this morning, and he said that I, well, there's a tumour... it's cancer, Madeleine.'

Madeleine couldn't help the gasping sob that escaped from her, and with one hand over her mouth, she lifted the other to wipe a tear from Thomas's cheek.

'I have to start radiotherapy straight away, which will go on for the next six weeks – and I'm going to have to come in for it every day,' he explained, repeating Donal's words.

Only the blind fluttering in the soft breeze behind them made any noise in the bright room as they looked at each other, trying to comprehend the devastating revelation.

'Oh, Thomas, it can't...' Madeleine cried, 'it can't be true.'

'I wish it wasn't,' he said, feeling slightly calmer after hours of solitary contemplation.

Sitting in silence, Madeleine realised just how much she had been taking Thomas for granted. And now, possibly too late, she saw that she had been so caught up with Donal that she never noticed how she had been falling in love with Thomas all along. Unable to think of a single word to say that would ease his pain, she leaned in closer to him on the narrow bed and stroked his hair, painfully watching as his heavy tears quietly dropped onto the pillow.

'I'll be here to fight it with you, you know,' Madeleine whispered, trying to smile as reassuringly as possible. 'I'll stay with you as much as you want, and I can come into the hospital with you too.'

Thomas looked gratefully at her, aware also of the new intimacy that his illness had stirred.

Eventually, their closeness was interrupted as a nurse came into the room, bearing a small tray of immaculately aligned syringes.

'Time for your bloods, Thomas, if that's OK,' she said, as if Thomas had a choice.

'Do you want me to stay?' Madeleine asked, watching him roll up his sleeve.

'It's OK. I'll probably go for a sleep after this anyway,' he said, smiling feebly at her.

Kissing him goodbye, as the nurse prepared the various vials behind them, Madeleine left the room quietly, containing her tears only until she had closed the door. She had tried to muster a smile for him before she left, but feeling too heavy-hearted, she could only manage a weak look of encouragement. She had tried to sound positive while she talked to him, but now, alone, Madeleine felt that, once again, she might be losing one of the most important men in her life.

\* \* \*

Kay sat back in the taxi as the car sped down the impressive tree-lined road. Declan had called the previous day to invite her to dinner in his house, to which she had agreed, deciding that with Ed due home on Friday, she might not get the chance again. Lying to Claudette had also seemed somehow easier this time, as Kay convinced herself that it would be the last time she would need to do it. Ed would be home soon, Declan would once again become a thing of the past, and she would look back and just remember him as a wonderful oasis of pleasure in her otherwise stressful marriage.

As on their first date, Kay had agonised over what to wear. At least when they were meeting in town, she thought, she had known to get dressed up. In his house, however, she wasn't sure if he expected her to arrive in a black dress and diamonds, or blue jeans and a tee-shirt. Deciding that she couldn't go too far wrong with something in the middle, Kay eventually settled on a dark red sleeveless linen dress, which accentuated her narrow waist and petite frame. She also wore a pair of kitten-heeled black sandals, and a light black cardigan in case the outfit looked too formal. Her smooth, olive skin was lightly dusted with translucent powder and with just a touch of sheer lip-gloss and dark mascara, Kay looked both naturally stunning and effortlessly elegant.

As the taxi turned into a wide driveway, Kay's mouth dropped in awe. The extensive lawns around the house were perfectly manicured, and dozens of flowers and shrubs, in every colour imaginable, spilled forth from each corner. Huge evergreens protected the house from the sound of passing traffic and Kay wondered who kept the garden in such magnificent bloom. Handing her money to the taxi-driver from the back seat, she got out of the car and walked towards the large steps. Giant terracotta urns flanked either side of the doorway, and, ringing the bell, Kay realised with a pang that she wished she shared this home too. She loved the flowers and the expansive redbrick façades. Everything about the serenity of the grounds signified to Kay the tranquillity that was conspicuously lacking in her own home. As long as she was with Ed, she thought to herself, a peaceful and happy life would elude her. Straightening herself up, then, as she heard footsteps walking towards the door, she knew that this was exactly the reason why she had to enjoy Declan's company tonight. It had been a long time coming, it wouldn't be happening again, and Kay decided that, without a doubt, she deserved this brief glimpse into happiness.

Growing louder with the approaching footsteps was the sound of a dog barking, and when the door finally opened, Kay was greeted by a smiling Declan and an excited golden Labrador. Any nervousness she had been feeling dissolved when she saw his welcoming face. Noticing a large unidentifiable stain on his tee-shirt, she couldn't help laughing.

'Honestly, I did look respectable a few minutes ago, before Major here ran into me while I was testing the sauce,' he said, indicating the wooden spoon in his hand. 'Come on in, though, I'm so happy you agreed to come over,' he finished, giving Kay a kiss on the cheek as she walked past.

He led her through the hall into a warm and inviting kitchen, which was considerably larger then her own, and pulled out a seat from the table for her to sit on.

'You don't mind if I just finish up here for a couple of minutes, do you?' he asked, nodding his head in the direction of the bubbling pans on the Aga.

'No, no, not at all,' Kay answered, impressed that he was doing all of the cooking himself. Ed could barely make toast, and she had expected to find cartons of takeaway food when she arrived.

Declan covered a deliciously garlic-smelling pan of creamy sauce, and then took a bottle of champagne out of the fridge and filled up the two glasses already on the table in front of Kay.

'Here's to your first visit to my humble home,' he said, raising his glass, 'and to the prospect of many more.'

'Indeed,' Kay agreed, unwilling to tell him that she wouldn't be able to come again. 'Whatever's cooking smells incredible,' she added, trying to take the focus off her non-committal response to his invitation.

As they chatted, Kay sat entranced by his every move, eagerly following his talented hands chopping and mixing and stirring the food, and she found herself imagining what it would be like to feel his hands move that way over her. She was snapped back into focus, however, as Declan repeated his question.

'Top-up?' he asked again, holding up the bottle.

'Oh, yes, that would be lovely, thanks,' she answered, mentally reprimanding herself for being so distracted. She didn't want it to look like her eyes had been glazed over with boredom.

'So, how long have you lived here?' Kay asked, watching the bubbles rise in her glass. She could remember the tiny kitchen in the rented student bedsit he had lived in when they were going out together – unquestionably a far cry from the impressive kitchen she was sitting in now.

'About seven years, I think,' he said, contemplatively. 'I actually bought it from an IT colleague of mine who moved to America. I hadn't really planned on buying a house. I was very happy in my old apartment, but as soon as I saw this place, I just couldn't turn it down.'

'I don't blame you,' Kay commented, looking around her. 'It's fabulous... well, what I've seen of it, anyway.'

'I'll give you the grand tour later,' he said with a flirtatious smile, 'and then you can tell me what you think.'

Even the thought of what might lie ahead made Kay shiver in anticipation, and Declan's expectant gaze suggested that he was thinking the same.

They laughed and chatted easily as Declan moved around the kitchen making last-minute preparations for their meal. The table had already been simply set for two, and, before bringing over the starter plates of steaming mussels, he dimmed the lights and lit the candles on the table. The atmosphere changed immediately from one of warmth and cosiness, to a seductive, intimate setting, and Kay was feeling more nervous and excited than she had done in years.

After medallions of lobster for their main course and a mouth-watering lemon mousse for dessert, Declan filled up their cups with freshly made, strong coffee. Kay couldn't help noticing the difference between this date and their last. While meeting in town had felt like an illicit affair, sitting in his house somehow seemed totally natural to her. She didn't know if it was the wine or simply the company, but the more the evening went on, the more Kay felt completely at home.

'So, how about that grand tour, now?' Declan asked, looking at her over the single flame of the candle.

Kay just smiled in response. Standing up as he offered her his hand, she picked up her drink and followed him out of the kitchen. From the wood-panelled dining room, they made their way into the drawing room, from where they returned to the hall and found themselves on the wide, carpeted staircase. As he took her hand once again, Kay felt a tingling from his fingertips as he tightened his grip around hers and led her up towards the landing. After briefly pointing out two guest bedrooms, the guest bathroom, and a large study, Declan led her eventually to the last door at the end of the corridor.

'And this is my bedroom,' he said as he opened the door before her and followed her in.

The room that they entered felt stylish and masculine to Kay. It was decorated sparsely. The walls were white and the plain black comforter covering the enormous bed in the centre looked imposing beneath a large print of Matisse's 'Red Studio'. She became aware of soft music in the background. Turning to find Declan, she saw him flicking the switch on the wall to dim the lights.

'You should really check out the bathroom as well,' he said, leading her into the adjoining room. 'I'd always wanted a Jacuzzi, so when I bought this house, I had one put in straight away – definitely my favourite toy!'

As he stood out of her way, Kay was faced with a huge tub sunk into the floor with steps leading down into it. The bathroom, decorated from floor to ceiling with slate-coloured tiles, seemed bigger than it really was because of the reflection of a large mirror on the back wall, and Kay was almost intimidated by its grandeur.

'It's amazing,' she said, looking around her in awe. Comfort and practicality had won out over style in her own house when she had had children; she'd always planned that when they had

244

grown up she could redecorate the way she wanted. That day seemed a long way off to Kay, however, as she stood now in the remarkably plush and luxurious bathroom, and she couldn't help the jealousy she felt at seeing how Declan lived.

'I've never even had a Jacuzzi,' she said, thinking back to hotel rooms she and Ed had stayed in, where watching her husband fall into bed drunk had been more likely then having a Jacuzzi with him.

'We could change that if you wanted,' Declan said tentatively, with a questioning look.

Without saying another word, they moved towards each other, and kissed gently. Declan's lips felt soft and tenderly eager. Although Kay knew that she shouldn't be kissing him, it felt absolutely right. She closed her eyes and allowed herself to succumb to the pleasure and happiness that was coursing through her veins. Her legs felt weak with desire and her mouth sought his hungrily as he put his arms around her and held her body tightly. Kay had been starved of affection for so long, and been taken for granted by Ed for so many years, that Declan's fervour was unleashing a passion in her that had been aching to be realised. The familiarity of his kiss was bringing back memories for Kay of a time in her life when she had been blissfully happy, and she sensed that Declan, as he lovingly cradled her head in his hands, was feeling the same.

'So,' he said, breaking away, 'how would you feel about that Jacuzzi?' he asked, looking into her eyes as if willing her to say yes.

Kay hesitated momentarily. She knew that if she agreed to this, it would be impossible not to return to him again, but casting her worries to the back of her mind, she nodded in agreement and entwined her fingers through his.

'Well, if you don't mind filling the bath, I can run down and get us some more wine,' he offered.

Kay found herself relieved at his suggestion, aware that she would rather get undressed without the focus of his intense gaze. It had been a long time since they had been together, and she was afraid that she wouldn't live up to his memory of her.

'Sure,' she answered, giving him another kiss. 'I'll be waiting for you.'

Before he left, Declan lit a couple of candles around the bathroom and turned off the light. The shadows playing on his face as he turned to go out the door made him look all the more attractive to Kay, and her initial guilt made way for a feeling of impatient desire.

In the bathroom on her own, Kay twisted the chrome taps, watching as streams of hot water cascaded out and heavy clouds of steam swirled up to the ceiling. While the water level slowly rose in the giant Jacuzzi, she removed her shoes and her jewellery, and undid the zip on her dress. Stepping out of it and turning off the taps, she put her toes into the water, cautiously testing the temperature, and then, placing her other foot in, she walked down the two steps into the tub, and sat languorously back. She noticed that the mirrors had become misted, and the candlelight was making the steam dance and whirl in circles with every movement and breeze from the door, which, left slightly ajar, seemed expectant of Declan's return.

A few minutes later, he arrived back with a bottle of chilled wine in his hand. Without uttering a sound, he filled up her glass, and, taking off his clothes, stepped into the Jacuzzi. Kay gazed admiringly at his fit, toned body, and longed to feel his skin against hers in the warm water.

'You look gorgeous,' he said as he sat down, reaching over to draw her towards him.

With one hand on her thigh, he flicked the switch on the side of the bath, and immediately, hundreds of tiny bubbles surged up from the jets to the surface.

As water fizzed and simmered around her, Kay became aware of teasing sensations shivering through her body, and when Declan smoothly moved his hand to the base of her spine, she felt her heart beat faster and her limbs melt with desire. Kissing her again, he encircled her breasts with his hands. Responding to his touch, she entwined her legs around his waist and moved in closer to him. Eventually, feeling that he could wait no longer, Declan stood up and reached for a fluffy, oversized white towel from the glass shelf beside them. Helping Kay to her feet, he enveloped her in its soft, cotton warmth, and, stepping out of the bath, he swept her up in his arms and carried her to the bed. Despite the balmy evening air, Kay shivered with anticipation, as Declan dried her gently and covered her in feathery kisses.

'I've thought about this for so long, Kay,' he said, lying beside her and protectively wrapping his arms around her.

'So have I,' she whispered softly as she kissed his neck. 'I just never thought it would happen.'

Aware that this moment was like a dream for them both, they kissed passionately and intensely, and Kay revelled in the thrill of feeling the weight of Declan's body above hers.

'Please come into me,' she moaned, straining her body towards his as she felt his growing hardness.

Answering her plea, he slid inside her, and they moved with increasing momentum as their arousal mounted with every deep and hurried breath.

Close to coming, Declan tried to hold off for as long as he could, but with a passion brimming that he had been waiting to unleash for years, he could eventually wait no longer, and released in a wonderful orgasm. As his movements slowed down, he could feel Kay getting faster until, seconds later, she too reached a shuddering climax.

They lay for a long time looking into each other's eyes, wordlessly communicating their pleasure and contentment through the simple touch of their skin. The blend of food and wine and lovemaking soon made their eyelids heavy, and before long they had drifted off into a deep sleep.

Kay woke with a start shortly afterwards, but seeing that the hand on the clock had only moved forward an hour, she lay back again and watched Declan sleep. Soon, however, as unwelcome thoughts of responsibility infringed on her magical evening, she kissed him awake.

'I have to go,' she whispered, affectionately stroking his arm.

'Oh, can't you stay a little longer?' he asked longingly, turning around and tenderly kissing her back.

'You don't know how much I'd love to, but I can't risk anybody at home getting suspicious, and Claudette will probably be awake until I get in,' she explained.

'OK,' Declan agreed reluctantly. 'I'll call you a cab,' he said, and reached for the phone on the bedside table.

When the taxi arrived, Kay kissed Declan a long goodbye, and unwillingly resigned herself, as she sat into the seat, to heading back to reality. After a twenty-minute ride back home through the quiet streets, a sleeping household greeted Kay when she opened the front door. Tiptoeing through the hall and up the stairs, she smiled to herself in the darkness. Quietly getting into bed and pulling up the covers closely around her, she could smell Declan's aftershave on her skin, and echoes of his touch seemed still to play over her. As she lay there, she was unable to let go of the memory of his body against hers. And when sleep finally came, Kay was reliving every moment of their evening together, taking the sleepy feeling of total happiness over into dreams that had, so often in the past, been filled with panic and distress.

\* \* \*

As warm yellow sunshine streamed in through the windows, Linda, Marie and Catriona came out of their rooms to find Nessa already in the living room. She was sitting back against the large cream cushions on the couch drinking a glass of orange juice, wallowing in the balmy breeze that was floating in through the open door.

'It's really beautiful here,' Catriona exclaimed, as she sat down in an armchair, 'and your apartment is just gorgeous!'

As she said it, she looked around the room, admiring the floating muslin drapes over the windows, the large pale cream couch and the beautiful plain rugs on the polished floor.

'And would you look at the size of the TV?' Marie exclaimed, running her hand along the length of the top of the screen. 'Do you know, I think what they say is true, everything is bigger in America. I wonder does that go for the men too?' she asked suggestively, raising a quizzical eyebrow.

'God, Marie, we're here five minutes, and you're already thinking about sex!' Linda answered with a smile. 'We can't bring you anywhere.'

The others laughed as Marie shrugged off her comment.

'It might be interesting to find out, though, wouldn't it?' she retaliated jokingly.

'Well, assuming you're not going to be finding it out this morning, Marie, could I get you an orange juice in the meantime?' Nessa asked, getting up from her seat and smiling as she walked past her into the kitchen.

'Do you know, you can actually smell the sea,' said Linda. 'Anyone for a walk before breakfast?'

'Early morning is the best time, while it's still relatively cool,' said Nessa, coming back in with a clinking jug of juice and a tray of glasses. 'And the other good thing is that it's still very quiet at this hour. We'll have the place to ourselves.'

True to Nessa's word, the glistening sand stretched out for miles, and there wasn't a soul to be seen.

Skipping on ahead towards the ocean, Catriona called back to them over her shoulder.

'I can't believe the water's so warm already, and it's only half eight, not quite Brittas, eh?'

The others laughed as she splashed at the water's edge, each glad that they were on this magnificent beach, thousands of miles away from their responsibilities at home. Walking along the hot, golden sand, Nessa pointed out some of the stunning houses whose owners she knew.

'I can't believe that people own these houses just to come out here once or twice a year,' Linda said, as Nessa showed them another seasonally deserted coastal home, 'I think I'd stay here all the time.'

'They must have more money than sense if you ask me,' Marie agreed, looking thoughtfully at her feet as tiny waves broke gently over them. 'I imagine I'd be here all year round if I had an apartment.'

'Ah, but, when you have kids still in school, and a family business back in Ireland, it's not quite as easy as you'd like it to be,' Nessa said, defensively.

'Oh, I know,' Linda reassured her. 'Sure, we all have a million commitments at home, but isn't it nice to daydream a little?'

'I suppose, especially when we're already here, and we left drizzling rain back at home yesterday morning.'

'Exactly, I know which place I'd rather be,' Catriona joined in, returning to the group.

'Now there's a girl with the right attitude,' Marie affirmed, putting her arm around Catriona's shoulders, 'but there mightn't be any more fun unless I get some food into me – I'm starving!'

'She has a point,' Nessa agreed, laughing, 'and with a twenty minute walk back across the beach, I think we should probably head back about now.'

'I wonder if it's still raining in Dublin?' Catriona speculated as they turned around and headed for home. 'I wonder what they're all doing?'

'Well, I'll tell you one thing,' said Nessa, 'they're not heading in from a nice brisk walk on a gorgeous beach to a fabulous

American breakfast of fresh fruit and pancakes with maple syrup and...'

'Stop!' Linda cried in mock horror. 'I can't *bear* it!'

They're probably playing golf, Catriona thought to herself with a shudder. And that's what we'll be doing soon too!

\* \* \*

After their game on Tuesday, Madeleine and Kay went for lunch in the clubhouse.

'You're playing brilliantly, Madeleine,' Kay said, as she stirred a spoon through her soup. 'I'm beginning to think I'll never beat you!'

'Thanks,' Madeleine replied, smiling at her friend, 'but I almost wish I wasn't.'

Kay looked at her in confusion.

'Well, it's just that with Thomas so sick at the moment, I find golf is the only thing that actually takes my mind off him, so if it meant that Thomas would be OK again, I'd gladly play terribly.'

'Oh, I'm sorry,' Kay said, putting her hand on Madeleine's arm. 'I shouldn't have said anything.'

'Don't be silly, sure how were you to know? Anyway, at least I'm in a good position now to play in the semi-finals of the Hannah O'Toole Cup – I'm to play Eleanor O'Reilly, so I need all the practice I can get!'

'Well, I just wish I didn't have to be your guinea pig,' Kay replied, laughing. 'It doesn't do much for my ego to keep losing, you know.'

'Judging from the smile that's been plastered on your face all day, I wouldn't have thought there were any dents in your ego – what has you in such a good mood? Has there been news of Ed?'

Kay looked carefully around her, watchful in case anybody might be listening.

'If I tell you, Madeleine, you have to promise not to say another word to anyone,' she warned in a lowered voice, though still unable to get rid of the smile playing on her lips.

'I'm hurt that you even have to ask,' Madeleine replied light-heartedly, crossing her fingers to show that Kay's secret would go no further.

'OK. Remember I told you that I bumped into Declan in the Belmont and he said he'd call?' she started, looking conspiratorially around her.

Madeleine nodded.

'Well, he did call, and I went over to his house last night for dinner.'

'Go on!' Madeleine said urgently.

'And we had a Jacuzzi together.'

'And...?'

'And we had the most wonderful, intimate sex I've ever had,' Kay finished excitedly, barely controlling her voice at a whisper.

'I knew he'd call!' Madeleine exclaimed, happy that she had been right all along. 'So, are you going to see him again?' she asked.

Kay pushed away the soup in front of her, knowing that it wasn't going to get eaten.

'I don't know, I suppose so,' she said, her words tumbling out breathlessly.

Madeleine hadn't seen Kay so happy in months, years probably, and her smile was so infectious that she found herself beaming back.

'You're not going to give me a lecture on this, are you?' Kay asked cautiously. 'Because, I know what I'm doing is wrong, but I can't stop it.'

'Kay, does this look like a face that's about to reprimand you?' Madeleine asked sternly, lifting her hands up.

Kay laughed at her friend's expression.

'No, I suppose not,' she laughed. 'Thanks. And just as soon as I figure out what I'm doing, I'll let you know. Anyway,' she continued, 'enough about me. You didn't actually tell me how Thomas is getting on.'

'Oh, he's doing OK,' Madeleine answered, the smile falling from her face. 'He's coming home on Saturday, but he has to go back as an outpatient every day after that. He's really being incredibly positive about the whole thing, but I just can't seem to be as optimistic about it. I'm worried sick about him, Kay.'

Kay looked at her despondently, wishing that there was something she could say to make her feel better; but, thinking herself that Thomas's situation looked bleak, she couldn't find any words to really comfort Madeleine. Eventually, she spoke.

'And have you heard about his job?' she asked, remembering that he had been unsure as to whether they would keep it open for him.

'They've actually been fantastic about everything,' Madeleine said. 'They've told him that he can come and go as he pleases, and that his job will be there for as long as he wants it.'

'Well, that's one less thing to worry about, isn't it?' Kay asked, trying to be hopeful.

'Yes, you're right, and I'm sorry, it's just that it takes so much energy out of me to be happy when I'm with him that I don't seem to be able to keep up the act around others.'

Any further intimacies were cut short by the animated conversation of a four-ball arriving in the clubhouse, heatedly discussing their scores.

'Actually,' Madeleine said, looking at her watch, 'I'd better get going. I said I'd visit Thomas this afternoon and it's already half two.'

'Oh, OK,' Kay replied, looking at the uneaten sandwich in front of Madeleine, worried that the situation with Thomas was affecting her more than she was letting on. 'Well, make sure you call me, won't you?' she asked, giving her a hug. 'Just to let me know how it goes.'

Madeleine smiled gratefully at Kay. 'I will, and you be careful driving home. It's not safe to daydream at the wheel, you know,' she teased, as she picked up the napkin off her lap and laid it on the table.

Gathering their bags and jackets together, they both headed outside. And while Kay left the sunny car park feeling refreshed, contented, and already looking forward to her next meeting with Declan, Madeleine got into her car, dreading what the coming days and weeks would hold.

* * *

Donal replaced the receiver gently on the hook, and silently deliberated the way things seemed to be turning out. Only a few weeks ago, with Madeleine apparently back in his life, he had never felt better, but now, control over his own happiness was once again eluding him. The chance he thought he had of getting Madeleine back was slipping through his fingers, and the future was clouding over with its predictable sameness. Without Madeleine, there would only be Judith, and as long as there was Judith, there would be no joy.

Madeleine had telephoned to say that she couldn't see or speak to him again, and although it would be hard for her too, Thomas's illness had made her realise that he was her priority. She had repeated herself again and again, and Donal hadn't been sure whether she was saying it to convince herself or to convince him. Either way, he thought, sighing with inexpressible sadness, it was over. Whatever ray of hope her homecoming had shone into his mediocre life, it was now being taken away from him again.

If he was honest with himself, he couldn't blame Madeleine for her decision. Thomas was an extremely nice guy, and he knew that if it was he who had to choose between the person who had let him down in the past and the person who adored him unconditionally now, the decision would seem fairly clear-cut. And so it was for Madeleine. As a result of his own fears, Donal had ultimately forced himself out of the picture, and he was left with no one to blame but himself.

Lost in his thoughts, Donal didn't hear Judith come in the door. She startled him by speaking in the quiet room, and he looked up, surprised.

'I didn't know you were back,' he said, hoping that she hadn't caught any of his conversation with Madeleine. 'Weren't you playing a match?'

'Yes, but it finished up earlier than I expected it would. I hit really great form, couldn't do a thing wrong in fact,' she gloated with a self-satisfied smile, 'and it was all over by the fourteenth. So, now I'm in the semi-final of the Hannah O'Toole.'

'Oh, well done,' Donal congratulated her unenthusiastically. 'Who will you have to play?'

'Catherine O'Neill, and then the winner of that match,' Judith chuckled slightly, as if the thought of losing was comically unrealistic to her, 'will play Madeleine O'Connell, who has apparently already won her semi-final.'

Donal tried hard to look nonchalant at the mention of Madeleine's name.

'What sort of players are they?' he questioned, hiding his discomfort.

'I'm not really sure,' Judith commented, oblivious to the effect that hearing her opponent's name was having on Donal, 'but they're bound to be pretty good to get this far. Whatever they're like, though, I don't plan on losing, so it's hardly an issue,' she finished, taking off her light jacket.

With her coat in one hand, she picked up a vase in the other, and looked critically at the drooping flowers standing sadly in it.

'The new cleaning lady isn't great, is she?' Judith asked, not really expecting an answer. 'I'll have to have a word with her – it's unacceptable to be so bad at something that requires so little thought.' She sniffed dismissively. 'I suppose I'd better see if I can do anything with them.'

255

With that, she walked out of the room in a flurry of disapproval to find the pruning scissors and some fresh water, leaving Donal once again alone in contemplation in the bright, quiet room.

After she had swept out of the room, he was aware of the relief he felt at her departure. He found her tiring in her relentless criticisms and over-zealous attitude towards success. He wondered whether she would win the tournament or not. He guessed that she probably would. After all, it was regularly the case that what Judith wanted, Judith got, an ethos that pervaded all aspects of her life. In fact, thinking about it, Donal realised that the only thing she hadn't got was a baby, but then, he supposed, that wasn't exactly something she could've had much control over. He had often wondered, though, whether he could have done more to help her. With his medical contacts, there must have been some avenue he could have explored for her, but then, she had never looked for or even seemed to want his help. Thinking about children, Donal's mind wandered back to the Medical Benevolent Fund dinner, and to his coincidental meeting with Frank O'Leary. He had been in Belfast for so long that it would be great to have him around Dublin again; they might even be able to grab a game of golf together some time, he thought. One issue that had remained unresolved since that night, however, was the fact that he was sure Judith had never mentioned seeing Frank to him. They had been great friends in college, so he was quite positive he would have remembered something like that. When he had mentioned it in the car, though, Judith had become angry, and irritably spat out that of course she had told him. It had also seemed strange to him that she had gone all the way to Belfast to see a doctor when there were plenty of good gynaecologists in Dublin, but after her initial reaction to his question, he hadn't pursued it any further. Whatever was going on, however, something didn't quite add up, and Judith's hasty retort had left Donal feeling distinctly uneasy.

# CHAPTER TWELVE

AS THE GENTLE SOUNDS OF THE WAVES BREAKING AGAINST the shore and the hum of the fan in the living room were drowned out by laughter, Catriona arrived out of the kitchen with armfuls of hot plates, her face red and flustered. She was almost sorry she'd offered to cook this evening, but she had been so tempted by all the fantastic food in the supermarkets that she had been dying all week to try her hand at putting a meal together.

'Dinner's up,' she announced triumphantly, as she put plates of steamed shrimp with spicy horseradish sauce down in front of them. 'Bon appetit!'

Awestruck by the impressive starter, Nessa, Linda and Marie were almost speechless when Catriona followed this with a main course of scrumptious chicken tortillas. She had made a mouth-watering coriander and tomato salsa to accompany them, and soon, having washed the rest of the meal down with a delicious Merlot, they all sat eyeing up the last one on the plate.

'I think I'm going to burst,' Marie complained limply afterwards, looking at her empty plate. 'I've eaten far too much.'

'No room for dessert, then?' Catriona asked temptingly, standing up to take away the empty plates.

Marie considered the offer for a minute. 'Oh, go on, then,' she acquiesced, reckoning that if it was as good as everything else they had just eaten, she'd be a fool to miss it.

Smiling, Catriona went off to the kitchen to collect the final course out of the fridge. She came back through the door carrying an impressive ice-cream cake, smothered in a rich, double-chocolate fudge and pecan sauce.

'You're not doing much for my waistline, are you?' Nessa asked, as Catriona dished her out a generous portion, 'but if it's just this once – and we are on our holidays after all,' she said, licking a bit of chocolate flake that had fallen off her slice.

'You're a real treasure, you know that,' Marie said to Catriona, who immediately blushed at the compliment. 'This food is better than you'd get in a restaurant. You should sack that chef you have in Redcliff, Linda, and put Catriona in his place.'

'Oh no!' said Catriona. 'That'd be terrible, I wouldn't...'

'Well, we could wait till he retires then,' said Marie soothingly. 'I'm only teasing, Catriona. But you could do worse, all the same, Linda. And she's started playing great golf, too. The climate seems to agree with you, Catriona.'

'Absolutely,' Linda agreed. 'I haven't eaten as well in a long time. And you have played very well, Catriona, it's true.'

'Well, you've all been so encouraging,' said Catriona, slightly embarrassed to be the focus of attention, but pleased too. 'And the holiday atmosphere has really helped on the golf course. I haven't felt so nervous.'

'I told you it was mainly a question of confidence,' Linda said. 'Right, now, you've done your bit this evening. It's up to the rest of us to clear up. You sit there and have yourself a little drink. Marie and I will see to the dishes.'

'We will indeed,' said Marie heartily. 'Thanks so much, Catriona, for a lovely meal. And thank you, Nessa, for a really great holiday.'

Getting up to clear the table, Linda took the first of the plates into the kitchen, while Marie handed Nessa the brandy bottle.

Catriona couldn't believe how nice everyone was being to her, and as the sugar-brown liquid was poured into her tumbler, she felt that everything was almost absolutely perfect. She closed her eyes and listened to the comforting chink of dishes being stacked in the machine in the next room.

It had been a wonderful holiday. Catriona had really come out of her shell. Marie had regaled them all week with hilarious jokes and her good-natured attempts to fix them all up with whatever good-looking men she could spot at the club or on the beach. Nessa was delighted everyone had enjoyed themselves so much, and was pleased that the apartment was being put to such good use. Linda had enjoyed it too, and had managed to put her worries about Ian to the back of her mind for most of the time.

'I think I'm ready for a drink, now,' Marie said, coming back from the kitchen and falling down exhausted on the couch. 'I still haven't got over the way that bitch in the outlet mall today stole the last size twelve of that gorgeous Givenchy dress.'

The others laughed, remembering the argument they had dissuaded Marie from having with a rather formidable-looking woman in the evening-dress section.

Three drinks later, Catriona sat cross-legged on the floor in the path of the breeze coming from the open door, and Marie, Nessa and Linda each sat sprawled out, relaxing on the other seats around the room. While Marie prepared their fourth drink, conversation turned to sex, and by the time she had taken her seat again on the couch, Catriona was disclosing her most embarrassing encounter. She had really opened up to them over the course of the week, and they were beginning to realise that there was a lot more to her than just a shy personality hidden beneath baggy clothes and a mane of long hair.

'God, I'll never forget the time when myself and my boyfriend first decided to have sex,' she began, putting her hands over her face at the memory of the night. 'At the time, I was really against the Pill, I didn't want any chemicals in my body. Given that I was smoking like it was going out of fashion at the time, it was a bit of an ironic moral stand to take, but at eighteen, it seemed like the right idea. Anyway, I wanted to use some other form of contraception, so I went off to the family planning clinic and they showed me how to use the cap, explaining that I had to use spermicidal jelly with it.'

Catriona ran her hand through her hair as if deliberating whether she should go on with the story, but seeing the interested faces around her, she knew that she was already in too far to stop.

'Well, as you all know, I can be quite shy at times,' she continued, at which the others laughed, 'and I was so mortified when they were giving me the instructions on how to use it, that I didn't really listen. I think I was concentrating too hard on not blushing or something, so I hardly took in a word of their advice, and left the clinic without having a clue about what I was meant to be doing,' Catriona said, taking another sip of her drink. 'Anyway, one night, when my boyfriend's parents were out for the evening, we decided to finally do it. Obviously, I was a bit nervous, and before I attempted to put in the cap, I had a couple of drinks which I thought would help to calm me down.'

'Oh, no,' Marie said, anticipating the direction of the story. 'I tried it sober once and couldn't get the hang of the damn thing.'

'Exactly, they're tricky at the best of times. I realise now, of course, that I hadn't a hope of getting it right when I was pissed, but sure I was totally unaware of the, well, the complications I'd encounter, at the time. When I think of it now, I can't believe how cheeky we were – we had decided to use his parent's bedroom – and I went into the *en suite* bathroom to get ready. I'd had so much to drink by this stage, that I think I must've been doing everything wrong, and ended up putting on far too much jelly. So, just after I had inserted it, I heard this really loud popping sound and the cap came shooting out, hitting the sink, and spraying the jelly all over the beautiful pale, beige carpet.'

There was an audible gasp as the others imagined the scenario, and Marie couldn't help laughing at the misfortune and naivety of it all.

'There I was, down on my knees, trying to clean up the mess, when my boyfriend came in, stark naked, wondering what was taking me so long,' Catriona said, mortified. 'He nearly had a fit when he saw what had happened, and we spent the rest of the night trying to clean the carpet – we didn't get to have sex at all.'

'Oh, God, that's awful,' Linda sympathised through her laughter. 'I hope you got it together eventually?'

Catriona nodded. 'Yeah, we did, but only after I decided to go on the Pill,' she finished, taking a sip of her brandy.

'Speaking of contraception,' Linda said, 'when I started the menopause, I went on the HRT patch, and shortly after I'd started to use it, we were invited on a business trip with Ian's boss and his wife. We were staying in this amazing hotel in Milan, and on our last free morning, we had arranged to meet them for breakfast before going sightseeing. I'll never forget the heat. It was nearly forty degrees, and Ian had put on the lightest pair of shorts he could find. Anyway, we were all queuing to be seated in the little café, and as we were chatting away, Ian's boss happened to glance down. "I see you're using the patch," he said to Ian, "Do you find it any good?" Ian, of course hadn't a clue what he was talking about, but looking down as well, I knew straight away what he was asking.'

The others sat forward too, wondering themselves what Ian's boss had been talking about.

'You see,' Linda continued, 'we had been having a bit of nookie that morning, and my patch somehow got stuck onto Ian's leg without either of us noticing. When we were late then for breakfast, we decided to leave our showers until afterwards, and just got dressed in a hurry so as not to keep his boss waiting. It turned out that his boss had thought that Ian was using the male testosterone patch for a bit of help with getting it up – poor Ian nearly died when I told him.'

'I can understand why,' Nessa said, imagining the embarrass-ment. 'Did he ever mention it again?'

'Thankfully, no,' said Linda, 'but I don't think Ian was ever able to be quite as relaxed around him as he used to be. Pass me that wine over there, would you? I need another drink just thinking about it.'

It wasn't just the embarrassment of having told her story that had Linda diving for the wine bottle, it was the thought of how well she and Ian had got on in those days, how well she had thought they were still getting on – until all this had started. Two days previously, she had tried repeatedly to call him at home. After listening to the dial tone ring out several times on their home phone, she had eventually got through to him early one evening, on his mobile. What Linda heard however, was something that she was totally unprepared for. As Ian hurriedly tried to reassure her that everything at home was fine and that, really, she had no need to worry about him, Linda had heard a woman's voice calling him in the background. For what seemed like an eternity, she remained silent at her end of the phone, dumbstruck that her husband could even consider entertaining a conversation with her while he had another woman there with him. Devastated, she had rushed her goodbye, and broken into tears.

That's when it had all come out. Nessa had found her in a snivelling heap on the sofa by the phone, and she had admitted that she was worried that her husband might be having an affair.

'But… but,' Nessa had stumbled, putting her arm around Linda's shaking shoulders, 'what makes you think that?'

Telling the others about seeing Denise's name flashing up on the screen of Ian's mobile, Linda began crying all over again.

'And worst of all,' she went on, 'he seems to be so happy at the moment that he doesn't even notice how upset I am.'

'Maybe there's an innocent explanation,' Nessa had said, trying to comfort her. 'Maybe…'

And then Linda decided to tell them everything. She explained how she had listened to the voicemail on Ian's telephone a couple of weeks earlier, about how he had lied about going to play bridge, and especially, about how he had seemed so happy that she was going away for the week. Nessa and Marie were astonished. Linda and Ian had seemed like such a solid couple that they just couldn't believe he would ever be unfaithful.

Pouring a large glass for herself now, Linda looked up at the group.

'Please, someone else say something,' she said, laughing. 'One of you girls must have a more embarrassing story than that? Take the spotlight off me for a while!'

'Yeah, go on,' Catriona joined in, beginning to regret having mentioned anything about her own experiences. The drink had momentarily loosened her tongue, and she was starting to regret it.

'I suppose I can remember one rather embarrassing experience,' Nessa said as the wine bottle got passed in her direction. Catriona sat back, a little relieved. 'Myself and James were staying with my in-laws one weekend, and after a particularly large Sunday lunch, which had been washed down with equal quantities of red wine, we decided to go up to bed for a rest.'

Marie looked sceptically at her.

'A "rest", Nessa?' she said, unprepared to believe that their intentions had been so honourable.

'Honestly,' Nessa replied, laughing, 'that's all we had planned, but, well, we got a little carried away...'

'Ah ha!' Marie said, 'I knew it.'

'... and one thing led to another, and we ended up having one of the best "rests" I've ever had. We forgot, however, that the bed was much smaller than ours at home, and we fell dramatically out of it and landed with a thud on the floor.'

'Oh, my God,' said Catriona, cringing herself as she imagined how embarrassed she would be if Mike's parents ever heard them. 'Where were your in-laws at the time?'

'Unfortunately, directly underneath us in the sitting room, reading the Sunday papers,' Nessa said, laughing, 'and we made quite a bang. After all, I'm not exactly small! Anyway, his father came rushing upstairs to find out what was wrong, and James, putting his hand over my mouth to stop me laughing, answered that a heavy book had just fallen off the shelf.'

'Some book! What was it, the Kama Sutra?' Marie said, winking at Nessa. 'And did he believe you?'

'Well, I don't know that he exactly believed us, but he certainly went back down the stairs quicker than he came up them. I think he must've realised what had happened. I don't know who was more mortified, though, when we went back into the sitting room, us or James's parents. Needless to say, we didn't stay for tea.'

'I'll bet you didn't,' Marie said, wiping away a tear of laughter, and helping herself to another brandy.

'What about you, though, Marie? You must have some shocking anecdotes to share,' Nessa said, relieved that her embarrassment was over.

'Oh, you know me, girls, the nuns had such an influence over me that I'd never do anything untoward or impolite.'

'Pull the other one,' Nessa said, raising an eyebrow. 'I'd say you've enough stories to put the whole lot of us to shame.'

'Honestly,' Marie replied with an innocent look. 'I can't think of anything interesting enough to tell you.'

'Oh, look,' Linda said, pointing out the window. 'I think I just saw a little pig flying past the window!'

The others laughed as Marie conceded to them with a nod. 'All right, then. You've twisted my arm.'

The others settled back, and Marie began her story.

'Well, when Billy and I were newly married, he went off to work one morning, earlier than usual, and I went back to bed for a while. He was gone about fifteen minutes when I heard his car coming back up the driveway. I just caught sight of the top of the red bonnet going past as I stood up. I assumed that Billy had forgotten something, and I decided to surprise him with a little more than he had come home for.'

Marie winced as a gulp of brandy slid down her throat.

'So, anyway, I ripped off whatever I was wearing, rushed down the stairs, stark naked, and threw open the front door before he had the chance to put his key in.'

She paused dramatically, while the others sat, eager to hear what happened next.

'"Take me, I'm yours," I shouted, only to find someone who quite definitely wasn't Billy standing on my front porch.'

Nessa burst out laughing, almost choking on her drink, and only barely managed to ask her question through the coughing and spluttering.

'Who was it then?'

'Well, it turned out to be the local Fianna Fáil TD, who was canvassing for the upcoming elections, calling early in the morning to catch all the mothers and housewives still at home,' Marie answered, by this time laughing mischievously herself at the memory. 'He just happened to have a similar car to Billy's, and I had jumped to the wrong conclusion. I don't know who was more embarrassed, me or the TD.'

'What did you do?' Catriona asked, captivated as much by Marie's nerve at flinging the door open stark naked, as at the idea that she flashed the local Fianna Fáil candidate.

'I slammed the door in his face and ran back upstairs, got into bed and covered my face with the pillow. I never told Billy, and for some reason, I've never been able to vote for Fianna Fáil since!'

They all laughed until tears began to stream down their faces.

'I think we should make a general pact, though, that not a word of this ever gets whispered up in Redcliff,' Marie suggested, imagining the comments she would get if some of the others found out about her exposing herself to a local politician.

'Absolutely,' Catriona agreed, already embarrassed at the idea of anyone else hearing of her cap debacle.

'Right,' Nessa said, standing up, 'if we're all agreed then, I think I might hit the sack. I can tell already I'm going to have a bit of a hangover tomorrow, which will be bad enough on the plane, but I don't want to add extreme tiredness to it as well.'

'Yeah, maybe you're right,' Linda said, picking her glass up off the coffee table. 'But before we go, how about one last toast to our holiday?'

'Yes, that's a good idea,' Marie agreed.

And with that, they all raised their glasses in celebration of a wonderful week, and taking one more sip of their drinks and hugging each other goodnight, they headed off to bed in Nessa's fabulous Florida apartment for one last time.

* * *

'Miss O'Connell?'

'Yes,' Madeleine answered, not recognising the voice at the other end of the telephone.

'This is Nurse Murphy from St John's. Thomas asked me to give you a call to see if you could come over here as soon as possible.'

Madeleine's heart skipped a beat.

'Is everything OK?' she asked. She knew, however, that something had to be wrong – he had never called for her before.

'Mr O'Sullivan will be able to speak to you when you get here. Shall I tell Thomas that you'll be here shortly?'

'Em... yes, yes, of course. I'll be right there,' she said urgently, already picking up her car keys from beside the phone. 'I'm on my way.'

Quickly replacing the receiver, and without stopping to grab her coat on the way out the door, Madeleine's pulse was racing as she ran down the stairs and out to the car. She didn't want to imagine what was wrong. When she had dropped Thomas off

266

that morning, he had seemed fine, more cheerful than usual in fact, and so she just couldn't understand how things could have deteriorated so quickly.

Driving along the busy road, Madeleine seemed to get stuck at every red traffic light. Her mind was reeling with the thought of what she would be told when she got to the hospital, and she drummed her fingers impatiently on the steering wheel trying to anticipate what had happened. She didn't even know what ward to go to when she got there. Thinking that Thomas would be anxiously waiting for her until she found him, Madeleine began to panic.

Eventually, having pulled quickly into a space in the hospital car park, she ran up to the entrance, interrupted another lady looking for a friend's ward, and frantically asked where she could find Thomas Killeen.

'Miss, if you could just wait one minute, I'll be able to help you after I deal with this lady here,' the receptionist said.

'You don't understand,' Madeleine pleaded. 'I need to find him straight away, I don't have time to wait.'

'Excuse me, but I was here before you,' the elderly lady in front of her pointed out in a rather annoyed fashion.

'I know, and I'm very sorry, but it'll only take a second for the receptionist here to tell me where I have to go, and then I'll be gone,' Madeleine appealed, growing more and more distressed thinking about Thomas.

'It's OK, Mary, I'll show the lady where to go,' a familiar voice said from behind her.

She turned around to see Donal walking towards the receptionist's area, and Madeleine felt herself relax a little. At least he would be able to give her some answers.

As they walked along the corridor, she realised that it was as if there had never been anything between them. He spoke to her as a consultant, and left his voice bereft of the emotion that it was usually filled with when they talked.

267

'So how are you?' he asked as they stepped into the elevator.

'I'm not sure,' she admitted, looking at him. 'I suppose I'll know when I find out how Thomas is. What's happened, Donal?'

'Well, I'm afraid that there's been a bit of a setback and I've had to admit him,' he said regretfully.

'What kind of setback?' she questioned, fearing what could have gone so wrong.

'Well, we've been constantly monitoring his progress, and unfortunately, the tests we took this morning showed a deterioration in his condition,' Donal paused for a second, knowing that his news would be hard for Madeleine to hear. 'You see, Thomas's white cell count is down, and his urea is rising, which means, in layman's terms, that he's in danger.'

'In danger?' Madeleine repeated, fighting back the tears that were threatening to fall. Her upper lip was beginning to quiver, but she didn't want to upset Thomas further by crying before she even went in to him.

'We're doing everything we can, Madeleine,' Donal promised, 'but at this stage, you should know that all we can really do to help him is to give him medication for the pain.'

Madeleine was speechless, and instead of finding anything to say to Donal, she stood numbly silent as the elevator doors opened before them.

Finding Thomas's room, Donal stood back and allowed Madeleine to enter on her own.

'Hello,' she said, as the door closed gently behind her. Instead of Thomas's usually healthy, olive complexion, his skin had taken on a yellow hue, and he seemed to look thinner than when she had dropped him off earlier that day.

'You got my message then? Thanks for coming,' he said, smiling at her as she came over to sit on the side of the bed.

'Of course I came,' she replied. 'You know that all you have to do is ask.'

'It's not looking so good any more, Madeleine,' he said, his eyes downcast. 'I'm scared.'

She hugged him close to her and with a kiss to his forehead, began to run her fingers soothingly through his hair.

'I'm always here for you, Thomas, you know that, don't you? I'm not going anywhere,' she told him, holding him tightly.

Comforted by her presence and her touch, Thomas started to cry quietly. Listening to his sobs echoing through the still room, Madeleine's own tears were unlocked, and soon both of them sat rocking in each other's arms.

Shortly afterwards, as Thomas drifted off into an uneasy sleep, Madeleine sat looking at him, wondering why this had to have happened. He had been so healthy, and so happy with her, that it seemed too cruel to take him away now. She couldn't help feeling selfish, wondering how she would cope if he died. Her thoughts were interrupted, however, by the click of the door, as a young nurse came in to check on Thomas's drip.

'You look really tired,' she said sympathetically. 'Why don't you give yourself a break and get a cup of coffee from the café downstairs? Thomas will be asleep for a while yet.'

'Thanks, I think I will,' she answered gratefully. 'You'll keep an eye on him while I'm gone, though, won't you?'

'Of course I will,' the nurse replied, putting her hand on Madeleine's shoulder. 'Take as much time as you want.'

Madeline realised that she was glad of the break. The sandwich tasted like cardboard and the coffee was watery, but she knew that stepping out of Thomas's room for a brief change of scenery had done her good. On the way back, she passed by the chapel. It had been a long time since she had been in church, but knowing that Thomas needed all the help he could get, Madeleine decided to go inside. Sitting into one of the hard, wooden pews in the peaceful silence of the small chapel, she dipped her head in prayer. She found herself bargaining with God, promising that she would do anything if only Thomas could get better again.

Through her tears, she looked up at the faded paintings lining the walls, and swore that she would go to mass more often, spend more time with her mother, and visit her father's grave every week, if only Thomas could recover.

'Please just don't let him die,' Madeleine finally whispered, wiping her eyes.

After a few minutes more, she glanced at her watch. Seeing that she had been gone for nearly an hour, she slipped out of the quiet chapel and ran into a bathroom to splash some water on her face, then hurried up to Thomas's room, hoping that she would get back before he woke up again.

* * *

The following few days passed by in a haze. Thomas drifted in and out of consciousness and Madeleine grew to know every inch of his small room as she sat by his side. He began to appear weaker every time she saw him. His smiles, when she came in, took more and more effort, and conversations became regularly interrupted through his tiredness or shortness of breath. Madeleine knew how happy he was to have her with him, but somehow, cooling his head with a damp cloth, or pouring him a glass of water seemed insufficient to her. She felt utterly helpless as she watched him struggling to put on a brave face, and wished that she could do something more worthwhile to really help him to get better.

Madeleine soon got to know all the nurses by their first names. She couldn't believe how caring and dedicated they were, but despite knowing that Thomas would be in good hands if she left, she still insisted on coming to stay with him every day. She also got to know Thomas's mother, and found that they took comfort from each other at times when he got really bad. Occasionally, having a quick cup of coffee together during the rare moments when neither of them was in his room, Madeleine began to realise that there was so much of Thomas's life that she didn't know about. And now it seemed that she would never get the chance to find out anymore.

A couple of days later, Madeleine was just about to leave to get something to eat when Donal came into the room. Sitting back down beside Thomas's mother, she knew instantly that something was wrong. In a sympathetic voice, Donal explained that Thomas had gone into renal failure. Mrs Killeen burst into uncontrollable sobs. Not wanting Thomas to hear her so upset, she left the room, supported by one of the nurses. Madeleine sat mutely by Thomas's side, looking at his peaceful face, while Donal hovered awkwardly by the door, unsure about whether he should stay or go.

Eventually, Madeleine left the room with Donal, and thanked him for giving them the news. Outside, she suggested to Thomas's mother that she should go home, to get some rest for a while. Although it wasn't said, they both understood that this would be the last time she would leave the hospital with Thomas still alive, and so, with a melancholy resignation, she agreed.

Alone again with Thomas, Madeleine was torn between wanting the tiredness and worry to be over, and wanting it never to end. She couldn't bear to think about him dying, and yet a part of her had become numb to the reality of it. While he was there in front of her, she found it difficult to ever believe he could die, and when he woke up, and made a concerted effort to be cheerful for her benefit, Madeleine's heart nearly broke just thinking about what he must be going through.

Not long after she had sat down, Thomas began to stir, lifting his eyelids slowly and smiling sleepily as Madeleine's form came into focus for him.

'Hello, you,' he said, covering her hand with his own.

'Hello, yourself,' she replied, trying to smile back at him. 'Your mum's just popped home for a little while to get some sleep, but she'll be in again before dinner this evening. Is there anything you want that I could ask her to pick up for you?'

'No, no, thanks. I already have everything I need with me here,' he answered, looking intently at her. 'Madeleine, I was thinking earlier... I never said it to you before, but I've felt it for a long time – you do know that I love you, don't you?'

Madeleine leaned in closer to kiss him. 'Of course I do,' she replied. 'And I love you too.'

Smiling, Thomas kissed her weakly back before resting his head down against the soft pillow.

'Just wanted to get that cleared up, you know?'

'Well,' Madeleine said with a laugh. 'I'm glad we've got it all sorted now.'

Noticing his eyelids beginning to droop again, she pulled the sheet up over his chest, and rubbed his forehead, whispering 'Sleep tight', as she watched him drift back into a deep slumber.

Two days later, Madeleine sat in the same seat listening as Mrs Killeen cried pitifully at the other side of his bed. Thomas had died peacefully in a heavy sleep, at seven o'clock. His departure from this world had seemed so subtle that for a moment, Madeleine hadn't quite known what had happened. In fact, it was only when the nurse asked her kindly to leave so that she could lay him out, that his death began to sink in. Together with Thomas's mother, Madeleine went out into the gloomy corridor, and the two women clung to each other as tears streamed down their faces.

'Can I drive you home?' Madeleine asked her gently, later on that evening, when there seemed no reason left for them to stay in the hospital. It had been nearly two hours since Thomas had died, and there was nothing to do now but to go home.

'Oh, yes, yes,' she replied wearily. 'That would be great, thanks. My sister is coming up from Cavan tonight, so I'll have someone with me,' Mrs Killeen added.

Thinking about the emptiness that she would have to return to, Madeleine simply nodded. She linked her arm through Thomas's mother's, and they walked slowly together out to the car.

When they reached Mrs Killeen's house, Madeleine put on the kettle for a cup of tea, and waited with her for her sister to arrive. Despite the heat still hanging in the evening air, the house seemed cold and empty, and Madeleine thought that Thomas's mother looked old and frail in the big house. When Madeleine heard a car pulling up in the driveway, she promised Mrs Killeen she would call her the next day, and left the house. She drove along the dark, quiet roads, back to her own empty apartment in Dún Laoghaire.

She ought to ring her mother, Madeleine knew, but instead, she phoned Kay, and as soon as she heard her friend's voice, she broke down in tears.

'Oh, Kay, he's gone,' she sobbed, feeling for the first time the magnitude of what Thomas's death would mean to her.

'Where are you now, Madeleine? I can come over straight away if you want,' Kay replied, unsure of what she could say to ease the pain.

'Thanks, Kay, but I'm really exhausted, and I think I'm just going to go straight to bed. I haven't really slept for the last few days. I just needed to call you, though.'

'Are you sure you don't want me there?' Kay asked.

'Positive, thanks, but if it's OK with you, I'd love to see you in the morning,' Madeleine said through a yawn. 'And Kay, if you'd just ring my mum for me, and tell her I'll phone her tomorrow? I just can't face it tonight. I'm too sad to talk to her.'

'Of course. I'll do that right now, and I'll be over as soon as you call me in the morning,' Kay reassured her. 'The kids will have me up at the crack of dawn anyway, so I can be there as early as you like.'

'Thanks, Kay,' Madeleine said gratefully. 'I'll call you when I'm up. See you tomorrow, then.'

True to her word, Kay arrived ten minutes after Madeleine rang at half past nine the next morning. Sensing that her friend was both physically and emotionally exhausted, Kay sat her down, and told her not to move while she got the breakfast ready. She had brought over some croissants, still hot from the bakery, and fresh coffee, and set about her preparations quietly as Madeleine sat contemplatively at the table.

'I just can't believe it, Kay,' she said eventually, taking her first sip of coffee. 'I mean, I know I've been watching him die for a few weeks now, but it all seems so surreal, I can't believe that he doesn't live upstairs anymore, or that I never get to see him again...'

As her words trailed off, Madeleine began to cry, and Kay rushed over to put her arms around her.

'I know, but isn't it better that you had him briefly in your life than not at all?' Kay said, stroking Madeleine's hair. 'And a blind man could see that he was mad about you, so you should be comforted by the fact that your just being there for him would've made his whole ordeal that bit easier.'

Madeleine broke away and looked at Kay through watery eyes.

'Thanks, I do know that, honestly, but I know that it's going to take so much time to accept that he won't be popping down from upstairs, to realise that we can't go for walks or meals together or weekends away,' she said, taking stock of everything in her life that Thomas would never be a part of any more.

'Well... I don't know what to say, Madeleine, except, I suppose, that whenever you're upset, I'm always here for you – whether it's two o'clock in the morning or four in the afternoon, you're to call me, all right?' Kay instructed her friend.

'All right,' Madeleine replied with an appreciative smile.

'Tell you what,' Kay said, going back to her own seat at the table and spreading butter on her croissant, 'why don't you come and stay with me for a couple of days, at least until the funeral is over? You shouldn't have to be here on your own at a time like this.'

Madeleine considered her offer for a moment.

'That would be great, actually, thanks,' she agreed. 'I didn't really fancy having to come back here without Thomas in the apartment above anyway.'

'Well, that's settled then,' Kay said, delighted to be able to look after her for a few days. 'You can pack a few things into a bag after breakfast and come straight back with me today.'

Madeleine was glad to have the distraction of the children while she stayed in Kay's house. As she played with them or settled arguments at dinner time, she found herself momentarily forgetting about Thomas, and she felt that the relief that came with the interruption to her thoughts was priceless. It afforded her a little time to unwind, leaving her in a better frame of mind to deal with her grief.

One thing that she did find a little difficult to deal with, however, was the change that had occurred in Ed since his rehabilitation. He had lost weight, and instead of the outgoing, gregarious and usually drunk man she had come to know, he was now withdrawn, introspective and moody – and Madeleine simply didn't know how to relate to him. Kay confided in her about his worry over the impending court case. As a result, he was proving to be little or no help with the children, and Kay admitted that she felt like she had just been given one more child to mind. She couldn't deny, though, that this new Ed was at least more considerate than the old one, and Madeleine was touched by his offer to go to the funeral with them.

The removal the following day was a brief and upsetting affair. They waited outside the church for the hearse bearing the coffin. Accompanying it inside, Madeleine wept discreetly as Kay guided her up the aisle. After some short prayers, standing outside in the chilly evening air as people milled around her, she wished that she could disappear from the crowds. She apologised to Thomas's mother for leaving so early, and, making her excuses to other guests a short while after they arrived in the nearby hotel for coffee and sandwiches, she went back to Kay's house. She knew that the funeral would be even harder for her, and so going to bed early seemed to be the best respite she could get from her mourning, at least until tomorrow came.

275

Despite foreseeing a hard day ahead, Madeleine was unprepared for how emotionally draining the actual funeral would be. When they arrived at the church, hauntingly exquisite phrases of Pachelbel's 'Canon' followed them to their pew, as the string quartet echoed the feeling of loss with the beautiful sadness of the music. Madeleine was both astounded and touched by the number of Redcliff members who had come to the church, and was struck by the irony that in such a sad situation, she really felt like she belonged for the first time since she had come home.

Madeleine managed to hold back her tears successfully for most of the service by squeezing Kay's hand and looking at everything but the coffin at the top of the aisle. She even stood up to read one of the lessons, containing her emotions just long enough for the microphone to carry her final, quavering words from the poignant passage across the dimly lit church. When a soprano stood up to sing Fauré's 'Pie Jesu', however, the dulcet notes seemed to carry with them all the pain that Madeleine was feeling, and as the soloist's voice soared to the eaves of the church, she wept into Kay's comforting shoulder.

After the final prayers and a silent drive behind the hearse to the graveyard, Madeleine stood beside Thomas's mother as she threw in a single red rose onto the coffin. Tears dropped silently from both their cheeks for the duration of the burial, and when the congregation followed the priest in the final words of a decade of the rosary, they hugged each other affectionately, bonded together in their grief.

* * *

That night, finishing her cup of tea after sitting up late talking about Thomas, Madeleine yawned tiredly and stood up.

'I think I'd better get to bed,' she said, rubbing her eyes, 'I didn't realise I was so exhausted.'

'Sure, of course you're tired,' Kay told her, standing up herself and ushering Madeleine towards the door. 'You've had a really tough day, and what you need now is a long sleep.'

'Thanks for getting me through everything today,' Madeleine said, stopping to face her in the hall. 'I don't think I could've done it on my own.'

'Don't mention it,' Kay answered with an affectionate smile, 'it's what I'm here for after all, isn't it? Anyway, goodnight, my darling,' she added, giving her a hug, 'sleep well and I'll see you in the morning. Hopefully the kids won't be up too early, and you'll be able to get a bit of a lie-in.'

Madeleine laughed, knowing that it was unlikely. They had woken her at seven o'clock that morning; and, having promised to take them for ice-cream the next day, she suspected they would have her up early again.

'Well, 'night anyway, and you sleep well too,' she said before continuing on up the stairs.

Although they were both aware of it, neither of them had mentioned Donal's presence, without Judith, at the church that day. And as Madeleine headed up to the guestroom's cosy double bed, for a brief moment, her thoughts of Thomas were interrupted. The image of Donal's concerned face looking helplessly at her, as if, somehow, her pain was his own, flashed before her eyes, and Madeleine found herself feeling relieved that he had taken off his consultant's persona for the day, to support her now as a friend.

# CHAPTER THIRTEEN

A CLEAR, BLUE SKY AUGURED WELL FOR THE FIRST DAY OF Open Week in Redcliff. The wind had stilled to a warm, gentle breeze, and with the temperature lingering in the early twenties, it seemed the perfect day to be playing golf. For Linda, Marie, Nessa and Catriona, the weather was almost reminiscent of Florida, and even Catriona was feeling good about the imminent game.

Meeting for a coffee and a sandwich before they went out on the course, the four sat in the dining room chatting, catching up on each other's news since they had come home. Nessa, holding her sandwich mid-air as if she had forgotten about it while she spoke, was telling them how James and her son Gavin had fared in her absence.

'You see, I had wanted to make sure they would be fed properly while I was away, so I cooked meals for them and left them in the freezer so they could take them out as they needed them,' she said, pausing to take a bite of her BLT, '... only, mm, sorry,' she laughed, swallowing, 'I needn't have bothered at all, because when I looked in the freezer when I got home, they hadn't touched a thing – they'd either eaten out or ordered in every night! I tell you, I won't be going to that trouble again.'

'Well, I got a nice surprise when I got home,' Catriona said. 'Mike said that while I was away, he realised just how much I did for him, and so he had dinner ready for me for a change when I walked in the door.'

'Sure, of course he missed you,' Linda said. 'Isn't he lucky to have you?'

'*And* your cooking skills,' Nessa added, remembering the mouth-watering meals Catriona had prepared for them on holiday. 'No offence to Mike or anything, but I'm sure that whatever he cooked, it wasn't half as good as what you'd come up with.'

'Maybe not, but didn't he do his best?' Linda said in a motherly tone. She knew how much it meant to Catriona to feel so appreciated, and winked at her inconspicuously as the others chatted on about her cooking.

'Well, speaking of cooking,' Catriona said coyly, 'I've got some news.'

'You've been promoted to chef in that restaurant you work in, I suppose,' said Linda.

Catriona looked crestfallen. 'Yes,' she said. 'How did you know?'

'Oh, I'm so sorry, Catriona. I didn't mean to take the wind out of your sails. That's great news. Congratulations!'

'Thanks,' said Catriona. 'The chef finally decided that full-time work didn't suit him, and so he left. And the boss asked me if I'd be interested, so…'

'I knew it!' said Nessa. 'I knew they'd discover you one day. We couldn't get to keep you all to ourselves, as our own private chef. The world was bound to find out. Congratulations, Catriona.'

'Well done!' Marie added.

'The thing is, though,' said Catriona, 'I'd just been about to ask Linda if there was any possibility of my taking over some of the catering here. Not put the chef out of work, of course, nothing like that, just maybe come up with some additional menus, on Saturday, for example, when the kitchen is low on staff... and then *this* happened!'

'Well, it's Redcliff's loss,' said Nessa. 'Just as well,' she added, patting her stomach. 'It mightn't do much for this if you had started here.'

The others laughed as Nessa licked her lips at the thought of Catriona's cooking every week.

'Oh, and just one other little thing as well,' Catriona said, almost forgetting about it herself. 'I've made up my mind, and I'm going to get laser treatment for my eyes and get rid of my glasses.'

'Well, you're certainly full of surprises today,' Linda marvelled, 'we'll have to take you to Florida more often.'

'Good for you, though,' Marie congratulated her, delighted that she was finally beginning to recognise that there was a fabulous-looking girl beneath all of her old and unfashionable apparel. 'You'll look stunning.'

'And with all these new changes,' Catriona finished with a soft giggle, 'you never know, I might even start to play better golf.'

'Well, you don't need laser treatment to help you with that,' Nessa said. 'You played really well in Florida. You beat me in that last game. So, if you need corrective eye surgery, then I don't know what I need!'

As the others laughed, Marie sat happily listening, thinking about the events her own return had provoked. The day after she had come home, desperate for some good sex, she had phoned Ciaran, something neither of them had ever done before. He was at work when she called, and if he was surprised to hear from her, he didn't show it. During their brief conversation, Marie told him that she was all alone and waiting for him to come over, and he agreed to call to the house later that day, during his lunch break.

In Florida, Marie and the others had visited the lingerie store, Victoria's Secret, when they had gone to Tampa on one of their many shopping trips. Marie had spent a small fortune, and left with bags full of new and sexy underwear, bought especially with Ciaran in mind. It was one of the more revealing ensembles that she wore beneath her robe when she answered the door, and as soon as Ciaran was safely inside, she slid the silk knot open, and let the robe fall to the floor. He smiled his approval of the black lacy basque with suspenders and stockings, and without saying a word, grabbed her eagerly towards him.

'How do you like your present?' she asked flirtatiously, as he ran his fingers beneath the intricate stitching around her bra. Instead of answering, he kissed her passionately on the lips, and, without even attempting to make it to the bedroom, they had sweltering sex right there on the hallway floor.

Marie was aware, however, that the girls would be shocked if they ever found out what she got up to, and imagined that it could possibly change things between them if they realised. She also knew that if people began to find out about their meetings, Ciaran's position in Redcliff might be jeopardised, so they continued to maintain their unspoken agreement not to utter a word of their affair to anyone. So, searching for some other piece of news since her homecoming, Marie talked instead of how well John had done in his medical exams, getting a secret thrill as she caught Ciaran's eye behind the bar, while the others congratulated her enthusiastically on her son's behalf.

During their conversation, Nessa, Catriona and Marie couldn't help noticing that Linda seemed to have something weighing heavily on her mind. They had each guessed that her suspicions about Ian's affair might have been affirmed since she got home, and no one wanted to ask her what had happened. Needing to share her problem, however, Linda broached the topic herself, casting her dilemma into the group's discussion to see of they could shed any light on the recent developments.

'I thought when I got back,' she started sadly, 'that Ian would have realised how much he missed me, and would want to spend more time with me once I got home.' She left her uneaten sandwich on the plate and covered it with her serviette. 'But since that day when he picked me up from the airport, I've hardly seen him at all.'

Linda looked around the table in the hope that somebody would be able to say something encouraging about the situation, or advise her on what to do. Instead, all she met with were blank, albeit sympathetic, faces.

'Well, I really thought that he looked delighted to see you at the airport,' Nessa offered hopefully, 'and that has to count for something.'

'I know,' Linda agreed, 'but it's what he's like when he's *not* with me that bothers me.'

Just as she finished speaking, a few of the ladies' golfing partners came over to join them. Nessa and Marie were playing with their brothers-in-law, Catriona had invited one of the waiters from work and Linda had arranged to play with Donal.

'Sure, we may as well all go out together,' Marie said. 'You're meeting Donal at the first tee anyway, aren't you, Linda?'

'Yes, that's a good idea, just let me grab my visor from my locker, I forgot to get it earlier,' she said, casting her problem to the back of her mind, as they all stood up to go outside.

A few minutes later, they made their way to the first tee. Wondering where her partner was, Linda looked around her.

'He's usually very punctual,' she said, slightly baffled as to where Donal could have got to. 'I hope nothing's happened to him, but of course he sometimes has an emergency at the...'

Her voice trailed off as she stared ahead of her in amazement.

Standing at the first tee box, with a beaming smile on his face, was Ian, dressed in full golfing regalia. From his Pringle sweater, down to his navy slacks, he looked like a well-seasoned golfer.

'Ian!' Linda exclaimed incredulously, almost lost for words as she took in the sight of her husband standing beside a golf trolley containing a very obviously new set of clubs, 'What are you doing here? You don't play golf!'

'Ah, but I do now,' he said with a smile. 'I've been taking lessons for the last few months in the hope that I might discover some natural talent for the game. And after playing with friends – on their courses, God help them, because I wanted to surprise you – here I am, hoping that you won't mind if I'm your partner today?'

Linda remained stunned as the others around them stood delighted at his revelation.

'You see,' he went on, coming over to her, 'I was just so proud of you when you became lady captain, that I wanted to do something really special for you, and you're always talking about what a pity it is that we can't play golf together, so I decided to fix that,' he said, picking her up and spinning her round. 'I will apologise in advance, however, for my bad golf.'

Linda laughed as he put her back down.

'But I don't understand. How did you manage to keep it a secret?' she asked, still dumbfounded that Ian would do something so wonderful for her. 'I never had any idea.'

'Well, I had all of the bridge group sworn to secrecy, and had them cover for me whenever I needed the excuse to go for a lesson. And then, Denise, of course, had the unenviable task of actually trying to turn me into some semblance of a decent golfer, and fitted me in whenever she had a cancellation, on top of all my regular lessons.'

'Denise?' Linda asked, realising how wrong she had been to so hastily jump to conclusions.

'Yes, that poor woman very nearly strangled me a couple of times,' Ian said, laughing, 'but we got there eventually and at least now I'll be able to tell you the difference between a sand iron and a driver.'

Suddenly, everything made sense to Linda, the calls, the messages, the unaccountable absences, and she was flooded with a sense of relief so great that she almost wanted to cry.

'Oh, Ian,' she said eventually, swallowing back her tears, 'no one has ever done anything so incredible for me before, and here I was, thinking all the time that...'

'Thinking what?' Ian asked, knocking his visor sideways as he kissed her on the forehead.

Linda knew that she couldn't possibly tell him what she had thought – that she had suspected him of being unfaithful, and that she had told the girls in Florida about Denise and his suspected affair. She felt dreadful.

'Oh, nothing,' she said, hugging him, 'it doesn't matter now.'

Hugging him tightly again, and wiping away the tears that had escaped, she began to comprehend just how much he had done for her, and in that moment, as they stood there together, Linda loved Ian more than she had ever thought it possible to love anybody.

'Well, nice to know I got something right,' he joked, as he looked into her eyes. 'And now... shall I drive off?'

Watching proudly as he selected his driver from the trolley, Linda caught Nessa's eye, and smiled. It didn't seem to matter any more what she had suspected. All that was important now, she realised, was that she had been wrong – thankfully.

* * *

'Well, that didn't last long, did it, your new-found sobriety?' Kay asked, her voice a mixture of disgust and disappointment. The sight was a familiar one. Red eyes, the stale odour of beer-laden breath, the slight, but unmistakable unsteadiness on his feet and, of course, the signature cigar waving expansively in his hand as he tried to justify his drinking. Kay felt sickened by what she saw.

'Ah, lay off will you? It was just a couple of beers. I'm well able to handle it,' Ed replied, taking off his jacket and throwing it on a chair. 'I told you I wasn't going to drink spirits any more. You see, I know that spirits don't agree with me, but beer is fine. A different story altogether. In fact,' he slurred, leaning intrusively towards her, 'you should be happy that I know what I can and can't handle. I realise now what spirits do to me.'

Ed sat down at the table and started flicking through the newspaper that was already open on it. This was much more like the man she was used to. Argumentative, self-assured, superbly confident and, just as it had been almost from the start of their marriage, not caring about what Kay might want. She realised she had been stupid to ever think that rehabilitation might have changed him. It had only succeeded in suppressing his true colours for a couple of months, but the old Ed was beginning to resurface, and now, Kay supposed, it would only be a matter of time before they went back to the way they were before the accident.

One of his friends had picked him up to go to a rugby match that morning and, as Claudette was on her day off, Kay had found a replacement to play in the open day for her, staying at home instead to mind the children. Initially, she had been happy that Ed was going out. He was due to go back to work the following week, and she had thought that a bit of socialising would be good for him to get used to being out again. Since he had returned from the Belmont, he had stayed at home most days, preferring to sit on the couch and watch sport on the television to going out with friends. Leaving the safety of the house had proven to have had the wrong effect however, and when Ed came home drunk that afternoon, Kay knew that whatever pretence they had been living under for the past couple

285

of months, the reality was coming crashing down around them now.

Throwing the paper aside, Ed got up and strolled over to the fridge. He swayed slightly on his feet as he surveyed its contents, and after a couple of seconds, roughly closed it again.

'I'll be back soon,' he said simply, without looking at Kay, and walked out of the kitchen. Seconds later, she heard the front door slam with a bang.

She prayed silently that he hadn't gone to the pub. Her nerves were fraying as things were, but if he came back even more intoxicated and obnoxious, she didn't know how she would cope. In a way, Kay's prayers were answered, as she heard the key turning in the door about fifteen minutes later. Standing back to let him pass in the kitchen, she watched with a quiet resignation as he took the familiar six-pack of beer out of a brown paper bag. Taking one out of its ring, and putting the remaining five into the fridge, he went into the television room, oblivious to the tear that had fallen down her cheek.

Kay listened to the children begin to argue and cry, as Daddy switched from cartoons over to the football, and she collapsed into a chair, trying to block out the sound of chaos descending in the next room. She couldn't believe that after all those weeks in rehab, the family days, the promises, that he could so easily throw away everything they'd been through. In a way, she wasn't surprised at all. Kay knew that she would never have been with Declan if she had known that things would be any better with Ed.

'Is this it?' she thought to herself, as she heard Dominic begin to whine for her, and call her name. 'Is this all that lies ahead of me?'

She felt sick thinking that the years rolling out before her contained nothing more than avoiding and placating a drunken husband, and trying to maintain a lie to her children that their father was still a good person. After things deteriorated to the way they used to be, Kay knew that they would only get worse again from there. She would always be afraid to let him look after the children. She could never be sure he would hear them if they hurt themselves and he was too drunk to notice, or that he wouldn't leave the grill on before he went to bed, and burn the house down. She wouldn't have three children, she would have four, only there would be nothing stopping Ed from abusing her efforts to look after them.

Picking up Dominic as he crawled through the open doorway, Kay thanked God that she had met Declan again. He was all she had been able to think about while she was listening to Ed slur his excuses, and the comparison between the two men had been startlingly clear to her. Kay knew now that Declan was ten times the man Ed would ever be, but her foolish naivety had been too dumb and impressionable to notice that at a time when it could have made a difference to her life.

Thinking about their evening together, Kay decided to call Declan later that night when the children would be in bed, and Ed would be inevitably passed out on the couch. As she stacked dirty dishes in the dishwasher and Dominic chatted to himself on the floor beside her, Kay hoped that she would be able, somehow, to keep Declan in her life. Because if she didn't, she knew that her hope for a happy future would slowly wither away before her, trapped in a role she never remembered asking for, and tied to a man that she couldn't abide.

\* \* \*

'Hi Mad, it's me, just wanted to say hello and see how you're doing. Give me a call if you want to. OK, well, eh, hopefully talk to you soon, then. Take care of yourself, bye.'

Madeleine listened to Donal's message again and again until she was able to repeat the words in her head as he spoke. Although she had made up her mind to ring him, it somehow seemed easier to keep listening to his voice message, than to actually call him herself.

It had been a couple of weeks since Thomas had died, and Madeleine still felt unable to lessen the feeling of depression that had descended on her since that last day in the hospital. She had moved home for a couple of days after the funeral, to avoid going back to her apartment, and on her own again now, she longed for the company of her mother. She had taken Snowy out for walks on the beach, glad of companionship that didn't require conversation, and spent countless hours sitting alone, interrupted only by her mum bringing in cups of tea.

Despite the comfort of being at home, however, nothing really seemed to help the sadness and isolation Madeleine was cocooned in, and she only felt more desolate and without purpose as the days went by. Gradually, as she searched for a way to move on with her life, the idea of going back to America began to form in her head. She knew that her mother would be heartbroken, but Madeleine realised that apart from her and Kay, there was nothing to keep her in Ireland. In New York, there were still numerous friends, a good job, and an apartment, which would be free for her to move into again in a couple of weeks. The only thing holding her back, as usual, was Donal; but, determining not to believe that he was a reason for staying, she finally picked up the phone to call him.

'Hi, there, Mad,' he said happily, recognising her name on his screen. Madeleine was a little unnerved, having expected, for some reason to ring through to his voicemail.

'Oh, hi… I was just ringing really to say thanks for the call, it's nice to know you're thinking of me,' she said, trying to sound casual.

'I'm always thinking of you,' he replied, 'and I've been worried about you. I actually wasn't even sure I should call, but I couldn't not check to see how you're doing.'

'Well, thanks,' she said, 'it is difficult, but then I don't suppose it's ever easy is it?'

There was a brief silence as they both considered what to say next. Madeleine was finding it hard to remain focused on her reason for calling. His voice and his concern were weakening her desire to tell him she was leaving. She knew, however, that if she was to go through with it, then she would have to remain distant. If she exposed her emotions again, he would be able to change her mind, and deep down Madeleine knew that this was exactly what she was trying to avoid. It was clear that neither of them knew what the boundaries were between them now, and it was proving difficult to uphold the platonic friendship she had previously instigated. Taking a deep breath, she continued.

'I had actually intended calling you, anyway,' she said confidently. 'I've been thinking, and... well, I just wanted to let you know. I've decided to go back to the States.'

'*What*?' Donal said, aghast. 'But why would you do that?'

'What's here for me Donal, really?' Madeleine replied, knowing already what his answer would be. 'I have friends, a job and an apartment all waiting for me in New York, and I seem to be running out of reasons to stay in Ireland.'

'But... but, you've friends here,' he said, frantically.

'Friends, Donal?' Madeleine asked. They were both choosing their words carefully to play around the subject neither of them wanted to bring up again, but the insinuation was heavy and each sentence spoken down the line was loaded with meaning. 'Exactly, I know I have friends, but you have to see that that's not enough for me.'

'Madeleine, can we not meet and talk this over?' Donal pleaded, desperation revealing itself in the urgency of his question.

'There's nothing to talk about,' she answered, not unkindly. 'I've made up my mind, and I know that this is for the best.'

'But... when, I mean... how soon will you be going?' he asked, stuttering his words.

'I'll stay to play in the final of the Hannah O'Toole, but I'll go pretty much straight away after that.'

Donal remained quiet. He understood why she was going, but he couldn't comprehend that she was actually leaving him again.

'You can't do this, Mad!' he said eventually, unwilling to accept that she had really made up her mind. 'You can't go.'

'I can, and I will, Donal,' Madeleine replied, affected by his obvious pain, but annoyed that, even now, he couldn't tell her what she realised she still wanted to hear. 'Nothing's changed,' she finished simply, 'and at least if I go back to New York, I can start rebuilding my life again.'

'Please, please,' he begged, 'just meet me, Mad, and we can talk about this together.'

Madeleine knew, however, that if she saw him again, for even a second, her resolve would crumble, and they would start on the roller coaster all over again. She couldn't see him. It was simple.

'I'm sorry, I just can't. Please trust me that this really is for the best.' She took a deep breath. 'Goodbye, Don.'

As she lifted the phone from her ear, she could hear a tiny voice calling her name, but quickly pressing 'End Call', she cut off Donal's pleas, and sat in silence, crying.

She might have been through separation from him before, but sitting alone with tears pouring down her face, Madeleine realised that it never got any easier. At least this time, she thought to herself, would be the last – she would never come back, and she would never fall for Donal again.

* * *

Donal kept the mobile to his ear for almost a minute, hardly believing what was happening. It had never crossed his mind that Madeleine would leave. His hands began to shake as the reality of her departure dawned on him. How could they keep doing this to each other? How could he keep hurting himself and the person he loved most in the world? Finally allowing his mind to acknowledge this truth, Donal felt worse than he had in years, since their first separation. Putting the phone on the desk, he fought the urge to call her back to try and change her mind. His pensive solitude was interrupted, however, when Judith opened the study door, and pierced the silence with the sound of her stilettos on the polished wooden floor.

'Hello,' she said light-heartedly, 'I heard you talking from the kitchen, who were you on to?'

'Oh, eh… it was just golf business, nothing you'd be interested in,' he answered distractedly. For once, he was not prepared to carry on their façade of being happily married, and instead, sat looking at her in silence. He took in her immaculate appearance, and noticed, as if for the first time, the flawless picture of the woman in front of him. She was tastefully dressed, and perfectly made up, but elegance, he realised, was all she exuded. There was no hint of personality emanating from her, and just as she would tidy a stray hair, or powder away a shine on her nose, so too did she cover all traces of the real Judith. Donal began to scrutinise her expression and to imagine the thoughts behind her cold eyes, and it suddenly occurred to him – he hated her. She was hard and emotionless, and compared to Madeleine's warmth and beauty, her character and attractiveness amounted to no more than a shop mannequin's. The cruel irony of their marriage struck him as he contemplated their loveless union, and the absence of children, at that moment, felt like his punishment for hurting Madeleine as much as he had. In the eerie stillness of the quiet room, Judith began to feel unnerved by his penetrating gaze.

'Why are you staring at me?' she asked uncomfortably. 'Is there something wrong?'

'Yes, and no,' he answered.

His enigmatic response unsettled Judith further. 'What do you mean, Donal, what's the matter with you?' she asked, trying to hide her concern with a tone of impatience.

'Well,' he conceded, 'I was actually just thinking about children, about what a pity it is that we never had any.'

'Oh, for God's sake, you're not going on about that again, are you?' she said defensively. 'You're not even really interested in having a family. You never bring up the subject, and your interest in those tests I took was minimal to say the least.'

Judith knew that she was treading on thin ice. Donal had tried everything he could to be involved with her at the time, but she hoped that maybe she would be able to deflect any more questions if she retaliated angrily.

Donal stood up from behind the desk.

'How dare you insinuate that I wasn't interested,' he seethed. 'No matter how concerned I was, you always brushed my questions off with vague answers and impatient replies, somehow making me feel guilty for even asking. Did you ever, even for a second, consider how I might have felt about the whole thing?' he spat out, not allowing her time to reply. 'No, Judith, you never gave me a bit of credit for possibly being upset about it. So the only choice I had left was just to support you by not saying anything, and by being as sensitive as I could when you came back from doctors' surgeries, time after time, without any answers or solutions.'

All of the anger he had felt at having to marry her and the frustration and hurt he was going through at losing Madeleine again suddenly became too much for Donal to bear. As they stood facing each other, the easy-going, laid-back husband that Judith was used to was now replaced by a man she had never seen before, and she was beginning to feel nervous.

'And why did you never tell me about going to see Frank O'Leary?' he continued, colour rising in his cheeks as he spoke passionately. 'And don't tell me you did, because I was in college with him, and I know I would've remembered.'

Unsure of what to say next, Judith decided that her only approach could be one of apathy, and stepping towards him, answered his interrogation condescendingly.

'I can't believe you're dragging all this up again, Donal,' she began, a little shakily. 'How many times do I need to tell you that I most definitely did tell you about Frank. It's hardly my fault if you don't listen to me.'

Judith looked at her watch, as Donal, lost for words, stared incredulously back at her.

'Anyway, I have an important client coming tomorrow, so can we drop this please?' she asked, without expecting an answer. 'I have a ton of work to do, and I want to get up to the driving range to practise for the Hannah O'Toole before I start it.'

With that, she stormed out, leaving Donal tired and frustrated, alone again in the room.

Although unable to prove that she had never told him about Frank, he was incensed by Judith's reaction, and he determined to confirm his point. He would love to be able to see Frank's files on the consultation, to find out what, if anything, she had been told. He knew, however, that ethically, he could never ask Frank to do such a thing. What went on between doctor and patient was strictly confidential, even when there were close friendships involved.

'There must be some other way of finding out what she's hiding,' he thought to himself, hearing Judith's car rev up and back out of the driveway. Suddenly, an idea occurred to him and a small smile crept across his face.

'Yes,' he said quietly to himself, 'that's it!' And sitting back down on the leather chair, he reached once more for the telephone.

* * *

Judith fumed as she drove towards the driving range. Her earlier nervousness had passed, and all she felt now, as she sped along busy roads, was anger that Donal should have the nerve to continue harassing her about her consultation with Frank. It had been three times now that she had had to pretend that she had told him, and it wasn't getting any easier. If anything, she thought, it was becoming more and more difficult to convince him that she had already mentioned her visit to him.

Well, she thought to herself, at least Frank had believed that story about the abuse, so whatever medical ethics he was bound by, his friendship with Donal would also work as an advantage. He would never devastate an old college friend now by telling him what he thought was the truth. Although she was sure her secret was safe, Judith was still unsettled by Donal's behaviour. She had never seen him so angry before. Judging by the rage and vehemence of his questions, he had been guarding his true feelings for quite some time. And all over children, she marvelled. They were godparents to enough little brats as far as she was concerned, they hardly needed any of their own.

Pulling in to the car park of the driving range, Judith decided to put the whole Frank situation out of her head. She knew that nothing could be revealed to expose her lie, and Donal was sure to have snapped out of his mood by the time she got home. In the meantime, she had more important things on her mind. The Hannah O'Toole Cup was only a few days away now, and although Judith could already see her name on the trophy, she knew it would be far more fun to put her opponent to shame by winning effortlessly. Some practice on her long putts and a bit of time in the sand area working on her bunker shots should do it, she decided, as she took her clubs out of the car. Victory would be sweet, Judith reckoned, smiling to herself as she thought about the other finalist. Winning the cup was one thing, but beating Madeleine O'Connell to get it would be the icing on the cake.

# CHAPTER FOURTEEN

'I CAN'T BELIEVE HE'S DRINKING AGAIN. HOW'S IT BEEN AT home?'

'Dreadful, I'm sick of this cycle of drinking and then apologising, and then drinking again, especially now, after everything we've been through.'

Madeleine had called round to Kay's house and, sitting in the back garden sipping cool glasses of lemonade in the early afternoon sun, they were catching up on each other's news.

'Ed keeps telling me that it's just beer, and that he can handle it, but drunk is drunk in my book, whether it's from beer, wine, or a vat of whiskey – the end result is always the same.'

'Well, at least his licence is gone,' Madeleine said, trying to grasp some shred of hope for Kay out of the situation. Ed's court case had been heard the previous week, and, charged with driving under the influence and dangerous driving, he had been fined, had had his licence revoked and had been sentenced to two months of community service.

'It's awful, Madeleine, but in a way I'm almost sorry that he wasn't sent to jail. He can more than afford to take taxis wherever he wants to go, and the fine will hardly even make a dent in his bank balance. In fact, the only thing that did him any real damage was the publicity,' Kay said, looking guilty for voicing her feelings out loud. Madeleine was the only person she would dare tell that she wished Ed had been sent to prison. 'He hates to think people might have a bad opinion of him, or that they might know about him knocking over that little boy.'

'No, but he's fine with getting completely drunk and abusing you,' Madeleine said, unwilling to defend him.

'Hmm, I know,' Kay agreed. She had gone past the point where she had any desire to excuse his behaviour either. 'And the thing is, it's almost worse that he can't drive any more. I mean, obviously I would never want him out on the roads when he's drunk, but now he thinks that because he doesn't have the responsibility of the car, he can drink as much as he wants. It's like some sort of vicious Catch 22, and I don't know what to do any more.'

Madeleine looked at her sympathetically.

'Have you talked to anyone in the Belmont Centre about it? Surely someone else's experience must be able to help you in your situation a little bit?' she asked, knowing that she could never fully empathise with how Kay was feeling.

'Yes,' she answered despondently. 'All they said, though, was that I should try to keep encouraging him. That just because he's fallen off the wagon, it doesn't mean he has to stay there. But, sure, when he won't go to any AA meetings, or even agree to have a sponsor, how can I help him? It's terrible,' she admitted, 'but I don't think I really care any more. The only reason I'm doing any of this is for the children.'

She took a long drink of her lemonade. 'Anyway, I'm sick of talking about Ed. How've you been getting on?'

'Well, as it happens, I do have some news,' Madeleine answered sheepishly.

'Go on...' Kay encouraged her, sensing that it was something big.

'I've decided to go back to New York,' she said tentatively.

'Oh, Madeleine, you're not!' Kay exclaimed, stricken with the idea of her friend leaving again. 'Sorry, I mean, of course I'm happy with whatever's best for you, but I just have this terrible sense of déjà vu, it's miserable when you leave.'

'I'm sorry Kay, but I have to do this,' Madeleine tried to explain. 'I've been thinking about it for a couple of weeks now, and I finally decided yesterday. I really think it's the best thing for me to do.'

'What about your mum?'

'It's funny,' Madeleine replied. 'I thought that she'd be devastated about it, but she's been great, and said that as long as I'm happy, she's happy. I know that she'd really rather I stayed, but she sees too that this is right for me.'

'And have you told Donal?' Kay asked, with a slight cringe.

Madeleine nodded. 'Yes, I spoke to him on the phone about it the other day,' she said, her voice adopting a sadder tone. 'In a way, he was probably the hardest person to tell. At least I knew that you and mum would be happy for me.'

She paused for a second.

'Kay, this probably sounds terrible, but while I was with Thomas, a part of me was relieved at the distraction he provided from thinking about Donal. But now that he's... well, now... there's nothing to stop me from getting totally wrapped up in Donal again. And I've learnt enough to know that that can't happen,' she finished quietly.

'I know, it's the last thing I'd want for you either. You're right to go,' Kay answered, putting her hand on Madeleine's arm. More than anyone else, she knew how painful separating from Donal had been. For this reason, putting her own feelings aside, she encouraged Madeleine's decision. 'So, have you decided when you're going to go yet?'

Madeleine looked apologetically at Kay, anticipating her friend's reaction. 'Next week,' she said. 'Wednesday.'

'Next week! But surely you'd need more time than that to get organised?'

'I know it's short notice, but I think the sooner I go, the better,' she said in a soft, though decisive tone.

'I'm going to miss you so much,' Kay said, a little calmer, pursing her lips in an effort not to cry.

'And I'm going to miss you too. You'll have to come and visit me.'

'Of course I'll visit, you couldn't stop me if you tried,' Kay said laughing. 'And God knows, I am going to need a couple of holidays judging by the way things have been so far. What made you decide on Wednesday, anyway?'

'Well, I'm playing in the Hannah O'Toole on Monday, so I knew I'd need a couple of extra days after that to get myself organised,' Madeleine answered.

'Oh, of course, I'd forgotten about that. I couldn't believe it when I saw that you had to play against Judith in the final,' Kay said, unsure as to how uncomfortable Madeleine would feel about it. 'And I hear that she's angling for the lady captainship next year as well,' she went on. 'Well, I tell you, if that happens, I'll leave Redcliff. I won't stick around to watch that bitch run the show.'

Madeleine laughed at her indignant attitude. 'You don't have to leave on my account,' she answered, quietly flattered that Kay would do such a thing for her. 'Or, more importantly, you shouldn't do anything you'd later regret – it would only be for a year, you know.'

Kay huffed in response. 'Well, we'll see.'

'Anyway,' Madeleine continued, 'I've already decided that as long as I imagine every ball I hit is her head, I should play OK.'

'That's more like it,' Kay said, delighted that she was finally openly admitting her dislike of Judith.

298

'But I don't want to start worrying about the game just yet,' Madeleine said. 'So, how are things going with Declan?' she asked.

Immediately a warm glow blushed over Kay's face, and her expression turned from one of unhappiness to bashful delight.

'Oh, Madeleine, I can't tell you how brilliant it is to be with him again,' she said, remembering her last evening with Declan. 'Arguments with Ed are almost bearable when I know I can talk to Declan about them, and for the first time in years, I actually feel like I've something to look forward to in my life.'

'But does he not mind that you're married?' Madeleine asked, thinking of her own situation.

'It would devastate Mark, Holly and Dominic if I were to leave Ed now,' Kay answered honestly, 'and Declan knows that. One day, though... My life with Ed is not for ever, I know, but both Declan and I are aware that sometimes, there are more important things to think about than ourselves. If there were no children involved, the decision would be easy. As it is, though, we'll just have to take our time.'

'I hadn't really thought about that,' Madeleine admitted. 'You're lucky that he's prepared to wait for you.'

'I know. I'm not deluding myself, and I can see that he's not entirely happy with the situation. Still, he knows that my children come first, and that, although I love him, if it came down to it and he wouldn't wait, I'd let him go.'

'Well, let's hope it never comes to that,' Madeleine said encouragingly.

'To be honest,' Kay answered with a smile, 'I don't think it will. He keeps telling me that he can't believe he has me back, so I don't think he'll be going anywhere!'

Madeleine put her lemonade glass back on the wooden table. 'And speaking of going, I'd better head off myself. I've loads to do this afternoon.'

'Oh...' Kay said, as they both stood up. 'I really, really am going to miss you, you know.'

'And I'll miss you too,' Madeleine replied, reaching over to hug her, 'but let's not talk about that now. If I start seriously thinking about it, I'll cry, and I feel that's all I've been doing recently.'

'Would you like a hand with packing or anything, or maybe a lift to the airport on Wednesday?' Kay asked as they gathered together their belongings and walked back up the garden path towards the house.

'Thanks a million, but it's OK,' Madeleine said gratefully. 'I hate goodbyes, so I think I'll just take Mum out for dinner on Tuesday night, and then hop in a taxi on my own on Wednesday morning.'

'OK, well, make sure you call me after the game anyway, to let me know how you get on.'

'Of course I will,' Madeleine smiled. 'Just keep your fingers crossed. If I lose this match, I think it might be just as well I'll be leaving the country. If I lost, it would just be one more thing for Judith to gloat about.'

After collecting her bag and keys from the hall table, Madeleine hugged Kay tightly. Neither of them wanted to say anything, but they both knew that this would be the last time they would be seeing each other for quite some time.

'You take care of yourself now, d'you hear me?' Kay said with mock sternness. 'And if at any moment you want to come home again, you just ring, OK?'

'Ok,' Madeleine answered, close to tears, 'and you look after yourself too. Don't let Ed get you down. And you know that whenever you want to, there's always room to stay with me in New York. We'll just put you on the couch, and the kids can sleep in the spare room.'

Kay laughed as she wiped her nose, unable to stop the tears that had begun to fall.

'Thanks for everything,' Madeleine whispered, as they hugged each other one last time.

'Thank you,' Kay answered, 'and good luck – you really are doing the right thing.'

With that, Madeleine walked out and got into her car before she had time to get upset all over again, looking back once to wave at Kay who was standing in the open doorway. For the second time, the two friends were left to navigate their separate ways through life, thousands of miles away from each other.

Backing out of the long driveway, Madeleine just wished that she could feel as confident as she sounded about her new plan. Her decision to go back to America had been a tough one, but it was made now, and there was no choice but to go back and start again – away from her grief, away from her lonely apartment and away from the married man she was still in love with.

\* \* \*

Madeleine and Judith met as arranged in Redcliff at two o'clock on Monday afternoon. The atmosphere in the locker room as they changed their shoes was tense and, although curt words were exchanged, both women guarded themselves against engaging in lengthy conversation. The competitive air between them was unmistakable, and from their attitudes to their outfits, intentions were clear. Both were there to beat the other, and with more to play for than just the cup, they had come prepared to compete in a battle of pride.

The day was perfect for golf. There was a gentle breeze, just enough to rustle through the fairway trees, but too soft to affect the ball, and the sun, just past its midday peak, shone warmly over the course. Conversation was sparse as they wheeled their trolleys up to the first tee box. After they had bestowed perfunctory wishes of good luck on each other, the game commenced. Match-play was the format. Having discovered that

Judith played off the same handicap as she did, Madeleine knew that it would be a tough and even match.

Despite her nerves – something, she noted, that was not affecting Judith in the slightest – Madeleine played beautiful golf, and after the first nine holes, they were all square. Balls were competitively driven down fairways, shots were chipped in expertly from sand bunkers, and birdies were successfully holed down the smooth slopes of the greens. In fact, Madeleine's game was so unexpectedly impressive that it soon became clear to Judith that winning the match might not be as easy as she had first thought. As Madeleine was about to putt her final shot on the green of the tenth hole, Judith suddenly had an idea.

'How many shots are you to here?' she asked, taking her own putter out of the bag.

'Three,' Madeleine answered, 'and you?'

'Well, I'm three… but I was sure you were on in four,' Judith replied, looking quizzically into the air as if trying to count their shots so far, 'but anyway, not to worry. Go ahead.'

Momentarily losing focus as she went back over the last three shots in her head, Madeleine missed the relatively easy putt she had set up for herself. She was annoyed that she had allowed her mind to become so distracted and, stepping off the green, she watched as Judith deftly landed her ball in the hole.

'Oh, my apologies,' Judith said saccharinely, 'you were right, it was just three shots. The sun must be going to my head! Not to worry, I win this hole anyway. Shall we go on to the next one?'

Irately collecting her trolley as Judith sallied forth triumphantly, Madeleine determined not to fall for such an easy trick again. It was clear that she was proving to be a lot better than Judith had expected, but she had never thought that the aspiring lady captain would stoop to such levels of childish deceit to win the game.

After Madeleine's ball stubbornly refused to budge out of the bunker on the eleventh, Judith won the next hole as well, but when Madeleine went on to make a birdie on the twelfth, the small gap between them narrowed once again. Tension was beginning to mount as, shot after shot, the balance dipped in favour of Judith one minute and Madeleine the next. Over the next two holes, however, with Madeleine confidently chipping onto the green and sinking her putts firmly, things seemed to be going her way.

A hair's breadth continued to divide the scores of the two women until, eventually, Judith decided that stronger measures needed to be taken. Suffering nerves that she never imagined experiencing, Judith's usual poise failed her at the seventeenth tee, and she drove her ball down the right-hand side of the fairway, and into the thicket of trees.

'Oh, shit!' she said, once she was within the copse of firs and out of Madeleine's earshot, realising how impossible her next shot would be. The ball was securely fixed between the gnarled roots of an old tree, and Judith couldn't see any possible way of unearthing the ball from its wooden web. With an idea springing to mind, she glanced quickly back out to the fairway to make sure that Madeleine wasn't looking, and surreptitiously dropped another Teitlist 2, the same as the ball she had used to drive with, onto a small clearing of soft pines. After taking a practice shot, she sent the ball shooting off towards the green and, smiling smugly to herself, she was about to leave the shelter of the dense trees, when an unexpected voice stopped her.

'I saw that, you sneaky bitch,' came the observation and, silently cursing, Judith turned slowly to see who had confronted her.

Marie had been having a practice round while she waited for Ciaran to finish his shift, when, in need of a quick pee, and unable to hold on until she got back to the clubhouse, she had snuck into the coppice to relieve herself. She had been surprised to hear Judith's loud 'Oh, shit!' and, coming out from her secluded shelter, she had watched quietly as the second ball got

303

hit out onto the fairway. Given the importance attached to the Hannah O'Toole in Redcliff, Marie was aware that today was the day of the final. Seeing Judith cheat so unscrupulously, it didn't take long for her to figure out what was going on.

'Now, I don't know what stage of the match you're at,' she started sweetly, 'but if I find out that you've won this competition, you can be sure that I'll have no problem telling everyone what I just saw here.'

Judith was speechless. Seeing no way to extricate herself from the situation, she realised that she had no choice but to comply with whatever Marie suggested.

'I am, however, very fond of your husband,' Marie continued, 'so if you... let's say you were to lose this game, then you can be sure that your miraculous production of that second ball will remain just between the two of us. It's up to you.'

Judith contemplated her situation.

'Well, I was losing anyway,' she said magnanimously, after a second's thought.

'Oh, well, that does make it easier then, doesn't it?' Marie replied, savouring every minute that she stood watching Judith squirm.

'Yes,' Judith muttered, beginning to walk away. 'I suppose it does.'

A somewhat shaken Judith reappeared from the trees to find Madeleine considering her own shot in the rough. She seemed so engrossed in her thoughts that she hardly noticed Judith's lengthy absence, and happily resumed the game once they were both back on the fairway. Even if she had wanted to win, Judith had been so distracted by Marie's threat, that she easily lost the hole to Madeleine. Biting her tongue, she turned with her hand outstretched.

'Well done,' she said through gritted teeth. 'There's no need to play the eighteenth, you win two and one.'

Madeleine was perfectly aware that she was two holes up with only one to play, but she had wanted to hear Judith say it. She knew that it was a childish wish, but somehow she felt that her victory would be greater if she heard Judith concede it.

'Thanks,' she said, unable to wipe the satisfied smile from her face. 'You played a great game.'

As they walked back to the clubhouse, Judith asked to be excused from going in to have the customary drink, pleading an urgent appointment. Happy that she wouldn't have to sit through twenty painstaking minutes of polite conversation, Madeleine readily accepted Judith's apology, and went on inside to see if there would be anyone else to celebrate with.

'So, how did you get on?' Marie asked, as Madeleine changed in the locker room.

'I won!' she answered, delighted to have been asked.

'Well, now, we can't let you go then without a celebration, can we?' Marie said, secretly thrilled at Judith's defeat, 'and I'm sure that that lovely barman upstairs would chill us a bottle of champagne if we asked him nicely.'

An hour later, Madeleine emerged from the clubhouse feeling elated. Everyone had seemed genuinely pleased to hear that she had won, and by the time she was leaving, several of the other members had come over to their table to join in the celebration. Her joy was tempered somewhat, however, as she phoned Kay to give her the good news. Once they had arranged that she would collect the cup on Madeleine's behalf, the silence on the phone turned into a reminder that they wouldn't be seeing each other again for a long time. Forcing a laugh, Kay announced that she was refusing to say any more goodbyes, and so with artificial joviality, she promised to call soon, and hung up the phone. Now that there was only dinner with her mother and some last-minute packing left to do, Madeleine suddenly felt the enormity of her decision. It was no longer an idea in the back of her mind, to be put into place sometime in the future: it was happening now for real, and doubts or no doubts, she would be getting on a plane in two days' time, to fly back to another life in New York.

\* \* \*

As soon as he arrived in St Emily's Hospital, Donal checked the operating lists for the afternoon. Having ascertained that Frank would be in surgery for a few hours yet, he knocked briefly on the door of the consulting room, and was greeted warmly by Betty, who stood up as Donal came over to her desk.

'There you are,' she said, picking up some aged, brown folders. 'I was wondering when you'd be in. I have those notes all ready for you.'

'Thanks, Betty. I just didn't want to hassle Frank with it this morning, I know how busy he is,' Donal lied, 'but I just thought that this opportunity would be too good to miss, and knew it would probably be easier to come in myself for the files.'

'Oh, you're right,' Betty agreed, 'you couldn't pass up a chance like this.'

On the phone earlier that day, Donal had told Betty that he was going to a conference in Belfast. He had lied about a meeting he had arranged with a visiting American gynaecologist, and explained how he had wanted to bring Frank's notes on Judith with him. They would be helpful, he had said, in case this doctor could offer any advice on more recent fertility treatments. Donal said he hadn't wanted to bother Frank over such a small matter, and Betty obliged by handing over the file.

Nervous that Frank would come back sooner than expected and find him in the office, Donal had left hastily. After driving some distance from the hospital, he pulled into a quiet lay-by. He felt his hand tremble slightly as his fingers leafed through the notes. Eventually finding the page he was looking for, he put the folder aside to read the single page of the radiologist's report. Under 'Hysterosalpingogram' the test results read 'No distal spill seen', which Donal knew to mean that, due to some blockage, the dye used in the tests had not been able to pass through Judith's Fallopian tubes. Confused, he read on, eventually coming to Frank's hand-written explanation for the blockage at the bottom of the page: 'Patient had a termination aged eighteen, leading to an untreated infection, which would explain inability to conceive.'

Donal was momentarily stunned. Why hadn't she ever told him about an abortion? His immediate reaction was one of pity. He could have helped her through it if he had known. Slowly, however, as his mind cleared the haze of confusion obscuring the truth, the enormity of Judith's lie unfolded before him. He hadn't known her when she was eighteen, he thought to himself, she was only in her first year of art college at the time and their paths weren't to cross until a few years later. Colour rose in Donal's cheeks and he began to shake with anger as it dawned on him that Judith could never have been pregnant when she told him she was. How could he have been such a fool? He couldn't believe that he had fallen for one of the oldest tricks in the book and, in doing so, had thrown away his chance of happiness with Madeleine. Casting the page aside, he switched on the ignition, and in a rage, pulled out onto the road again. Judith had made a mockery of his life and their marriage and, for once, Donal was going to ask the questions that he should have made her answer years ago.

* * *

As Judith put her key into the front door, her thoughts were still on the game. She couldn't believe that she had lost, and for the duration of the journey home, she had fumed with the anger of being caught. Judging by the vindictive pleasure Marie had taken in issuing her the ultimatum, however, Judith knew that any attempts at persuasion would have been in vain. The woman obviously didn't like her, and knowing that Marie had witnessed the whole scene, she couldn't risk her secret getting out. It was a fact that Judith was uncomfortable with, but she knew that she had had no choice but to lose.

Walking into the kitchen, she stopped, startled, as she saw Donal sitting silently at the table. She had been so preoccupied with her own thoughts that she hadn't noticed his car in the driveway.

'Hi,' she said, throwing her keys on the counter. 'I lost.'

'Why?' Donal asked quietly.

Judith scrunched up her face in irritated confusion.

'What sort of stupid bloody question is that?' she retorted, annoyed. 'I lost because she won,' she said, taking off her jumper and hanging it over the back of the chair.

'Why?' Donal repeated, staring at her. 'Why did you do it to me?'

Judith looked at him properly for the first time since she had come in, and noticed the frightening intensity with which he was staring at her. From his face, her eyes gradually descended to look at the brown file he was holding loosely between his hands, and she saw her name printed across the front in faded black ink.

'Do what?' she asked, a flicker of fear registering in her question.

'Set out to destroy my life,' he replied, refusing to alter his gaze.

'What the hell are you talking about, Donal?' Judith asked, unsure of what was going on, 'What do you have a file with my name on it for?'

'I've been reading all about you, Judith,' Donal started, spreading open the folder, 'and for the past hour, I've been trying to figure out why exactly you would want to ruin my life.'

Judith remained numb, rooted to the spot, as she began to figure out what his revelation might be.

'You see,' he started, raising his voice, 'it may have taken me ten years to discover the truth, but I've finally found out about your lie. I know about the abortion, Judith, about the infertility, about the fact that you couldn't possibly have been pregnant when we married, and, assuming that all the above information is correct, that you even faked your miscarriage.'

The air was thick with his accusation, and for a moment, as they stared at each other, Judith realised that the only way out of the situation was to work on his compassion, or what she hoped was left of it.

'I hoped you'd never find out,' she started, veiling her face in an expression of sadness that Donal knew too well to believe was genuine, 'but you see, I just loved you so much that when you told me you were going to finish with me, I panicked, and told you I was pregnant.'

To perfect her tone of remorse, she paused for a second.

'Please don't hate me for it,' she went on. 'I really didn't know at the time that I couldn't conceive, and I had honestly intended getting pregnant as soon as I could after we got married, but things started to go wrong, and I thought it would only hurt you to tell you the truth. I couldn't bear the thought of losing you.'

As she spoke, she moved towards him, trying to force a tear from her eye. Donal, unmoved, stood up to indicate that he didn't want her to move an inch closer.

'Judith, grant me a little intelligence,' he spat out, disgusted by her excuses. 'You were never concerned about losing me – all you cared about was that you married a husband with suitable credentials, and my consultancy provided that, didn't it?'

Judith tried to answer, but finding her throat too dry to speak and her mind too shocked to find any words, she stood mute, wishing for some miracle to turn back time, and avoid his catastrophic discovery.

'Anyway, I'm leaving now,' Donal said quietly, picking up the file from the table, 'and when I come back, it will only be to collect some things. I can't bear to be in the same room as you, let alone live with you,' he finished venomously.

She put out her hand to stop him. 'But, Donal, think about this for a minute,' she pleaded, desperate to say something that would make him stay. 'What will you do, where will you go? We have a pretty good set-up here, don't we?' she argued, realising that his compassion was bled dry. It was time now for pragmatism, and she needed him to see that it would be foolish to throw away what they had together. 'We have a beautiful home here, successful careers, you're the captain of the golf club, and with any luck, I will be too in the next year or two. We operate well together, Donal, we can give each other space – don't you see? Why would you jeopardise everything you've earned for yourself over something that happened years ago? We could forget all of that and start again.'

Judith's usually immaculate appearance looked dishevelled and distraught. Donal, however, remained impassive. Having waited for her to put forward her plea, he looked at her with contempt.

'I'll tell you why, Judith. I'll tell you exactly why it makes perfect sense for me to walk out on you without the consideration of a second chance. Because I can't stand the sight of you,' he said, his voice dripping with disdain, 'and because every time I look at you, I see what you did to me, and I know that I can never reclaim the years you drained from me. And most of all, because, although I have absolutely no respect for you, I at least still have some for myself.'

With that, he walked past her into the hall, where he had left a small bag packed, and ready to go.

'Goodbye, Judith,' he said finally, turning to look at her pathetic figure, her eyes still wide with disbelief. 'Anything further between us will be conducted through solicitors.'

Picking up his bag, he grabbed the keys to his car without a backward glance, opened the front door and left.

As the sound of the banging door echoed back to where Judith stood in the kitchen, she straightened herself up. She refused to believe that Donal would ever actually leave. Deciding to give him some time to cool down, she went out to the mirror in the hall to fix an errant hair that had fallen astray of her ponytail. She would go for a shower, she thought to herself, and by the time she was done, he would, doubtless, have already come back. This, Judith considered, was not a part of her plan, but she was sure that it would prove to be nothing more than a temporary crease that she would be able to iron out. Trying to convince herself of this as she walked up the stairs in the eerie silence of her newfound solitude, she fought hard to deny the voice in her head telling her that this time, she might just have gone to far.

\* \* \*

Waiting to depart, Madeleine looked out the window of the Aer Lingus airbus at the grey drizzle that had begun to fall. The soft humming of the engines and the quiet conversation of the other passengers suited her mood, and she sat in contented contemplation. Leaving again somehow seemed conducive to thinking back over everything that had happened since her return to Ireland, and the highs and lows of the last six months ebbed and flowed in her memory, until they merged into a collective impression. She loved Ireland, there was no denying it, but Madeleine was aware of how little there was to make her stay any more. Donal had tried to call her the day before. She knew, however, that even his voice could dissuade her strongest resolve, and so, ignoring the call as it flashed on screen, she had also left his message unheard.

Madeleine had made the decision to leave the apartment and spend her last night at home. It had been hard to leave, especially as the familiar smells of fresh baking, Pear's soap and her mother's perfume had mingled in her nostrils long after she had sat into the taxi. At least, she thought, she had been able to control her tears until she was safely away from the house, saving her upset until she was alone, so as not to make it any harder on her mum than it already was.

Crossing her legs and rooting a book out of her bag, Madeleine was secretly delighted that the seat next to her was unoccupied. Feeling as emotional as she did, the last thing she wanted was to have to make small-talk with an over-friendly fellow passenger. She opened the first page of the Deirdre Purcell novel she had bought in the airport, and, settling back to immerse herself in the fiction, she felt the seat beside her dip under the weight of a late arrival.

'Hiya, Mad,' a familiar voice whispered in her ear.

As she turned to face her companion, a slow smile spread across her face.

'Hiya, Don,' she said in delighted amazement, feeling, at last, his arms wrap tightly around her.